# THE CITY ISLAND MESSENGER

*James Gregory Kingston*

ISBN: 1541134184
ISBN 13: 9781541134188
Library of Congress Control Number: 2016920853
CreateSpace Independent Publishing Platform
North Charleston, South Carolina

*To my best friend, Andy.*
*Without your encouragement and support,*
*I'd still be sitting on the edge,*
*wondering if I should jump into the deep end*
*of this pool called "writing".*

# ACKNOWLEDGMENTS

*The City Island Messenger* was inspired by Howard Rittner, an actual Western Union messenger on City Island during WWII. The first time I met him, he was living two lives: South Bronx social worker by day and Julliard-trained musician by night. His experiences convinced me that there was a story worth telling to honor all the young, unsung telegram messengers on the home front. The characters, buildings and social order created for this story are fictional, but the heavy burden of a small job borne by young messengers across the U.S. was real, and had yet to be fully expressed in novel or film.

During more years than I care to remember, this story was developed in New York writers groups and widely disseminated through the Hollywood community.

Working as a writing partner on another youth oriented project with Dyan Cannon let me build on her insights into the characterization of younger teenage girls.

The L.Harry Lee Literary Workshop in Rocky Point helped formulate the story line with cinematic style drafts. Will Chandler and Annette Handley-Chandler of the Sag Harbor Writers Group bluntly told me what to throw away and never look back. The sharp criticism of the Westhampton Writers Group, under the direction of Donna McGullam, nursed the bare bones back to life, providing a forum for noble failure.

Staged readings by Todd Suprina and Robin Windels Ruggiero in endless public forums brought the characters to life, entertaining hundreds of guinea pig listeners.

Logan Kingston's editing helped polish the piece with a final coat of consistency.

It takes a village. I am indebted to you all.

# CHAPTER 1
# IVORY KEYS
# BORE'D 1880

*I was bore'd Black. I stayed Black 'til I was 12.*

*I was bore'd on The Road To Nowhere. It weren't no more'n two wagon wheel ruts wanderin' through a maze of shanties, 'afore sidlin' down to a lonely path, and that path trickled to a lazy trail. But still, it was a road.*

*My father was a travelin' man. He could finger the strings on every instrument a high-hatted gentleman could name. He was a picker and a strummer of the ultimest kind. Come winter and come summer, he would ride the music circuit from Atlanta to Savannah, from Charleston all the way to Richmond town, playin' at the most festive of fests, makin' dancin' music for the merriest of souls. Twice a year he'd arrive home, comin' up The Road To Nowhere with banjos and fiddles trussed up on his back, sometimes with a new mule or a huntin' dog of the first order, just in time for the spring plantin' or the fall harvest. He be lookin' so fine in his Sunday-go-to-meetin's that my Mama would fairly fall out on the floor for want of breath.*

*My father showed me how to plow and play.*

*My father taught me how to fret and string.*

*My father gave me life in his music, and he made it mine.*

*My father wasn't there when I was 12.*

*My father wasn't there the day I stopped seein' Black or White.*

*My father wasn't there the day I got blind.*

*My father was a givin' man. He give me pretty near everything, everything but a name. He call me "boy", sayin' that be my for-now-name, and when the time come, I'd find the name I was meant to wear. A name I could earn. A name I could grow into and make my own. A name strong enough to last a hundred years. My father was a wiser man that most.*

*But even a no-name blind boy loves the warmth of the risin' sun specklin' down on his naked face. Most days I would hear them birds singin' their get-up song, and that's when I knew I could beat the sunrise. And sometimes when I stood in them ruts waitin' to bid good mornin' to that fireball, my mind would see the Road snakin' and back-switchin' to the floor of the spread out valley below. Everything got green in the valley 'afore it got green up on the hill. And it stayed green way far after the skeletons of our trees and bushes faded to boney brown. The valley was a green growin' place. That's why it was so mean and mystifyin' that valley people could not be trusted, and Mama reminded me and my two little sisters of that fact, loud and often.*

*To the sunset side, the wagon ruts ran up to a stand of magnolias, each bud light as air, each beautiful as life. Some folks swore they'd seed the dyin' flowers fall up instead of down 'cause they was so light. But I, myself, never did believe such a fact, and owned it up to the folly of old folk toward the young.*

*Now livin' on a road, even a unused road, was a far sight more important and way more powerful than livin' on a path. And Mama insisted that we walk in them ruts every day, blind or sighted, wind or water, mad hot or froze cold, keepin' weeds and such from fillin' them in.*

*"Makes no nevermind if it be a road to nowhere," my Mama say. "It be a road! And we can hold our heads up, our eyes meetin' any man's eyes, 'cause we lives on a road." And in Lumpkin County, Georgia back in 1892 that meant somethin', and most likely still does.*

*My cousins and my cousins' cousins, all had names. But them that had no road, was knowed to bad mouth me and mine from time to time.*

*The jealousy in their worrisome words meant nothin' to me. Seein' or not, named or nameless, I was proud to be sittin' in them ruts, warmed by the Georgia sun and feelin' that clay slip through my fingers, replenishin' The Road To Nowhere.*

*But I growed up, left them precious ruts behind, and like my father, I rode the circuit and lived the life. I wedded, bedded and had one son. Smoked too much and drank too little. I gave and I took. Found new friends. Buried old family. Made some good luck. Made some bad. And I grew in wisdom, but didn't always heed it.*

*I settled in New York and aged, kept on searchin' for that magical sight my Mama talked about, the sight that lets a blind man see into another man's soul. And I finally met that soul on City Island and come to know what I was meant to know: that God puts some men on His earth for no other reason than to be killt by some other man.*

*Life was good, 'cept for that first week in July of '42.*

*But the story I'm fixin' to tell you ain't about me. It's about the balls and strikes the big game throws our way. It's about livin', and it's about dyin', but most of all, it's about being 12.*

*Due to the nature of my present circumstances, I find myself a short-timer. Therefore I shall waste no more of my words nor your attention, only to tell you that every happenin' is true, 'cept maybe for them parts that I had to fill in 'cause I wasn't there when they was hatched, or for them parts that was passed on to me by somebody I deemed an unreliable prevaricator. But every word is true as best I can remember.*

*And that part what ain't word-for-word true is mostly true.*

*I know, 'cause I was there.*

# CHAPTER 2
# THE SANDLOT
# JULY 1, 1942

*Most folks might say this here story started out one mornin' on a hot summer sandlot.*

*Now this ain't no broken glass, dog shit sandlot. This here was the Yankee Stadium of sandlots: dirt in the infield and green weeds in the out, cardboard for bases and a not-too-rusty chicken wire back-stop. Nobody asked who owned this half block of paradise. Nobody cared. The big brothers and sisters of them kids who was usin' it on this day, cleaned it out back when they themselves was 8 and 12. But by now they be gone off to the shootin' war leavin' their legacy behind. This next generation treated it like some kind of war memorial. And in truth, I guess that's what it had become.*

*This empty lot, stitched in between a few bungalows and the sea, was the closest thing to a park that we got here on City Island. And since we was way out in the ass end of the Bronx, which the Manhattan politicians treated like the ass end borough of New York City in the first place, we knew that we was livin' halfway to misplaced and one step short of forgotten. With 642 people on this little island, there ain't enough votes to get a rag picker elected. The last time any voters turned out was to repeal prohibition, and that was only out of a sense of national duty, since there never was no real prohibition on City Island. So Islanders learnt right early not to count on any outside help. When you live on a island, you get what you get. And some days you get nothin'. You learn to take care of your own. And like a "savin' woman" once taught me, you keeps your mouth shut.*

*Near most half everybody was related to near most half everybody else in some round about cousin way, whether it be by birthin' or marriage or just plain old neighborly sex. Now that ain't to be misconstrued. This here was a church goin' island and most of the local gentry was God-fearin' good people.*

*Most but one.*

*Some folks said that killin' would be too good for him. But that be the best we got, so I guess it might just have to do.*

A dozen boys and a few girls played the last inning of a close game. As was traditional for the morning contests, the players had to be between 9 and 12 years old to walk on that field. That rule was never written down. It was never spoken. It just was.

The most vile, the most hideous of punishments awaited any other-aged player who dared approach the chicken wire with a mitt on his or her hand. In recent memory, no one had tried. In fact it had been so long that no one really remembered what the vile and hideous punishment was, but it must be something horrible or the field would be filled with anxious eight-year-olds.

The teenagers played in the afternoon. They never seemed to be awake in the morning.

Howie Logan was one of several 12-year-olds on the diamond that day. He held his white ash Louisville Slugger high, brand name up so the hard wood wouldn't splinter on impact, waiting for that perfect pitch. He lived for the game. His ultimate goal in his young life was to play first base for the Yankees ten miles to the west. If he failed at that, he'd play second. If that didn't work, he'd try out for short stop. He didn't even care if he held down the last spot on the last squad. He just wanted to play.

But "want to" and "can do" are often a dream apart.

"Strike one!" Blind Ivory Keys' familiar voice called out.

Big Stevie, also 12 but already the size of an older, afternoon player, squatted his 150 pound frame behind Howie at home plate, where he easily intimidated most batters. He was having a tough time shaking up Howie, but for the last eight innings he had enjoyed what he saw, from behind his wire mask, as the best part of a catcher's job: keeping the pressure on.

"Four times up, Howie. Not a hit yet. You're gonna blow this one, too. Yeah, you watch. You're gonna blow it."

Howie wanted to give him a little push, just hard enough to tip him over. He could imagine hearing the other kids laughter as Stevie hit the ground.

Howie tapped his bat on the cardboard and brushed the stray dark strands out of his eyes. He should have listened to Mom and let her cut his hair.

The pitcher made his move, and Howie answered.

"Strike two!" called Ivory in an authoritative tone.

Ivory was, indeed, the 60-year-old, Black, sightless, sunglassed ump. His hands rested on Stevie's triceps, monitoring every slight movement, every muscle twinge, as the horsehide sailed into the catcher's mitt. Seasons of sandlot, combined with his musician's heightened kinesthetic senses, had taught him to call the balls and strikes by sound and by feel. The ball's solid WHAP! as it buried itself into the sweet spot of the catcher's mitt, combined with a minimal arm movement, let Ivory know when the ball was in the strike zone. And his decision was final. Always.

Ivory bent down behind Stevie again. Inside his face mask, the tight gray hair and short need-a-shave beard always matched one of his two daily clothing choices: black and white, or white and black. Perfect combination for a live-alone blind man.

For the first few years behind the cardboard plate the previous generation had been known to retort, "You're blind ump!" after each close strike call. But that grew old as the kids grew up, and the bonds between Ivory and his multi-generational charges were forged in this legendary diamond dust. Respect for his authority at home plate translated to a natural reverence off the field, while still allowing Ivory to regain that childhood stolen from him at the age of 12 in Lumpkin County, Georgia.

Stevie raised his catcher's mask and stood up in Howie's face. He called out to anyone in earshot.

"Another strike. What'd I tell ya? I said he'd blow it, and he blowed it. Am I lucky or am I a genius?"

"You're both lucky *and* a penis," answered Howie.

"I said 'genius', Howie, 'genius'. Very funny."

"Play ball!" came Ivory's call.

Big Stevie set himself to receive the next pitch. Ivory bent over behind him, his hands resting back on Stevie's arms. The ball sailed into Stevie's glove a little wide, and silence told the catcher that Ivory sensed the lateral move in his body. Stevie's disagreement with the call arrived in the form of a long fart aimed at the umpire behind him. Ivory waved it off.

"Hey, Howie."

"What?" Howie's tone told Stevie he was getting annoyed. That was the reaction Stevie was waiting for.

"How come the army put your father in jail?"

Howie's jaw clenched as he stepped out of the drawn-in-the-sand box. "He's not in jail."

"Then where is he, huh?"

A wave of Howie's wrist let Big Stevie know that he was still holding the bat. But the authority in Ivory's voice dominated everything.

"I said, 'Play Ball'!"

Howie knew Stevie's tactics, and he knew he was falling for them. He moved back to the plate, and looked to the runner on third base. Kim Nakamura was not the biggest player on Howie's team. She was neither the oldest nor the most talented. She was the prettiest. But more importantly, she was fast.

He knew her. He knew she was going to run if he hit the ball and probably run if he didn't. Stealing home was one of the toughest moves in baseball, and that was why she'd do it. She seemed driven these days to prove something, maybe that a Japanese girl could play an American boys' game.

Howie knew he had to get a solid hit, or Kim would die between third and home. Stevie's annoying voice snapped him back.

"Did they take your old man 'cause he's a traitor, Howie? Is your Pop a Jap-lovin' Benedict Arnold traitor?"

Howie wanted to tip Stevie over worse than ever, but the pitcher had already sent the ball on its way. Howie took a mighty cut. A wobbly grounder. He ran to first. Kim, with a big lead off the cardboard, charged for home. The second baseman fielded the ball and threw it in, more confident that Big Stevie could make the play than little Mungo at first base. Stevie moved to tag her just as Kim crossed the plate. She looked safe, more or less.

"You're out!" declared Stevie with the roar of a lioness that has just felled prey for her cubs. "You...are...out!" The pride would eat tonight.

Kim refused to accept the call.

"Am not! I was safe. Tell him, Ivory."

Ivory flipped his thumb over his shoulder. "Blind man gotsta go with the player holdin' the ball."

"See? You're out," insisted Stevie. "This game is ovaaaaa! Boop-boop-a-doop."

"I was safe!"

"Out!"

Kim was in his face. "Safe! Safe! Safe!"

Stevie shoved Kim away. She fell backwards into the dust. Both teams gathered in close, each yelling support for its squad. Howie charged in from over-running first and pushed his way through. Kim jumped up and raised her fists, but Stevie easily tossed her back down. Ivory groped his way in to separate the young people as best he could.

"Boys! Girls! Hold up there! This is the sacred game of baseball we're playin'. Respect the call!" But the spectators were too busy screaming to hear him.

Howie lunged into Stevie, but the bigger opponent threw him down on his face. He jumped on Howie, pushed his cheek into the dirt and was about to punch him in the head when suddenly the crowd parted.

The chill had crawled down the back of Ivory's neck even before the children had looked up. Stevie only caught a glimpse of the approaching figure as it loomed into view. Howie was too busy trying to defend himself to notice.

Suddenly Stevie took in the full picture and just as quickly backed off.

Bad Bill Logan stared down at the two amateur wrestlers. The tall 53-year-old's broken nose and longshoreman's meat-hook hands told a dozen bad luck stories in just one wordless glance. The intense look in his steely eyes said this is a man who goes down hard and comes up swinging.

Stevie kept backing up until it was apparent that he was more halfway to leaving than halfway to staying.

"This ain't over, Howie. Come on guys."

But Kim wouldn't let him off that easily.

"I was safe!"

"Yeah, but so was the fleet at Pearl Harbor."

She looked down, ashamed and embarrassed for a lot of reasons and not really knowing which one to pick, then hurled her sharpest arrow in Stevie's direction.

"Well I got a brother fightin' in the Army. That's more'n you got."

But it was too late. Stevie ignored her final desperate attempt at retaliation. His teammates followed their captain off the diamond. Kim helped Howie to his feet, and the game dissolved. Bad Bill had melted away as quickly as he had appeared. Thoughts of an afternoon splashing in the Long Island Sound filled most of the players' heads, most but two. Splashing was not in their daily routine any more. Howie and Kim had jobs waiting for them, but they were in no hurry to get there.

"Kim, you gotta respect the call."

"Yeah," she reluctantly admitted. "I know...Sorry, Ivory."

Ivory nodded his acceptance. "You ain't just playin' ball when you step foot on my field. You playin' life. Sandlot lessons feed the soul. Best ones be bitter and hard to swallow."

Howie righted his hand-me-down Columbia two-wheeler, and they tied their mitts onto the handlebars, then walked along side the bike, navigating the street by the sea. The original 1936 red paint was wearing away in spots, but the brand name sky badge on the center pole was rust free and serial number A5429 was still visible, imprinted on the frame between the pedals. Ivory remained behind surrounded by half a dozen sandlot refugees. He found his guitar against an old bench made out of a fallen telephone pole along the first base line, and started to strum *Froggy Went A Courtin' And He Did Go, Ah-huh.* Howie wished he had picked a different song.

They walked for over a block before Howie finally broke the silence. Silence was tough.

"No free passes for that jerk, Stevie, when I make the majors."

"Which will be never," said Kim.

City Island unrolled before them, and they were oblivious to its unique beauty. The blue-collar marina held a dozen commercial fishing boats, but half of them were idle now either because there was not enough gas to go around or the fishermen had joined the Navy. They were up on blocks at the height of the season. That was not only bad for the economy of the Island, it was also bad for the dinner table. With one not-so-busy entrance road, fewer and fewer groceries made it as far as City Island. Victory gardens and chicken coops were becoming a survival necessity within eye-shot of the distant, towering Gotham skyline. In the land of plenty, the shadow of want was on the wall.

Still, Island resiliency was undaunted. Young women walked babies or rocked them on the many bungalow porches that almost touched each other. Older women rocked themselves, waiting for gossip from and about the younger. There were few men and fewer cars. They had gone to that unforgiving, all-consuming war. The war that followed The War to End All Wars. The war that would change City Island, and the outside world forever.

Kim spit on her handkerchief and wiped an emerging scratch over Howie's left eye. It would bookend the one already on his chin, framing his still-boyish face nicely. Howie had a winning smile, which he hadn't been able to find since his grandmother's funeral. But he was still looking.

Kim spit again and went to work on his chin.

"I was safe, Howie."

"Respect the call."

"A blind ump! We're probably the only place in the world that has a blind ump."

"Sometimes those real umps at the Stadium look like they call 'em blind."

"Did you ever ask Ivory, Howie...how he got blind?"

"Nooo...Nobody knows. Nobody asks, and nobody knows. And he ain't tellin'. So forget it."

"Ask him."

"*You* ask him, Kim."

"He likes you best, so ask him."

"I ain't askin'!"

Howie decided maybe silence wasn't so bad. But this time Kim broke it open again.

"You didn't have to step in like that. I could lather any two of those guys."

"Yeah, sure. And three on Sunday."

"I mean it. Big Stevie ain't so tough. Tatsu taught me how to fight before he joined the Army."

"Where is your brother now?" asked Howie.

"I don't know. He never writes. Probably on some secret job or somethin'."

"Well, you're my buddy, Kim. And buddies got to stick together. So that's why I jumped in. I didn't really think about it or nothin'. It just happened. And believe me, Stevie *is* tough...You want me to spit for you?"

"No. I'm okay. You took most of the licks. But you didn't jump in 'cause I'm your buddy. You jumped in 'cause I'm a woman."

She spit again, but now it was too late. Howie had stopped half a step behind her. He winced.

"Would you cut that out?! I hate it when you say that. You are *not* a woman."

"I can't help it. I *am* a woman. Look at me."

Howie covered his ears. But his eyes took in a 12-year-old tom boy with a boy's figure and a boy's mitt who, only moments ago, had played a game that was normally played by boys, and finished the last inning by fighting with a boy. It's just that on City Island you couldn't find enough boys to have a game, so both genders had always been invited into the dust. It was tradition. But Howie was applying tradition selectively.

"I don't want to hear it. That's it. Just drop it."

Kim couldn't do that anymore than she could have let Stevie off the hook. She tried but she couldn't.

"Okay dunce head, what *do* you want me to be?"

"I just want you to be, well, to be what you've always been."

"What's that?"

"Your old dumb-ass self."

Kim punched him in the arm.

"Dunce head," she laughed.

"Dumb-ass." He punched her back.

"Dunce head."

"Dumb-ass."

This was going nowhere, but it made them both feel a lot better. They punched and wrestled and rolled and laughed. Finally exhausted, they collapsed into the grass that clumped on the side of the small dunes, only to make fun of the cloud formations overhead, and spit on each other's faces until Stevie's souvenirs were washed clean. On their backs, they spread their arms wide and looked for shapes in the clouds, unconsciously embracing all the beauty that surrounded them.

When the laughter and the spit both dried up, it would be time to go, but until then, these were the days of innocence and wide-eyed imagination, the days of seabirds above and sails beyond. This was the first day of the last week of their childhood.

# CHAPTER 3

# THE FIRST TELEGRAM

# JULY 1, 1942

Howie rolled his Columbia to a stop, and Kim jumped off the wide handlebars. They had reached their destination, Nakamura's General Store and Western Union Office, half hung over the water's edge on twenty barnacle-caked poles. Mr. Yoshi Nakamura's small skiff was tied to the dock in the rear. Nowadays it was used to fetch the supplies and staples seldom delivered by the gas-starved trucks.

A poster in the window facing the street announced the City Island Annual Fourth of July Dance at the Legion Hall, which was directly across the street. It, too, was hard by the sea.

The Legion Hall was little more than a weathered barn-like structure, boasting both a bar and a kitchen. To the rear, double doors opened to a veranda with a waist high fence that protected the initiates and inebriates from falling to a watery grave after a night of drink and dance. Inside, posters told that all proceeds from this year's event would go to buy war bonds. The largest gem of the collection, the obligatory, finger-pointing "Uncle Sam Wants You", dominated directly opposite the little area set aside for the band.

The Legion Hall and the general store stood like wooden sentries, each guarding its part of the southern entrance onto City Island, each bearing a face of cedar shakes in varying tones of silver, brown and gray depending on the angle of the sun and the force of the rain on that day. If buildings indeed could be described as friends, these two would be from the old school of camaraderie, willing and ready to sacrifice themselves so that the other might continue to stand.

Memorable storms had hit from both directions and each building had its turn blocking the wind and protecting the other. The general store had actually been land bound like the Legion until the big blow of '38, "The Long Island Express", undermined much of its foundation. It was about to crash into the cold sea, but the Legionnaires rushed to the general store's rescue with poles and pilings, some torn right from the walls of the Legion itself. Indeed, just as many of the island's inhabitants were intertwined, so these two buildings shared the same blood. So much so, that they were even known to creak to each other as they contracted in the cool of night after a hot summer day. The natives called it "the talk". It was a groaning sound to be remembered forever, each building mimicking the other. And then it would stop.

On many a summer night, Howie and Kim had wrapped themselves in blankets and rested on the general store porch rockers waiting for the talk to begin, usually sleeping through it. The older brothers, Vinny and Gene, or Tatsu, would periodically check on the two children, or sometimes even sleep with them until the sun dawned across the Long Island Sound. The two families were intertwined even as the buildings were, and neither storm nor turbulence could ever dissolve this bond. And each family weathered the forces that drove against the other.

Standing tall like a solitary sentry in the midst of these two old friends was the Legion flagpole, inordinately high so that it would always rise above the sloop or ketch masts that, before the war, had bobbed on either side only a hundred yards away.

Atop the peak of the general store's porch, near Kim's bedroom window, was a small bell attached to a wire that disappeared inside. By this means, the telegraph operator would always be alert to any incoming transmission while he tended to the other tasks a family operation required.

Howie propped the bike up against the general store's porch.

The bell rang and both children automatically looked up.

As they entered the store, Yoshi Nakamura was taking telegraph tape from a clattering typewriter-like machine that produced the finished message. He cut the tape into sections, using his special quick-glue to fix them onto the yellow Western Union paper. Telegrams didn't arrive everyday, and they always brought the other operations to a halt.

Groceries and hardware filled the shelves. Posters urging conservation and victory gardens competed for wall space with Tatsu's high school diploma and signs about rationing. Tires and 19-cents-a-gallon gas were already restricted, and food rationing was about to start on the East Coast as soon as the booklets were distributed. The West Coast would be spared until December.

The telegram had taken precedence over some waiting customers, and Kim stepped behind the counter to finish tallying up their orders. She donned a white apron like her father's. No one was disturbed by the delay. Besides, this being the only store on the island, that telegram was for one of their neighbors or family members. And telegrams were always important. The customers strained their peripheral vision in vain attempts to get a head start on its contents. But years of experience had taught Mr. Nakamura that a telegram, like a religious experience, was best served when not indiscriminately shared. He adroitly protected his charge while avoiding offending the secret gawkers.

Mr. Nakamura gave the slightest of bows to the two children. But they didn't nod back. To the contrary Kim seemed momentarily embarrassed.

"Ah, Howie! You are just in time. I have groceries and a telegram to be delivered. Get your cap."

Kim finished with the shoppers while Howie wired a makeshift basket over the bicycle's rear wheel. He knew not to ask any questions about a telegram until the solitude and sanctity of Western Union had been restored. Once the last customer had left, he approached Mr. Nakamura.

"Who's the telegram for?"

"Mrs. Mable Trent."

"What's it say, dad?" chimed Kim.

"My function is merely a vessel. The words pass through me, but I do not read them. They are not mine."

"Oh, dad. What is it? Company rules, right?"

"It is called respect, something that your mother and I obviously overlooked in your upbringing."

The mention of Kim's absent mother sent the slightest wince through Howie and he hoped that the subject would not be mentioned again until he was on his way. He reached up to the shelf that was his own domain. It held the badge of his station, the celebrated gray-green Western Union cap. He carefully removed the hat and polished the visor with his sleeve, then wedged the telegram into the lining and pulled the hat down close to his ears. He double checked the little belt at its rear, making sure it was tight enough to lock in its valuable cargo. He turned the peak deftly at an angle and hoisted the two bags of groceries. He had never bothered to fill the small loop on the side that was meant to hold a pencil. No one had. This priceless piece of history held more memories than Howie could count. Mr. Nakamura reached over to straighten the cap with hardly a look, but he held Howie's head still, questioning the facial scratches.

"Fighting?"

"Baseball."

Once he reached his bike, Howie slipped the peak back to the side. Stevie had called him "Little Lord Fauntleroy" once. He didn't know who the Little Lord was, or why he was disliked so much, but he did know that it was something to be avoided. Aiming his hat to the side was the height of jauntiness, and jauntiness was something to be pursued.

Not only was he jaunty, but he was jaunty on the job. He and Kim were the only two of their circle of friends who had real jobs. And Kim worked for her father so that might not even count. Howie's job came with a uniform. People liked to see men in uniform, especially during these times. So what if it were only a hat. What's *under* the hat is what's important.

The never-on-time bus had just circled the flagpole at the end of the road. No one got on. No one got off. No one ever did. Howie reached over and held onto the open rear door letting the bus coast him up City Island Avenue. Mom would have a conniption if she saw him, but it was worth the chance. Besides, his brother Vinny used to do it all the time. And he suspected that Gene had done it when he delivered telegrams for Mr. Nakamura before Vinny. Old Joe the Bus Driver, not only expected it, he deserved it. In the summer he would always ride with the doors open, making it impossible for any boy on a bike to resist. Especially Howie.

Three blocks on the bumpy asphalt and Howie let the bus go as he made the turn to Mable Trent's house. Mable had the palsy. She shook when she walked, and she shook when she didn't walk. Her hands shook, and her neck shook. And on a bad day, her voice shook. At 45, her trembles made her look 70. She was a good woman. She must have just been born old.

Eddy, her son, made a career out of doing for her, but he was the first Islander to enlist in the Navy after Pearl Harbor. Since then, it had been difficult. Howie's brother, Gene, however, had

Eddy beat. He joined the army five years ago and was in Hawaii when the bombing started. He almost stayed there, the hard way, in the ground.

Howie propped his bike up against the bungalow porch and climbed up the two steps. Pete the Dog bounded in anticipation.

Pete the Dog was what a tour guide would have called "local color". He loved visitors, loved the freedom of the Island, and loved his evening beer. Pete the Dog was seven years old. That was about fifty in people years, well old enough to legally consume alcohol. Legend had it that his mother had taken up with an off-Islander after the traditional Fourth of July fireworks display and Pete the Dog was one of a litter of seven delivered later that year. When the family left in the winter, Pete the Dog flipped out of the truck as it bounced over the shaky bridge. Nobody was sure if Eddy Trent found Pete the Dog, or Pete the Dog found Eddy. Either way, they had become inseparable. A picture of Eddy in uniform even hung a few inches over Pete's dog bed.

Howie never could figure out if Pete the Dog was a white dog with black spots or a black dog with white spots. But Pete probably didn't know either, so it really wasn't too important. No one had ever filled out papers for a dog license on the Island, and no one probably ever would.

Howie reached the porch as Pete the Dog was just getting into his happy bark.

"Telegram, Mrs. Trent."

"Open it for me Howie."

Howie was glad to hear those words. He didn't want to wait awkwardly by as she tried to tear open the simple yellow envelope. He placed the interior paper into her shaking hands, and rustled his own hands around Pete the Dog's head and neck.

"Oh, it's for my birthday, from Eddy! He's in the Pacific, you know, but I don't know where. Now you stay right here, Howie. I won't be a minute."

Howie knew that there were "minutes" and there were "minutes". Hers were a lot longer than his, but most grownups progressively lost their sense of time as they gained in years. He played with Pete the Dog until she returned with a nickel in her hand.

Mr. Nakamura never bothered to have anyone sign a copy or a check list to verify that a telegram had been received, even though Western Union expected it. City Island groceries were on the honor system, generally charged in a ledger and paid somewhere down the road. So telegram delivery had become part of that honor system as well. And when it came to getting a signature from shaky Mrs. Trent, Howie loved the honor system. Besides, he would never lie about delivering a telegram, and hardly ever about anything else. He already had one lie scratching inside of him, clawing to come out.

Mrs. Trent placed her shaking hand against Howie's scraped cheek and his whole face vibrated like an angry headache.

"You're hurt."

"Baseball, is all."

He pocketed the coin with a "Thank you, and Happy Birthday."

Howie hopped back on Columbia. The groceries may have suffered in the heat, but telegrams always took priority, no matter what. His was a sacred trust.

Pete the Dog briefly chased the bike, then turned tail. Howie reached Mrs. O'Reilly's nearby bungalow before Pete the Dog got home. The hereditarily challenged canine had been given his rather lengthy name to distinguish him from Old Pete the Clammer and Old Pete the Fisherman. But when the two Old Petes passed on, never returning from a watery adventure one stormy, alcoholic night off eerie Hart Island, no one thought to shorten Pete the Dog's moniker. Perhaps it would have given too much closure, acknowledging that the old salts were never coming home. But every Islander knew that bodies lost in this part of the swirling Sound, seldom surfaced.

Mrs. O'Reilly rocked a patient syncopation and rose as Howie landed. She wore rosary beads around her neck, the only jewelry he had ever seen her don. Her matronly appearance belied the wildness of her misspent youth. Legend had it that she had hoofed three years on the stage as a Flora Dora Girl, and if, by some twist of fate, this weren't true, the midnight dreams of at least a dozen Island girls would be dashed tonight.

Howie propped the bike against a big tree, the biggest and probably the oldest on the island. This little lawn was always shaded and grass only grew in sporadic colonies in the sandy soil. Local residents named most important objects on City Island, and this was no exception. Through the decades, the big tree had been known by many, more personal names, but this generation simply called it "The Big Tree".

He carried the groceries up the two steps as Mrs. O'Reilly opened the screen door for him, glancing at his bruises.

"Before you ask, it was baseball. Okay?"

He brought the bags to the kitchen, and no sooner had he plopped them down than he started to unpack. Howie had been here so often that this was practically a second home for him.

"I see you have your cap on, Howie. Who's the telegram for?"

"I'm not supposed to say. Western Union policy and all. If I went around tellin' every time somebody got a telegram, I'd get fired."

There was a long pause. Neither said a word. Howie tried to be strong but he was not good at any silence that lasted close to a minute. The walk home with Kim was his best effort so far, and he had failed at that. He had to blurt it out before it could fester inside.

"Okay. It was for Mrs. Trent. It's her birthday. Her son sent it. She really misses him. You could tell."

"We all miss our sons. Which reminds me, I got a letter from Charlie yesterday. He said he left something for you hanging on his headboard. Go on. Go on. Get it."

"Yeah. I know Charlie. It's probably used up chewing gum."

Charlie's room, walled with trophies and banners, was a monument to a young man's baseball career. Pictures of high school teams, and Topps baseball cards stared back at Howie. Autographed photos filled the few bare spots. Bats and balls were scattered just as Charlie had left them six months ago. He and Howie were linked by the same dream: to play professional ball. In the center of the wall was an autographed picture of Joe DiMaggio.

"He sure loves Joltin' Joe. Don't he?"

"Yes he does," Mrs. O'Reilly called in from the kitchen.

"He hit in 56 consecutive games last year. That's a major league record. Nobody will ever break that. That's why he got to be the MVP. The Yanks won the league by 17 games, ya know, before they murdered the Bums in the series. What a year! It makes you wanna move to the Bronx."

"This *is* the Bronx, Howie."

"I mean the Bronx Bronx. The real Bronx. Where the people live. Across the shaky bridge."

"I'd suggest you wait and see how they do this season, before you make any sudden decisions."

"Don't worry, Mrs. O'Reilly. They're gonna be champs again."

His eyes finally tore themselves away from DiMaggio's picture to search the headboard. Hanging alone, in plain sight, was a baseball mitt, well worn beyond the point of being broken in. To any outsider: a glove destined for the trash heap. To Howie: a legendary treasure.

Every ball player on City Island knew this particular mitt. Charlie had played so well on the City All Stars team thanks to this glove, that he named it "Magic", which later faded to the more colloquial "Maggie". But the young fielders who looked up to their Island idol held that glove in reverence. They refused to diminish it by any name corruption, and in fact, went the other way. They always accorded it a full "Magic Maggie".

Howie's eyes swelled. He mouthed a silent "Magic!" as he brought it into the kitchen like he was carrying a baby chick in two cupped hands.

"Go ahead. Try it on."

He slipped his hand warily into Magic Maggie; a little big, but he didn't see it that way.

"It's perfect!"

Howie lifted the bike from The Big Tree and hopped on. He had planned to ask for a new glove this Christmas, but now he set his hopes on a kickstand. He looked back at the bungalow, thinking of the last time he had come to the house with his brother Gene, who was Charlie's best friend when they were young. Gene...now somewhere in northern California. And about Kim's mother who was stuck out west, probably not that far from Gene. He drifted to Gene's wife, Teddy, who would be squeezing the oleo coloring right now in preparation for dinner two blocks away. She did it the best. She could make it the same color as butter. She could make it mound up like butter. If only she could make it taste like butter.

He looked down at Charlie's mitt swinging from the cross bar and once again mouthed, "Magic."

Suddenly Stevie appeared in front of him with a baseball bat already crashing down in his direction. The blast hit the bike's handle bars and knocked Howie off. He careened into the big shade tree and came up with blood trickling from his nose.

Stevie stood over him. "*Now* it's over."

Little bright lights danced in Howie's head. He caught a glimpse of Stevie triumphantly turning away. But a large hand grabbed Stevie from behind, spinning him around.

Stevie instantly knew it was too powerful to be Howie, and his worst fears materialized as he looked into the eyes of Bad Bill Logan. The back of Bill's hand cracked across Stevie's face, knocking him down. Bill picked up the bat and gave Stevie a look that could kill. Stevie was a breathing dead boy.

But Bill swung the bat as hard as he could against the tree. The bat shattered as Howie, below, grabbed his hat and scrambled for safety, all the while screaming.

"Uncle Bill! Noooo!"

Bill picked Stevie up by the throat. His raspy voice spilled out, "Don't ever be touchin' me blood again."

Stanley the Bookie would have made odds that Stevie was about to die, but he wouldn't have counted on Pete the Dog's barking jaws snapping at Bad Bill's ankle. Bill sunk his shoe into Pete's belly, kicking him free. Pete let out a whimper as he received the blow and bounced across the lawn, wisely retreating to safer ground. But it provided enough time for Mrs. O'Reilly to make a hasty exit from her front porch. Her ear-grabbing hold probably saved Stevie's life. She took charge of the screaming boy, and Bill backed off.

"I've got him, Bill. Leave him to me."

"Ohhh! Ah! Ow! Ow!"

She ear-walked Stevie along the street toward his home.

Bill turned his attention to Howie who was fighting to get his hat on his head. Bill picked him up and carefully straightened his cap, then backhanded him across the face just as he had done to Stevie. Howie sprawled onto the ground, losing his cap again.

"And you!" growled Bill. "You be stayin' away from the likes of them slant-eyes!"

Bill disappeared down the street. Howie sniffed back the tears and felt the welt rising across his face. Clearly this had not been his day. Pete the Dog returned for a few good face licks before Howie pushed him off.

"Good boy, Pete. Go home, boy."

Pete cocked his head and slowly moved toward the Trent house.

Howie found the cap, climbed on his bike, dusted off Magic Maggie and pedaled home, passing Mrs. O'Reilly who navigated Stevie as if his ear were a tiller.

"Bad Bill wouldn't get away with that if your Pop was here," she called out to Howie. "Shame Pop got arrested like that, the day the war started. Still your mother should have seen it coming. What with him living in Tokyo now and again, and speaking all that Jap talk, and all."

She clutched the rosary beads to her ample bosom.

"Remember me to your mother, Howie. The saints preserve the poor woman...Tell her not to worry. I'm on the beads!"

# CHAPTER 4
# MAKING A PIRATE
# JULY 1, 1942

*If'n a boy get hisself in a beat-up, the last place he wanna go is home, 'cause his mama most likely gonna whup that boy again. But if'n he done nothin' wrong, and if'n his mama don't wear no blinders, he got nothin' to fear. And his mama can be his best friend. Sometimes mamas need to be boys' best friends, even for just that little bitty time. That little bitty patchin' time. 'Cause after the patchin' come the talkin'. And mamas like the talkin'.*

Howie stared at the picture on his living room mantel while his face got painted brown. He tried to concentrate on the dim radio music playing in the background, hoping it would distract him from the pain.

The Logan house was one of several old captains' homes that had safeguarded families while the salt men set to sea for year-long journeys. The small verandas that encircled the pinnacles on the third floor allowed the wives to pace a continuous walk as they watched the horizon in anticipation of their husbands' safe return. But they didn't always return as safely as hoped, and the narrow balconies were christened "Widows' Walks". These were the only Island homes with fireplaces and mantels, and thus a place to display the family photograph.

This picture showed the three Logan boys in younger and happier times.

Gene in his sergeant's uniform, the stiffest one in the photograph, threw his chest out. Each hair in his military haircut stood at attention.

But Vinny, the middle brother, the Fordham University senior, beamed. He was enjoying four years of the usual Jesuit indoctrination without question. If he had questioned it, he probably would have gone to hell, or worse, failed out. Vinny didn't seem to care. But Mom would never accept the former, nor Pop the latter. And there was no percentage in crossing Pop. But now younger Vinny was a commissioned officer, and older Gene was not.

Howie, smaller and chubbier last year, was the only one left not fighting the war, well not in the traditional sense. Secretly he was glad it would be over before he could ever get called up. It couldn't last much longer. Not with the Americans in it now. Everyday the big ships lined up in the Sound only a few miles from his upstairs window, waiting for their European bound cargo. The war would end soon. It had to.

Howie glanced away from the picture and toward Gene's wife on the sofa. Teddy was knitting something beyond recognition. At this point it looked more like a rag with legs than any type of baby clothing. Yesterday it resembled a wash cloth with a head. Eventually someone would have to speak to that girl. She lacked what Ivory would call "direction".

"Ow!"

Mom hit a tender spot as she cleaned and painted Howie's multitude of minor facial wounds from three encounters that day:

Stevie, Stevie and Bad Bill. The iodine was turning into warpaint. She blew on it to temporarily lessen the pain.

"Gee, Mom! Why don't you just decorate me with lipstick?!"

"It's too hard for a woman to get, to waste it on a little boy," added Teddy. She and Mom shared a laugh. It was a woman's joke that he felt no need in pursuing.

Teddy was only 22 and hardly looked it. She had been one of those increasing numbers who came to the Island each summer. Only one summer she didn't leave. She married Gene instead, right before he shipped out to Hawaii. He sent for her as soon as could be arranged. But when she came home, she came home pregnant. The good news was that she not only missed Gene, she missed the bombing. The bad news was Gene didn't.

"Ow!" Mom did it again. "Can we stop now?"

"Almost done."

"Ya know, Mom, Stevie is just sooo mean to Kim."

"When someone's mean to me, I write their name on the sole of my shoe. When it's gone, so is their meanness."

"That's silly."

"Silly or not, it works."

"Mom! That hurts!"

"You think that hurts? You're lucky it wasn't your father's hand you felt."

"You think Uncle Bill hates me?"

"Hates you? He's family, and there is nothing more precious in this world than family. Even Bad Bill Logan."

"Is he really bad?"

"Well, he never had the opportunities that Pop had. They both worked on the docks, but Pop went on to Mitsui Importing, and Bill...Bill went to Panama. But he's a great man. Always remember, he built the Panama Canal."

Teddy was quick to offer her opinion. "If you ask me he should have stayed there."

"Some men just get bad when they drink," said Mom. "He can't help it. But it might be wise, Howie, to stay away from him next time."

"It's like he's watchin' me."

Teddy wasn't finished. "Well I think he's worse these last two months since Nana died."

That was one memory that rampaged through Howie's brain in broken pictures. Bad enough that he couldn't control these random thoughts about his beloved Nana during the daytime, but now they were crashing into the peace of his dream land world. His gut felt queasy. He fought it off.

"There. We're done."

Mom gathered up her cure-all, makeshift, collected-over-twenty-years medicine kit. It had nursed the entire family back to health at one time or another, as well as a weird assortment of friends, neighbors, pets and the occasional summer stranger who washed up on their shores.

Howie had to get this out.

"I think Bill's been worse because he couldn't save Nana. He tried to grab her, but he missed, so he blames himself. That's why he never comes over here anymore."

"The shame is that the War Department wouldn't let Pop be here for his own mother's funeral. That's the shame." Howie could hear the slight elevation, the heat, the underlying antagonism in his mother's voice. "But soon he'll be home again, and everything will be fine."

Howie knew she was the optimist in the family and had to end that conversation with a positive observation. If she had not, she would have felt guilty all evening and well into the night.

The screen door blew open as Vinny and his blonde fiancée, Lillian, bubbled in. Vinny carried a bolt of fine Japanese white silk. He spotted the painted Howie and couldn't pass up the opportunity to comment. Vinny bent down to examine Howie's bruises. His dog tags dangled in front of Howie's mouth. For a moment Howie envisioned himself biting the tags off, but then again, it would probably hurt. A white tee shirt and army fatigue pants completed the Vinny-look. Hair always in place. Teeth and eyes always bright. People liked to be around him. He just made them feel good. In spite of joining the army and using his college education as a step into the officers' ranks, he still managed to hold down a part time job: teasing Howie, because that's what big brothers do for and to little brothers. It had become their ritual.

Howie couldn't wait for Vinny to get married and get out. His leave was almost up. But with the wedding only a week away, Howie could tolerate anything Vinny said or did. He just hoped that Lillian was not moving in with them, too. One absent brother's wife was quite enough. If only Pop or Gene would come home, the sides would be a little more even.

"Oooh. Rough day on the diamond, squirt. In my day, the bat was for hitting the ball, not each other."

"Very funny, lieutenant."

"Who knocked the snot out of you?"

Howie hesitated for a second, looking over at Mom before answering. "It was...Big Stevie."

"Now, Vincent, don't get any ideas about kicking Stevie's arse," warned Mom.

"Well, listen to the Irish comin' out the woman. Mom said 'arse'!" laughed Vinny.

"You did!" Howie jumped in. "You said 'arse'!"

"I said 'ass'. I mean...nothing. Forget it."

Vinny turned back to Howie, mouthing the word "arse".

"Take my advice, little brother. Until you guys can get along on that diamond, collect 10 pounds of scrap iron and go to Yankee Stadium for free. It's a lot safer."

Lillian took the ream of material down from Vinny's shoulder. She was not like Teddy, her future sister-in-law, at all. Lillian was always moving, always laughing and presumably not pregnant.

"I brought back all the silk. My mother won't let me use it for my wedding dress train. She said it was better that I get married without a train than use this Jap…and then she used a bad word. I'm sorry, Mrs. Logan."

"You'd better get used to calling me 'Mom'. Just think. Gene and Vinny, my two oldest boys, married. Now let's see. Who's left?" Mom's eyes searched the room finally landing on Howie.

"Not me! I ain't never gettin' married!"

"You stay with me, Howie. You'll be the joy in my old age. And Lillian, dear, I can fully understand your mother's feelings. Japanese silk is not 'in' this season."

Mom was gracious as usual.

"I didn't even know you could get that silk anymore, 'Mom'," Lillian responded, pushing out the word.

"You can't. Pop brought this back with him on his last trip to... ah...Tokyo." Mom had to take a breath after that statement. "So you'll wear your sister's veil and train?"

"It'll be perfect," answered Lillian.

Vinny struck his handsome pose, pointing to his own face with both hands. "And you'll look beautiful. Almost as beautiful as... (clicking his tongue against the roof of his mouth - *tuk*)...me!"

He had this exciting way of making little tongue-clicking or lip-popping sounds as he paused before every important announcement. It said "ta-daaaa" without sounding self-serving. Howie loved to hear him talk, but right now he'd love to hear him talk long distance.

"Vinny, stop teasing. No one's going to look at *you* on your wedding day," said Mom, raising her voice.

Vinny grabbed Lillian, bouncing and dancing to the radio music.

"We'll be the All-American war bond couple! We'll travel coast to coast. People will wait hours for our train to pass. They'll have to buy war bonds just to behold the magnificence of...(*tuk*)...us!"

*How does he do that sound?* thought Howie.

He took his own personal inventory of his own personal skills. That one was not listed, neither was dancing. Vinny was a great dancer. Howie was a great dancer for a 4-year-old. Unfortunately he was 12. Dancing and tongue tukking and lip popping were added to his long-term life goals, way behind playing ball, and pretty far behind playing the sax. Long-term goal setting, however, sapped a lot of energy that could better be spent figuring out how to get back at Vinny for 12 years of teasing, six of which he was aware of.

Now Gene, on the other hand, didn't lip pop or tongue tuk but loved to dance. He and Howie always understood one another. They were muckers, Irish buddies. The day he came home might be the day that Howie had something better to dream about.

"You're sick, Vinny. You know that? Sick up here in the head. Don't marry this guy, Lillian. He snores."

Howie headed toward the bathroom mirror.

Lillian whispered close to Vinny, "I know" which reminded her of something else. "Mom! When does Father Aiello hear the last confessions?"

"Four o'clock."

"Come on, Vinny. We can just make it."

She dragged her betrothed out the door in a whirl. Wherever they went, they seemed to leave an invisible wake of flying energy behind.

Mom looked around the suddenly quiet room.

"That girl's got so much religion, I swear she pees holy water. But I like her anyway. Let's go, Teddy. It's time for your daily beer."

"Are you sure beer is good for a pregnant woman?"

"Guinness wouldn't put it on their posters if it wasn't true."

"Mom!" Howie screamed from the bathroom. "Look at my face!"

"You look like a pirate."

Silence filled the void while Teddy and Mom waited for his response. There was still a little boy left inside the emerging man. It saw its opportunity and took advantage of it. The women smiled at his answer.

"Yeah! A pirate...I like it!"

# CHAPTER 5

# THE FIRST TALK

# JULY 1, 1942

*Right minded folks would say that buildings cain't talk to each other. That's just a accepted fact. But most folks on this island don't know no better. So they just accept the fact that they can. And if lighter-than-air magnolias can really fall up instead of down, it ain't so surprisin' that 100 year old buildings might'a picked themselves up a few speakin' words here or there...or at least sound like they did.*

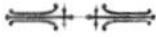

The air was still. The heat was gone. There was a good chance that the two buildings would talk tonight. They had a lot to catch up on. City Island hadn't had a hot day followed by a cool night since last summer. It would be a long and meaningful conversation.

Howie could see both the Legion and the general store from his spot on the back steps of the old house. He had practiced in the quiet of the evening and knew that his musical message was traveling out to the big ships sitting in the Sound. He hoped a sailor heard him. That would be an easy way to help the war effort. He was confident that he had enough blow power to send the music that far. He named the unkown sailor "Fred."

Ivory's number one rule was etched in his mind.

*It's all about the lungs.*

He had run through the full routine that Ivory insisted he practice on his tenor saxophone every day. It had lost its shine and bore proud dents that told of some previous owner's hard-knock life. But it stood up to the demanding blues and jazz melodies that required long riffs and stretched Howie's wind capacity, always without notes on paper. Written musical notes meant nothing to a blind man. It was the note-blower that mattered. Ivory had plans for Howie that Howie didn't even know about yet, long range plans.

He sat on the same step where he had been the night Nana died. Since that evening, the saxophone had become Howie's reality anchor. It seemed that the only time he could completely escape his memory of that fateful day was when he concentrated on creating his music.

He looked up at the second story window and tried to forget, but the earlier conversation had planted a seed that was now harvested for better or worse. He had to cheer himself up and the only way was with a cheer-up song, one that Ivory had insisted he add to his repertoire even though it made no sense on the sax. It was not a sax song, so he played it all the harder: *Get Out the Way Ole Dan Tucker!*

It was a tough blow, and it took a lot out of him. By the time he finished, he found himself standing, foot-tapping, and physically spent. His puffy cheeks hurt, but his mind was clear. He dropped back down to the step.

Mom had come out to listen. She sat by his side and took his hand. He was still young enough for her to do that. And he knew it. Howie looked down at her hand. She wore an extra ring, a silver

Irish ring showing two hands encircling a heart. He knew it well. Nana had called it her Claddagh ring.

"You're wearing Nana's wedding ring."

"I'm saving it for Pop. It's more than just a wedding ring. It was Nana's tether to the old sod. City Island reminded her of where she grew up, in a little fishing village on Galway Bay called Claddagh. So she insisted that this is where she belonged. Where we all belonged...And where she should be buried...You alright? I heard you scream again last night."

"Just a bad dream."

"Sounds like you get a lot of bad dreams lately."

"It'll be okay, Mom."

"You didn't eat much tonight, either."

"Wasn't hungry."

"What's the matter, Howie? The bruises?"

"Nah. I didn't know if I should tell Vinny that Uncle Bill laid me out. He might do somethin' crazy. I just hate lyin' to him."

"You didn't really lie. You just didn't tell him the whole story. That's the fun of it. Besides, Vinny's already got a war and a wedding on his mind. And that's enough for any boy to handle."

"Do you think maybe Bill's tryin' to take Pop's place? He *is* the older brother."

"Nobody can take Pop's place. Here or not, he's still the head of this family, and he'll deal with Bill when he comes home."

"Bill said I should quit workin' for Mr. Nakamura. Do I have to?"

"What do *you* want to do?"

"Well, Vinny had the telegram job when he was my age. And Gene had it before him, so I kinda feel like I should do it, war or no war. I mean, Mr. Nakamura didn't start the war. It's not his fault. I think Pop treated Mr. Nakamura more like a brother than he did Uncle Bill. How come?"

"'Treats' not 'treated'. Dunny's not gone forever...I guess it goes back to the bananas."

This made no sense to Howie. "What bananas?"

"It was a long time ago and you were very young."

"I hate bananas."

"You used to love them. But I think you ate so many that...well... Things change."

"That's the whole problem, Mom. Everything's changin'. It's all gettin' worse and worse. Everyday it gets worse. I just want...I want everything to be the way it was before. Before Pop went away. Before Gene got bombed. Before Nana died. The way it was when I was 11."

Mom tried to edge the blues out of him.

"Twelve's a lot more grown up than 11. I've known people who have been 11. I've heard them talk."

"Yeah, me too. Eleven was easy. Twelve is work."

They looked at each other for a moment, then broke out into a smile. Mom had done her job, and she had done it well, helping him put a little order in a life caught in a growing web of problems and priorities. She gave him a hug. He was still young enough to get a hug, too.

"What do you think Pop would say about me being the messenger?"

"Pop...Hmmmm...Pop's his own man. He would say, 'Don't let anybody make your decisions for you.' But then nobody could ever tell Dunny Logan much of anything."

Now, the hard question.

"Is Pop a traitor?"

And the easy answer.

"Of course not."

"Then where is he? Why did the army take him away in handcuffs? It's been six months and we don't even know where he is!"

Mom saw this as a matter-of-fact business.

"Back when I first met Pop and he was working on the docks, they took him away in handcuffs a couple of times. And he always came back. My parents were not too happy, but he kept on showing up at my door. I told him he'd have to change if he wanted us to get serious. One night, he was walking through the docks with that big club he used to swing around so important like, and he beat up three guys who tried to steal a load of silk. The importer, Mr. Mitsui, was so impressed, he offered Pop a job. They sent him to Yokohama and he saved another load. The next thing I know I'm raising three sons, and he's escorting shipments back from Tokyo. So sometimes change *is* good...We'll ask him where he was when he comes home."

"*If* he comes home."

"Don't worry about that, Howie. He'll get home. Hirohito, himself, couldn't keep Pop away from his family."

Mom gave Howie a knowing wink. She waited for him to wink back, and he did. He was her baby-of-the-family, and he would be until the day she died.

"I'm gonna go listen to the buildings talk tonight."

"Okay, but take a blanket."

"And Mom," laughed Howie, "you did say 'arse'!"

When he reached the general store porch that night, another body was already blanket-wrapped on a rocker, waiting for the creaking talk to begin. Kim knew he would arrive. She had heard his saxophone drifting across the evening air. Now the dominant sound, overpowering the soft breeze and sea ripples, was the lonely echo of Ivory's piano rolling out of the Legion Hall across the sandy circle.

Howie's iodine markings weren't the only things he was showing off tonight. He also wore a red bandana over his hair, tied to one side.

"Think I look like a pirate?"

"A dumb-ass pirate maybe...Don't worry, Howie. I'll help you scrub it off tomorrow. But you *gotta* take that rag off your head."

Kim kicked the "boy" right out of the little man.

"Yeah, I know."

He slid the bandana off.

Howie pulled a big wooden rocker tight to hers. They settled in for the night and shared their blankets across both chairs. In other lands, in other times this closeness they exhibited might have been scandalous. But these two City Island families had healed and comforted each other for a generation. They would not let 1942 come between them.

Kim had popcorn. She had lemonade. She had all the tools required to stay awake until the talk began. They vowed to keep each other up so they wouldn't miss this first talk of the summer. They would eat the popcorn, drink the lemonade and pee in the bushes if they had to.

They were asleep by ten.

They never heard the steps of another lone figure who came to hear the talk.

Across the street, Ivory's feet followed his faithful cane to a weathered bench in front of the Legion. The feet raised up and the body stretched out. A pants pocket gave birth to a shiny half-pint flask that promised to keep its owner company until the talk began.

The night was cool. The talk rose slowly. Echoes, creaks and groans. First the general store, next the Legion in response, then the general store again. They talked of storms in nature, and storms in nations, and family storms yet to come.

His flask wet the lips. His ears absorbed the talk. His mind drifted back to other summers and other nights, and other beautiful sounds. The sounds of Lumpkin County, Georgia. The sounds of the first and last time he had ever seen a piano. The sounds of the last time he had ever seen.

He replanted the flask in his pocket. When his hand emerged, it held an old white rabbit's foot. His thumb gently rubbed what was left of the soft fur in a continuous circular motion, painting a faint smile across Ivory's sleepy face.

# CHAPTER 6

# THE PICKIN'

# JULY 2, 1942

*Sometimes bein' a messenger can just be no more'n deliverin' words that ain't gonna hurt nobody.*

*And sometimes bein' a messenger can be a God-awful burden. Now at least a bag-man runner gots somethin' that he can measure and count when he arrive. But a "word" messenger? All he gots to tally up is the look on that face staring back at him. When I was 12 and flat out, down in that green valley, a stranger-messenger 'bout my age had to climb The Road To Nowhere to reach my Mama. That was one happenin' that I hoped I would never have to re-live by tellin' it to another earth-bound soul, 'cause I wear the shame to this day that he had to deliver my bad news and get paid with a bad news look in return. A boy gonna carry that look inside his own-self forever.*

*I never knew his name. He'd never forget mine.*

⊰⊱

The telegraph bell had rung early that morning. Howie missed the never-stops-anyway bus so he had to push the pedals himself.

He cruised his Columbia Roadster with hands locked behind his head. The Western Union cap was jaunty, the wind was in his eyes, and he was king of the Island.

Random women on random porches smiled at his coming and going. He knew them all. He knew a lot of people in his 12 years. The last time he had counted, it was 439 including relatives. Working in the Island's only store had made that easy. He passed Mrs. Giardello's house, and she waved to him as she rocked her morning rock.

"Hello, Mrs. Giardello."

"Good morning, Howie. Who's the telegram for this time?"

"Mrs. Sabatini."

"Oh! What does it say?"

"I don't read 'em. I'm just the messenger. Western Union Policy. If I read the telegrams I deliver, I'd get fired."

Mrs. Sabatini lived only three cottages down from Mrs. Giardello. There was no local newspaper on City Island so they both had taken on the awesome responsibility of finding out everything about everybody on a daily basis. And they both considered the other one to be the Island busybody.

But the most amazing part about the two women was that they both had moved to City Island on the same day 30 years ago. Knowing that they could never be "natives", the ladies waged an unwinnable rivalry as to who was more "local", each claiming to predate the other by minutes. But the most amazing, amazing part was that they were sisters.

And like so many others on the island, they both had sons at war. Cousins.

Whenever Howie and Kim were hungry, or maybe just bored, they would stop by one of the houses, allowing themselves to be grilled for the latest gossip over some cannelloni or a small calzone. They always knew in advance what they were going to divulge and how slowly to let it slip out. Sometimes they even visited both houses on the same day. And when Stevie reported to the gossip columnists, he usually brought along young Mungo.

Mungo never spoke. Nobody knew why. He generally tagged around behind Stevie, but in a pinch he'd tag along behind Howie, too. He didn't field, hit or throw very well. Although Ivory had tried to introduce him to the drums, he really couldn't play an instrument of any kind. And he was always speechless. Always. But if you wanted some quiet time, he was an excellent friend to have handy. All the other kids liked him. He made them look good by comparison.

Visually, Big Stevie and smaller Mungo were opposites. Stevie was heavy boned, assured of himself, at least on the surface, and sported a dirty blond crew-cut that would grow into corn silk by the end of the summer. Little Mungo, however, always looked pale. He had a pale complexion, pale floppy hair and even a pale smile. Sometimes Kim would rub dirt on his face just to make him look alive. And when he needed recharging and thought he could get away with it, darting his eyes from side to side, he'd pop his furtive thumb into his mouth for a quick 10-second power suck.

But today Howie was alone and on the job.

Mrs. Sabatini grinned as she dropped a buffalo head nickel into Howie's palm. She turned around and screamed down the street to Mrs. Giardello, "It's a boy!"

"Wait a minute, Howie."

She was back in an instant with a second nickel.

Howie smiled confidently.

*Today was going to be a lot better than yesterday. A lot better! Nothing could go wrong today.*

Howie snacked with Mrs. Sabatini, much to the angst of Mrs. Giardello, and made it to the sandlot in time to stare across home plate at Stevie as they chose up sides. That was the good part about growing up on a small island. No matter what differences the kids might have on Monday, they had to be over it by Tuesday, because you never knew who might be your teammate tomorrow. It wasn't like there was an inexhaustible supply of back-up players. Something serious had to happen to keep anyone out of the game. And something serious hardly ever happened. Everybody was picked and everybody played.

Deciding who picks first was a sandlot ritual. One captain vertically tossed the bat to the other. Then they would hand-over-hand the length of the bat working upward. Whoever squeezed his hand in for the last grab, would have to hold that hand over his head and encircle his body with the bat three times. If he still held on, his arm was out-stretched and the opponent got one kick to knock it out of his grasp. If he managed to hold the bat at the end of that gauntlet, he got first pick. But the other team would be first at bat. It had always been done that way, and no one remembered why.

As their names were alternately called, the boys and girls moved behind either Stevie or Howie. Kim waited anxiously to be picked. In spite of being one of the best players, she was toward the bottom of both mental lists today.

Howie took his time, casually tossing his old mitt in the air as he made his picks. He didn't bring Magic Maggie to the game today, still apprehensive about actually using something that was City Island's version of a national treasure.

Ivory meticulously cleaned off the cardboard home plate, using the back-up home plate, a slightly smaller piece of cardboard he kept folded in his back pocket. He owned a whisk broom, but it was misplaced in the unseen recesses of his small cottage. He normally would have Howie or Kim or Big Stevie locate it, but he thought, perhaps this time it would be a good job for Mungo. It was a stretch for a blind man and a silent kid to communicate, but Ivory liked to stretch.

Stevie picked.

Howie picked.

Stevie picked.

Howie picked.

The pool was shrinking. Only Sue Ellen, Mungo and Kim remained. Kim was obviously the best player and should have been selected much earlier, but she wasn't, and the expression on her Japanese face was anything but inscrutable. It gave away every insecurity that she owned.

*Why didn't Howie pick me already? What if nobody picks me? What am I gonna do? Can you really be "not picked"? Has anyone ever been "not picked" before? If you're "not picked", where do you go?*

Stevie said the fated words. "Sue Ellen."

Howie wanted Kim to be on Stevie's team. He knew that if they had to play *with* each other instead of *against* each other, maybe they'd be friends again. His plan was coming together perfectly. Only two players were left now, Kim and the 9-or-10-or-maybe-even-11year-old, useless looking, silent Mungo. Howie would choose Mungo, the daisy-picking kid who didn't even know how old he was. Stevie would have to take the last player, Kim. It *was* a good day.

Mungo drove his fist into his mitt, working on the pocket. He had to. It was an inherited catcher's mitt, thickly rounded and thickly padded. He knew that Howie would pick his best friend, Kim, even though she was a girl. And he knew that Stevie would never let him be a catcher on his team, even though Mungo had the right glove for it. Stevie was always the catcher. The "even thoughs" were stacked against Mungo today. He'd have to man first base with a catcher's mitt again. He was getting used to it.

*Next year Howie and Stevie will both be too old to play the morning games, and I'll be the captain. And I'll catch!*

He picked last week's elbow scab while he waited for Howie to call Kim's name.

But Howie called, "Mungo".

Mungo was so surprised he almost said something. Today he'd be the catcher, the almighty caller of finger signals, the wearer of the mask, the stopper of runs at the plate. He could be a hero. There's always a chance for a catcher to be a hero. Celebrating, he balanced his glove on his head, flapped his arms like a bird and flew around behind Howie. He stood on one leg, crossed his arms and grinned.

*Today is a good Mungo-day.*

It was Stevie's turn for the final pick, and Kim was the only candidate left. He looked her over, hiked up his pants and did his best James Cagney.

"I ain't gonna pick you. Seeee? You ought to be in the internment camp with your mother. Seeee? They don't allow no American baseball in Japanese internment camps."

"Come on, Stevie. You gotta pick her."

"I ain't pickin' her, Howie. She ain't picked. Let's play ball!"

Ivory was listening intently and his expression told a story of disapproval as the other players ran to their favored positions. Kim remained alone to the side of home, staring at the ground. Howie turned to Ivory.

"Tell him, Ivory. He has to pick her."

"Stevie's the captain, and a captain gots his 'drothers. Now if'n he 'drother pick nobody than Kim, it be up to him. But he gots to live with his pickin'. So no mealy mouth bitchin', Stevie, when you lose. 'Cause without Kim on that team, you *will* lose. Sorry ass truth delivered. Feed on it...And while we're at it, next time I make a call you don't like, don't be passin' no gas either. Or you ain't gonna be your own team's squattin' catcher no more. 'Cause this ump gots his 'drothers, too. Fact stated...Play Ball!"

Howie tried to say something to Kim, but no words came out. Of all times to find out how to keep his thoughts to himself, this had to be the worst. She let her mitt slip to the ground and walked away.

Howie moved slowly to the glove. His feet dragged in the dust. He picked the mitt up and appeared as if he were going to follow her, but Stevie yelled again, this time from his catcher's stance.

"Let's go, Howie. Ball time!"

The sacred ceremony of baseball had begun, and Howie was wanted at the altar. He weighed his loyalties to his best friend, and he weighed his loyalties to the game.

With a torn-apart look at the disappearing Kim, he pulled himself back to his team.

Howie's squad was up first. He had failed to kick the pickin' bat out of Stevie's hand.

# CHAPTER 7
# TATSU'S FIRST LETTER
# JULY 2, 1942

The store was finally quiet. No customers. No telegrams. No deliveries.

Mr. Nakamura took advantage of the lull to remove two strands of old flypaper strategically placed in front of the south-facing windows. They each boasted dozens of multi-eyed residents, and there was a waiting list anxiously buzzing through the aisles. He unfurled the new sweet-smelling amber and dangled it from the ceiling with a thumb tack. But this was his last roll, and he treated it with a special reverence. To maximize its effect, he had decided to plant it near his work station. But the sticky paper tape was now located over the counter, perhaps a little too close to the customers, not the safest of locations. He would need a crystal ball to predict if, or when, another case of this little piece of life's necessities might ever get delivered. Supply trucks saw no need to use up their precious gas traveling to City Island when they couldn't even fill the needs of their mainland customers. It was worse than usual now that rationing of cars, gas, and tires was in effect. Food item restrictions loomed on the not too distant horizon.

As of yesterday, bicycles had become the latest victim to fall under the rationing system's hatchet. Nakamura decided to withhold this bit of information from Howie. He wouldn't take it well. The good news was that the government had decided to postpone the banning of sliced bread for one more year. After that, the metal used in the slicing machines would turn into bullets.

Although the store still had all the staples, some items were running low. Butter was temporarily non-existent. If no supplies came soon, he would have to sail the skiff over to the Bronx Terminal Market, or follow the Sound into the East River and down to Harlem's 125th Street pier. That's when he could have used his son's help. Two men could secure the craft's cargo and navigate much more safely than one. He would have to draft Kim or Howie to do the job his son Tatsu had done before the boy went overseas. After all, this was war, when 12-year-olds became 18 over night.

Mr. Nakamura stood behind the fly paper, dangerously close to the sticky surface, and whispered a warning to any unseen, prospective tenant, "Fly away."

But as he stepped back to admire his work, a lone fly inaugurated the new insect mausoleum. Instead of smiling, a hint of sorrow slipped across his face and he breathed a little "ooooh". The fly buzzed in vain.

Nakamura carefully lowered an old metal box from a shelf above his desk. He opened it, lifting out three letters tied together with a red ribbon. His hands separated them, selecting the first one. The envelope was addressed in both English and Japanese characters, but the letter inside was written in Tatsu's impeccable Palmer Method cursive script.

*September 1, 1941*
*Dear Father,*

*Today I have arrived in Tokyo. As soon as my foot stepped off the ship, I realized that coming to the university was truly a wise decision. It is good to be among one's own people. Tomorrow I will visit the House of Mitsui for the interview which Pop Logan so graciously arranged.*

*The home of our cousins is well-appointed and close to the university. Everyone here travels by bicycle the way we would use a bus at home. They think I speak with an accent and ask me many questions about my life in America. I think they do it just to laugh. I am expected to teach English to my cousins every day. I fear that sleeping on the mats will take some getting used to. I actually enjoy eating their seaweed, but I still miss mother's cooking.*

*I was saddened to hear that grandmother has grown more ill, requiring mother to travel all the way to San Francisco to be by her side. When I left her, she seemed much improved. I hope that all will be well shortly, and that she will return as soon as...*

"Are we gonna get locked up in some internment camp?"

The loud question broke the letter apart in Nakamura's mind as Kim charged through the door. He folded the letter neatly and replaced it in the envelope.

"Are you worried?"

"Are we, Dad?"

"Truthfully, if this were the San Francisco Bay instead of the Long Island Sound, we would have been sent to Colorado by now."

"What's the difference?"

"The government in Washington is too busy to care about a handful of New York Nisei. But a hundred thousand Japanese in California, that's a lot of sushi."

"No jokin', Dad. I'm serious. Are we goin' or not?"

He put his arm around his daughter.

"Do not say farewell to your friends, yet. Only West Coast Japanese are being taken away."

"Well, if we go, I hope we go to Owens Valley so we can be with Mom. Why did Grandma have to get sick?! Why did

Mom ever have to go back to San Francisco anyway?! I hate San Francisco! I *hate* it!"

"Kim, you've never been to San Francisco."

"It's all Grandma's fault."

"It's nobody's fault."

"Some day they *will* get us! In the middle of the night! They'll come, and they'll get us! And no one will ever know where we went! Ever!"

She started to cry and buried her face in her father's shoulder.

"Not Tatsu. Not mom. Not nobody."

"No, that won't happen. I believe we have a guardian angel watching over us. Protecting us from harm."

"What angel?"

"Saint Donovan."

"Dad, saints can't be angels. There are saints, and there are angels. But there ain't no guardian-saint-angels."

"It must be difficult to be so young and yet so wise."

She sniffed the last of her brief tears away.

"I read the newspaper, Dad. It said that they arrested 30 Germans and three Italians in New York so far. But I only heard about two Japanese, and I never saw that in the papers, only on the radio."

"There's been more than two."

"Are we gonna get arrested?"

"Do not worry, Kim. Only spies get arrested."

"Is that why Pop Logan got arrested?"

"He's no more spy than I am."

"Well, I wish they would arrest us. Just so I could get sent away! I hate this place. I hate everybody here!"

She clutched in tighter to her father, and he stroked her long black hair. This was the first time she slowed down enough to notice the letter in her father's hand. Before she could question it, the sore moment was healed by another voice from the doorway.

"Even me?"

Howie blocked out the sunlight. He stepped closer and held Kim's mitt out in her direction.

"Especially you! You didn't pick me!"

She wiped away the last vestiges of crying eyes. Howie had seen her eyes cry before, just as she had seen his. For 12 years they had laughed, cried, fought and made up, and fought again. They had sweated, played and prayed together so much that his Catholicism and her Buddhism had gotten lost in the mix. The few mysteries they did not know about each other by now, they would never understand.

She stormed by Howie and marched onto, and off of, the porch on a desperate journey to nowhere in particular.

Howie tried to rush after her, but his spontaneous burst of motion brought him directly into the newly hung flypaper, and it wrapped around his head as he turned. He swung his arms wildly in the air, but the flailing movements only succeeded in ripping the tack out of the ceiling. The golden mess fell into his hair like an amber python. With a sputter and a spin, he escaped his inanimate attacker, peeling its last gluey remnants off Kim's baseball mitt.

The yellow paper settled at wide-eyed Nakamura's feet. Howie ran for the door with a hasty "Sorry!" thrown behind him.

Nakamura's open mouth was speechless. He knew there would be rejoicing in the local insect community tonight, and that he'd have to sail in search of supplies earlier than anticipated. The lone captive fly broke loose, staggered on the floor for a moment and quickly buzzed through the closing doorway.

Howie caught up to Kim at the flagpole in the middle of the road. The two old buildings stared down at them as if they had strategically positioned themselves a hundred years before just to eavesdrop on this particular conversation.

"Kim, wait."

"You didn't pick me."

"I'm...I'm sorry. Okay?"

She stopped and formed her battle line, putting the flag staff between them. As Howie stepped around so he could see her, she inched backward, forcing him to follow her circular path, slowly circumnavigating the pole.

"How could you?! You picked Mungo over me! Mungo! Go back to your team. You're the captain!"

"No, I'm not."

"Yes, you are."

"No, I quit."

"Captains can't quit."

Howie let his devious smile escape. "I made Mungo captain."

"Mungo!"

"Yeah. Serves 'em right. Here, take your glove."

"I don't want it."

"Yeah, you do. Come on. Take it."

She held her ground, swallowed a long breath and her shoulders heaved up and down. Her eyes came to rest on the sticky spots decorating her mitt.

"What's this?!"

"Flypaper."

"Flypaper?!"

"Yeah. A little vegetable oil will get this right out. Don't worry. Whatever it is, we can fix it."

"Okay...Thanks for getting it."

"You're welcome."

He handed her the mitt, and her eyes locked into his. She smiled a different smile than he had grown used to. It was a smile that made him uncomfortable, and he looked down to find his foot inexplicably drawing something in the road sand. He tried to stop it, but the movement was uncontrollable with a mind of its own. He was afraid Kim would see it, too, and ask what it was. He had no idea, and if he told her about it, she'd label him "the dunce head", which is probably what he was. He hoped his foot would walk when needed.

The ringing of that small, but all-demanding bell shattered the moment. In unison, their eyes shot up to the roof peak of the general store. A telegram was coming in.

# CHAPTER 8

# 439 SOMEONES

# JULY 2, 1942

*Bravery be somethin' that you don't know you got for sure 'til after you be done with it. And it be done with you. When it come to bravery, the sayin' and the doin' are a giant step apart. And if you ain't scared when you do the doin', then you ain't really brave. You just too dumb to know better. When I was 12, I was in a place I oughtin' a been, and I was too dumb to know better.*

Howie and Kim hurried back inside. She saw her father replace the letter into a small pile of two or three others. He moved to the receiver as the message typed itself out. Howie automatically got his cap. It was good that he had left the game today. He was needed here. He put his mitt on the counter and waited.

"Who's it for?"

"Your sister-in-law, Teddy."

Howie froze. He had been waiting for the first military death telegram to arrive. They all had. He knew that sooner or later someone would die in this war, and he would have to carry the message home. It would be some one of the 439 people he knew, some one of the 642 who called this island home. It was more than probable. It was inevitable.

Kim's face grew tense. Howie's mouth went dry. Finally, Nakamura finished the cutting and gluing process. He fanned the paper in the air to dry and sealed it in its yellow envelope. Howie could restrain himself no more.

"Is it the death one?"

"Have we ever received a death telegram on this Island since the war started?"

"Not yet."

"Then what are you worrying about? Do not worry about what you cannot change."

"But someday it'll come in."

"Perhaps. And what will you do then, Howie? Run and hide?"

"I'll...I'll do my duty, I guess."

"Like a brave soldier on the home front."

"Yeah, like a brave soldier."

Howie wanted the telegram but Nakamura used it like a pointer in the air.

"If all the brave soldiers decided to run and hide, on both sides, there would be no one left to fight this war. If there is no war, there are no telegrams. And your burden would be lifted."

"Gene wouldn't run. Neither would Vinny."

"Ah, Gene is in the hospital, so he cannot run. And Vinny is in love. A man in love is capable of doing the most unpredictable things. And of the three brothers, that leaves just you."

"Me? I wouldn't run. Not from those dirty Nazis. Not from those dirty Nips."

Howie caught himself and let his eyes slide downward, realizing he might have offended Mr. Nakamura's feelings. But the reply came back with a smile.

"Not from Big Stevie?"

"Not even Big Stevie."

"You are not afraid of him?"

"Oh yeah, I am. But I wouldn't run."

"Then, obviously, you are a man. Perhaps not yet a bright one, but a man nonetheless." Nakamura smiled at him and handed over the telegram with a look of confidence in Howie's abilities. "I know that when the time comes, you will, as you say, do your duty."

Howie slid the telegram under his cap, turning the peak to the side.

Kim stopped him at the door and handed him his mitt.

"Howie, I...I'm really proud of you."

He was a little embarrassed, but he liked her attention too much to care. He just hoped his foot wasn't going to start drawing again.

By the time he got home, a dozen different scenarios had flown through his mind. He knew that Gene was still alive, or Mr. Nakamura would not have delayed in handing over the telegram. *Speed and accuracy, that's what makes Western Union "Western Union".*

As he came in through the rear screen door and heard it whap that familiar WHAP! behind him, he was confident that this would be a good day at last. Teddy had just brought in a basket of early pole beans from her victory garden. It was hard to get anything to grow in this sandy soil, but she came from farm stock and knew how to cajole Mother Earth into offering up her wares.

*They must have a pact. At least she's a better grower than a knitter.*

He didn't want to alarm his sister-in-law, but he had a job to do. Her hair hung in her face, and she looked tired as she snapped off the bean ends. He remembered when she first came to the big house. She was so young and so beautiful. Teddy was a girl who had married a man. Gene always seemed old, grown up, able to make quick decisions, like Pop.

A string bean hit Howie in the face. Without even looking, he knew Vinny threw it. This was no time for games. He slid the paper from under his cap.

"Telegram, Mrs. Logan."

All three stopped abruptly, totally caught off guard. Vinny's string bean game was over. Howie held the telegram in Teddy's direction. Her expression fixated somewhere between pain and apprehension. One hand rose to cover her mouth while the other rested on her near-term pregnant belly.

Howie moved closer. "Don't worry, Teddy. I think Gene's okay."

Teddy reached for the telegram and had it opened before her hands came back to her body. She read it, dropping the envelope to the floor. Tears welled up in her eyes, but they were tears of joy.

"Oh, dear God in heaven! Gene's been released from the hospital in San Francisco. He's coming home! He just changed trains in Which-eee-ta!"

Teddy squealed. Mom squealed. Grabbing their hands, and Howie's too, Vinny danced all of them into a circle singing "Which-eee-ta! Which-eee-ta! Which-eee-ta!" When they stopped, Mom hugged each one and cupped Vinny's face in her hands.

"Do you know what this means, Vinny? You're brother will be home for your wedding!"

"Now if only Pop was here," he lamented, as much as Vinny was capable of lamenting.

"Underestimating your father has been the downfall of many a man. Come on, Teddy. I'll help you get your room ready."

The women exited into the parlor and up the stairs. Teddy showed the telegram to Mom. Teddy's voice trailed off as she asked, "Where is Which-eee-ta?"

"It's pronounced Wichita, dear. It's in Kansas."

"Kansas...Oh, yeah. Dorothy and Toto, and the *wicked witch*!..."Witch', 'Wichita'... I should have known that. It all makes sense now."

Howie had done his duty. But that one flash of fear in Teddy's eyes was scary. He wasn't sure he was man enough to deliver the death message, in spite of what he had told Mr. Nakamura a few minutes before, especially to someone he knew. And he knew 439 someones. But the people in this house now, and the people he hoped would be in this house soon, were the people he loved. Gene would finally be safe, but Pop was missing, and in a few days, Vinny would be married and shipped out. Pop was tough, but Vinny was silly, crazy, reckless Vinny.

Although only two years younger than Gene, he was still a kid. *Who in her right mind would want to marry Vinny, the college boy? Poor Lillian. What if reckless Vinny didn't come back?*

He wanted to hug his brother. He needed that physical contact to reassure some part of his brain that feared the worst, the unspeakable. He was young enough to hug Mom, but too old to hug another man. Men didn't hug men. Boys did. Men especially didn't hug their older brothers, unless they wanted to get hurt. Yet words alone wouldn't do.

Howie walked a ten-foot mile, crossing the seemingly endless kitchen. It took guts. With one quick, awkward motion, he threw his arms around Vinny and gave him a back-slapping hug, then stepped away waiting for a reaction, hoping it was an understanding smile instead of a right jab.

"Hey, squirt. What's this all about? Disappointed that you're not going to be the best man now that Gene's on his way? Ahh, you'll be more relaxed playing that saxophone of yours in the back of the church next to Ivory. I swear the way you carry that thing around now makes it look like you grew another arm."

"I'm gonna miss you. Be careful over there, okay?"

"Come on. Knock it off. I don't even know yet if they're sending me out of the country. You don't see me sweatin' it, do ya?

Nothing's gonna happen to Invincible Vinny. I'm always lucky, right? Invincible Vinny."

Howie didn't want to answer. Vinny always thought he was invincible, but he wasn't always as invincible as he thought.

"Right?"

"Yeah, you're always lucky."

"Right. So don't worry. I'm gonna be back here, kid. Back to kick the green out of your Irish 'arse'."

Vinny got him in a headlock, knocked his hat off and nuggied the hell out of the boy. Howie tried to break loose, laughing, but Vinny spoke calmly and held firm.

"This headlock does it every time. Don't even struggle. Just learn from the experience. Enjoy it. You're a fortunate boy to have *me* for a brother. I don't do this for everybody. So don't give me any of that 'miss you' shit. Besides, I'm a second lewey. Hey, I got it... (popping his lips)...made!"

Howie hoped that he was right. Vinny relaxed his grip.

"Okay, Howie. Now you do me. Let's see what you got."

"I got nothin'."

"Squeeze in. Pull the head down, and do it fast."

Howie switched places with his brother, wrapped his arms around Vinny's head and locked in tight, but he couldn't get Vinny's head lowered. Vinny laughed.

"That's it? Come on, kid. Put some weight behind it."

Howie let his legs collapse, leaned down hard and brought Vinny's face right to the floor. Vinny began to choke, cough and laugh, all at the same time. Howie only laughed.

"Hey, Vinny. You got snot comin' outta your nose. You're a lucky boy, you know. I don't do the snot-hold for everybody."

Vinny wrestled to break free and finally pried Howie's arms loose.

"That was...ah...that was good. I was going to teach you the groin kick next, but I think that's enough for one day."

*Headlocks and groin kicks. Maybe Vinny really was becoming a fighting soldier.*

Earlier, as Howie had ridden away from the traffic circle by the general store on his Western Union run, Mr. Nakamura had stepped out the back door to tend to his small sail boat. Kim took advantage of his absence to search out the letters she had seen her father read a short while before. They weren't hard to find. She climbed a stool and slid the box down from the shelf.

Sitting on the floor behind the counter, she read all three letters until her eyes burned and her heart pounded. Sobbing louder than she would have thought possible, she gathered their pages and crushed them up into one indistinguishable mass, looking up just in time to see her father looming overhead.

"Tatsu! I hate him! How could he do this to us?!"

"I cannot explain your brother's actions," her father said as he lovingly retrieved the pages, smoothing them back into legible shapes.

"Why didn't you tell me?"

"Would it have helped?"

"No."

"Then you did not need to know. As for these letters, Kim, treat them with respect."

"Burn them! Burn them now!"

"We will save them for his mother."

He revived the crumpled papers and reverently replaced them in their envelopes, retied the ribbon and secreted them away.

Kim secreted their memory into a deeper place.

# CHAPTER 9

# CHANGING TIDES

## JULY 2, 1942

*Every time my father come home from the music circuit, he left behind him new strings for my banjo or a new bow for my fiddle. But the most important thing he ever left was a stick drawing in the Georgia clay. When I was still a seein' boy, he outlined 88 small boxes and placed my fingers on the keys, hand over hand. Together we would play the dust piano, drawin' out the notes from every hidden throat place we could find, our own fingertips touchin' the right squares at the right times. I knowed, and he knowed, that I could play the piano long 'afore I'd ever seed one.*

*Through plantin' and harvestin', through season and season, we practiced in the red dirt. We played* Dixie. *We played* Mine Eyes Has Seen the Glory. *We played* Bringin' in the Sheaves. *Then the plantin' season was gone and so was he. On misty mornin's, I'd look down The Road To Nowhere for him to appear like a angel high-steppin' through a cloud, a piano strapped to his back. Knowin' it could never happen. Hopin' that it would.*

*Music, be it rejoicin' happy or blues singin' sad, is a marvelous wonderful thing. Somehow it know when the world be off key, and it set it right again.*

The day was fading as Kim searched for her best hair ribbon. She wanted to look good in case it turned out to be a special Kim day. She hadn't fully decided yet what this evening would hold in store.

As her father closed up downstairs, she moved quietly to the small Buddhist shrine on the shelf in the corner of their living room. It held only a few flowers, a small hanging bell and a statue of the sitting Buddha representing peace and tranquility. She would much rather have had the reclining Buddha to symbolize entering into death unafraid.

Kim knelt down and tapped the bell, producing a tingling vibration that flowed across the room. She took a small incense stick and lit the end, wedging it upright into the sandy bottom of a decorated cup. As the sweet smelling wisp of smoke started to rise, she pulled it into herself in a purifying motion, and brought her hands together, pointing skyward. She closed her eyes and bowed several times, finally touching her forehead to the floor.

Howie welcomed the approaching evening at home in his own way. He had important business to take care of. Shoe business.

He sat in the empty up-stairs window where Nana had been only two months before, saxophone by his side. Any high point on sea-level City Island held the promise of a beautiful sunset. He gave in to temptation and tore his eyes away from the coral colors spread out behind the newly built Whitestone Bridge and the distant Manhattan horizon.

In the opposite direction, City Island's enticing, bad-girl sister beckoned to him. Hart Island, flat and sparcely treed, was almost lost in the encroaching darkness. Floating between the tiny, ill-named Rat Island and Devil's Stepping Stones, it sat hoping to welcome any and all City Island citizens who might someday wish to take up residence there, permanently.

Hart Island's one light flickered like a twinkling Bethlehem star, a hint of happiness in an unhappy place. Howie tried never to look at it too long, or he could be easily tempteded to visit just by the sheer mystery and rumors that surrounded that small island and its Mortuary Man. Instead he stared down at the spot of green where Nana's body had come to rest.

*That was a bad day*, he thought. *A very bad day.*

As usual, he had been sitting in the backyard practicing his saxophone in the early evening, when the daily sea breeze fades and the stillness settles in. His notes carried far out to sea this way, instead of back into the island. The neighbors never complained. But they never would. Not on City Island.

As the foggy half-truths of the scene replayed in his mind, his 75-year-old Nana hung out the clothes from the second story window above him, where the pulley line started its run across the yard to the telephone pole. And as all City Islanders know, back yard telephone poles were installed so that there would be a place for clothes lines to anchor. Any electric and telephone wires were merely an after thought to justify the pole's existence.

But the horror always came in flashes. Nana loses her balance as Bill's big hands reach out trying to save her. But she slips through his fingers. He's too late. She falls out of the window, crashing to the ground only a few feet from Howie, and her piercing downward cry echoes in his brain like the last note he hit on the sax.

Howie had worked hard to get rid of these images, but they just wouldn't give up. He tried to think of something else.

A small pencil came out of his pocket and he propped one foot up on the opposing knee. He didn't have much faith in Mom's advice about solving problems by writing friends' names on shoe bottoms, but he had run out of options to win Stevie over. They used to be good friends, but Stevie seemed to grow up fast. Too fast. And Stevie liked the feeling. He liked armpit sweat and pubic hair and saying "shit" when things went bad. Howie wrote one word on the sole of his shoe: STEVIE.

The sun was almost gone, and Howie ascended the narrow stairs to the third floor widow's walk. He opened the windowed door and climbed outside. Pop had told him not to go up there until he got around to repairing or replacing the railing the way he had intended. But Uncle Sam had other plans, so Howie carefully avoided getting too close to the edge. He could still see the sun's rays from here.

Howie double-checked the sole of his shoe. Stevie's name was still intact.

Stevie did not have a good start in life. His father left when he was too young to know, let alone care. His mother had raised him as best she could while working as a nurse's aide at Fordham Hospital, across the shaky bridge in the real Bronx. Sometimes she was home; sometimes she wasn't. Stevie got in the habit of eating wherever and whenever he could. It was his good fortune that often Islanders accepted family and friends alike, into their homes at mealtime. And Island generosity was probably somewhat responsible for keeping him alive. If anything, Big Stevie was over-fed.

Ivory had given him free lessons hoping to teach Stevie the magic of the drums. He had what Ivory termed "ability" but he never said the boy had talent. And Stevie wasn't a serious student, anyway. But now that Howie was maturing into the natural love that he possessed for the saxophone, Stevie realized he was being left behind and began drumming in earnest. He lived on a small island, had few skills and fewer real friends. He was destined to disappear by the time he was sixteen, sucked somewhere into that life beyond the shaky bridge. And Howie was scared for him.

From high on his third floor perch, Howie played the plaintive notes of *The Saint James Infirmary Blues*. Ivory had learned it from a New Orleans vamp when he played piano in a house of joy, and he insisted that Howie know this particular song for those particular occasions when only the bluest of blues would do. It was bluer than the *Jelly Roll Blues*, even bluer than *The House of the Rising Sun*. It was a song of tragedy, the death of a loved one anonymously lost on a public hospital slab, and the melody told the tale.

Nana's death crushed his mind, and he played on until the notes came automatically, without thinking about where or when his fingers should move. The music came out of the end of his horn as if it magically happened all by itself. His eyes flowed across the sun and the sea while his fingers flowed across the brass. It was so easy, he didn't want the sound to end.

Transport ships sat waiting in Long Island Sound. Fort Totten in Queens and Fort Schuyler in the Bronx had guarded both sides of the Sound a century ago, protecting New York from the east. Now they were alive again and he could see their flags being lowered on opposite shores. As the sun set, the lights began to dim, and the city that never sleeps practiced its version of the black out. There would be no more night games at Yankee Stadium until this war was over.

A lone shadow walked along the beach, finally stopping at the water's edge. Although there was not enough light to illuminate the face, Howie knew it was Kim by her boyish body and long black hair.

She removed her shoes and stared at the water. Finally she walked in, fully clothed, and kept on walking. There were no waves that could be called "waves", only strong ripples. But the nearby rip currents in the unforgiving Sound were swift and had been known to carry swimmers, pets and candy wrappers immediately out of sight.

Howie stopped playing in the middle of a bar. He didn't like what he saw and instantly headed for the ground level, dropping his sax on the second floor.

No right-minded Islander would be swimming in the Sound at night and alone. He was raised on the water and, like any other Island kid, knew how to respect it. It was never the locals or the natives who drowned. It was always the summer people. First generation locals listened to the weather. There was no glory in riding out a storm at sea. But Island-born natives were so attuned to the ways of salt water, that on a calm day they could even hear the tide change. First, the ripples grew quieter, and again still quieter, until the sound of the water hitting the beach pebbles stopped. A few seconds of silent calm hung in the air, until the pebbles started to push each other in the opposite direction, and the tide had shifted, unnoticed to all, except those who were born by the sea. And Howie was. But so was Kim.

Howie reached the beach to find Kim floating face down, fully extended, fifty feet off shore. He dove into the water and stroked to her body. He knew he had the lung capacity to swim her back in and hoped it wasn't too late. He'd straddle her on his hip holding her chin up as he side-kicked for dry land, just as Gene and Vinny had taught him and just as he had seen them do a dozen times before. They called it "the big swim".

*It's all about the lungs.*

As he reached her, he forcefully lifted her face up out of the water, grateful that he wasn't fighting the deadly rip tides that surround the Legion Hall. She yelled.

"What are you doin'?!"

"I'm savin' you."

"When I want you to save me, I'll tell you."

They each splashed back to the shoreline. Obviously this wasn't the big swim.

"What's goin' on?"

"Nothin'. I...I was just hot. That's all."

"That's not all. You don't go face down with all your clothes on just because you're hot."

"I do."

"At night?!"

"Well..."

"Somethin's wrong. What is it?"

"Nothin'."

"Nothin', huh?"

"All right, everything."

"Everything what?"

"Forget it. Just leave me alone."

He could see that he wasn't going to get anywhere with her. Not tonight. Like the unnoticeable shift of the tide, Kim had been subtly changing, and Howie hadn't listened for the signs. He should have been a better friend, and he knew it.

"Come on, Kim. I'll carry your shoes...You are a dumb-ass. You know that? Look at your clothes."

"Oh yeah? Well at least I took my shoes off. Now who's the dumb-ass, dumb-ass?"

She punched him in the arm and ran. Howie threw a shoe at her. He missed. But the second one caught her square in the butt. The day was looking better all the time.

# CHAPTER 10

# THE LONG FUSE QUARTER-INCHER

## JULY 3, 1942

Howie wanted to go on the boat in search of supplies but Nakamura decided he would take Kim, instead. Maybe her father wanted her company. Maybe he didn't want to leave her alone due to her recent erratic moodiness. Maybe it was just her turn. But whatever the reason, they had been gone longer than expected. He was probably having a tough time finding what the island needed.

The store had been busy that morning. The discussions about rationing and the upcoming stamp system had stirred a small feeding frenzy, and Howie was holding the bait. By noon the hunters and gatherers had returned to their lairs. A lull was approaching, and as soon as the palsied Mrs. Trent made it to the counter, Howie would have the store to himself. No one new had come in all morning, and his "someones" count still stood at 439. He uncapped a bottle of orange Nehi as a reward for a morning's work well done.

The door opened, and another body slipped in, but it was only Stevie. Howie figured that Stevie might know less than 100 people; 150 at most. He thought that there probably was some kind of rating scale that measured the intelligence of a person by the number of people that person knew. He had already lost track of several of his 439 and his count could be slipping downward. At the same time, 439 seemed to be an awful lot of people. He didn't see how anyone could really know 500 at the same time. But with 642 people on this island, he might get there if he worked feverishly, and if almost all of them came shopping.

Howie helped Mrs. Trent shake her groceries onto the counter, added them up and recorded the total in the 30-day ledger. Most accounts were settled at the end of the month. Except for those that weren't.

He put the bags into her unfolded, wire-framed, two-wheeled grocery pull cart.

"I don't know what I'll do when they start using ration coupons," she confided.

"The blue stamps will be for the canned goods. The red ones are for the meat. You'll be able to remember that 'cause it's the color of meat. Get it? Red. It'll be easy."

"If you say so."

"You sure you don't want me to deliver these for you later?"

"Thank you, no, Howie."

She started for the door. Her tremors were acting up today. From behind the shelves, Stevie stepped in front of her, blocking the path. He shook in a mirror image of the old woman.

"D-D-D-D-Dance with me, Mable."

Howie interceded. "What do you want, Stevie?"

"Ack-bay off-yay. Or do you want some more of what you got the other day?"

Howie started to climb over the counter. "You and what army?"

But Mrs. Trent waved him off.

"Don't trouble yourself, Howie. I've always been able to handle Steven. Pete!"

Pete the Dog rounded a display case and came to a face-to-face confrontation with Stevie. Both of them growled. Pete the Dog meant it.

Stevie bared his fangs. So did Pete the Dog. Pete meant that one, too.

Stevie stepped back and smiled his nervous smile.

"Wow, Mrs. Trent. You are a good sport. And Pete the Dog always knows how to take a joke. Don't you, Pete the Dog? Don't you?"

She stared him down with a frozen look that seemed to transcend the palsy. It was clear, strong and almost steady.

"Come, Pete the Dog."

The duo exited onto the porch and across the street. Howie breathed a sigh of relief.

"I love that dog." Stevie sounded honest. He didn't have a lot to love.

"What do you want?"

Stevie turned his attention back to the counter. He looked around to make sure they were alone, and took a long-fuse, slow-burning quarter-inch firecracker out of his pocket.

"When they gonna start them ration stamps you was talking about?"

"How should I know? Soon, is all."

"Well, when they get here, I want some, a whole sheet of the red."

"Am-scray ou-yay."

"You know, I could accidentally dump this little quarter-incher down your pants. How would Kim like that? Nothin' left to hold on to."

Howie's temper fired up. His hands gripped the counter, and he turned his mind to the sole of his shoe.

*If I do somethin' now, all that good name-wearin'-away time will be for nothin'.*

Stevie lit the miniature firecracker and casually tossed it at Howie. It bounced off his belt and onto the counter.

*And then again, why am I wastin' my time with this Stevie jerk?*

Howie jumped the counter. He attacked with such speed and surprise that Stevie stood flatfooted, mouth open. Howie shoved him into Vinny's patented headlock and pressed his ear into the counter inches from the small, smoldering firecracker. Suddenly Howie scooped it up, but instead of tossing it away, he pushed it into Stevie's open mouth and squeezed his jaws shut. Stevie's tongue started to burn. He went wild. Pain competed with fear, but Stevie could not shake Howie loose.

"Mmmm! Mmmmm!"

"Take it back! Take it back!"

"Mmmmmm!"

"Do you take it back?"

Frantic nods said he did, and Howie let go. Stevie spit out the firecracker. It was still alive, and the long fuse hissed. Stevie coughed and scratched his tongue. He grabbed the closest bottle that he could reach. Fortunately, it was the orange Nehi. He drank furiously as Howie and he stared at the fuse. It fizzled out.

"Whoa, Howie! Son of a bitch! Hey, you burned my tongue! What'd you go all looney tunes for? It's only a dud."

"You'll live."

"Think I need a medic. And I'm not payin' for this Nehi!"

"It's worth it to see you squirm."

"You're a real Bogart, Howie. Ya know that?"

"Got that headlock from Vinny. But Kim's right about you. You're not so tough."

"Yeah? Well, don't go spreadin' that around, or you're gonna find out different."

*BAM!* The firecracker exploded! Stevie jumped back.

"Whoa, shit!"

But he collided with Howie who had beat him off the mark.

"Yeah, shit," Howie echoed.

At last they found something they could agree on, and they laughed about it. The shrill sound of the boat whistle broke the magic in two, each boy taking a part of the memory with him, wearing it close to his soul. They had faced danger together and both had survived. Such a moment may never come again.

"Mr. Nakamura's back from the docks. You wanna help us unload?"

"I ain't no yellow man's piss-ant slave. Not yet anyway."

Stevie and the Nehi took off out the front door, and Howie watched him head north toward the center of the island. Howie knew that they had made that first step in meeting each other once again on equal ground. Maybe it didn't matter how many people you knew, but rather how you treated the ones that mattered.

Howie checked his shoe. Part of Stevie's "V" had been worn away

# CHAPTER 11
# THE BELL TOLLS
# JULY 3, 1942

Nakamura maneuvered the small boat into the slip behind the store. The sloop had a light inboard motor as well as one mast, a mainsail and a jib. It could move in a heavy wind, a light breeze or even when the Sound was still. Today, the sails did the job. Nakamura let the jib luff as he turned into the wind and slacked off the mainsail. Old tires nailed to the side of the dock served as bumpers. Kim jumped from the boat to cleat the lines as Nakamura reefed the sails. Two dozen crates of food were stacked on the aft deck and a few live fish flipped around between them. Howie climbed aboard to help unload.

Kim's mood was up. The cruise must have been good for her spirits.

"Look what we caught on the way back!"

Nakamura philosophically gathered the fish into a wooden box from the dock.

"The day we eliminate the fish from the sea is the day mankind dies. Meanwhile, we have dinner."

Howie loaded up but he could tell that Nakamura did not bring in as much as the store had sold that week. He would have to do better if they were to keep up with the Islanders' demands.

"Not a lotta crates this time."

Nakamura cast his eyes down, knowing that his response would acknowledge what Howie knew all along: that the store owner was carrying the burden of the Island's welfare on his small shoulders. And he didn't know how long he could do it.

"I had difficulty locating all the fresh fruits and vegetables we need. But we can survive."

"It's gettin' hard to find enough good meat and butter, too," added Kim.

Howie thought back to the days of unlimited butter a year ago. Butter on pancakes. Butter on popcorn. Butter on butter. Life was all changing, and not for the better.

The ringing of the rooftop bell plowed through his daydreams. It froze them all, each pinned in anticipation of his or her own imaginary telegram, but Nakamura recouped and strode calmly into the store. Howie and Kim waited awkwardly, then continued off-loading supplies. Finally Howie spoke. He couldn't endure that long a silence.

"How far did you have to go?"

"We picked up most of it at the Bronx Market, but had to go across the Sound to King's Point for the produce. People will still complain, though, 'cause it's not very good stuff."

"Yeah, but if it wasn't for your father, this whole island would starve."

"They ain't gonna see it that way. They're gonna say that it's because we're Japanese. And maybe they're right. You should'a seen the suppliers, Howie. People who sold to my father for ten years. They looked at him like givin' us supplies was committin' treason. It hurt him. And it hurt me to watch. I'm glad you weren't there. He would have lost face in front of you."

"Me?"

"In his eyes, you represent your father."

"But after all, I mean, he's my boss."

"But he's your Pop's friend, and they have some kinda bonds between them."

"Oh yeah, the bananas."

"What bananas?"

"I don't know 'what bananas'!"

They carried the first of the crates up the wooden planks and through the store's rear door as Nakamura carefully slid the telegram into its envelope. His somber mood cut the children's conversation short. He looked up at Howie. His expression was a cold wind coming off the Sound at the end of March, fierce and piercing and reaching down to the bone. Kim dropped her crate, but Howie simply traded his weighty burden for one that was physically much lighter, but mentally and emotionally straining – the Western Union cap.

Nakamura spoke the first direct order that he had ever given to Howie.

"Take it off. I'll deliver this one."

"It's the death one. Ain't it?"

"Yes."

And Howie, for the first time, defied him.

"I'll do it."

"I think it would be better if I delivered..."

Howie took his words away by pulling the envelope out of Nakamura's hand.

"I said, I'll do it."

"Howie, listen to my dad."

"Look around, Kim. There's a war on. We all have jobs we don't wanna do. But we do them anyway. And we keep on doin' them. That's what war is. This is my job, my own war. And I gotta fight it."

Silence swept the store like a new broom. Howie looked at the name Nakamura had written on the envelope. His pale expression froze, and he rubbed a hand across his face as if to re-start the blood flow. He would have to reduce his 439 someones by one.

Howie slid the telegram underneath his cap, but this time he straightened the symbol of his office directly to the front. He stepped out onto the porch and mounted the bike that had been calling its playmate's name all morning. This ride would be different.

Nakamura and Kim never moved.

"How come he sounds so old, dad?"

"The war found him. War steals children, and gives back little soldiers."

"That's...crazy."

"Yes. I'm afraid it is."

The bus-that-hardly-ever-comes-and-is-never-on-time drove past Howie and he didn't reach for the open rear door. Death deserved no free ride. The bus glided by, on its way back through the real Bronx to the City. He pedaled down the all too familiar streets, bypassing the all too familiar neighbor women who smiled and waved from their porches. But their waving went unacknowledged, and they quickly realized that their greatest fears had been fulfilled. The war had finally come to City Island.

Two blocks farther along the bus route, Big Stevie and Mungo sat in the grass. Stevie untwined the fuses from a string of short fuse quarter-inchers as he explained the fine points of firecrackery to his silent tag-along friend.

"See, Mungo, if you light the fuses when they're all stuck together, you get fast loud noises, but then they're gone in like one big thunder boom. You could scare somebody to death. But if you only twist two or three fuses together at a time, then people start jumpin'. And you want people jumpin', not dead. Jumpin' is good. Dead is bad. You could try blamin' the firecrackers, but dead is still dead. So, you wanna try it?...Do ya?...All you gotta do is say you wanna. I got 'em right here...Come on. Just tell me...Say 'I want some firecrackers'. Go ahead, Mungo. It ain't hard...Okay, ya know what? Maybe you don't speak English. Did you ever think of that? Maybe you speak somethin' else. All we gotta do is figure out what. Here, try this. Everybody speaks Pig Latin. If you wanna say 'book', you just take the first sound and put it at the end. Then you add 'ay'. So 'book' is 'ook-bay' and 'read' is 'ead-ray', and you don't do nothin' to the 'the' and the 'a' and all that other small stuff 'cause it's too small. So you got 'ead-ray the ook-bay'. Try it...Go ahead...Oh! Some words got no sound in front, so you just leave them alone and add 'yay'...like 'up' is 'up- yay'. That's it. Easy right? Try it...Say 'ead-ray the ook-bay'...No? Okay. Say 'Ungo-may'...Come on. I know you can say your name, 'Ungo-may'...Cooome on."

Mungo pointed down the block as Howie rode into view. Suddenly language didn't matter. Stevie shared the firecrackers and lit them up.

Howie made his turn and caught a glimpse of Stevie and Mungo tossing the little explosives at his tires. He swerved but never stopped, even as they blasted around him. But he did stop at a bungalow. It took him a long time to get off the bike. It seemed like hours but was really only seconds. By now, he had no way of knowing. His blank brain was defending itself. With a deep breath, he ascended to the porch climbing the steps one at a time, eyes down.

Mrs. Giardello had been rocking and first spotted Howie when he was still halfway down the street, his impending arrival announced by the exploding firecrackers. As he got closer, her synchronized motions decreased until they stopped all together. When he dismounted from the bike, she had slowly pulled herself out of the rocker. Their eyes met at the top of the stairs. The ends of his facsimile smile wavered and pulled his mouth down. He had choreographed this scene in his mind for days, and now spontaneity ruled with a vengeance.

He lowered his head, removing the telegram from under his cap. His mouth would no longer vocalize, and he simply held the envelope out to her. Mrs. Giardello's hands started to wring some imaginary thing invisibly clutched between them, as she looked off into the distance. But they made no move toward the message. Tears choked behind her eyes as she thought of a thousand excuses not to take it, and one reason why she should. Howie stubbornly refused to pull his hand back.

"Mrs. Giardello...you have to take it."

"No. I don't."

"You have to."

He took hold of her moving hand and slid the telegram between its worn fingers. It was too much for her to bear. She slowly peeled the envelope open, removed the telegram and silently mouthed the words to herself. The first tear found its migratory path down her once-apple cheek.

She reached for Howie taking him by both shoulders, bringing her face close to his, as if pleading for him to undo what had already been done.

"No, Howie. No...Not my Danny. Don't take my son."

Howie stood helpless as Mrs. Giardello let the paper drop to the floor and collapsed back into her chair. He looked for assistance. Nothing in City Island transpires in a vacuum and other women would be watching from their windows, porches and yards. He called to the closest, but several were already on their way. The urge to flee from the scene of his crime was a fast growing seed, but he weeded it out, knowing she could not be left alone.

"Mrs. Sabatini! Mrs. O'Reilly! Come here!"

The first neighbors arrived to relieve him from his self-imposed guard duty, trampling over the suddenly disregarded, yellow paper. It had served its purpose and now was both used up and useless.

Amid her growing wave of sobs, Howie reached between the sturdy women's sturdy shoes, rescued the telegram and wedged through the adults, replacing it in Mrs. Giardello's now limp hand. He knew that this simple piece of paper, her last contact with her Danny, would be kept forever. As the numbers of consoling neighbors increased, Howie faded into the background, mounted Columbia and slowly removed himself from the tableau of pain.

But after a few feet, his legs deserted him, refusing to move. He realized that his heart was racing. He could actually feel it thumping through his shirt. The bike coasted to a stop, unwilling to carry him any farther. He dismounted, letting it fall at his feet. He took one last indelible look at the misery he had unleashed, before his legs gave way, and he sank to the roadside grass. Slowly, his eyes turned from the unbearable scene behind him.

Howie sat staring out to the sea, physically unable to walk away, held captive by the peace of the blue water and pale sky. The sounds of firecrackers echoed in the distance, but he was oblivious to it all. His fingers pulled a blade of grass from the sandy soil, then another, and still another. He found himself uncontrollably ripping out large green clumps, and he had to sit on his hands to make them stop.

Howie felt tears crawling down his cheeks, and only then did he realize he had begun to cry. He wiped them away and studied his wet fingers.

This was a bad day. Anything that gave birth to that much grief must be an evil deed. He should go to confession, or better yet, talk to Ivory. Ivory's piano made everything okay. Almost everything. Even for just a little while.

# CHAPTER 12
# TO DANNY
# JULY 4, 1942

*In that mad hot summer of my twelfth year a cousin's cousin rumored to me that he saw a piano one time at the big house in the green valley. Mama told us 'bout letters and ciphers and fear of the Lord. Mama told us there was nothin' to be gained by venturin' into the valley. Mama was right, but I was 12. And when 12 comes up aginst "right", 12 always wins.*

*One fierce hot night, when the bedstraw was soaked and moisture rolled across my hairless lip in little beads, I thought I heared my first piano singin' into my sleepy ears. Rubbin' myself awake, I stepped off of them old worn boards that arrogantly called themselves a porch. I sat in The Road rut, lookin' off to where my Pa might be approachin'. I knew he couldn't be carryin' no piano, yet the distant music, real or imagined, gloriously persisted like no other I ever did hear.*

*I hoped I was awake. But sometimes a body just cain't stick his head up outta that dream as quick as he want. You don't know where that dreamin' life end, and where that wakin' life begin. You be stuck in there like a little turtle trapped inside his little shell, when the puddle dry up and the cakin' mud lock in all around him. Of all the dreams we dream, them stuck-in dreams be the muddiest. But somethin' tell me, deep down, this ain't no stuck-in dream.*

*I followed that sound aroma along the path, down the trail, through the smell of the sweet hay grass where the hill ends and the valley starts below. With bright stars to light my way, I thought that just a few years separated me from some underground railroad runners that the folks still talk about on lots of nights like these. I felt their fear shudder through my body, a momentary shiver in the heat of a moonless night.*

*I never knew if I really heard that sound up on the hill, but a hour later when I reached the big house, it magnetized my ears, drawin' me like a honey bee to a magnolia. I was hopeful. And I was helpless.*

*I crawled closer to the front columns, intoxicated for the first time in my young life, followin' the sound to a open window. This was the wrong place for a colored boy to be, I told myself over and over again, but myself refused to listen. Crouched like a frog, unable to pull away, I raised my eyes and peered over the ledge. The window was open, the glass panels throwed back. I had seed glass 'afore, store-bought and clean, but never this bright and this clear. Yet instead of trying to run my fingers along its magical surface, I searched for the source of the all-consumin' music.*

*Candles bathed the piano in a brightness that could only be worthy of enlightened saints and redeemed sinners. The ivory hands that kissed the ivory keys ran up to the arms of the young missus. Her slight frame sat perched, eyes closed, wearing nothin' but her all-together in the unbearable summer heat. The beads of moisture driftin' downward made her shoulders shimmer in the light.*

*My eyes wanted to follow the droplets on their path across her bare body, a truly unique and wondrous sight, the likes of which I had never seed 'afore. But they would not, could not, be pulled away from the sole object of their desire...the piano...the likes of which I had also never seed 'afore. I was in love, whether it be affliction or affection, with that piano. I prayed that someday, somewhere, I would become a piano man, and I resolved to take its name for my own. And hence I chose, right then and right there, to be called what my eyes perceived as the most beautiful part of this most beautiful of sights: Ivory Keys.*

⁂

Howie rode against the storm. Wind blew his cap off and into the Sound, sending a dozen telegrams free falling across the waters. He skidded sideways, laying the bike down for 15 feet, and righted it again. He battled the wind and the rain, trying to get home before it turned to sleet or snow. The doors to the house were wide open and he could see Nana on the third floor, holding onto the widow's walk unstable railing. He rode Columbia into the house, up the stairs, reaching the walk. Nana had her hand outstretched, her Claddagh ring sparkling, and he gave her the telegram. As she accepted it, the old railing finally gave way. She started to fall, but Bad Bill's rescuing hands reached out of nowhere to grab her. It was too late. The old woman lost hold of the telegram, and it ripped free as she fell to the ground screaming Howie's name. The yellow paper floated peacefully away.

Howie bolted upright to find himself in bed. Sweat drenched the sheet, and he was out of breath. Looking around, he assured himself that this was but a dream, and what he saw now was the real thing. But he was just asleep enough not to be sure which one was the dream. He hoped it was the other.

He groped for his security anchor, the sax next to his bed, promising himself that a few quiet notes would restore reality and chase away that dream. It always had. He wet his lips and blew, but only a snarly "SQUARK!" came out. His second effort was no better. His panicky lungs had failed him. He re-hoped that maybe *this* was still the dream. But it wasn't. Slow deep breaths were all he had left to calm his racing heart.

Danny had grown up with Howie's brothers, Gene and Vinny. With City Island's best ever ball player, Charlie O'Reilly. With Ivory's son, Corey The Cook. With the palsied Mrs. Trent's son, Eddy. With Kim's brother, Tatsu, and a half a dozen more. They had each stolen one another's homework, cheated on tests together, dated each other's girlfriends and skinny-dipped off the shaky bridge. If one had it, they all ate it, drank it or caught it. They had forged rock-hard friendships on an anvil of two indelible decades. Now one of them was gone, and the others would never be the same.

Danny was one of hundreds of casualties that kept trickling in from the Battle of Midway, the first naval engagement fought by ships that never saw each other. American sailors and flyers had stopped the Japanese armada and destroyed three aircraft carriers while losing the Yorktown.

At dinner last night, Mom had wondered if some form of recognition, a plaque or a carved stone, would be forthcoming for Danny. Howie tried not to listen, fearing the worst, hoping that there would never be a City Island family discussing a monument for one of the two Logan soldiers. He removed himself from the conversation and slipped out the back door.

He found Ivory playing the well-worn upright piano at the Legion Hall. It was where he spent his evenings when the bar was open, with a tip glass on top of the soundboard, and his cane hanging from an old Rough Riders' gun holster tacked onto the piano's side. He supported himself through small gigs and lessons for the Island children, having never worked on the books long enough to qualify for any pension, governmental or otherwise. But he alone was the official house band for the hall. And for big occasions, he recruited a few locals to back him up. Tomorrow night, Howie would play his first Fourth of July money paying job.

The Legion Hall had grown up from an 1840's barn to a fish house. By the 1920's it had evolved into a dance hall. But now from a combination of sheer size, age and location at the southernmost end of the Island, this general gathering spot held the place of honor among all local structures. It boasted a full kitchen with two gas stoves and a big sink. Over 200 merrymakers could enjoy Legion hospitality before they would be forced to expand onto the waterside terrace. A veritable museum of Great War memorabilia hung behind the long bar, with a Rough Rider's dented bugle at the center.

Instead of unloading on Ivory, Howie stared up at the "Uncle Sam Wants You" poster and listened to the notes. He pointed his index finger at Uncle Sam's and let the two finger tips touch, but was slowly drawn back to the old piano. The blind man's music seemed to have all the answers. Well, some of them at least. The poster only had demands. Finally, Ivory finished the set, and Howie sat down on the bench. Ivory could sense who it was. Howie was the only one who ever shared that space.

"Where's your axe, boy?"

"I...I'm outta music today."

"Jumpin' Jehoshaphat! A music man with no music! Somethin' must really be wrong, or the repo man found out where you be hidin' that saxophone. Ha! A music man's best friend be his axe, his workin' tool, even if it just be no more'n a hummin' comb or a pair of spoons. Any time I walks into a strange room and hears a piano playin', feelin' its vibes risin' through the floorboards, its voice fillin' the air...well, then it ain't no strange place at all. It be home. And all I wanna do is tickle that old friend, just a bit, and hear her laugh out loud. Now that be a friend you can depend on. That be a anchor, and every soul on this earth need some one or some thing for to be their anchor. Fact."

"Danny Giardello is dead."

Ivory fell silent. But Howie couldn't.

"The war got him. I delivered the telegram to his mom...It made me cry."

The over-heard words buzzed down the bar, a hush falling over the patrons. Ivory's head dropped. The keys clinked as he folded his hands on the keyboard, said a silent prayer and began to hum a blues tune that Howie had never heard before. Ivory knew a lot of music and a lot of other things that Howie had never heard before. Slowly Ivory's fingers joined the melody and expanded the musical notes.

"Don't just stand there, boy. Get your axe. We got work to do."

"What kinda work?"

"We gotsta drive the blues to heaven so they can reach that poor boy's soul. And our music be flowin' all around him when he glide in proud through them Big Pearlies."

Howie had complete faith in Ivory's wisdom. He had never been wrong. That's why he was the ump. Eyes or no eyes, he called them like they needed to be called. Of all the adults in his life, Ivory rode him the hardest, never accepting a weak note nor a weak excuse.

As Howie left the Legion, he passed a new arrival who marched in with a confident swagger. Pete the Dog stopped long enough for Howie to pet him, then walked to the end of the bar, tail held high. He barked, laid down and crossed his paws. His bark was met with a few random, "Pete the Dog!" greetings from those residents already seated on their stools. Bartender Johnny placed a saucer of beer in front of Pete who made no immediate move to lap it up, but just lowered his head and rested.

In a few minutes, Howie was standing by the piano, playing back up to Ivory's lead. There were no written notes. There were no words on paper. They all existed in the soul of a man who had lived the blues for 50 years. Howie, at 12, was an infant in Ivory's world, yet he blended instinctively as if he knew where the blind man was leading him before he was ever told.

Ivory had followed the music circuit on everything from a mule to a Greyhound. "Yes, sir," he used to tell Howie. "I been doin' the dog from Memphis to Natchez, from N'Orleans to New York Island. Music brought me the gravy life, and if I die tomorrow, may I die givin' more than I took. 'Cause that's the most any soul can hope for."

Ivory stopped playing. The few patrons in the room quieted down. He lifted a shot glass of inexpensive Philadelphia Blended Whiskey that had been sitting full on top of his piano, untouched for the entire evening. Finally, he spoke the words, loud and clear, that Howie had been waiting for, the words that would bring some closure, even if it were only temporary, to Howie's self-inflicted pain.

"Danny died givin' more than he took. We celebrate him today. We'll mourn for him tomorrow. Amen."

He downed the house-liquor drink and exhaled a long low, appreciative "Ahhhhhhh," as he finished. Then he spoke in a thunderous voice, "I said 'Amen'!"

And his "amen" was met with a chorus from those at the bar as the others drank to Danny. Two old Legionnaires, Lubisch and Antonsic, stood with their hands over their hearts. Pete the Dog barked and lapped his beer. Bartender Johnny poured a Philadelphia shot and slid it down to Howie. Not sure what to do he awkwardly picked it up and stared at the small glass, the smallest he had ever held. The brown liquid looked like castor oil, smelled like turpentine, and it was still a "no thanks" away from his nose. He had the feeling that he was about to make one of life's million momentous decisions. He hesitated, drawing a hush of unwanted attention, and raised the glass.

"To Danny."

Howie's toast was met with "To Danny" from several mouths, and he downed the shot just like he had seen the men do before, but followed it with a coughing spell and only succeeded in embarrassing himself. It tasted horrible and burned his throat worse.

Obviously not his best momentous decision. He nodded a forced smile back to the drinkers.

Howie wanted to wash his mouth out but felt the shot rebounding up from his stomach. He backed into the kitchen and made a speedy exit out the rear door, just in time to heave into the un-cut grass. Slipping back inside, he held his mouth under the kitchen faucet and spit into the sink. It felt cold, and it felt clean. He did it again.

But Ivory started to hit the keys once more. Duty called and Howie was forced to answer. This time, it was one he knew. He slid back inside and easily played along as Ivory began to sing *Danny Boy*. His raspy voice, the voice of the ages, brought Bartender Johnny to the edge of tears. He had to step away from his domain and sit on a stool. The song was slow and seemed to last too long, or maybe it was the drink.

By the time it was over, Ivory was spent. He closed the keyboard, stood up and removed two quarters and a dime from the tip glass. He smoothly slipped his cane out of its holster like a Dodge City gunslinger. Holding it out-stretched, he aimed his feet toward the door, but first his hand found Howie's shoulder.

"Damn war. Sometimes, boy, life's a hard row to hoe. Maybe harder for the stalks still standin', than for thems what got plowed under. But you know what? You don't get to choose your row. You get what you get. And how you deal with the plowin' is what's gonna make you a man. There's nothin' wrong with sobbin' like a babe today, 'long as you know that your mama ain't gonna be there to wipe your nose tomorrow. And nobody's gonna put your hat on when it rains.

"Bein' a music man is harder than bein' anybody out in *their* world. We got our own set of rules. Unforgivin' rules. And maybe the hardest is puttin' on that face...that gig face...Tomorrow you gotsta be wearin' that Fourth of July gig face, no matter what you feel inside. I cain't see it, but I can still feel it in your music. And the people, they needs to see it. That be a awesome burden the

Good Lord loaded us music men down with, and He ain't 'bout to lift it just 'cause Danny pass."

Ivory stepped into his long-memorized path toward the exit but stopped and turned before he hit the evening air. His vibrant voice grew preacher-loud, dominating the room and drawing every patrons' attention.

"Life's a bitch, boy, but you gotsta grab her, and you gotsta ride her! You ride her wherever she take you! And when she finally fly you up into the yonder, you scream with joy that you got the best out of life, and life got the best out of you!"

His deep laughter echoed across the bar, and a few drinkers nodded in agreement.

"You and me, son, we got some long-ass ridin' to do, 'cause this here war ain't goin' nowhere. But you and me, we gonna make this turn out the bestest it can. Fact stated! Ha! Now walk with me and rejoice, boy, 'cause you lookin' at a man with sixty cent in his pocket!"

Pete the Dog lapped up his last Knickerbocker and followed them out.

But all that was last night, and now a new day beckoned. Howie's strong lungs and their deep breaths had calmed his body down. He pulled back the damp sheet and climbed out of bed, trying to forget his Nana nightmare but hold onto the rest of his yesterday. He glanced over at the top of his dresser.

Two quarters, a dime and an invisible load of responsibility.

# CHAPTER 13

# TEN POUNDS OF SCRAP IRON

## JULY 4, 1942

From his bedroom window, Howie inhaled another beautiful dawn. Two new liberty ships rested in the Sound between City Island and Queens awaiting their precious cargo. Little boats flitted around the big gray ships, buzzing with activity on a continuous search for German submarines. Rumors had it that they were running up an unbelievable damage count in the off-shore shipping lanes. So it was conceivable that, at any minute, a wolf pack might come into the Sound on its deadly mission.

Several of City Island's larger wooden-hulled sailing boats had been painted gray and moved farther east to join the Suicide Regatta: a volunteer Coast Guard fleet being assembled to locate and sit over enemy subs until help arrived. With no engine, these sailboats were immune to the submarines' sound detection system. On the other hand, with no heavy guns they were sitting ducks for any hungry sub that happened to poke up its periscope.

This morning the sun was bright, the air was clean and there was no haze over the city. But something was out of place. As well as the crying terns and laughing gulls, the silent cormorants and the gently rolling swells, one lone object stood out against the watery backdrop: Kim. She sat on the barrier rocks that protected the shifting sand and stared down the beach. Howie hoped she wasn't getting "hot" again. He located his blue denim dungarees where he had left them last night, tossed on the floor in a corner of the room.

Turning the pockets inside-out produced several nickels, a button and a shell. He combined the coins with the change on top of the dresser and threw all of it into a large can by the side of his bed. It produced a dull *clink* as it melded with five pounds of assorted change. He hastily scribbled in a few numbers at the bottom of a column in a motley black and white covered notebook and tallied them up. When he closed the book, the title "Need $52.99" stared back at him.

In a few minutes, he was sitting beside Kim. She didn't seem surprised. She was wordless, and that was one aspect of their relationship that Howie knew she was better at than he. He couldn't take it and spoke first. She knew he would. That little power game was one of the few joys she had left.

"You're up early."

"Couldn't fall asleep," she admitted.

"I had a hard time stayin' asleep. I woke up with this nightmare that Nana's death was all my fault...I don't wanna ever kill nobody, especially Nana, even in a dream."

"Death. At least she's at peace."

That brought the curtain up on another show of silence. Howie couldn't think of anything intelligent to say and wished he had brought his sax.

Kim pointed to the far end of the narrow beach. Ivory stood facing the sunrise, arms raised, feet spread apart.

"Why does he do that? He can't really see the sun."

"I think it's like a bath for his brain," answered Howie.

"Then we should do it, too. He has powers, ya know. Maybe he gets 'em from the morning sun."

Kim led him off the big rocks. They stood side-by-side, holding hands and squinting into the rays, looking across the water, beyond Hart Island toward Connecticut's brilliant morning light and distant rolling hills. After a few quiet moments, Kim lowered her eyelids. Howie glanced over, saw her eyes closed, and shut his, too.

"Gettin' any powers yet?" she asked.

"Don't think so. All I got is little red dots. But if I do, I'll squeeze some over to you."

They silently waited for the magic to happen, as the warmth of the summer sun caressed their hopeful faces.

"Do you ever think about suicide, Howie? I mean really think about it?"

"Catholics ain't allowed."

"Yeah, but *do* you?"

"No."

"It's very honored among the Japanese."

He could feel his toasting face scrunch up with the next question and was glad she wasn't looking at him. "Do *you* ever think about it?"

"Not really...Well, sometimes, maybe a little."

"Don't, okay? Promise me."

Lost in her private moment, she ignored his request, substituting a new agenda.

"Ya know what I want to do, Howie? I want us to go on a date."

"A date?!"

"Yeah. A real date. A date-date. Feels like I'm never gonna go on a real date before I die."

"Don't you need a...a 'boyfriend' for a date?"

"No, just you."

Howie knew he was cornered, but if he had to go on a date-date, he was not going to sell himself cheaply.

"Just suppose I did take you on this date-date, would you promise me somethin'? That you won't think about that suicide stuff no more?"

"I could try. But ya know, what's in your brain is in your brain."

"And you won't tell nobody?"

"About the suicide?"

"No, dunce head! About the date."

"Yeah. I promise."

Howie had to think this one through. He would do anything for his best friend, even go on a date if he had to. But on the other hand, if his not-so-best-friends found out, they would never let him live it down. Stevie would stretch it out for at least a year. He worked up all the ramifications, but Kim could wait no more.

"So?"

Howie felt his voice leaving him, and, for a brief moment, he forgot about everything else on his mind. Again one of life's million momentous decisions threw itself in his face. A date-date! He coughed his voice back to life.

"Ah...Okay, yeah. We'll do it."

They opened their eyes and turned to face each other as Howie finished.

"Can you get your hands on 10 pounds of scrap iron?"

Noon found them standing in front of the Legion Hall waiting for the bus-that-sometimes-comes-and-sometimes-doesn't. Ideally, it would reach the end of the black top right here, drive around the flagpole circle, and continue on its journey back toward Yankee Stadium. Today it would stop.

Howie's and Kim's feet were surrounded by two baseball mitts, 15 feet of chain, two old flat irons and a small anchor. They had tried to guess the weight by putting bits and pieces on the produce scale that hung in the general store and now felt confident that they had the required 20 pounds between them. In actuality, it was probably closer to 40, but they were taking no chances. Not today. Not with a real date-date on the line.

Joe drove into sight, swinging the bus in a big circle, and they gathered up their iron tickets. The chain fell loose as they entered. Howie grabbed one end, dragging it aboard, and it noisily rattled up the step, drowning out Joe's laughing greeting.

"Two for the game!"

He knew them by sight. City Island kids started waving to Joe early in life, the way children in Iowa wave to the train engineer as he crosses their flat terrain. Only here the driver never changed. And on the few instances when they actually rode the bus, they took delight in waving back to their friends who remained within the safety of the island.

The bus pulled out with its two sole passengers. The flag flapped its 48 stars from half mast on the tall pole behind them and a large sign over the Legion entrance proclaimed "Annual Fourth of July Dance TONIGHT!"

Outside, as the bus passed the sandlot diamond, the morning contest was in its ninth inning. Neither Howie nor Kim had returned to the teams since that last pickin' day, and Howie missed it. He just had to get back to the game, but work and dating had pointed him in other directions for the moment. They would have normally yelled out the window and waved, but this was a date-date and neither one was really sure about the rules.

Stevie was up at bat with Ivory behind home plate. Silent Mungo waved to Joe, and he acknowledged it back, but Mungo spotted Kim and Howie seated behind the driver. Surprised, he looked to see if other teammates had spotted them too. Apparently no one had. He knew this information should be shared, but it was his alone. He opened his mouth as if to speak, hesitated for a second, and turned back to the game instead, just in time to see Ivory call Stevie out.

"Strike three!"

Kim witnessed Stevie smash his bat down against home plate and responded with a spontaneous "Respect the call, Stevie!" through the open window. She smiled her first smile of the day. Howie was preoccupied with the headlines in the *Daily News* tossed on the seat across the aisle.

112,000 AMERICAN BORN JAPS REMOVED FROM WEST COAST
COLORADO, UTAH CAMPS AT CAPACITY

He didn't want Kim to see it and distracted her while he casually cleared the paper off the seat and slid over in its place.

"Hey, look! I brought Charlie O'Reilly's mitt."

"Wow, Magic Maggie!"

"Yeah. He wants me to have it."

"For keeps, or just 'til he gets home?"

"For keeps, I guess."

"Ya know, Howie, maybe he doesn't figure on comin' home."

"Nah. He'll be back. I know he will."

But Howie didn't know, and she knew that he didn't know.

By the time they reached The House That Ruth Built, there was a line of grown-ups and children, each carrying ten pounds of scrap iron, each proudly aiding the war effort, each donating his American eagle or her bust of Napoleon. The weight-man handing out receipts gave Kim a half glance.

"Chinese?"

"No."

Her negative answer caught him off guard. He looked up, this time administering the full glance treatment.

"Not Jap?"

Howie chimed in with a laugh.

"American."

He handed them their coupons with a sarcastic smile, rattling off his instructions.

"Right. Over my red-white-and-blue ass. Here. Take this to the ticket booth. Get goin'. Weisenheimer kids. Who's next?!"

As they happily approached the ticket line, Howie noticed small groups of men staring at Kim and commenting to each other. He switched sides, putting himself between Kim and her not-so-much fan club.

The scrap iron had gotten them as far as the outfield bleachers, the best seats in the stadium where the die-hard Bomber fans sat on wooden benches. No arm rests. No backs. No shade. Just baseball. Howie was starting to like this date stuff, and he watched the game intently.

Kim edged closer across the board and slipped her mitted hand over Howie's Magic Maggie. She was comfortable. She was happy. Here she was safe. Everything else that had invaded her little corner of the universe in the last six months couldn't follow her through that turnstile. She rested her head on his shoulder.

"No more suicide talk, Kim?"

"I'll try...Think we got any powers today? Ya know, from the sun?"

"Yeah, I think we did."

Kim closed her eyes. She hadn't slept, and it was catching up with her.

"Someday, I'm gonna play here," said Howie.

"Yeah, right. If they ever start a band."

Howie smiled but never looked away from the game. DiMaggio was up next.

# CHAPTER 14

# TATSU'S SECOND LETTER

# JULY 4, 1942

Bad Bill's weathered hands worked at a rough wooden counter as he and two boat yard friends opened little neck clams. They were "the kind". Anything on City Island that could be measured in gradation might ultimately reach this top rating. They celebrated this morning's harvest, and the empty beer bottles told even the dullest eye that these clam knives were now as dangerous to the wielders as they were to "the kind".

Tomorrow, they would drop the bulk of their catch at the Bronx Market, but today, they kept the best for themselves. This was turning out to be a good Bad Bill day.

Several dry-docked party boats rested on blocks, only useful to support the clammers' ten foot long rakes. These boats had taken thousands of half-day fisherman into the Sound every summer, and now stood idle, destined only to watch out-of-work boat mechanics shuck nature's bounty for their own appetites. They had just performed a job they thought beneath them, yet were lucky to have any job at all. Their scraped and scratched hands opened another round of beer and washed down another round of could-a-been. Could-a-been's were hard to choke down.

The general store had fallen quiet this afternoon following a busy morning. Officially, it was a holiday, but word had spread about Nakamura's recent acquisitions, so he knew he had to open. Most of the local ladies had come in earlier to shop and exchange stories about Danny Giardello. There was talk of naming the American Legion Post after him or at least placing a plaque at the foot of the flagpole. A ceremony to initiate Mrs. Giardello into the ranks of the Gold Star Mothers was inevitable.

Now alone, Nakamura finished sweeping, leaned the broom against the counter and locked the door. He swatted at a fly but missed, and hung up the "closed" sign for the holiday afternoon. Taking down the box from above his desk, he untied the red ribbon that secured the envelopes together and removed his son's second letter.

*October 1, 1941*

*Dear Father,*

*My eyes have opened at the wonders and treasures I find among my people. I am one with my homeland. Never did I realize how the American ways served only to maintain our subservient position in their decadent society. I urge you to dispose of your worldly goods and follow me home. The All Nippon Students' Society has made me aware of the ignorance of our lives. It has not been your fault, and you bring no shame upon yourself for falling under the influences that surround you. But now the oppressive ways of the United States, its demands on the Imperial House to withdraw from Manchuko, the embargo on both oil and steel, the freezing of Japanese finances in American banks and a dozen other offenses have made clear to me that we can no longer exist as foreigners in a foreign land…*

A violent crash made Nakamura spin around only to get hit with a spray of broken glass as a porch rocker smashed through the front door. Bad Bill Logan blasted in behind it. He picked up Nakamura and threw him across the room with an insane scream. Canned goods and boxes scattered. Bill was drunk and staggering.

"Arghhhh! It's all your fault, you dirty slant-eyed bastard! A woman's son gets killed. And you yellow scum killed him! Then you deliver the yellow death notice! Well, I'm *your* death notice. Right here! Right now!"

Nakamura grabbed for the broom to defend himself, but Bill drove him into the floor before he could reach it. Trickles of blood spread over Nakamura's eyes. Bill lifted his victim up and back-handed him across the aisle, smashing a shelf to the floor. Bill stumbled through the can goods as a crawling Nakamura finally found the broom. He expertly spun it around and slid the handle between Bill's feet, bringing the mad man down. His head hit the base of the counter. He didn't get up.

A few neighbors entered as Nakamura struggled to his feet. In the middle of the little group was Bill's wife, Cathleen. Born in Ireland, she still wore the brogue that accompanied the map upon her face. But that map barely hid one remnant of a facial bruise that quite possibly had been inflicted during Bill's last binge. She was embarrassed by this latest display, but humiliation could only knock this woman down, not out. She set about making the best of what she could salvage. She was used to it.

Nakamura poked Bill with the broom and got no response. A wave of fear that he had killed the big man washed across his face. But Cathleen examined her husband and put Nakamura's fears to rest. Bill stirred.

"Ahh, sure, and there you are Bill. He's okay, thank the Lord."

She tried to laugh at the modest proportions of Nakamura's physique, allaying his fears and apologizing at the same time.

"There ain't no one on this island man enough to kill Bad Bill Logan, especially one your size. But I am sorry he's makin' such an arse of himself. I think he's just fearful that we'll be receivin' one of your telegrams about Bill Jr., someday. You know how he gets when he dips his beak."

"Yes. I know. He's one man who should not drink."

She spoke randomly to the neighbors, who now included Vinny.

"Well, don't just stand there like sheep in a meadow. Give me a hand getting Bad Bill home. Ah, Vinny. Grab your uncle's arm there like a good lad."

Vinny stepped through the small crowd. He hefted Bill's 200-plus pounds, draped him over his shoulder and dragged him away. Cathleen faked a laugh as she tried to pick up the pieces of a splintered door and a splintered life.

"If I didn't know better, Vinny, I'd swear you was Simon the Cyrene, carrying Christ's cross on your back."

"He's getting heavy. Can we crucify him now?"

"Perhaps, it is you, Cathleen," interrupted Nakamura quietly, "who is carrying the cross. Maybe I have something that will help that bruise heal faster."

"Best tend to yourself, lest Bill pay you another visit."

Cathleen turned her face away, speaking to the group.

"He's really not such a bad man. He did build the Panama Canal, you know. I'm sure that was quite a task. Takes a special man to volunteer for that kind of dangerous work. But that's Bill, always putting his country's needs above his own. He's America through and through, he is."

Having exhausted her list of meaningless excuses, she followed Vinny up the street.

Seeing blood on his shirt, Nakamura realized he was cut. A woman insisted on examining his wounds, pressing a handkerchief against the most severe one above his eyebrow. He sat down on the counter as a few other neighbors came in surveying the landscape and organizing the debris. A second woman moved to tend to Nakamura, but he waved them both away. His eyes were already on Tatsu's letter spread at his feet, and that quickly became his priority. He tenderly picked up the pages, reassembled them in the correct order, put them back in the envelope and retied the red ribbon. As he began to replace the packet in the box, however, a drop of blood fell onto the letters.

Nakamura wiped it off with his thumb, but the stain was already there forever. His expression showed the emotional pain he was enduring internally, yet he ignored the cuts and bruises that populated the exterior of his body. Almost ceremoniously, he returned the box, and took in the vista of destruction. It looked like a tiny whirlwind had just blown through a barn. Except for the door, the damage looked superficial, and the more neighborly Islanders were already restocking dented cans and replacing fallen shelves.

Islanders were trained from birth to clean up their own problems.

Later that afternoon, Stevie sat on the bench in front of the Legion Hall, waiting for the bus-that-got-there-when-it-felt-like-it. He squirmed uncomfortably and adjusted a hammer tucked into his belt, sticking him in a most personal of places. He stood up several times, anxiously pacing and peering down the street. When the bus finally came into view, he wished someone else could be there to meet it with him, but even Mungo had finally given up and gone home.

The two veterans of Yankee Stadium saw the general store's broken door even before they climbed down the last step to the sandy, blacktop road. Mismatched boards had been awkwardly nailed over the broken panes of glass. Kim came eye to eye with Stevie as she stepped off the bus.

"What happened?!"

"Bad Bill got drunk and beat up your dad."

Kim dropped her mitt, ran across the circle, onto the porch and lunged for the door handle. It was locked.

As the bus pulled away, Howie added her mitt to his. He and Stevie were a step behind her, but she vaulted over the porch's side railing and darted for the back door on the waterside of the building. The boys started to awkwardly climb over the railing together, but quickly decided to run around it instead. Howie saw Stevie remove the hammer from his waist.

"Stevie, you nailed all these boards up?!"

"Yeah. Pretty good, huh?"

"You did that for Kim's dad?"

"Nah. Old man Lubisch gave me two bits."

"Two bits?"

"Alright, two bits and a roll of flypaper. My mom really misses flypaper. So what do ya want from me? I sorta had to."

Charging upstairs, Kim smelled the incense even before she found her father kneeling and bowing low in front of the Buddha.

"Dad! Dad!"

Only when he faced her did she see the white cloth wrapped around his forehead with a wet red patch bleeding through. But just confirming that he was still alive had a calming effect, and she caught her breath.

"Oh, Dad. Let me see that."

"It is nothing."

She unwrapped his head to examine a small but deep gash above one eye. Howie and Stevie arrived behind her, bumping into each other, and they winced when they saw the wound. Kim replaced the large bandage.

"I think you need stitches, Dad."

The word was repulsive to both boys, and their expressions showed it. Kim moved closer to them and whispered the word again.

"Stitches. Is your mom home, Stevie? She's the best."

In a few minutes, Stevie arrived at his house, dropping his hammer as he entered the small bungalow. His mother spent more time at Fordham Hospital than she did at home and he was lucky to find her there. As a nurse's aide, she was the closest thing to a medical professional on the island. He called as he headed for the kitchen.

"Ma! Ma! You gotta come do some stitchin'. Here. I got you some flypaper."

She had several steaming pots on the gas stove and looked up to see Stevie's urgent expression. She was accustomed to dealing with the Island's small emergencies. They had become routine. Her face brightened as he handed her the two-inch high, cardboard cylinder.

"Did you steal this?"

"No, Ma. I earned it. From old man Lubisch."

"Okay. Let me turn everything off. Who's hurt?"

"Mr. Nakamura. Bad Bill beat him up. I'll get your bag."

Stevie ran out of the kitchen.

His mother went rigid as she heard Nakamura's name. She calmly struck a match and relit the flames, throwing her words behind her.

"Don't bother. I've got too much to do here. I'm workin' a double tonight, makin' that good holiday pay. I may not even be back tomorrow, and these meals ain't gonna cook themselves, ya know. So, I can't go."

"Ma!"

"I said, 'I can't go.' That's it."

"But Ma. Mr. Nakamura needs..."

"You heard me! And I told you to stay away from that Nakamura girl...Stevie?"

The spring-loaded *WHAP* of the closing kitchen door made her turn from the stove and yell through the screen panel.

"Steven!"

The return trip to the general store seemed to take longer, and Stevie found himself only walking by the time he climbed the stairs to face Kim. His eyes looked down as the words came out.

"She won't come."

Kim's right hand formed a fist as she marched toward the exit.

"Come on Howie. I gotta take care of somethin'. Stevie, you stay."

"For what?"

She gave Stevie the stare that crawled up from her belly and fired out her eyes. He backed up a step and raised his hands in surrender.

"I'm stayin'. I'm stayin'."

In two minutes, Howie and Kim were standing in the Logan kitchen as Mom searched the cabinets for her first aid kit.

"Stitching's my specialty, Kim. So don't you worry. I'll have your Dad ready to dance at the Legion Hall tonight, before you know it. Remember old Pete the Fisherman? That guy was too proud to have a woman sew him up. Used to do it himself. But then, he used to pull his own teeth, too. There was this one time when he got a hook caught in his tongue, and he couldn't get it out. With those crossed eyes, he always had trouble looking in the mirror and working in reverse. While I'm trying to remove it, he insisted on telling me how it happened. Every time he tried to talk, he just made these little jibber-jabber sounds like...Ah! Here's my first aid kit. Think your father would like to be a pirate, Kim?"

"No."

In the livingroom, Teddy propped herself up on the couch and put down her knitting, whose shape resembled nothing yet known to mankind. Lillian, next to her, slipped Teddy's gold wedding ring onto a long thread.

"If it swings straight, it's a boy. In a circle means a girl."

They waved to Howie and Mom who headed out the back door toward the general store, but Kim never made it outside.

She detoured upstairs to Howie's bedroom. She quickly searched through his closet, pulled clothes from the corners and crawled under the bed, finally locating her sought-after treasure. She rose, running a hand down the sleek lines of the Louisville slugger, then stepped back and took a practice swing.

As Howie and Mom reached the store, Howie looked behind him but found no trace of Kim.

"Hey, Mom. Kim's gotta take care of somethin', and I think I better help her."

He jogged back toward his house, but when he re-entered the living room, he found Lillian on the couch, letting the ring arc like a pendulum above Teddy's exposed, pregnant belly. Howie came to a crashing halt with a crunched-faced "Eeeew!", and turned his head away, throwing back, "Did you see Kim?"

"Probably at the sandlot," said Teddy. "She just left with a baseball bat. You got a game?"

"This ain't no game."

Howie bolted out the front door, catching Lillian's fading words behind him.

"It's swinging straight so it's a boy. It's definitely a boy. I think. No, wait...Yeah, it's a boy."

Kim was already standing on the porch of Bad Bill's bungalow. She summoned up her courage, knocked on the door, spit in her palms, then stood in a batter's stance with her weapon high and off her shoulder.

The door sat motionless on its hinges.

For the first time, Kim started to look the slightest bit nervous. She took a practice swing, then knocked again, louder. The door opened and Bill's wife looked down at a now embarrassed Kim.

Kim held her position and forced a smile.

Cathleen Logan casually called back inside and let the door close.

"Bill, it's for you."

A moment later, semi-sober Bad Bill filled the doorway. Kim hesitated for just a split second as she looked over her shoulder and twisted the bat to make sure the Louisville insignia was pointing upward. She still could not take that chance of cracking Howie's bat. The corner of Kim's eye spotted Bill's approach, and she swung wildly in his direction. But Bill didn't hesitate at all. That split second bat adjustment was enough for him to move in, lift his hand and catch the bat in mid-flight. He easily pulled it out of her hands and laughed at her futile effort, throwing her weapon into the road.

Bill towered over her. A deep growl rocked his big frame, while his liquor-breath wrapped around Kim's head and smothered her senses. Her feet were too scared to run. Sheer survival brought her fists up in self-defense, but Bill simply covered her face with his large palm. A little shove sent her sprawling backwards, tumbling down the porch steps.

"Get lost, chopstick."

He laughed himself back inside, but she could still hear his ridicule slipping out the screen windows into the late afternoon air. Flat on her spine, she climbed to her feet and headed for the bat. Howie got there first. As she reached for it, he snatched it up and hid it behind his back.

"Are you crazy?!"

"You're ain't me, Howie. You don't know."

He pointed her away from the bungalow, and they slowly walked back toward the flagpole circle. Kim felt defeated. But she knew that Howie had her best interests at heart and couldn't be mad at him for interfering. That's just the way he was.

In the general store apartment, Mr. Nakamura looked peaceful as he lay on the kitchen table. Standing over him, however, Stevie was turning pale. His left hand held a small lamp so Howie's mother could see better. With the right, he gently squeezed the skin together around Nakamura's wound, stopping the blood from flowing into Mom's suture area. Stevie let out a low, gasping scream as each stitch entered and exited Mr. Nakamura's forehead. But the silent recipient of the little semi-circular needle's thread never changed his expression. Mom laughed at every one of Stevie's moans.

A few minutes later, Kim and Howie entered. A body was on the floor, and the scene brought Kim to a startled halt.

"Is he dead?!"

Mom smiled.

"Stevie? No, he just passed out. And your father, thank you for asking, is fine."

Mom put a wet compress on Stevie's forehead. His eyes popped open as he looked up from the floor at a circle of laughing faces above him.

# CHAPTER 15
# THE DANCE
# JULY 4, 1942

*Music is a religion with no beliefs. It mystifies the soul and sets the mind free. Music equalizes mankind, whether it be playin' or singin', listenin' or dancin'. Music is a lover who gives and gives, and asks nothin' in return. Music is a friend who holds your hand in joy or sorrow. We don't see it or feel it or taste it, but it's in us all. And that Fourth of July in '42, the music from a little bitty, thrown-together, playin'-for-tips dirt band lifted up a lot of people who needed liftin' up in their uncertain lives.*

As tradition required, sunset saw the half-masted flag first rise to the top of the pole, then slide down toward the waiting hands of Legionnaires Lubisch and Antonsic. A simplified Glen Miller tune flowed out of the Legion Hall. The Fourth of July music pulled in off-Islanders of every shape and size known to exist on the other side of the shaky bridge. Navy, Army and Coast Guard uniforms intermixed with a few civilian outfits.

Automobile usage was at a premium. To see one car was not unusual. But to see 40 passing on one City Island street was enough to bring old folks and young children to their windows. Each arriving car overflowed with bodies, and, for the first time this year, the island held more males than females.

Lubisch and Antonsic lowered the flag with military precision. Three laughing couples skirted around them and rushed inside. They were the scrap metal of life, and the music was their magnet.

The Stars and Stripes reached the safe arms of the Legionnaires without touching the ground. Satisfied that they had completed their chore, they began the traditional triangular fold, moving progressively closer together. The two old men had to raise their voices over the inside music, even as they reached each other.

"A lot of cars, Lubisch."

"Brings in a lot of customers."

"With gas restricted to four gallons a week, every car must be packed."

"Good for them. The young people deserve their fun tonight. Who knows how many will be back next year?"

"But all these lights, Lubisch. What a target we make of ourselves."

"Americans celebrate. We can't help it. We're shmucks. It's who we are. It's what makes us great. So quit your kvetching and get back behind the bar."

A thunderous round of voices came roaring out of the hall as the slightest of pauses allowed the dancers to vocalize "Pennsylvania-six-five-oh-oh-oh!"

The two ex-soldiers headed inside.

"Lubisch?"

"What?"

"Think Ivory will play a polka tonight?"

"If you ask."

"Me? I'm not going to ask. You ask, Lubisch. He's close to you."

"Lubisch don't polka."

Their overly loud voices were lost as the light-hearted crowd swallowed them up.

Ivory was swinging on the piano, leading a talented but strange conglomeration of make-shift musicians: two seasoned work horses on trumpet and trombone, a hip housewife-type slapping bass, Howie on sax, and a still weak-kneed Stevie as a last minute replacement on drums. A sudden Independence Day impulse to enlist on the part of the scheduled drummer left Stevie, one of Ivory's many students, as the closest thing to a percussionist available on an hour's notice. Ivory drilled the rhythmic combinations into Stevie's hands.

"The piano grabs the music's soul. It's the laughter and the tears," he had explained to Stevie. "The brass be its personality, and the bass its breath. The sax...well, the sax be like its mind when it's lost in deep, deep thinkin'. But the drums, the drums be its heart. Without the beatin' of the drums, everything else dies. So, try not to kill the music, boy."

This was over Stevie's head. He wrinkled his brow and looked frustrated.

"Just show me what I gotta do."

Ivory did, and so far Stevie was managing to keep pace with the others. They overpowered him and covered for his mistakes. Ivory made "ba-pa ba-pa ba-pa ba-pa bop-bop-bop" sounds as he moved his head and lips in time with the proper beat. And Stevie kept his eyes on Ivory's every move. But he was also showing Howie that he could play. At times Howie was impressed with Stevie rising to the occasion. But his glare had no pity whenever Stevie skipped a beat. Stevie knew it and tried not to let his eyes stray in Howie's direction.

Ivory's old jazz schooling brought him to the fore, and some people gathered so close to the piano that any seeing man would have felt smothered. But it just renewed Ivory's energy, and at times he stood up to play backwards, dancing in place and even spinning completely around without missing a note. This always drew an exuberant ovation from the crowd and an influx of tips into the glasses atop his piano. Tonight was a night that many a young serviceman would carry with him into battle.

Lubisch and Antonsic placed the flag under the bar and resumed their duties as Bartender Johnny's sidekicks. Orders were backing up and he was glad to see them return. They had insisted that the lowering of the flag came first, drinks second. Johnny had to agree. After all, this was the Legion.

Hardly noticed, Pete the Dog arrived at the entrance and stopped short, contemplating the noisey crowd. Dropping his head, he turned tail and left.

The hall was so full that dancers spilled out of the double doors onto the terrace and even to the railing that overlooked the swiftest waters of the Sound. A few fool-hardy drunks always sat on the edge of the rail, and every year they ran the risk of losing one or two over the side and into "the Labrador Express." Any body that took that watery fall would disappear, easily swept out into the Sound. Next stop: bouncing off Hart Island, waving goodbye to old Fort Totten and the farms of Bayside, Queens, and vanishing into the Atlantic. The 111-acre fort, built during the Civil War to protect the north entrance to New York Harbor, now played temporary host to anxious soldiers, some preparing for that ever-possible submarine attack, some preparing to join their waiting troop transports. The Sound would be unforgiving to anything or anyone who tried to make that crossing tonight.

Pregnant Teddy sat at the far end of the bar, precariously balanced on a high stool. She sipped on her beer and spoke over the music to Mom and Lillian.

"I shouldn't be drinking when I'm pregnant."

"Why not?" Lillian asked.

"It makes me pee a lot."

"Personally, I like to pee a lot."

"Wait 'til you have somebody sitting on *your* bladder, Lillian, kicking it just for fun. Oh yeah, everybody loves it at first. They find their cutesy little Betty Boop voices and say 'Oh, look, honey. The baby's kicking.' But pretty soon the kid puts on combat boots and learns how to goose step. I hate these parades."

Teddy hesitated before asking the question that had bothered her since Mom mentioned it a few days ago. She leaned in close to her future sister-in-law and spoke confidentially.

"Lillian, if you pee holy water, do you have to drink it first, so it, you know, goes through?"

"Nobody pees holy water! I think it might be a sin. It's probably in the Bible."

"But Mom said that you..."

Mom laughed as Vinny emerged from the crowd and pulled Lillian to the dance floor.

On the terrace, a semi-sober Bad Bill went to the well once too often. He sat perched on the railing, back to the water. A small group of men sat around him as he spouted rot-gut wisdom.

"Give me a gun. It don't even have to be loaded. And I will personally blow the ding-dong off of every damn pretzel-bending Heinie kraut in this great country of ours. God bless America and the horse she rode in on."

The temperature in the kitchen was a few degrees higher than the bar. Even though she was still upset, Kim had rallied to meet her commitments, just as her father would have expected her to do. Wiping her forehead with a rag, she finished washing a rack of glasses, then edged to the swinging doorway to watch Ivory and Howie exhibit a mystical connection as they played.

On the dance floor Vinny and Lillian showed off their best moves. And while they were practiced to perfection, they were still two dancers. But the sax player and the piano man were one.

The music got hotter. The crowd grew louder. Teddy had a tough time speaking over the noise to Mom.

"I wish Gene was here. I know he can't dance. He never could, even before he got hurt. Sure, he thought he could. He loves dancing. And that's what I love about him. He thinks he can do anything! Why won't he tell me how bad he's hurt? I gotta pee."

She signaled Lubisch for another beer, then cut the line to the ladies' room.

On the terrace, Bill had drawn in a fifth listener to his audience.

"There was this spaghetti-suckin' I-talian wop when I was pourin' the canal. 'The Big Ditch' is what we called it. He slid right into the c-ment. He just sorta created this...this grease stain when he went down. They can't help it. It's hereditary. You gotta put talcum on the bullets before you shoot a damn I-talian. Otherwise it kinda slips right off. Never hurts 'em. Never."

From the kitchen, Kim waved to Howie and he winked back, motioning with his head for her to come out. But she held up a dish-rag indicating that she was busy.

Vinny and Lillian slipped away from the dance floor and found the one quiet spot in the hall. They squeezed behind several stacked tables that had been moved to the unused coatroom. It was impossible for them to be so close and yet, not get as close as they wanted.

They sank below the tables holding onto each other. Vinny was at the peak of his virility: strong, powerful, and uninhibited. Lillian was at the peak of her desire: engaged, ripe and ready. Trying to balance this with the Catholic Church tap dancing around their brains was driving them insane. A few more days and they'd be legal explorers in the world of wiz-bang. But for now it was catch as catch can. And today's catch was only two whispers away.

"Oh, Lilly."

"Oh, Vinny."

"Oh, Lubisch, I don't know what you did with them extra beer glasses."

"I didn't put them away. You put them away. Antonsic, I think your mind is starting to snooze."

"Lubisch, if I put them away, I'd know where they was."

Legionnaire Antonsic moved a table. Vinny and Lillian popped into view, straightening themselves a little and smiling. Vinny jumped right in.

"Nope. No glasses down here, gentlemen."

"You kids should be out there having a good time. Antonsic and me, we'll find the glasses. Go. Have fun. Dance."

The couple laughed and escaped back to the dance floor. Lubisch and Antonsic shared a smile and shifted another table.

Johnny was still backed up at the bar, moving as fast as a tired bartender is expected to move. But by the time Teddy returned to Mom, her next beer was waiting. Mom was nursing her Knickerbockers tonight. Teddy had already nursed three.

"I know the Guinness people said beer was good for a pregnant lady, but you might be overdoing it a little, Teddy."

"Good, 'cause I don't really like it. I'm just drinking it for the baby. Gene says that he should name all the boys, and I should name all the girls. What do you think, Mom?"

"As long as it's a saint's name it really doesn't matter."

"Oh, Lord. I gotta go again. What is it with this kid? I think he does this on purpose. I swear I can hear him laughing at me... Lillian told me it's a boy...I bet I could pee in this glass and no one would ever know."

"I think it's time I took you home, missy."

"Is Gene home?"

"Soon, Teddy. Soon."

"I want him home *now*. He's my husband, and I want him home."

"Believe me. I know how you feel. Pop's been gone since December 8th, the Feast of the Immaculate Conception. That's 211 days and 211 nights, which I estimate to be a couple of hundred slaps and tickles, not to mention a few delicious 'oom-pahs'...Oh, I miss the oom-pahs."

She closed her eyes, tossed back her Irish red hair and made a slight "mmmm" sound as she relived her last oom-pah experience. But Teddy brought her back.

"You count them? You count the days?"

"You don't?!"

"Hmmm, no. I never thought about it."

Mom patted Teddy's hand and gave her a you-poor-little-innocent-thing look.

"Every morning when I wake up, before I open my eyes, I reach over to see if maybe Pop might just be there. But he never is. One day he was here, and one day he was gone. They took him away with no explanation. No nothing. And not a word since. So, yes. I count the days, and the hours and the minutes too. And if I thought peeing in that glass would bring him back one second sooner, I'd do it right now, right up here on the bar. I'd do it to music with a rose in my teeth and a feather in my hair! I'd do it upside down, on a trapeze swingin' across this room, screaming Dunny's name! But he's the only one who can get himself home. Now let's get *you* home before you wet your drawers."

They slid off the stools and wedged their way through the crowd, Mom easily parting the merrymakers.

"Pregnant woman. Coming through!"

On the terrace, Bad Bill had just finished that one drink that slipped him over the edge of sobriety and into the chasm of inebriation. He entertained almost a dozen listeners.

"The Japs...The damn Japs...There ain't nobody in this world as sneaky as the Japs. Damn slant-eyed, yellow midgets is what they are. And we got one laughin' at us, watchin' every move we make...

How come, how come FDR banned everyone from having a wireless radio, and that nip across the street has a godamn Western Union telegraph? Don't nobody think no more? Look at those ships right out his back window! Don't tell me that this is some kind of coincidence. 'Cause it ain't. No coincidence ever killed an American G.I. And no coincidence is ever gonna kill a son of mine. I say we string that nip up by his ding-dong 'til his eyes straighten out, once and for all, and the horse he rode in on."

A growing number in his audience responded with support while just a few laughed it off and slipped away. As the crowd thinned, one small body became visible on the ground with his back to the rail. The ever-silent, ever-observant Mungo rose with an angry expression and moved inside. He didn't stop until he reached the kitchen and squatted down again, watching Kim dry glasses and shuttle them to the bar. She winked at Mungo as she carried her next load out to Bartender Johnny, earning a smile in return. He was still smiling when she got back. His angry face was gone.

Inside, Mom had a tougher time than anticipated getting Teddy out the door. When she turned around, Teddy was kissing her way across the room, stopping at everyone she knew, and some she didn't, to say goodbye and finish long lost conversations.

Vinny and Lillian bypassed them, sneaked through the kitchen and out the back door. Mungo hardly looked up, but Kim waved a soapy hand to the fleeing couple. They were too consumed by love to notice anybody. She wondered what true love felt like. She wanted to know before she died. Kim loved her family and she loved Howie. But she had always loved him and didn't know if there was a difference between love and true love; and if so, could one grow into the other? Or do you know your true love the first time you see him? She never heard any bells or whistles when she was around Howie, which was most of the time. And she was glad because it would have been awfully noisy all day long, if that were really the case. But people said that when you kiss the one you truly love, you hear those bells and you hear those whistles. How could Lillian always be smiling with all that noise in her head? Maybe it was destroying her mind. She'd have to find out for herself.

## CHAPTER 16

# THE CANE

## JULY 4, 1942

The dance ended before 11:30. It always did. Most of the revelers and workers wanted to be outside for the traditional midnight fireworks display, so closing up was never a problem.

Kim had dried and stacked what seemed to be a thousand glasses that night, but more likely was the same hundred over and over again. The music stopped, and she knew her chores were almost done. Kim stepped onto the deserted dance floor to collect a dozen empties from on and around Ivory's piano as the band packed up, and she glistened with pride when she saw Howie get approving handshakes from the three older musicians.

Howie and Stevie dumped six glasses that contained a serious amount of tip money. It overflowed a table, and they started an excited count. Stevie was feeling confident for not getting kicked out of the band halfway through the night.

"Did you see that, Ivory? The way those ladies were lookin' at me tonight?"

Ivory lifted his head, then lifted his sun glasses.

"Oh, yeah. I forgot...But, Howie. You saw them, right? They *always* go for the drummer. I'm tellin' ya, I'm thinkin' of makin' a career outta this. I didn't know how good I was."

Ivory furrowed his brow. Stevie swore that Ivory was looking right at him.

"I don't know how Howie ever talked me into lettin' you sit in," Ivory said.

"I have...ah...potential. Tell him, Howie."

"Sorry, Ivory. I should have told you to pick Mungo. You gave him six months of lessons, right?"

"Don't listen to him, Ivory. I'm gonna play great at Vinny's wedding. You watch. Besides, Mungo's only ten years old" Stevie retorted. "Or eleven, maybe! What does he know?"

"More than he says. Next time, Ivory, pick Mungo."

"Hey! Howie, don't say that! I'll practice. I promise. Okay?"

"I'll make that decision." Ivory's authority ended any debate. "And you, Howie. You gotsta play like there's nothin' out there but a dry desert. You're too distracted by them glasses clinkin' and them people laughin'. Or else you gonna be playin' beer halls and cat houses for the rest of your natural-born days."

Stevie illuminated at the idea. He marked it down as a long-term career goal: *beer halls, cat houses.* But Howie had other plans.

"You know I'm gonna be a ball player."

"God already made you a music man. Don't go sucker punchin' the Lord when you sportin' a battin' average below two hundred. All right boys, let's pay the rent."

Stevie and Howie came up with $32.50 in tips, and they divide it among the six musicians. It was a good night's work.

Ivory went back to the piano as the others packed up. Bartender Johnny brought him a shot and a cigar. He lit up and then lit into his favorite New Orleans jazz.

As Howie pushed his tips into the deepest recesses of his pants pocket, he found Bad Bill standing in front of him.

"Messenger boy, I thought I told you to stay away from the Jap."

"I have a job to do, Bill. I'm fightin' the war my way. So I ain't quittin'."

Howie brushed by him, heading for the kitchen, but Bill's voice brought him to a stop.

"Hey Howie. You know what the Romans did to a messenger who brought bad news?"

"What?"

Bill made a slicing motion with one finger across his neck, then broke into ominous laughter. A momentary shudder caught Howie off guard. He tried to look the part of a brave young man, but turned like a scared little kid and entered the kitchen just a bit too fast, tripping over his own feet. Echoes of Bill's laughter burned his ears even after the door had swung shut.

Kim was the last of the kitchen crew to leave. As she finished sweeping a push broom across the kitchen floor, she heard Bill's laughter, and the derisive tone automatically told her that it must be at Howie's expense.

All of the kitchen staff had been aware of Bill's attack on her father, yet no one had spoken directly to her about it. She didn't expect condolences from her fellow workers, but she didn't anticipate the stares she got, either. Compared to Bill, even Big Stevie seemed like a reasonable person, and she found herself promising to give Stevie a second chance. But not Bill. Bill had become her enemy, and now, seeing him defeated was all she needed for a reason to keep living.

When Howie gracelessly stumbled into that kitchen, he was the brightest color in her rainbow day. Even Bill's laughter couldn't darken that. Kim abandoned her broom and tucked Howie's sax into the closet. She took his hand and led him out the same back door that the lovers had used to flee a short time before.

Mungo, left squatting against a wall, realized that he had been forgotten. He stood up, crossed the room and picked up the broom. He weighed the heft of the handle, and examined the lie of the broad bristles. Satisfied, he experimented with the best possible grip for pushing the broom across the floor.

In the barroom, Ivory heard Bill's laughter die away, and called to him without letting his fingers leave the keys.

"Hold up there, Bill."

"What?"

"Tellin' ya like a friend. So take it like a friend. You gotsta slow down and think 'bout what you doin'. You a wheel on fire. You gonna run downhill 'til that flame turn you into ash and ember. Fact. Sorry ass fact, but true."

Bill came back, closing the gap.

"You've been on this island for a long time, old man, and I guess that gives you a right to your own opinion. But this war's changin' our whole life here. Half the boats I work on are up on blocks. There's no summer trade. The war stole our Island sons, yours and mine included. And now the food's about to get rationed, and that Jap controls who eats and who don't. You *know* he's slowly stranglin' the life out of the Island's supply line. So yeah, you're entitled to your opinion."

Bill worked his way around the piano.

"And you can work all that voodoo of yours out in the sandlot, gettin' them kids under your spell. And pretty soon they start listenin' to you more than their fathers. And lookin' up to you. And walkin' away from their fathers. And they don't write, or call, or nothin'. They turn their back on their own family, but somehow he writes to you. Well, your voodoo ain't gonna work on me, old man. You ain't as smart as people say. You can bullshit everyone else, but I know."

Bill tapped an ominous finger against Ivory's dark glasses, distracting him, as he silently lifted Ivory's cane out of the holster nailed to the side of the soundboard.

"In there, you're seein' everything. You're seein' it all. You ain't foolin' me. I know you ain't blind. Nobody's that smart that they could do what you do and know what you know, with no eyes. So you take your opinion and shove it where the moon don't shine, but don't go tellin' me how to run my life."

Bill slammed his hand down on the keys. The music crashed into a discordant silence. He leaned in and spoke softer, but the soft tone made it all the more threatening.

"When I'm done with that Jap, I'm comin' back for you. And once everybody else knows about them eyes, you and me gonna dance a few rounds."

Bill thought he had the last word. He was used to having the last word. But Ivory wouldn't let him go. He calmly leaned away from the piano and puffed the cigar out of his mouth.

"If'n you really wanna dance with a seein' man, Bill, then you gotsta wait a spell, 'cause we gonna be dancin' on the other side of the grave. You best mend your ways 'afore you burn out or boil over. Time you stopped lookin' at people with open eyes, 'cause all you ever gonna see is what they look like and where they come from. Close them baby blues, and maybe you find out just who they are. I know things be a heap more complicated in a seein' world, so I ain't gonna write you off yet. But if you need help seein' what you really gotsta see, well, you know where I be...right here...like a friend."

Bill, cane in hand, started for the door, but Ivory still wasn't ready to let him go.

"And Bill."

"What?"

"The cane."

Bill laughed. "I *knew* you could see!"

He broke the cane over his knee, and tossed the parts across the room. One rolling piece headed for the door, stopped only by a shoe coming down hard. Bill followed the shoe, ankle, leg upward to Cathleen's sullen face. Arms crossed, she swirled out of the Legion into the clear night air.

Bill threw a look back at Ivory that silently shouted now-see-what-you've-done, then quietly followed behind his wife. He'd be sleeping on a chapel pew again tonight and needed to get a pillow before she chased him out of the bungalow.

Ivory went back to his tune as he called out to Bartender Johnny.

"Mr. Bar-tender, they done with that sweep-up broom yet?"

Johnny left the bar and stuck his head into the kitchen.

"Kim?"

But she was gone. In her place Mungo marched across the room as he practiced sweeping the already swept floor. Bartender Johnny smiled and flipped Mungo a quarter, carving a high arc across the short distance. Mungo stretched up and executed a perfect one-handed catch, his best fielding move so far this summer, never losing control of the broom.

"You grow up some, kid, and come see me next year. Maybe I'll have a job for you. Now, scram."

Bartender Johnny took the broom back into the bar, heading toward the piano.

Mungo looked around, assuring himself that he was alone. Satisfied, he flashed a smile at the coin making a new home in his palm. He closed his hand around his reward and slipped his thumb into his mouth. Ten seconds later he confidently stepped out the back door that had just played host to both lovers and friends, now a wealthy man of the world, or at least a working stiff with financial prospects and ball handling skills.

This was a good Mungo day.

# CHAPTER 17

# THE BEACH WALK

# JULY 4, 1942

As Howie and Kim walked along the small dunes, they could hear the last 20 or so party-goers singing on the terrace behind them. They sang *Over There* and *Yip Yip Yaphank* and other songs reminiscent of The Great War.

Kim didn't want to let go of his hand, and she swung it to the music.

"Your pocket's clinkin', Howie, everytime you take a step."

"It's the tips. I made over six bucks."

"Wow. That's a lot of money."

"I know. It's heavy."

"Do you have your 52.99 yet?"

"Close. I got 32."

"What's it look like?"

"A herd of shiny buffalos. You're gonna have to help me carry 'em when I go to big Fordham Road."

They continued walking, and Howie's off kilter weight made him lopsided. He held his pants pocket with his free hand to minimize his clinking coins and spoke over the jingling.

"Vinny says this is probably the last fireworks 'til the war is over."

"Must be collecting all the gun powder. This is just the left over stuff they hafta get rid of before it blows up...I heard Bad Bill laughing at you back inside."

"If we had a cop on this island, he'd a been arrested for beatin' up your father."

"You're scared of him. Ain't ya, Howie?"

"No...Yeah. 'Cause he's so mean, and 'cause maybe it's in the blood. I don't wanna grow up like him."

"Then don't grow up."

"How could you not grow up?"

"Well, you could...die."

"Kim! No suicide talk, remember?"

"Ya know, Howie, a submarine could come up out there, right now, and shoot us all to death. I heard they already sunk a hundred ships."

"Yeah it could, and fireworks could fall down on our heads and turn our brains to sparklers. Don't worry about the 'might-happen' stuff. There's enough real stuff to go around."

"I mean it. They could come tomorrow morning and take me away to an internment camp. But at least maybe I'd be with my mom then."

"Can't she just tell them that she really lives in New York and that she was only back in California to take care of her sick mother?"

"She tried that. They don't care. She's stuck."

"They wouldn't take you away. Anyways, I wouldn't let them. I'd...I'd tell them that you was a skinny little dumb-ass. And we all know they don't take no skinny little dumb-asses to internment. They're too skinny and they're too dumb."

Kim couldn't stand that one. She punched him in the arm. It seemed like Howie was getting hit a lot these days. He tried to retaliate, but she ran away, laughing. He followed her along the dune line. When he caught up to her, she was sitting in the moonlight with her head back, her black hair dripping into the sand. Her silhouette looked like a picture from a fashion magazine, except for the flat chest and the round shoulders.

"You think you're so great, Howie. Don't you? Just 'cause you get to play in the band. Well you know what? Maybe you're half right."

"How come you didn't come in to hear me?"

"I could hear you fine from the kitchen."

She imitated Howie playing the sax with lots of exaggerated moves to avoid answering the question truthfully. She knew that she ran the risk of making herself a target for anyone's misplaced wrath over Danny's death. And she felt safer in the familiar kitchen where she and her mother had performed their familiar tasks for as long as she could remember.

"You coulda heard me better inside."

"Someday, I'll hear you in a big theater. You'll be the only one on stage. They'll put a spotlight on you. And I'll say, 'That's my Howie. I knew him when he was a dumb-ass, when he used to go in the water with his shoes on!' And then I'll punch you, or maybe if I'm in the balcony I'll just throw my shoe, 'cause even if you're not a dumb-ass anymore when you grow up, I'm never gonna let you forget how dumb you used to be. That's how good a friend I am."

Howie could hear her laughing in the dark, as she ran farther along the sand ridge. But she quickly fell silent, and he abandoned the chase. By the time he strolled up to her new position, she was on the ground and peering over the crest of another small dune. She lifted one finger to her lips, signaling for him to be quiet. He pressed himself into the sand and followed her gaze.

Below them, and 15 feet down the narrow beach, Vinny and Lillian were stretched out, arms wrapped around each other, lips locked in delicious rapture, oblivious to the world around them. Kim craned her neck, trying to get her head in the same position as Lillian. Finally satisfied, she turned her attention back to Howie.

"You can kiss me if you want."

This could be the moment of bells and whistles, if, in actuality, such a moment existed. She hoped for the best and prepared herself for the worst.

Howie looked suddenly self-conscious. He couldn't say he didn't want to kiss her. She'd never forgive that one. He wondered where he went wrong.

*It was probably the hand-holding thing,* he thought. *Yeah. It was definitely the hand-holding thing. Why did I let that happen? At least at the stadium, we had mitts on. It was sorta "long distance". But this. This is the real thing. What if I do it wrong? What if I just punched her in the shoulder instead?*

It was time for yet another one of life's little momentous decisions. They had never come so rapidly before. He made it.

"Okay. Get ready."

"I'm ready," she giggled.

"Then stop laughing!" She stopped.

He cleared his throat, loosened up his shoulders, rotated his neck.

He leaned in and gave her a peck on the lips.

"Not like that. Like *that*." She indicated Vinny and Lillian, who were starting to passionately roll in the sand.

"Like that?!" A hint of panic in his voice.

"Yeah. Like that."

Howie strained to get his head up higher so he could take mental notes of Vinny at work and play. Then he slid in close to Kim, speaking in a loud whisper.

"Okay. Here goes."

Kim put her head back and opened her mouth.

"I can't kiss you."

"Why not?"

"Your mouth is open."

"It's supposed to be open"

Howie took another look over the crest, positive the answer was "closed".

"Is not."

"Is too."

"Is not."

"Is too."

"Wait a minute. Stay right here," he challenged. "I'll go ask Vinny."

"Believe me. Okay? I know."

"How do you know?"

"I just know."

"How?"

"Well...I...I kinda tried it already." She eased out her shy admission.

"Oh? With who?"

"Nobody."

"A person or an animal?"

"Howie!"

"Pete the Dog! Right? You did it with Pete the Dog!"

"A person! Of course a person!...Sue Ellen, last week. Just to see if we could breathe."

"Could you?"

"No. It sorta crushes your nose closed. But I was good at holdin' my breath. Not as good as you, but good. You shoulda' seen me."

Howie let this sink in. He could visualize the two of them trying it out. But then his mind went a step further.

"I'd eat a live toad before I'd kiss another boy."

"You eat a live toad, *nobody* is gonna kiss you."

"I guess not."

"Toady breath."

"Quit it."

"Toady breath."

"Kim! Stop."

"Toady..."

Howie's toughest stare brought her down. They peeked back over the top of the dune. Their mouths dropped as they saw Vinny unbuttoning Lillian's blouse. The lovers' words were barely audible over the lapping waters of the Sound.

"No, Vinny."

"We're practically married."

"Don't."

"Lilly, I love you so much. I can't stand it any more."

"Holy-Mother-the-Church doesn't allow it."

"What Holy-Mother-the-Church doesn't know, won't hurt."

"No. I want to be in the state of grace when we get married, and so do you."

Howie and Kim sank down, giggling behind the dunes. Howie summoned up his kiss courage, then brought his face close to hers.

"Okay. Here goes. And don't laugh."

Howie looked left, then right like a pitcher checking out the leads on first and third.

"The wind up. The pitch. It's a fast ball down the..."

Kim's hand across his mouth cut him off. "There's no talking during kissing."

He baptized Kim with an awkward eyes-open kiss that grew into a comical gymnastic embrace. Their lips parted, and they laughed.

They each took a few deep breaths. The kiss was simple, but it had the slightest ember of passion that might grow to a flame if fanned, fed and tended over time...a long time...a long, long time... years if not decades. Howie licked his lips. Yeah, "decades" worked for him.

"It's a long fly ball. It's going...It's going...Its gone!"

Kim laughed again at the way he dealt with his feelings. She laughed and unbuttoned the top of her blouse.

"Do you want to touch my bosoms?"

"You don't have any bosoms."

"If I had bosoms, would you want to touch them?"

"No. Just cut it out. Okay?"

"I thought that's what boys wanted to do, touch bosoms."

"Big Stevie's got bigger bosoms than you and I don't want to touch his, either."

This time Kim laughed a little too loud, but Howie quickly quieted her.

"Shhhhhh!"

"Ya know, Sue Ellen runs to the mirror every morning to see if she grew bosoms overnight. I just look to see if my eyes grew rounder...like yours. I'm doing exercises. See?"

Kim began a ridiculous set of wide-eyed, cheek-contorted facial gymnastics. Howie stopped her, putting his hands on her face, thumbs under her eyes, fingers by her temples.

"They look great to me. Oh, wait. Hold still."

He suddenly nuggied one eyebrow, with a Three Stooges style "nyat! nyat!"

"I love you, Howie, but..."

"Can't take it, huh?"

He buttoned her blouse back up.

"You know I love you, too," he admitted. "Just don't go tellin' nobody."

They looked over the dune, but the other couple was gone. They stood up to gain a better vantage point.

"Howie, I...I have a confession to tell you."

"What?"

"When you kissed me, I didn't hear any bells or any whistles. That means you're not my true love. I'm sorry."

"Well, I got a confession, too. That was not my good kiss, my home-run-bottom-of-the-ninth-with-bases-loaded kiss. That was only my ground rule double. I didn't want to hurt you. The good kiss could really do some damage. For that one, you gotta close your eyes."

"But don't ya get dizzy?"

"Well yeah! That's the good part."

She laughed again, but Lillian and Vinny's louder laughter floated in the distance. Howie pulled her in like he had seen at the movies. He fumbled onward with his best Bogart kiss, and she lifted one foot off the ground like a starlet on the rise. It truly was his best kiss so far. It was also only his second kiss so far. The first was a learner's permit. This time the car was bucking in low gear, and Howie had no idea how to use the clutch.

Kim wished that she were wearing a hat so that she could hold it on her head as her neck tilted back. Their eyes were closed, their mouths open just enough. Kim leaned back a little more. And then it happened. Howie's pocket change shifted. He tried to stop it but...

"Uh-oh!"

They lost their balance and tumbled to the dune.

"You're right, Howie. That kiss does hurt."

Kim shook the sand out of her hair. "No bells. No..."

A whistling light soared into the air above.

"...whistles."

The first explosion lit the sky. It showered a spray of red rockets, each one exploding in turn again. The fireworks filled the night air, and Kim laughed so hard now that she had to clasp her hands over her mouth.

Howie knew he had saved the day for his team. That ball was still traveling out of Yankee Stadium and over the Jerome Avenue el. They probably heard the crack of his bat across the Harlem River in the Polo Grounds. That kiss would be tough to equal. But the fireworks part! That would be impossible to duplicate. He tried to act nonchalant as all truly great heroes should at the moment of their most amazing triumph.

The voices of the other couple pulled Howie and Kim over the dunes once more. They could only make out their forms against the fireworks as they reflected off the Sound, but it was obvious that they were stripping off their clothes and rushing toward the water.

Lillian's voice was the louder of the two. "Come on. Let's go swimming! Just keep your underwear on."

"Sure."

"I mean it now, Vinny."

"Don't worry." Vinny lost his shorts as he followed her in.

Their loud splashing drowned out the specific words, but Howie knew that they were playing in the majors, and he was still only on the triple-A farm team, after all.

Kim wasn't sure that what she had seen was what had actually happened.

"Did he take his clothes off?!"

"Peeled like a potato."

"All of his clothes?"

"Yeah. Bare, butt-bone naked. And Lillian was taking most of hers off, too."

She thought about the way they had imitated the older couple's kissing technique and hesitantly took it to its logical conclusion.

"Howie, we should take off our clothes and go swimming."

"I got a better idea."

Howie pushed his coins deep in his pocket, slipped over the crest of the dune and belly-snaked his way along the high tide line. Kim quietly followed his lead. This had become a beach-head action worthy of any European invasion tactician, especially the 12-year-old ones.

The fireworks continued to ignite the sky in the final display of New York's Fourth of July fervor until the war would be concluded. No doubt the German U-boats sitting in the shipping lanes and re-charging their batteries on the surface that night were puzzled by this outrageous display in time of war. It had no rational explanation. But then, by Third Reich standards, Americans were famous for their irrational practices, such as annual elections and multiple parties. It was said that entire crews of submarine wolf packs, up and down the Eastern Seaboard, gathered on their decks that night to share this final fiery panorama of viewing pleasure with their military and civilian enemies a few dangerous miles away.

Between the fireworks delayed echoes, voices from the distant terrace behind the Legion drifted across the large body of water. They rang out in choruses that built and reverberated as if other voices in other smaller communities around the Sound were joining in. But voices on the Sound have a way of bouncing back in strange combinations.

As Howie and Kim commando-crawled through the sand, toward a trail of lovers' discarded clothing, one set of terrace lyrics dominated the others, covering their surreal action.

"Over there, over there,
Send the word, send the word over there
That the Yanks are coming, the Yanks are coming
And we won't come back 'til it's over, over there."

The two crawlers were swallowed up in a maze of old songs and flashing lights that rolled across the dark water and rained down from the starlit sky, small morsels of humanity in a giant exploding universe, yet unexplained and unexplored.

# CHAPTER 18

# THE SOUND OF AMERICA

## JULY 5, 1942

*The power I puts into playin', it gotsta come from somewheres else in my bein'. That Fourth of July hoopla night stole from several of my faculties, leavin' me used up and worn down.*

*It weren't walkin' home in the dark what bothered me. I been walkin' in the dark near all my days. And there ain't never been no crime on City Island, 'cept a few years back when a deck-hand drifter accidentally killt. three ducks during a week-long amorous and amoral interlude. Instead of sendin' him to a sledgehammer jail house for six months makin' little ones out of big ones, a Bronx judge put that poor boy in the hospital. So even that indiscretion may not qualify as a full blowed crime spree.*

*No. It was definitely the lack of faculties that made me sleep instead of walk. And greedy that I was, that night I hoped to witness sounds even more magical than music...the talk of them two wise old buildin's...but mostly slept deep instead.*

A warm breeze rose with the sun at 5:07 that morning to find the debris of last night's celebration spread around the Legion Hall. Most of it was on the terrace where the late night singers had encamped, but a pile of newspapers strewn across the bench at the blacktop circle stood out of place. They were too organized, too utilitarian, and they were moving. They slipped to the ground as Ivory emerged from underneath the newsprint. He struggled to recall how he had come to this resting place last night. But then, last night seemed so long ago, and he really couldn't remember.

Since his boy Corey had joined up, like all the other eligible sons on the island, Ivory didn't seem to make it home every night. But he still liked to get up with the sun, and he still liked to feel the warmth of the dawn rays flow across his face.

He rose, staggered a second, then realized where he was. He felt around in his pants pockets, produced the old rabbit's foot, smiled and tucked it away again. He groped along the bench. and his brain strained to remember why he was there, and with an unfamiliar substitute cane: the too-long handle of a barroom push broom.

Bartender Johnny and he had traded stories with Lubisch and Antonsic until long after the fireworks had ceased and the patriotic songs had melted away. As always, the Legionnaires spoke of the passing of old friends, but this time they added the death of young Danny. They spoke of the war and the country. And they spoke of "the talk". Each one bragged about when he had heard it, or at least thought he did. But Ivory had no doubts. He had experienced the talking buildings many times before, and he challenged the others to sit it out with him tonight. He had no takers. No one really wanted to spend the night with a hard bench for a bed. Besides, ignorance was the better choice. This way no one would be in a position to deny City Island's oldest legend. It was part of the community's heritage that set it above any other seaside village, part of what made these two ancient buildings so important, and part of what kept these two outdated companions alive.

Slowly, the entire night's proceedings came back to him, and he started to remember hearing the buildings talk before he drifted off to sleep. Their barely decipherable repetitious echo of one simple word, called and answered by both structures, rang through the night: home. Ivory thought he might know what it meant.

Now, however, he heard a new sound, a slightly offbeat flapping on the flagpole. He felt his way to the staff, got his bearings and straightened up for the memorized walk home. It sounded too loud, as if it came from several flags all at once. But he saluted anyway, because a blind man doesn't take chances with nature, nation or God.

Ivory wore a false sense of comfort knowing that after a rowdy, festive night, either Lubisch or Antonsic had pulled himself out of bed for the dawn raising of his nation's wartime symbol of sovereignty, and it felt like dawn. Ivory fingered the warmth of the pole to confirm what his face had told him. The sun was already up.

He lit a cigarette, took a long puff and exhaled the smoke skyward.

He was about to start the refrain from *God Bless America* softly to himself for his journey home, when the I've-got-a-mind-of-my-own bus pulled into the circle on the first of its early morning trips. Or it could have been the last of its only-going-if-I-have-a-passenger-which-hardly-ever-happens late night runs. He wasn't sure.

Ivory heard the wheels squeak to a stop. He knew no one was getting on or he would have already been greeted by that someone's voice. Therefore, some other someone had to be getting off. The sound of an army duffel bag hitting the pavement gave him the first clue. Then two crutches met the road, followed by the sound of one foot. He waited for the other to fall but it never did. Instead, he heard a strong arm hoist the duffel bag over one shoulder, then the movement of the entire ensemble away from the bus.

"Good luck, soldier." Joe the Bus Driver's words remained as he pulled away.

Ivory took a step closer before he asked, "Mornin', soldier. Do I know you?"

"As well as you know that lung duster you're sucking on."

"Gene! I knowed it gotsta be you. Them buildings been tellin' me all night that you was comin' home."

Ivory held out his hand and the soldier shook it.

"That was what *you* used to call them. Wasn't it, Ivory? Lung dusters?"

"Yeah, but the way I feel now, I shoulda called them lung *busters.* I cain't fairly play the brasses no more due to lack of internal wind power. This young thoroughbred lookin' more like a raggedy old plow-horse every day. Quittin' someday, though. It's all about the lungs...So how the hell are ya, son?"

"Been better. Been worse."

Ivory handed Gene his newly lit cigarette. He took a drag.

"Keep it. So where you comin' from?"

"Hickam to Pearl. Frisco to home."

"Shit. A heap of stumps in that row."

"Yeah, it was...ah...somethin' else."

Gene shifted his 60-pound bag in tighter. He slipped the long strap across his chest and hefted the weight on his back. With two good legs there would not have been a problem, and he refused to let the inconvenience of one missing appendage become an excuse for not carrying his own load now. That was not his way, and never would be. He had spent a lifetime developing this strong, lean frame, and one lousy leg, more or less, was not going to throw him off balance.

Ivory turned his face up to the sun, soaking in the long, early morning rays.

"What a splendorous mornin' for a homecomin'."

Gene looked around at the City Island he had left in better times. Little that met his eyes had changed. The gulls still cried.

The salt air still filled his nostrils with the clean smell of the sea. Then his eyes rose up the flagpole, and a laugh fell out of his mouth.

"Welcome home, boy. We all been waitin' on ya."

"Ivory, just so you know, I'm comin' home minus one leg. I'm actually glad you can't see me right now."

"I could hear it in that step off the bus. Other than them smells that some folk send my way now and again for the sheer fun of it, you and everyone else in my world is beautiful. I don't see no lost teeth, no broken noses, no crossed eyes...no missin' legs. All I hear is voices, and all I see is souls. The trees are always green, and the sky is always blue. And when it rains, it's rainin' through sunbeams or moonbeams or any other personal beams you got. So Gene, you always be a beautiful sight to me. But now that you back from the hell fire, I gonna be checkin' on you. Time to punch your ticket for a soul check. Yes, sir. Big time soul check."

"If you see anything down there, be sure and let me know. 'Cause I ain't seen it in a while."

Gene nodded a silent nod. Ivory listened to the sound of the crutches moving away. He could hear Gene stop periodically to square his shifting load, barely managing to maintain his balance, yet refusing to give in. It was the sound of fierce determination. It was the sound of City Island independence. It was the sound of apple pie and small town America and everything else Ivory had sought after, until he finally stopped his rambling and found this speck of dirt so many years ago. And he had to sing its praise. His half-pint flask emerged, and he faced the flagpole. He raised the shiny container in the direction of the flapping sounds and then again in the direction of the disappearing Gene, swallowing with a good-to-be-alive swig. He half mumbled the words his early-morning brain recalled, humming those it didn't.

"God bless America,
mmm, mmm, mmm, mmm"

If he had been able to see, the wonders of the pole would have revealed most of Vinny's and Lillian's clothing tied in place of the flag. They flapped in the breeze with Vinny's military underwear topping the display.

Gene stopped at the front walk to the Logan house. He looked up at the century-old captain's quarters. The small lamp-post sign that he had etched in wood-shop a dozen years ago was still legible: Home Sweet Home. He rubbed his hand across its carved out lettering.

Gene inhaled the last gasp from his cigarette butt as long as he could and savored it as long as he could. And he delayed as long as he could. Finally, his fingertips began to burn and he knew his as-long-as-he-coulds were all used up. The butt dropped to the ground and he crutched it out. He took a deep breath, then mounted the porch and opened the heavy old white door, making a mental note. *I need to paint this door again.* City Island doors, with the exception of the Legion and the general store, were never locked. It would have been tantamount to accusing friends and neighbors of criminal activity. Most older houses, in fact, had no keys that actually fit anything current.

Gene entered devouring his first bacon smell of non-institutionalized breakfast in over six months. He navigated across the wide-board floor and into the kitchen archway. It framed his one-legged military bearing in the manner of a Civil War stereoscopic photograph. In an earlier time, the kitchen's occupants would have turned to welcome the captain home from a long and dangerous sea voyage. He would have brought them pineapples, and after a few days, one would have been placed on the porch table, announcing to the world that he was healthy and now accepting visitors. Before that time, a well wisher would only be expected to leave his *carte de visite* in the bowl on the table, acknowledging the captain's return.

But this South Pacific traveler dealt in no such symbols and civilities. Only a broken body and a soul struggling to stay whole.

Teddy carried eggs in a wooden bowl balanced on a larger abdomen, as she walked toward the stove where Mom had already started to cook up that good bacon Nakamura had put aside for her. She was getting ready to pour off the excess fat that she needed to save for dinner. Teddy sensed physical movement in the archway and glanced over as she spoke.

"Howie, how do you want your..."

She saw Gene where she expected his younger brother to be. Her eyes and mouth went wide and her voice was barely audible.

"...eggs?"

Her eyes fell to his missing lower leg. She raised her hand to her mouth and spontaneously dropped the bowl. A dozen large browns cascaded to the floor. Her gaze fought its way back to meet his eyes staring into hers. She ran to her husband's arms, crushing shells beneath her. Mom jumped at the sound of the crash, speaking before she looked.

"Teddy, what happened?...Oh, my God! It's Gene!"

After a moment's hesitation, she pulled her stare away from his pinned up pants leg, and ran over to join the group hug. Gene's crutches hit the floor and his duffel bag slammed down beside them. He braced himself against the wall and wrapped his arms around his wife. But he opened them once again to accept his mother's face resting on his other shoulder. Teddy cried into his uniform and held him tightly.

Any normal man would have responded with his own tears, but Gene had seen things and lived things that would forever prevent him from rejoining the ranks of normality. Forty minutes of hell in Hawaii would take a lifetime to heal.

His eyes caught Howie's across the room, staring at the missing leg. Gene's nod floated through the women's hair and Howie returned it with one of his own. Howie knew that if the roles were reversed, he would be crying by now. But Gene lived in a world where men don't cry, and little brothers look up to big brothers forever.

Gene's silent nod said, "I'm not whole, but I'm home."

Howie's answered, "You're my brother. You're my hero."

# CHAPTER 19

# AFTER WAIPAHU

# JULY 5, 1942

Breakfast in bed tasted as good as it smelled. Gene and Teddy spread out on the old four-poster. Everything in the bedroom was in perfect order for Gene's homecoming. He liked order. He liked to line things up, physically and mentally. His collection of six cigarette lighters was set up in the inconspicuous far corner of the high dresser just as he had left them before shipping out for Hawaii. The progression went from smallest to largest, with gold taking preference over silver where number three and number four tied for size. But the stack of dollar bills underneath them was a new addition.

Teddy's large bare belly exposed her pregnancy, and Gene caressed it with an awe only reserved for the male of the species. Seeing her for the first time in seven months made him fully comprehend the life of his unborn child. He glanced over at some amorphous yarn growth spread out on the nightstand.

"What are you knitting?"

"I'm not sure. The needles haven't told me yet. The doctor says I could deliver any day now, even any minute. Just knowing you're home makes be not afraid anymore."

"I missed you so much, Teddy. You know, sooner or later you're going to have to say something, anything, about the leg. I couldn't tell you in a letter. I didn't know how to do it. Tried a couple of times, but I couldn't. Besides, I wanted to be there to catch you if you fainted. But I think we should talk about it. That's what they said to do...talk about it a lot."

"It's my fault. I should never have left Hawaii," she said, looking away.

"Don't start that game. I've played it all before."

"But if I'd stayed there with you, we would have still been living in that little apartment up in Waipahu. You wouldn't have moved to the base."

"And when the Japs bombed that morning I wouldn't have been in that rack. And I wouldn't have gone back into the barracks. And my leg wouldn't have been blown off...I'm not playing that 'if' game anymore."

"But it's true. It's 'cause of me that you were there that morning."

"Yeah. Yeah. It's your fault for coming back to the states. And it's the baby's fault for making you do it. And it's my fault for knocking you up. That game never stops. It's a game you can't win. I lost it a thousand times before I stopped playing. But you know what does make sense?"

"What?"

"Those three G.I.s that I yanked out of there before I got hit, they all made it. So maybe God put me there for a reason. And maybe you coming back here was part of it. Part of some big plan or something. I can't explain it for sure, but this shouldn't happen to me just no reason. This leg's got to be worth something, worth those three lives, I guess. At least that's what I tell myself. I have to...And then this little runty buck private, Higby, comes looking for me. I'm stuck in there, shooting back at those Jap zeros through what was a roof before it fell on me, and here he comes, screaming my name. The whole place is burning, and he comes looking for me. I mean, this Higby kid was five foot nothing with broken glasses, and he comes in and lifts those beams off of me like he was a bulldozer. All the time I'm yelling at him to get out of there and get his weapon, and he ignores everything I'm telling him. He just keeps saying 'I'm gonna get you outta here, Sarge.' And he does. This was a kid that I was down on every day, thinking that he doesn't really belong in this man's army. I figured he hated my guts about now. And here he is, saving my ass from total destruction in the middle of the fires of hell...It was all God's plan. You were where you were supposed to be, and I was where I was supposed to be. And I had no control over what would happen. That was the worst part."

"You're right."

Gene usually was right, at least he could always win an argument. But Teddy knew to let him win was the only way she could eventually ignore him and do what she had to do in the first place. She had a way of convincing him that everything she did was exactly what he really wanted her to do after all.

Gene slid out of bed, and hopped over to the dresser for a cigarette and lighter. "What's all this cash?"

"It's the $110 that I saved to pay for the hospital and the doctor bill. You don't know how good it makes me feel that my baby doesn't have to start its life off in a city hospital charity ward."

He removed the money from under the lighters and counted it. He trusted his math better than hers. Then he noticed her wedding and engagement rings carefully placed nearby. Not carefully enough for Gene, however. He moved them into a better line with the lighters.

"They don't fit, anymore, Gene. I'm too fat."

"No wife of mine is going in to have a baby without a ring on her finger."

"And bells on her toes? We can't afford another ring."

"We have $110!"

"That's for the baby. Put it back, Gene. Please."

Gene reluctantly put the money under the lighters and then set up each one in a perfect row on the edge of the bills, which were now face up by presidents.

"Look at me. What am I good for? I can't even buy my wife a godamn wedding ring!"

"I already have one."

"I can't work. I'll never get any kind of a decent job unless the army takes me back. We may never see this much cash money again in our entire lives."

After working her way up to a seated position, Teddy covered her belly and folded her arms. She wanted to stamp her foot on the floor, but it would take too long to build the momentum she needed to roll out of bed.

"Gene, I do not want my child born on a 60-bed city ward."

Gene never gave in to Teddy, at least not that he knew about. He was proud of his ability to make decisions, to bark orders, to make men do what they had to do. Although not a tall man, he always walked taller than he was. But with one leg, he found himself newly dependent on her, and he hated it. He backed off, and it hurt.

"Teddy, whatever you want."

She knew that this discussion should have been good for 15 minutes. He gave up too easily. He was changing and she was a part of it, for better or for worse. She pulled him back to her unborn child and held them both tightly against each other.

"You always said, Gene, that there wasn't anything you couldn't do. Well, you can't do everything for everybody. It's time that somebody did for you."

They were quiet for almost a minute. The familiar sound of multiple seagulls chasing the one with the spider crab in its beak, harassing it until it dropped its breakfast, drifted in through the open window. They had played that game of survival for untold centuries. Gene's survival game was new, and he had to learn how to play from scratch.

"If it's a boy, I'm naming him Higby."

"Higby!"

"Higby...went back in for his weapon. Never came out. Higby Eugene Logan."

"No, not Higby. I don't know any saint named Higby."

Despite what Lillian and the ring-on-a-string had predicted, she now knew she definitely wanted a girl, but started working on her own alternate name plan, just in case. At a minimum, she'd get the word order switched around on the birth certificate.

Today, she'd start including a lot more pink in her knitting.

# CHAPTER 20

# THE CHURCH

# JULY 5, 1942

The Church of St. Peter, the Fisher of Men, was small, white and pressed against the sea. It was said that a good breeze could lift an altar boy's cassock over his face if he turned his back to the open front door. It wasn't built by the Diocese of New York. There weren't enough people to warrant a church on this ass end of the borough that is in the ass end of New York. So ruled the cardinal's building committee from some basement meeting room behind St. Patrick's Cathedral, several times.

By 1934, Mrs. Irmagard Lubisch was tired of waiting. She left Yonkers every summer for the idyllic serenity of City Island, preferring the smell of the Long Island Sound to that of the Hudson River. She saw no need to re-cross the shaky bridge every week and travel as far as Gun Hill Road to fulfill her Sunday obligation.

Her husband, Otto Lubisch, was a gentleman aluminum smelter, with several works in Pennsylvania and Indiana. When the depression hit, Otto refused to surrender. He vowed to work at the smelting furnaces side by side with any other company worker who understood the low-pay cut-back measures necessary to survive those desperate times.

Irmagard Lubisch waited for her husband.

He cut wages but not jobs. His company survived. His workers survived.

Irmagard did not.

She passed away during a flu outbreak in the summer of '35 at her 100 year old captain's house without the benefit of clergy. Otto returned from Pennsylvania to bury his wife on City Island, according to her wishes, in the small church graveyard that overlooked the sea she loved. Only there was no church. And there was no graveyard. Only Irma. So Lubisch put his money and his workers to good use, transporting several here to build what New York would not.

The church was really no more than a chapel with a capability of saving less than 100 souls at a time. But it stood beside the graveyard and Irmagard. Her monument, a chiseled marble replica, faced the water. The sculptor, Jon Antonsic, working from photographs and paintings, created what he deemed his masterpiece. He became so enamored by his own work, that some say he fell in love with the woman that he had never seen. When he had completed his commission and the monument was placed by the grave, both Lubisch and Antonsic were rumored to have wept in each other's arms. And so Antonsic, as well as several of the imported church builders, remained here after his work was done.

Nowadays Lubisch made the island his home to be near his beloved wife whom he had left for the sake of his workers years before. He had few remaining pleasures in life. Smoking a good Cuban and swapping stories with Ivory were high on his list. Arguing with Antonsic, the rival suitor consumed by a woman he never knew, also took up much of his day.

Close behind that, however, was watching the Island children play ball on the sandlot that he counted as his smallest, yet most valuable of worldly possessions. No one knew he owned it. No one ever would.

This morning he performed his greatest joy, as he did every morning, rain or shine. He sat by the side of Irma's lifelike statue, reading her favorite selections from Byron, Shelly or Keats. To him, loving Irma was an act of perpetual motion.

Kim passed by Lubisch as he finished the day's reading. His grandfatherly expression invited her to sit and listen, if she so cared. She and her sandlot buddies at times had joined him and at other times escaped. Listening to those old fashioned words that nobody understood anyway reminded them of school, and school was out. Today, she had direction. She needed help, and Lubisch was not the one who could provide it. She waved and entered the simple church with its white cedar shakes, small organ and its one under-sized stained glass window featuring St. Peter with a sprawling net.

Outside, Antonsic and Bartender Johnny approached the graveyard. A U.S. flag from the Legion Hall was folded under Antonsic's arm, and they both wore military style hats. Lubisch put his on as they met. The assembled trio marched out of the cemetery on a mission of their own. Antonsic cast a last look back at Irma's statue, and Lubisch pretended not to notice.

Kim knew Father Aiello wouldn't be around. The Diocese called this unauthorized, self-built church a "mission" and he was only allowed to come to the Island two or three times a week. Today was a "p.m. day" and this was the a.m.

Since she knew she would have the chapel to herself, she had brazenly shown up in her dungarees instead of the generally accepted skirt or dress. Howie had explained that the no-pants-for-girls-in-church regulation was a small-c-church-rule, not a big-C-Catholic-law, and since she was only a part time Catholic, she felt comfortable following part of the rules part of the time. Before she crossed the threshold she pulled a handkerchief out of her pants pocket and placed it precariously on her head.

She dipped two fingers into the holy water by the door, blessed herself, genuflected on one knee and knelt in the last pew. She hoped the breeze wouldn't come up and steal her headpiece. To have her head uncovered would probably be considered a violation of big-C law and maybe a venial sin for a female. It would be better to wear her underwear on her head than go against the bare-hair regulation.

She wasn't so sure about all these rules. She had persuaded Howie to tell her as much as he knew. And since she was traveling back and forth between both her parents' and her friend's religions, a lot of it didn't make any sense. The only thing more puzzling in her day-to-day routine was the Logan household no-meat-on-Friday rule, which, if violated, could possibly send everyone at the dinner table straight to eternal hell. Her Buddhist side, however, didn't believe in eternal hell, so it probably didn't apply to her. All she knew for sure was that boys could be bare-headed and therefore this God must love them better.

She looked up at the unfinished 14 depictions of the stations of the cross. There was hardly enough room to squeeze them in, seven on each side wall. Antonsic had been slowly painting them for years. *Why is he insisting on 14? It's too many for this little chapel. Artists are crazy people.* With all the beatings, thorny crowns and nails through the body, this was not a happy place, and she was a little afraid to be here alone. She felt a sense of comfort when she concentrated on the kinder looking Mary and Joseph statues straight ahead.

"God and His saints listen to everybody," she whispered and began her prayer.

"Dear Saint Donovan, please send my mom home. She doesn't live in California. She was just takin' care of my sick grandma, and the interners caught her. Now they're holdin' her like a slave... And watch over my dad. Don't let anyone hurt him or take him away. He never hurt nobody. His name is Yoshi Nakamura, and he lives over the general store. He said he thinks you're watchin' over us. I hope he's right. Amen...Oh, I forgot the bad part. They're Japanese, Buddhist Japanese...So am I. So if you don't want to do it, I understand. And I'll try 'n' find somebody else. Amen...again."

She lit a small candle and dropped two cents through the slot in the gray metal container under the bank of a dozen other quiet candles awaiting benefactors of their own. The pennies hit with a *CLANK*. Everything seemed louder in an empty church. Finally she stepped back into the sunlight just in time to catch a glimpse of a hatless Howie passing on his bike. He was on a grocery delivery, and she was about to call out to him when she saw Vinny and Lillian heading for the beach. They carried a blanket and towels, and had a picnic basket stretched between them. Howie had already targeted them and rode within shouting distance.

"Hey! Vinn-EEE! You lookin' for your underwear?"

Kim tried to stifle her laugh and made a rapid retreat into the graveyard's safety. Lillian smiled, blushed and put her hand up to her lips, signaling Howie to quiet down. Vinny laughed a laugh that was no more than a thinly disguised sneer.

"Yeah, Howie. That...ah...That flagpole thing. Pretty funny. You got me, but you'd better sleep with one eye open, 'cause you *know* I'm gonna get you back."

Howie hadn't been sleeping well at all; so one eye closed or two eyes closed, it wouldn't make much difference.

He rounded the corner in time to see Mrs. Giardello on her front porch receiving the folded flag from Lubisch and company. A dozen neighbor women stood ready to support her should the need arise. He stopped and watched from a respectable distance as the small ceremony took on a life of its own. The flag was unfurled and draped over the porch railing. A gold star was placed in her window, and several words were said. Then Mrs. Giardello wiped away her tears and hugged each of the ex-servicemen. Neighborly cakes and cookies appeared, and the group moved inside.

Howie walked his bike until he reached the smallest bungalow on City Island, directly across from Mrs. Giardello's. Ivory stood at his door as if he were watching the activity 100 feet away, but his ears did the job that his eyes refused to undertake.

His cottage had no porch, and it had no rocker. It was a simple house for a simple man. A bedroom for him. A living room couch for his son, Corey. The walls held his old instruments: banjo, guitar, saxophone, trumpet. Drums in one corner. Several harmonicas in another. The closet boasted only black or white clothing, so everything always matched. His needs were few, yet with the possible exception of Lubisch and Pop, he had been more places and lived more life than anyone on the island. He had a depth about him, and Howie knew that this old man was his mentor for life. It was not as if he had a choice. It had just been ordained that way. They were married by their music, and a lot more.

Howie lifted two bags of groceries from his basket and headed for the doorway.

"What's going on over at Mrs. Giardello's?" he asked.

"The Legion is making her a Gold Star Mother."

"What's that?"

"Well boy, it's sort of a club, I guess."

"How come she got in?"

"She lost Danny to the war. That's a club that nobody wants to join, but you cain't say no when they comes to your door, 'cause it be too late by then. Once they gots ya, you stay got."

"I hope nobody else here joins. I feel real sorry for her."

"What a shame it is. What a shameless shame. I can remember just last year, her son and my Corey was makin' wishin' plans right here on this very step. And now one's gone glimmerin'. What a shame. Come write me a letter to Corey. He gotsta know. Thank God almighty, he's flippin' that Navy chow in San Diego, California. You remember readin' that to me a couple of letters back?"

"Yeah, sure. Gene just got home from California...San Francisco."

"Glad he's safe. I already greeted the boy. Sorrowful thing that he done lost him a flipper. You think he's gonna make it?"

Howie followed Ivory into the kitchen, and started to unpack. He handed each item to Ivory so the old man would know exactly where he had tucked it away. When he got to the can goods, Howie named each one so that Ivory could put it on the "corn shelf" or the "peas shelf" or whatever shelf was mentally designated for its new home. Ivory's system was the best way to avoid a mouthful of surprises at dinner.

"Yeah, Ivory. Of course he's gonna make it. String beans."

"Sometimes you lose more than what you can see."

"Tuna."

"Sometimes they take away part of your body, and you lose part of your soul."

"You can't lose part of your soul. Twenty Mule Team Borax."

"I been there, boy. When I was just 'bout your age, and with no pa around, neither. I lost a little bit of my soul, but some sweet folks found it and give it back to me. Who gonna give it back to *him*? Knowin' Gene, he ain't lookin' for no love nor pity. Not him. Teddy gots the baby comin'. So who be left?"

Ivory was applying pressure, and Howie didn't know if he had anything to offer.

"Me, huh?"

"Yep. You...You be his anchor. When the time come that he need you, you'll know it 'afore he does."

"Gene? He never needed anybody in his life."

"Time'll come. Gospel fact. But today, rejoice that him and my Corey and all them other Island sons still be safe. All but Danny. Amen for him. Now I'm fixin' to write that Corey-letter."

Howie procrastinated, looking for anything else to do. He picked up a few bits of debris that had fallen into the oblivion of the blind: an unused cigarette, two spoons and a guitar string. Ivory retrieved a fountain pen and some paper from a kitchen drawer, knocking a few letters out. Howie picked them up. He had read them out loud before. Most of them were from Corey, but one had a different name on it: Bill, Jr...Bad Bill's son. Ivory had been his anchor. Howie replaced the envelopes and closed the drawer.

Ivory held the writing instruments straight out, waiting for Howie to liberate them from his grasp.

There was no way to avoid this next task. The lie slowly eating away at Howie was about to be served another helping.

# CHAPTER 21
# THE TWO BEST CUSTOMERS
# JULY 5, 1942

Ivory had given Howie a lot to think about. It kicked around his brain for most of the day. He had walked the two blocks to the diamond with Ivory, even though the blind man knew every step by heart.

Howie didn't play well. He couldn't get his head in the game and found it easier to blame it on lack of concentration rather than lack of talent.

*Tomorrow I'll break out Magic Maggie,* he thought.

Ivory's words stayed with him later when he sat on the back steps and practiced his saxophone for the unknown "Sailor Fred" and all the ships at sea. The notes temporarily erased that haunting image of Nana's fall, and Bill's valiant but unsuccessful effort to save her. The closing of the screen door behind him took his mind off the recurring dream. He looked over his shoulder without interrupting his sax melody. Vinny smiled down at him, making a pointed finger gun motion and that patented lip popping sound.

Howie knew that meant, "I'm still gonna get you." He made a mental note not to go skinny-dipping at the shaky bridge until

Vinny's two-week leave to get married was over. Howie had yet to climb the bridge like his brothers had done so often. And if he gathered the nerve to try, he'd hide extra pants in the rafters, just in case his clothes ended up on the flagpole.

Howie played louder as Vinny exited the back yard and headed in the direction of the church, sending haunting notes to follow his brother, hoping they'd say, "Don't mess with me." Vinny looked preoccupied, however, and probably didn't get the message.

In a few minutes, Vinny was kneeling uncomfortably in the confessional waiting for the small wooden panel to slide right to left. It did, and Father Aiello's voice whispered its way into his ears. Vinny responded with his traditional opening.

"Bless me Father, for I have sinned. It's been four days since my last confession."

"Welcome back, Vincent."

The tone in the priest's voice said the opposite of the words that came with it. This was Vinny's third trip to confession since he'd been home. He'd been busy.

"Thank you, Father. I had six impure thoughts and two impure acts. Well, actually, it was seven impure thoughts, but one of them turned into an impure act when the fireworks went off. So does it still count as a thought, as well as an act? Or once it becomes an act, do you just get a free ride on the thought? I don't know. I get confused."

Vinny could see the shadow of Father Aiello shaking his head from side to side. He heard him exhale a sigh of exasperation.

"Maybe I should go out and start again."

He wasn't sure if Lillian's Holy-Mother-the-Church allowed that. Probably she would have known, though. She had all the rules down. She knew which ones were mortal sins and which ones where venial, and even about original sin, too. She could name the seven deadly sins faster than he could name Snow White's dwarfs. She knew about baptism by water and baptism by fire and several other baptisms that Vinny swore she made up. She knew about wearing green or brown scapulars around her soft neck, and which indulgences wiped away the most time in purgatory. She was up on patron saints and archangels, seraphim and cherubim and the seven other angelic rankings in the celestial hierarchy that Vinny couldn't even pronounce. He was glad she never wanted to be a nun. He was really glad. Any more glad and he'd have to change his impure thought count in mid-confession. And that would be a sacrilege, something else to confess. His toll was mounting when Father Aiello's voice snapped him back.

"Refresh my memory. How long before you and Lilian get married?"

"About 72 hours."

"It's a good thing this is not a holy week, or you two would be creating a traffic jam on my lines out there. As it is, you're my best customers in a slow season. I ought to appreciate the business...But I don't!"

Vinny's head shot back at the unexpected force in his confessor's voice. Where was Lillian when he needed her?

"Now Father, we're all in this together. Lilly and I are trying very hard."

"Obviously, not hard enough."

"Don't take it personal, Father. It's not your fault. You're doing a great job! Actually, we're recommending you to all our friends. Well, not the married ones, of course...That's a joke."

"Confession is not a joking matter. Now say a good Act of Contrition. And don't let me see you back here for the next three days."

"I'll try."

"Three days, Vincent!...For your penance say three Our Fathers and..."

The church looked empty as Lillian entered, a handkerchief balanced on her head. She was dressed for a religious experience, wearing small white gloves and carrying a white purse. Her bright yellow sun dress contrasted dramatically with the blue jeans that Kim had so brazenly worn earlier that day. It was too hot for a sweater, but she draped one around her shoulders anyway, trying to de-emphasize her come-hither breasts. Small drops of perspiration escaped down her neck. If they ran any lower, they'd be what Vinny called "love dew". The thought made her smile. Vinny loved "love dew". He said it tastes like pretzels.

She removed her right glove, blessed herself with holy water and flicked the excess into her face to cool off as she walked down the short aisle to the confessional. Whispers came from the other side of the heavy ruby-colored curtain and she knew that someone had beaten her to penance today. But waiting was part of the whole reflection period.

Vinny was just finishing his confession as Lillian arrived outside the booth.

"I firmly resolve with the help of thy grace to confess my sins, to do penance, and to amend my life. Amen."

"Remember, Vincent. Seventy-two hours!"

The little wooden door slid closed with a final, forceful *CLICK*.

Vinny turned, poked through the curtain and exited all in one athletic move, nose bumping right into the center of Lillian's chest with a surprised, "Lilly!" Her poorly camouflaged breasts were exactly at eye level, and he stared transfixed like a salivating cat waiting for two goldfish to jump out of their bowls.

*I'm trying, father. I'm trying,* he thought. But the words that spilled out were "Aren't those hot?...Ah...*you* hot?" His instant correction came too late.

Lillian laughed and answered affirmatively, "Ah-huh."

He wanted to press his lips to hers, but instead simply lifted the back of his hand to that area just below her neck, and wiped away the moisture. She took his hand before it could be lowered, and kissed it softly. He smiled a self-conscious smile, then fumbled for the right words.

"I'm...ah...I'm going back in there, now. Will you be here when I get out?"

It sounded like he was going away for a stretch in the big house. She nodded, then added, "I won't stand so close next time."

He bravely pulled back the curtain without taking his eyes away from hers until the last moment. She threw an almost overlooked whisper after him as he disappeared.

"Vinny, will you be long?"

Vinny knelt and squeezed his thighs together. *I already am.*

# CHAPTER 22

# THE BANANAS

# JULY 6, 1942

*When I dreams, I dreams in sight and pictures most likely 'cause I was a seein' boy when I was bore'd. But somethin' like a automobile or a aeroplane, I done never seed. And although I can imagine what they do look like, such things never dream themselves into my dreams. I guess they be only in my day brain, not my nighttime sleepin' mind.*

*Now Howie, he seed it all, and he dreamed it all. And them Nana pictures just wouldn't leave that poor boy alone, but kept comin' back and comin' back, fixin' to torture him no end, night after night. He figure he be the only-est one who got the sleepin' miseries. He figure wrong.*

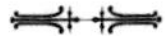

Howie strained to see the water as a green-gray, on-shore mist flooded toward him. His visibility from the back steps went from endless to zero in a few seconds. The fog grabbed at his ankles. He pulled his legs in tight against his chest, but never missed a note on his saxophone. He could see that the cloud cover was only ten or fifteen feet off the ground, and the sun was still smiling above the western horizon.

A noise, a dull, unrecognizable noise, sifted through the mist and slowly built into a relentless, low scream, reaching its crescendo as it swelled over the sax music and blotted out every other natural or man-made sound for miles around. His ears knew that sounds carom and echo off fog banks in the most outrageous combinations. But his eyes followed the direction of the noise upward as if guided by some unseen hand. The scream was Nana's, and he could see her lose her balance in the window above him. A foreboding urgency made his fingers play faster than the notes allowed.

Suddenly, she flew out of the window and disappeared into the green fog beside him, but the screaming never stopped. Bad Bill appeared in the window and stared down at Howie as his fingers froze around the sax, and the music died. But the scream didn't.

Terrified, Howie sat up straight, finding himself in his own bed, the victim of that terror-filled, persistent nightmare. But this time it was different. He could still hear the scream. He was sure he was awake, but he could still hear the scream.

And then it stopped.

And then he breathed again.

Howie got out of bed and unearthed his dungarees from a pile of clothes on the corner chair, then headed downstairs to suck in the fresh, healing air of an approaching dawn.

In Teddy's bedroom, she wiped the sweat off her husband's brow as Gene stopped screaming. He was not yet fully awake, and she held him until he realized where he was. As he quieted down, his chest stopped heaving, and he felt the overriding need to splash cold water in his face. Gene swung his body over the edge of the bed and stood up, but just as quickly crashed to the floor. He looked at his missing leg.

"Damn! I gotta get use to this."

Gene hopped back along the bed, reaching the crutches that leaned against the headboard. He was getting good at hopping.

Howie had been parked on the fogless back steps for fifteen minutes before Gene arrived. It was still dark, but the stars in the east were fading under the sun's constant onslaught as dawn pushed its power earthward. He could see the masts at the old yacht club by the water's edge. There had been talk of using it as a submarine chase station, but it fell by the wayside as Lubisch and his cronies formulated plans to revive boat building in the idling yards. Lubisch's connections and his love of America in war and peace, but especially war, were slowly eating away at Washington's bureaucracy. Late one night, as the old men sat around the bar at the Legion, Howie had heard him predict that PT boats would be rolling off the iron rails, splashing into the Sound within months.

If the boat builders came back home, City Island would again become the bustling, self-propelled, happy place that it had been before everything started changing. Quietly, anonymously, Lubisch would make it happen.

The beams of Execution Light to the northeast and Stepping Stones Lighthouse to the south slowly rotated, each flashing at its unique signature speed. Some suggested that they be closed down because they were offering submarines an open door to New York City. But in truth, the subs didn't need them. They had enough equipment to find their own way into the harbor if they really wanted to visit. For now, the lights persisted.

A third light flashed. It was Gene lighting his cigarette. He had chosen a silver lighter with an army emblem as this morning's selection. The screen door clanged shut behind him.

"Did I wake you up, Howie?"

"No."

"Then you're the only asshole on this island who doesn't know I got the screamin' sweats. You want a smoke?"

"I'm only twelve years old."

"Yeah. I guess you're old enough to buy your own."

Howie remembered why he had missed Gene so much. While Vinny teased and antagonized, Gene kidded and amused. Howie sensed that Gene, who hadn't gone to college, must be the more intelligent of the two. Leg or no leg, he was glad the rest of Gene was home.

"Does it hurt?"

"The sweats?"

"No. The leg."

Gene hit his good leg, then feigned panic.

"My leg? My God! What's wrong with my leg?"

Howie laughed at Gene's antics. "You know, your other leg."

"I was wondering how long it would take you to notice." He got confidential. "You think Teddy noticed?"

"Yeah. I think she did."

"Well, hell! There goes the surprise!"

Gene gave Howie a chance to stop laughing, then answered seriously.

"No. It doesn't hurt. But every once in a while I get a muscle cramp in my calf, and I go to rub it, and there's no calf there. But the cramp is real. It's weird."

"I was afraid to look at it. I was afraid to look at *you.* I knew that you were hurt pretty bad. Everybody did. But it's funny. Nobody knew what was wrong and nobody asked. We'd look at each other like we knew. But we didn't. We were all scared of the answer... Maybe we didn't wanna know."

"Well get used to it, kiddo. It ain't like baby teeth. They don't grow back. You ready for a real look?"

Howie didn't want to see anymore, but this was his brother. He was going to have to make the inspection sooner or later.

"Yeah. Do it."

Gene rolled up his khaki pants leg exposing his reddened stump. It was all healed over and Howie exhaled a safety breath.

"Don't up-chuck, kid. I like sitting here."

"Okay, Gene. Guess it's not *that* ugly, once you see it."

"What'd you expect? A bone stickin' out? I *was* gonna save it and stick it through my nose, but I figured that might really scare you. Hell, that would scare me. You're gonna see a lot more of it, 'cause I intend to be 'round here for a while."

"Yeah, maybe we can play ball."

"It's just a good thing that it was my left leg, 'cause I happen to be right footed. Yeah. Really. I am one lucky sonofabitch."

There was a pause that grew longer than it should have. Howie wanted to speak but he wasn't sure how to say it. Finally he blurted out the words a little too quickly.

"I had to deliver a telegram to Mrs. Giardello. Danny died. For a minute there, I thought I killed her with the news."

"Shit. Danny was a good boy."

"Yeah. It was hard to give her the telegram, but I did it. Before that the hardest thing about the war was Mayor La Guardia cancelin' the night games at Yankee Stadium. Too much light, he said. That and no butter."

"He's probably right. Night bombing, you know. Hey, it's *the* Yankee Stadium."

"I didn't know if I could ever deliver another telegram like that again. But I think I have to try, 'cause that's the only way I got of fightin' this war."

"You don't have to fight the war. Leave that to me and Vinny."

"When Uncle Sam says 'I want you', he's talkin' to me."

"You're a brave kid, Howie. I never had a chance to be brave like that."

"I'm just glad you're home. You *gotta* play ball with us, today."

"My ballgame days are over. Besides I'm too old for your game."

"Nobody would dare say nothin'. Not about you. You went to war, and you came back a hero. Maybe you could help me with my swing."

"I never went to war. War came to me...with a vengeance."

"But you saved guys' lives."

"Everybody was saving lives. If you weren't saving lives, you were either shootin' or dead. What I did, happened a thousand times that day. I was lucky I even got any shots off. I was too busy trying to survive. I'm no godamn hero, and don't you go tellin' people that I am."

"You are a hero. Teddy showed us the commendation letter from the War Department. You got that purple heart medal and the other one, the silver star."

"Yeah, 48 other GIs got the silver star that day, but they probably deserved it. I didn't do nothin' special, and I still got no clue why they picked me anyway. That and a nickel will get me all the way to Times Square. So forget about that hero shit. The war I seen isn't about heroes. It's about puking and dying and pissing in your pants."

This wasn't the same Gene that had left City Island with his bride a year ago for the beautiful Hawaiian Island of Oahu.

Howie had to change the subject, to get Gene's mind off his role, or lack of it, in "the war that came to him". It had changed him like it was changing everything else, and Howie couldn't stop it. He remembered Ivory's words about Gene losing part of his soul and needing Howie to be there for him. Maybe this had been the start.

"Tell me about the bananas."

"The bananas?" Gene laughed.

"Yeah, what about the bananas?"

"Whew, that goes back a long time. Let's see...Yeah. You were about two years old. Your hair fell out, and you almost went blind. They figured out you had a potassium deficiency, at least that's what the doctor thought. I said it was from jerkin' off."

"No. Come on."

"Yeah. You were pretty sick, but the few chemicals they could get, you just threw up. So you were as good as dead."

"Gene, be serious."

"I am."

"Really?"

Gene's tone got a little more somber. "Yeah. God's honest truth. We all thought you were going to die, and the doctors couldn't help. Nobody could. Well, nobody but Mr. Nakamura. He said, 'Feed him bananas. Lots of bananas.' The few you ate, you kept down. So they gave you more. But the Depression was on, and bananas were almost impossible to come by."

"How come I didn't die?"

"We couldn't afford the funeral."

"You're an idiot."

"For a year Pop and Mr. Nakamura combed the waterfront in his boat, bringing home every single banana they could get. Right off the ships. Pop used to work on the docks when he was startin' out and must have had some connections there. Sometimes they'd get two bananas, sometimes they'd come home with a hundred. When Pop went to Tokyo, Nakamura did it for another year on his own, every day. And then you got better."

"So that's why Pop treats Mr. Nakamura like a brother."

"Yeah. That and somethin' about how they met in Yokohama. Pop pays his debts."

Howie let this revelation sink in for several moments before turning to Gene for one last question.

"Who'd want to bomb Yankee Stadium, anyway?"

"Who else? The Brooklyn Bums! Yeah, I mean it. You know those guys they got hanging in big baskets with machine guns under the Brooklyn Bridge? They're not looking for East River submarines. They're really Dodger fans waiting for the Yankees to attack Ebbets Field. You know, I think I could do that job. I got 'squatting' down. Maybe I should be a professional squatter."

"Or a one legged baseball catcher! Hey, we already got a blind ump."

By now, they were both laughing. Maybe fate had put them here, at this time and place, solely for each other's support like Ivory had foretold. Or maybe it was just a few bad dreams.

Morning finally shed nighttime's cloak and spread triumphant across the eastern sky.

Ivory stood alone upon the small beach, waiting for the heat of the new-born sun to bathe his aged face and nourish the child that lived within the man. His stance was wide as he raised his hands above his head. Slowly, he spread his arms to embrace the warmth, and felt the glow energize his body for another day. Cries of laughing gulls merged with distant buoy bells. Nearby rhythmic wave breaks caressed his ears. The smell of salt air smothered his lungs and brought a smile to his lips. His body swayed. His spirit danced, choreographed to the unheard music of yet another miraculous dawn.

"Good mornin', Mr. Sun!"

Today would be a good City Island day.

# CHAPTER 23

# THE ANGEL OF DEATH

# JULY 6, 1942

Lubisch dropped a tin of tobacco and some rolling papers on the general store's counter. He resided alone and his needs were few. He had no children from his marriage to Irma but had silently adopted the children of the Island as his own. His door was always open, and someone from his household staff would dispense temporary supplies to any family that found itself in need. The residents were too proud to go outside of their own borders to admit that they needed help in financial or family matters, but they were not above looking to each other.

Nakamura swatted at a passing fly and missed, then started to wait on Lubisch as Kim finished with another customer. Kim casually leaned a little closer in her father's direction.

"I prayed at the chapel yesterday. I asked Saint Donovan to send mom home."

"Next time ask for flypaper."

The remark brought a smile to Lubisch's wrinkled face, but it was wiped away by the ringing of the small bell. Howie was stocking shelves, stamping blue ink prices on the tops of the new canned goods. He closed his eyes as he heard the unforgiving bell ring again.

Excusing himself, Nakamura moved to the telegraph desk. Lubisch knew the significance of the sound, as did every Islander, native born or imported. Kim stepped in to calculate his payment. Lubisch merely nodded at her tally, and she added it to his bill in the old gray ledger. He handed her a paper with his housekeeper's grocery order for the next several days. But he knew that the telegram would take precedence over everything else.

"Fill this when you have time. There's no rush. You can deliver it later, Howie, after you take care of..."

He motioned toward the telegram that Nakamura was printing out. The transcriber clicked away, and Nakamura started to give the slightest of negative side-to-side head shakes as he read. His usually stoic veneer wore thin.

A nod from Howie acknowledged Lubisch's instructions, and the old man backed away from the counter. Big Stevie's wood that temporarily covered the absent windows in the front door cast a dark pale across the store. Lubisch had to shade his eyes as he exited into the sunlight of a beautiful summer day.

Howie moved next to Kim, watching Lubisch walk past the flagpole, and whispered, "Wish I could just walk away like that."

In a few minutes, he was on his bike wearing the Western Union cap, turned straight to the front. With a pounding heart, he carried out the mission that he had trained for, yet dreaded to be part of. Fearing that this time he may not have enough physical energy to complete his task, he held onto the rear of the running-on-fumes-and-a-prayer bus as it pulled him northward on City Island Avenue.

Joe the Bus Driver knew when an island son was attached, and he knew when he wasn't. He made sure not to make any sudden slow downs, priding himself on his spotless thirty-year-plus record. Joe wasn't prompt. Joe wasn't efficient. But he had never hit anything nor anyone. He knew his people and his neighborhoods. He knew what to anticipate. Retirement with his perfect record intact was his obtainable goal, and he made sure that Howie would not be an uneraseable blemish on his life's work. As he reached Marine Street, Howie's hand slipped away, and Columbia coasted to the right. Joe checked his mirror and saw Howie's reflection disengage. Satisfaction crossed Joe's face as he mentally marked off another accident-free day.

Several of the women congregating around their porch rockers noticed Howie with his cap and no groceries, and they whispered as he peddled down their block. Another, who was about to come out her front door, quickly changed her mind and watched Howie through a slit in her white curtains as he rode by. She breathed a small sigh of relief when he passed her house like an angel at Passover, allowing her first-born son to continue to exist, unmolested.

Finally, he stopped in front of a cedar shake bungalow. It faced south like half the other Island houses, and the wind and sun had taken their tolls on the shingles that met them broadside. They had to be replaced every twenty years, and this cottage was overdue. In that aspect it was similar to every other house on the island. The woman who lived here, however, had no son to help reshingle. The woman who lived here had no son at all and didn't know it. Howie did.

The woman who lived here was the stoic, palsied Mable Trent.

She came to the screen door as she heard Pete the Dog bark in response to Howie's footsteps on the porch. The dog jumped up and licked Howie but could not get his usual convivial response. It didn't stop him and he jumped even higher.

"Howie! Another birthday telegram. Now who could this be from? Sit, Pete the Dog."

Pete responded, waiting for a second chance.

"No ma'am. It's not for your birthday." His look was solemn. His voice bordered on a quiver.

She took the envelope from his hand.

"It must be. I mean, why else would anybody want to send me a..."

She hesitated long enough to look away and let her teeth grab hold of her lower lip for strength and reassurance.

"I can open it for you."

After a long, courage building pause, "No".

Her hands shook more than usual, but she tried to rip the envelope herself. She pulled and slipped and shook. Howie started to take it away from her, but she held it back.

"It has my name on it. I'll open it."

Try as she might, her fingers were useless. Slowly she gave up, and just as slowly, Howie removed the letter from her hands. He effortlessly opened the envelope and handed it back to her.

"It's from the War Department. It says my Eddy was killed. This must be a mistake. It *is* a mistake. Isn't it, Howie?"

He couldn't answer. She reviewed her name at the top, but it hadn't changed.

"Yes, it says Mabel Trent. All right, then. No, I guess the War Department doesn't make mistakes. Does it?...I have a lot of arrangements to make, but, for the life of me, I don't know what they are. Thank you, Howie. Oh, here."

She reached behind the door and found her old black purse. Her shaking hand fumbled through it, until it fell to the porch floor spilling its contents across the gray wood. Howie started to retrieve the items but she shooed him away, then found a nickel and held it up.

"That's okay, Mrs. Trent."

"Here. You take this."

Her outstretched hand shook in his direction, and he could only look away. He had to say something, but didn't know what. Summoning up all his courage, he let his words slowly come out.

"Mrs. Trent...Eddy is dead."

And she summoned up her own.

"Yes, I know."

She forced the tip into his hand, and he started down the steps, emotionally spent. The woman's voice stopped him, and he slowly turned, stoop-shouldered like he was carrying a rapidly increasing weight. He thought this might be the huge emotional outpouring that he had expected. He thought wrong.

"What about Charlie O'Reilly? They were serving together, you know."

He took a breath to compose himself and then slid a second telegram out from under his cap.

"Yes, ma'am. I know."

Pete the Dog trotted along side the bike, continually looking up at the rider, anticipating the usual playful neck rubbing he had come to expect. Howie's thoughts were fighting in a different arena and he ignored Pete's small plaintive woofs.

"Go home, Pete."

In less than a minute, Howie would arrive in front of the O'Reilly house. The last time he had delivered groceries here, he rode away with Charlie's sacred baseball mitt. That was a good day, until he ended up sprawled at Bad Bill's feet. This time he would leave with no more than an empty space in his heart. He was still reeling from the brave mask that Mrs. Trent had chosen to wear and knew that this visit would be different.

Several mothers whisked children into their arms as he rode the one block between houses. Another simply covered her child's eyes. He had become the Angel of Death, and the Island's young had to be protected from him. It made no sense, yet to them it made all the sense in the world.

Howie leaned his bike against The Big Tree, the same tree that Stevie had once hidden behind with a baseball bat. He couldn't see Stevie doing that now. It was missing a chunk of bark where Bad Bill had smashed the bat only a few days before, days whose overwhelming problems seemed so minuscule now. If he ever got time, he would check the status of Stevie's name on the sole of his shoe. Hopefully, it would be gone. But somehow a name that had been so important four days ago was so unimportant today.

Pete the Dog bounced high again as Howie left the bike behind, and again he was ignored. Finally, Howie exploded.

"Go home!!!"

Pete jumped back at the volume of Howie's voice. It was a new sound to him, and he didn't fully comprehend the rejection.

Howie started for the first porch step, but once his foot touched that weathered piece of wood, there could be no turning back. Everything would be final. The steps looked so high, and he felt so small. He stood before them, unable to make the climb. Instead, his feet paced across the sandy lawn, crushing the sporadic grass. He grew unduly hot and took his cap off, holding the telegram away from the dog, securely against his body.

*A speedy delivery. A speedy delivery...Get back on that bike and ride away.*

That was something he could not bring himself to do. Yet he couldn't face those two porch steps either. He had nowhere else to go but follow his aimless feet on their aimless path for as long as he could make this moment last.

Pete tugged at Howie's clothing in a vain effort to find the boy he knew was inside them. But Howie yelled even louder, chasing Pete several feet away.

"Get away from me, Pete! Go home!"

Pete the Dog stopped at the end of the grass and barked. Howie dug a stone out of the soil, threw it at Pete, and the rock found its mark, hitting him in the flanks. Pete whimpered, but refused to leave and sat down instead.

Howie was on the verge of tears as he started to pick up another rock, but his movements were cut short by Mrs. O'Reilly's voice.

"Howie?"

A sheepish reply was the best he could muster. "Yes, Mrs. O'Reilly?"

As he answered, he popped his cap back on and the telegram loomed like a flag in his hand. The tone of his voice betrayed his apology for what he was about to do. She steadied herself at the top of the stairs, a deep breath chasing after several shallow ones.

"Are you looking for me?"

Tears welled up in her eyes as Howie moved toward the porch. Still standing on the ground, he handed her the telegram, and reciprocal tears began to inch down Howie's cheeks, as well. She ran her finger around the perimeter of the envelope, never looking directly at it. Howie couldn't bear to face her and dropped his focus to the wooden cross swinging helplessly on the end of the rosary beads suspended from her neck.

"Now, I…I don't even have to open it. Do I?"

"No. You don't."

It was all he could do to choke the words out. Her sobs exploded, and she opened her arms to hug him. They met halfway up the dreaded steps, sat and held onto each other's heaving bodies. Slowly neighbors emerged from their homes as if air raid, all-clear sirens had sounded.

Howie wished this could have been another day, any other day but this one. This particular day had become the worst in his long and knowledgeable life. He would have easily settled for Big Stevie and his baseball bat all over again. For today he rode with death. He had brought it with him. He was The Death Bringer, and that memory of those faces would never leave.

## CHAPTER 24

# THE HIDEOUT

## JULY 6, 1942

An hour later, Kim wandered down the street. Howie was overdue back at the store, and she was worried. She knew that the burden of his office was getting heavier every day, and this was too long for her to sit idly by while he faced that task alone.

The red bike stuck out like a beacon, and when she saw it still propped against The Big Tree, she ran the last half block. Consoling neighbors were visible milling around inside the O'Reilly house, but she was afraid to enter. A Japanese face might not be welcomed right now. She edged up to the porch and looked through the window, but could find no hint of Howie anywhere.

As she headed for the bike, she saw Pete the Dog resting at the base of The Big Tree. She sat down next to him on the spotty grass and rubbed his neck. Everyone on the island recognized that messenger bike by sight, and even though bike theft on City Island was non-existent, she knew Howie would never leave faithful Columbia alone for long.

"Where's Howie, Pete the Dog? Where is he, boy?"

Pete the Dog lifted his head and looked straight up. Kim looked up, too. Directly overhead, Howie sat precariously perched on a long limb. His eyes were red, and he sniffed his nose dry. Kim stood up and leaned against the tree.

"What'cha doin'?"

"Hidin'."

"From what?"

"Just hidin'. Okay?"

"Okay...Can I hide with you?"

Howie didn't answer immediately. But when he did, it reluctantly betrayed his need for her company.

"Yeah. I guess."

Kim put a foot on the bike seat, pushed her body against the trunk, and climbed into the tree. She slid next to Howie. His Western Union cap hung off the tip of his right shoe, swinging slowly in mid-air.

"When you hide, you gotta hide from somethin'. Or else people'll think you're crazy. Are you goin' crazy, Howie?"

"I don't care what people think."

"Just like 'Big Stevie' and 'Pete the Dog' and 'Bad Bill', they're gonna start callin' you 'Crazy Howie' or 'Hidin' Howie' or maybe 'Big Tree Howie' or..."

"I don't care. I'm never comin' down."

"Then neither am I."

They sat for a long minute, watching his right foot swing back and forth, waiting for the cap to fall off. It didn't. Finally, he broke the silence.

"You think people are right footed, like they're right handed?"

"Sure. Everybody who ever played hop-scotch knows that. But what nobody knows is that if you're right handed, does that mean you can't be left footed?...Ears. Yeah. That's a whole 'nother story. I bet people are right eared or left eared. Even though I throw righty, I think maybe I'm left eared. Is that weird?...I think I like

'Big Tree Howie' the best...Do you ever wonder how old this tree is? I do. I bet we could jump from here and not even get hurt... Gravity. I love gravity. Gravity's the best thing they ever invented. It's always there when you need it."

Kim spit on the ground, making sure to avoid Pete the Dog.

"See that? That's what I love about gravity. If we didn't have gravity, that would'a bounced right back and hit me in the puss. Kaploosh. Try it. You can always depend on gravity, and it won't ever leave you, either...So I forget. Why are we never comin' down from here?"

"It's this hat."

"Oh, yeah. The hat...What about the hat?"

"It's a death hat. Every time I put that hat on, somebody dies. I hate that hat."

"Too bad. I thought you looked kinda good in it."

"I'm killin' people, Kim. This time I got Eddy and Charlie. Who's gonna be next? It ain't never gonna stop. As soon as I go down there, it's gonna start all over again."

"Then don't go down. We'll stay up here forever. We'll eat leaves and laugh at people when they walk by. We'll be like Tarzan and Jane. Maybe get us a monkey. Or maybe just make monkey noises, so we don't have to put up with all that monkey you-know-what. 'Cause it stinks! Remember the zoo?"

"We can't make monkey noises, Kim."

"Why not?"

"People'll hear us and know we're up here."

"And like with that red bike of yours sittin' down there, they ain't gonna know already?"

"Well, yeah. I guess they will."

Again, they sat silently, watching the movements of that swinging hat. It edged closer to the tip of his foot.

"But I gotta do somethin' to finish this," said Howie. "Maybe you were thinkin' right. Maybe if I wasn't around no more. If I ended it all, then it would stop. Maybe..."

Kim cut Howie off before the "suicide" word snaked from his lips. He had wiped it from her vocabulary list, and now she scrambled to do the same for him.

"Or *maybe*, Howie, *maybe* it's not you. Maybe it's the hat. If you get rid of the hat, maybe that'll be the end of the telegrams. No hat, no messages. No messages, nobody's dead. What d'ya think?

"I don't know."

She looked at Howie, smiled devilishly and kicked the hat off his foot. Pete the Dog wandered over and sniffed it.

"There. It's gone."

But Howie wasn't satisfied.

"That ain't 'gone'...and I think it's starin' back at me."

"It ain't movin'. I don't think it's alive. You know, I don't think it *can* stare back."

"But it sure looks like it."

"Well then, you can't leave it there, lookin' up at you for the rest of your life, Howie. You gotta do somethin'."

"I know."

"So are we gettin' down, or what?"

"Yeah. We're gettin' down. This ain't a good hideout anyway. You can't see the clouds from here."

"It's a big tree, Howie."

They hung on the branch, then dropped to the ground. Howie put the hat on. Kim followed him and Columbia down the block, finally stopping at the water's edge.

The innocent beauty of a City Island summer was all around them. Gulls floated effortlessly, riding the soft onshore breeze. A monarch butterfly drifted inches over the hat, fluttered as if it were about to perch, then followed its timeless multi-generational summer migration route back south to Mexico.

But Howie was too single minded to notice any of it. He put down Columbia, walked into the water and didn't stop until he was up to his waist. Memories of Kim, floating face down, ran through his mind. But instead of imitating her, he stood still and removed his hat.

Kim hesitated at the water line, but the shifting tide sent periodic ripples up to her feet. With a why-not exhale, she took a deep breath and followed her best friend in, shoes and all. She stood by his side, waiting for some motion on his part. Finally, Howie rubbed his hand around the interior of the hat band as if removing some non-existent sweat, then put the hat back on his head and stared blankly at the horizon.

"Well, what are you gonna do, Howie?"

"I'm gonna throw it in."

"When?"

"I am. I gonna throw it."

"Yeah. When?"

"Now. Right now."

But he couldn't bring his hand up to retrieve his badge of office. He looked over at Kim, and she saw the hesitation in his eyes.

"I *am* gonna do it. Watch."

Kim watched, but still no movement. She watched, and she waited. And she watched some more. But watching wasn't good enough.

"Give me that!"

She ripped the hat off his head.

Kim wound up and threw it out into the Sound, but the hat didn't sail through the breeze as far as the strength of the throw had led her to expect. They both watched as the soft wave action brought the hat drifting back in their direction.

Slowly, a satisfied grin etched itself across Kim's face. She looked over at Howie.

"Are you peein'?"

"Yeah."

"Me, too."

In a flash, Pete the Dog shot by them, bounding into the water. He swam out to the hat, rescued it in his teeth and headed back toward dry land.

Kim took Howie's hand and they stepped back to the sand. But by the time they turned around, the hat had completed its dog-borne return trip to the shore.

Pete the Dog dropped it at their feet and sat hoping for a second throw. The hat circled aimlessly in a newly-formed tidal pool. Howie's wet shoe nudged it, and it answered with a bobbing nod. He scooped up the hat, poured its water in a splash across his face, then spoke directly to it.

"You're never gonna go away. Are you?"

"Then leave it. You and me, Howie. We could run away from this place. Or ride away on Columbia. Or even take my father's boat. We could leave it all behind. Maybe go west to California. Get to that internment camp in Owens Valley where they got my mom. It's called Manzanar. I have the address on an envelope. We could do it, you and me. She'd take us in. Maybe they take dogs, too. "

"We ain't goin' nowhere."

"Come on, Howie. We could do it."

"No. This hat'd just follow us, or go on somebody else's head, or somethin'...It's a bad hat, Kim. It's a death hat, and it ain't goin' away. So I gotta fix it."

"What if it don't wanna get 'fixed'?"

"Then I gotta kill it."

Howie slapped the hat against his leg, chasing the last of the water out, then placed the cap on his head, but he still felt drips edging around his ears. He hopped on his bike and motioned for Kim to climb onto the crossbar. Pete the Dog gave them a quick shower with his rippling full body shake. They snapped their contorted faces in the opposite direction in a vain effort to keep dry.

"You think that dog just shook our pee back on us, Howie?"

"Nah. Pee's warmer than that."

Pete fell in beside them. A few minutes of pushing pedals and they reached the sandlot, finding the second game of the day already into the seventh inning.

Kim's mouth dropped open as she realized Howie had no intention of slowing down. Columbia bounded through right field distracting the batter, allowing the pitcher to send a strike across the plate. Surely that mysterious, age-old, vile and hideous punishment was about to befall the two of them. She closed her eyes and held on.

Ivory's voice boomed, "Strike one".

The batter stepped out of the box and pointed his Louisville wood in their direction. Cries and threats from 30 teenage mouths filled their ears. Howie kept churning the pedals, finally skidding to a halt that made the pitcher jump off his imaginary mound. They dismounted. Kim held the bike while Howie walked halfway to home plate. Pete the Dog put his nose to the ground, following some unseen but more interesting trail off the field and into the higher grass.

Sneers and jeers turned to curses until Ivory emerged with his hands outstretched.

"Time! Quiet down! What is it, boy?"

Howie took his hat off, and the crowd noises dissipated in apparent anticipation of some sort of inadequate apology that it could immediately reject and get on with the mandatory stoning.

Kim was afraid to glance around for fear of finding handfuls of rocks looking hungrily back at her. Suddenly, the pitcher reclaimed his turf and kicked the bike out of her hands.

"Get your yellow ass off my mound, cracker-jap."

Columbia tumbled into the grass with one wheel still rotating, and Kim quickly moved behind it, safely out of the pitcher's reach. Her fists clenched, ready for whatever came her way.

Howie summoned up what was left of his lung power. He started to speak, and a few unruly voices shouted him down, trying to chase him off the infield. But Ivory refused to tolerate it.

"Listen up or leave! The boy's got somethin' to say."

That immediately dropped the noise level down.

"I know I'm a first-game player, and I ain't allowed on the field, but you all know that I'm the messenger. So I'm here whether you like it or not. Charlie O'Reilly is dead. He was the best ball player that ever come outta this sandlot. Could play most any position. You all seen him when you was in the morning game, and he was in the afternoon. I heard once he hit a ball all the way into the Sound, and it just kept on sailin'. Gone for good. He was on a hittin' streak in the minors when the war broke out, and he was a few days away from goin' to the 'bigs' for sure. We all knew it. But now he's dead. He ain't never goin' to 'the show'. And he ain't never comin' home. I just told his mom, and I thought it was my job to tell you, too. Maybe I'm breakin' the Western Union messenger code, or maybe not. If I am, I'll get fired. And if I do, then I do. And that's that."

His words drove a sledge hammer of silence through the crowd of teenagers, mowing them down to a man. Some sat. Some shuffled. Some just walked away.

Howie marched the remaining 30 feet to home plate and dropped his hat on the cardboard. He took the slugger from the batter's hands, raised it over his head and slammed it down into the symbol of all the death that had been brought to the island. He hit it again, and again, grunting with every swing, but the cloth hat merely rebounded upward, challenging him for more, silently screaming, "Is that the best you got?"

Dust rose and mixed with the hat's watery surface, turning the cap a muddy brown. Finally, with his most powerful smash, he cracked the visor, but still it held together. Oblivious to the noise around him and all-consumed by his invincible target, he readied one more burst of strength that might end it all.

A pair of arms rushed from the sidelines, wrapped around Howie's chest and locked his elbows in place. They picked him up and walked him off the field, the bat dropping from his hand. Exhausted, Howie yielded to their size. They deposited him in the grass, and he landed on his butt. He looked up to see Big Stevie shaking his head.

"What are you doin', Howie? You gone nuts?"

"But it's Charlie, Stevie. It's Charlie."

Howie stretched out on his back looking up at the clouds. He fought off a last sniffle and spread his arms wide to the sides. Stevie leaned down, speaking softly.

"You ain't gonna bring him back."

"I know."

Kim wheeled up the rescued Columbia, the wet and wounded hat resting in the bike's rear basket.

"Remember when we used to look at clouds, Kim? We don't look at clouds no more."

She put Columbia down for a well-earned rest, then spread out in the grass.

"Yeah, Howie, I remember."

"If we don't start lookin' at the clouds again, pretty soon we're gonna forget how."

Stevie's eyes self-consciously searched the ball field to see if they were being watched. But the teenage boys and girls had gathered in small groups, digesting the unwanted news. Apprehensive, he stretched out on the other side of Kim, reluctantly completing the trio. He lay on his back in imitation, feet together and arms spread wide.

But after a moment of inactivity, Stevie popped up and took one last look around. Finally satisfied that no one was observing them, he dropped his head back down.

"Is this dumb? It feels dumb. I'm doin' it, but it feels dumb. We look like three Christians gettin' nailed to a cross, or somethin'... What are we lookin' for, Howie?"

"Nothin', Stevie. We're not lookin' for nothin'. We're just watchin' the clouds. A cloud gets wasted if nobody looks at it. One minute it's here, and then all of a sudden it's gone, forever...like Charlie. After a little while you can't even remember what it looked like."

Kim, in the middle, let her hands find Howie's and Stevie's. She held tight and whispered.

"Don't worry, Howie. We'll remember."

Pete the Dog ambled in between Stevie and Kim. He made a quick circle, laid down and dropped his head onto Stevie's stomach. Stevie pulled his hand away from Kim's and gently petted Pete's head.

"You stink, Pete," said Kim.

"Just smells like a wet dog," answered Stevie.

Pete closed his eyes.

Half an hour later Columbia was leaning against the general store porch. Inside, Kim watched Howie hold out the damaged and discolored Western Union hat to Nakamura, whose eyes were even wider than when Howie had destroyed his last precious flypaper. He received the hat as if it were more than a co-worker returning from assignment. It was an injured friend coming home from war.

He needed an explanation.

"Fighting?"

And Howie supplied it.

"Baseball."

# CHAPTER 25
# THE RABBIT'S FOOT
# JULY 6, 1942

*Howie's heart stones was growin' too fast for his body to carry. He unleashed the weight on me, and I come back at him sharin' my own burden. Now maybe unloadin' on the boy wasn't the best of choices I coulda made. But some people tend to think a dead-eyed blind man might just be wiser than he look, 'specially if he listen more and talk less than the average sighted specimen of God's little joke on this universe. 'Tain't necessarily true, and that day I spoke more than I ought.*

Pete the Dog trotted into the Legion, barked and received the mandatory "Pete the Dog!" acknowledgement from Bartender Johnny. He poured the canine's daily saucer of beer and placed it on the floor. Pete laid down beside it, crossed his paws and yawned.

Within an hour Vinny's bachelor party would be in full swing, but for now Howie's sax struggled to keep up with Ivory, whose fingers roamed over the keys, freeing the blue melodies held captive in that worn out, bar-beaten piano. Finally, Ivory stopped.

"You are one spit-sour player tonight, boy. What are them Island sons up above gonna think when they hear your sickly gruntin' on that seasoned piece of work in your hands, pukin' up them raggedy-ass notes? Now play the blues like I learned ya!"

"I don't feel too much like playing anything tonight."

"Don't *feel* like it?! Did I hear you say you don't *feel* like it?! There be three boys waitin' on us. I'm sure there be better things to do in heaven than sit on one's ass waitin' for those of us left on God's green earth to feel like playin'."

"Yeah, I know, but you had to be there today, Ivory. Deliverin' those telegrams was the toughest thing I ever did. I cried at Charlie's house, but I don't think nobody saw me. I hid in The Big Tree...I wish Pop was here."

"It ain't the outside cryin' what matters. It's the inside tears that'll drown ya."

Ivory let his hand run across the stubble of gray growth on his chin. Behind his dark glasses he wore the expression of intelligence like a naked thinking statue that Howie had once seen in a book about art or Greece or Rome or someplace important. The boy knew he had come to the right man. Ivory pushed back from the piano, removed his glasses and rubbed a long rub into his empty eyes.

"When I was your age an unfortunate occurrence happened that caused me never to see the light of day again, and my Pa wasn't nowhere 'round for to reach out to. It ain't important how it come to pass, or why. But what do matter is that my Mama was the only-est person that I had. And when they sent a poor boy up the hill to tell her...some farm boy just 'bout your age, too...I was much oppressed that any soul had to carry such a heavy and loathsome burden as my bad tidings. I could feel his footsteps trudgin' through that Road To Nowhere, into the most beautiful of places that boy had ever trod, with wide valley views that see as far as a hawk could fly. Maybe he wanna fly away too, but he cain't 'cause he got hisself a job to do. And then the boy, I 'spect, he take a deep breath tryin' to hide the shake in his young lip. But it ain't no good. So he just hope that nobody seed. 'Cause if they do, maybe they think he ain't growed enough to do the deed.

"That deliverin' deed what that boy done, that's one deed that no man should have to do for his fellow man more than once in his life. But if he do, each time it make him more of a man, until he conquer it or until it crush him into the dust. That be the time that a boy needs his pa. I needed mines, and you needs yours. But mines wasn't there then, and yours ain't here now. So we keeps on plowin' that stumpy row, hopin' and prayin' that we're goin' straight, and swearin' at that lazy mule what gotsta be an obstruction to progress. We don't choose our rows. It's just what we got.

"Now them telegrams is your mule, and you gotsta push it forward. And if he shits in your path, you step right in it and push on harder until the job be done...or you quit. You just quit. You turn your back, and you look at that view, and you quit. You be the hawk and you just fly away. Either way, you gonna play the blues.

"But for now, we gotsta honor these three boys. If you cain't stroke it, son, step aside, 'cause there's shit in the row, and I'm plowin' on through."

There was a long pause, and Ivory never touched a key. Howie could feel the pain behind Ivory's words. If it weren't for the hugging rules, he would have put his arms around the old man. But Ivory broke the mood as he downed a shot from the small glass on top of the piano. He let out an "Ahhhhhh", took a deep reflective breath and finished his thoughts.

"But then again, I'm just another deacon in the Church of the Good Time Charlies. So what the hell do I know?"

He put his glasses back on and started to play again. Just when Howie thought he was coming to grips with his own unique situation, Ivory's final words derailed everything that he had set in motion.

Howie stared out the open door.

*Maybe I should just fly away.*

But he could feel that pointing poster of Uncle Sam staring over his shoulder.

Outside, he saw the stars and stripes slide down the flagpole to the waiting arms of Lubisch and Antonsic. Rumors were circulating that Lubisch would be traveling to Washington on some aluminum war production problem, leaving Antonsic behind to have that statue of Lubisch's wife all to himself.

*He has to be crazy to fall in love with a woman he carved but never met. Maybe he only loves the statue.*

One phrase that Ivory had used, "The Road To Nowhere", pushed Howie to dig deeper. This one took courage. He edged onto the piano bench and asked the question that had long been the subject of both first and second-gamers, alike.

"Ivory, I know you never talk about it, but did you lose your sight on that Road To Nowhere?"

"That's one song better left unsung. Besides, you gots bigger stones to lift than old Ivory's troubles, what nobody cain't do nothin' 'bout, no how. So you take care of number one. Don't fret 'bout number two. Ain't much worth tellin' anyways, 'cept some bad mojo that don't need no diggin' up. The trouble with other folks' troubles is that they like weeds. They plant themselves in your brain and then you gotsta extricate 'em. Mmm-hmm. Extrication! Just the *sound* of that word tell you it gonna hurt...Everybody all over the world thinks their troubles be so special. Well, read all about it! *Nobody* be that special, 'ceptin' to the ones that love 'em... Pass the basket. Sermon's over."

"Ivory, you think they got kid messengers doin' the same thing in Kansas and Colorado, maybe even Germany or Japan?"

"Ain't you a sight to behold! Thinkin' with your brain as well as your heart. Sittin' there with all them smarts fixn' to come out! Yeah, you right, 'ceptin' you know most every soul on this lump of dirt and sand. You know 'em like they was kin. So you liftin' a heavier burden 'cause you carryin' their stones, too."

"I wish Pop was here."

"Yeah, and I wish I had somebody to wipe my ass for me when I got the general miseries, but it ain't gonna happen. Case closed."

Lubisch and Antonsic entered the hall and tucked the triangle of a flag behind the bar. Pete the Dog slobbered down his last beer laps, barked his thanks and sniffed his way to the door. He stopped at Howie to get a quick pet behind the ear, walked into the twilight and headed home.

Ivory lifted his hands from the keys, reached into his pants pocket and pulled out the small white rabbit's foot. It's ragged appearance easily gave away its age.

"This here ain't much, but it's all the good mojo I got. Maybe it can chase some of that bad juice away. You rubs it when you needs it. I give it to Corey when he join up, but he worry about me bein' here alone, thinkin' that his daddy need the juice more'n him. He only goin' as far as California, so he send it back my way. It been good to me, but that don't mean it gonna be good to you. A rabbit's foot only be lucky when someone give it to you. You just cain't go out and catch you a rabbit. You wind up takin' all four of them feet and what you got? Nothin' but a dead rabbit. Yeah, you got dinner, but you ain't got no luck. I'd ditch my dinner any day for a potful of luck. So you keeps it as long as you needs it, then you pass it on to some other soul who needs a little good mojo in their life."

He handed the rabbit's foot to his young protégé but then engulfed Howie's hand locking it between his own. His words flowed out in a momentarily ominous tone.

"But don't never, *never* let nobody steal your rabbit's foot, son. 'Cause if'n a man steal another man's mojo, well that mojo thief gonna get tattooed with a bad luck shadow that follow him right into the grave and out the other side. That be a walkin' dead-man curse you don't wanna wish on your best enemy. 'Nough said. Now, less words. More play. And let me hear you stand straight and blow strong. Build them lungs, boy. It's the only-est ones you ever gonna get."

Howie admired the rabbit's foot, then tucked it deep in his pocket.

They played the blues.

# CHAPTER 26

# MILKIN' THE CHICKEN

# JULY 6, 1942

An hour later Howie and Ivory had finished their first upbeat set. The tempo had changed as the bachelor party exploded around them. Ivory nursed another shot, then followed his slightly scratched, replacement cane away from the piano. Howie and his sax escaped the cigar smoke cloud by exiting through the glass doors to the waterside terrace. But first he touched his index finger to Uncle Sam's as he passed the "Uncle Sam Wants You" poster, then saluted the flag standing near the doorway.

Vinny and Gene bellied up to the bar and laughed with Lubisch who was pulling Knickerbocker drafts. Gene downed an entire glassful in one long swallow, slammed his hand against the bar top, wiped his mouth and picked up a full one.

Two dozen boisterous locals played poker and craps as coin and paper changed hands. Young men of draft age, however, were noticeably absent. President Roosevelt had successfully asked Congress for the first peacetime draft in 1939 and the fruits of his labor had now depleted the Island. But most of these boys would have volunteered anyway. Raised on a spit of land stuck out into turbulent waters, they were used to living in harm's way.

Sitting alone outside, Howie replayed the blues that he had earlier shared with Ivory, their deeply moving rhythms temporarily interrupted by the fast-paced demands of the raucous bachelor party crowd. His solitary melody divorced him from the outbursts of background laughter. Barely visible liberty ships dotted the darkened Sound behind him, the ultimate recipients of his plaintive notes. It was all he could do to brighten a fighting man's monotonous day. He hoped he was reaching the unknown "Sailor Fred". A hushed mantle of stars wrapped itself around his boyish shoulders, protecting him from the world of man.

Howie had heard Ivory speak of his mythical Road To Nowhere only once before, when he'd had too much to drink, a lot too much. After his wife's death, Ivory had locked himself in the Legion Hall for three days, playing the piano until his fingers bled. Sometimes it was more like slamming than playing. Then he smashed the bench against the piano and broke anything else he stumbled across, before he passed out. Pop made everyone stay away until he carried Ivory home in a wheelbarrow. Then Lubisch quietly paid for the damages, and the incident was erased from City Island's unwritten history. The Logan house was home to young Corey Keys for almost a week, and it was here that Howie's mom distracted Corey from the loss of his own mother by teaching him how to cook, a skill that would become a necessity living with a blind father. It came so easily to him that his friends starting calling him Cookin' Corey. Now he was cooking for Uncle Sam.

Once during that turbulent time, when Pop had sent Howie to check on Ivory, he heard the incoherent ramblings about The Road To Nowhere. As Ivory's head and hands healed, Howie had questioned him about it. Ivory only replied that The Road To Nowhere was a hallowed and dignified place where questions and answers no longer mattered, where everything was simple, where he was born and where he intended to die. And they never spoke of it until today. The mere fact that Ivory would mention it again signified the importance of their conversation.

A cannonade of laughter on the other side of the glass doors snapped Howie's attention back to reality. He pondered the puzzle before him. Existence on City Island had always been seasoned with peril. Each succeeding generation of natives had grown more used to the uncertainty of survival, never knowing if their menfolk would return from an hour or a day or a year at sea.

Now three of their own had died. A tragedy of this magnitude would have brought any other small community to its knees, humbling it before God and man. But tonight he watched them celebrate the coming marriage of another Island son. It was as if they had heard the collective voices of generations of lost boys say, "Rejoice in my life today. Mourn for me tomorrow." Howie worried about Vinny's tomorrows.

Inside, Gene guzzled another beer and crutched toward the crap game, catching up with Vinny.

"I'm your best man," said Gene. "I'm supposed to throw your bachelor party! Who's paying for all this, anyway?"

"Maybe you've been replaced. We'll find out who did it when there's...(lip popping sound)...three of us waiting at that altar."

Gene's eyes searched the room, settling on Lubisch behind the bar. The old man's wink answered his question. What he didn't know was that Lubisch was simply throwing his own going away party, and Vinny was a convenient excuse.

Howie watched Gene lower himself on a crutch and into a one legged squat with all the grace and poise of a milk stool in heat. He threw some bills down hard enough to bounce them off the wooden floor. His jaw set tight, ready for competition at any level. He didn't care whom he went against or why. He wanted to be the best at everything he did. He demanded it. And when the war wouldn't give him that chance, he searched for anything that would. Vinny once said that Gene's toughest opponent was himself. Howie still couldn't figure out what that meant.

A hand reached up from behind the bar and scooped away two drafts from a group of look-alike friends that Lubisch had liberated from their wooden keg only a few moments before. The overflowing mugs sloppily disappeared from view. An instant later Stevie duck-walked from behind the bar carrying the two frothy brews. Blending into the crowd, he stood up and navigated out the door, setting a course for Howie on the terrace.

New York's drinking and draft ages officially coincided at 18. But not only did City Island's unwritten law frequently disagree with New York State law, it often superseded it. Islanders were well known for their subjective legal interpretations, especially those dealing with personal freedoms: anything relating to licenses, from dog to marriage; one way streets; parking regulations; opening hours; closing hours; selling beer on Sunday; stealing beer before your 18th birthday.

Many Islanders knew deep down that they were not really part of the Bronx. In fact, most felt that they did not actually belong to New York City. And more than a few suspected that, if challenged, the original 1895 contract transferring them from Westchester County to the City would not hold up in court. But what if Westchester didn't want them back? Maybe Connecticut would. Otherwise, they'd be left in a limbo-esque state of independent existence with far reaching international ramifications that were too mind boggling for the grasp of the average Islander, let alone Stevie. He was just happy to snag the beer.

Howie's sax solo carried across the evening air, and Stevie followed the sound with his eyes closed, just for the sheer challenge.

*How does Ivory do this blind thing all day long? He must see somethin'.*

He walked into a picnic bench, sloshing beer out of the glasses.

"Whoa shit!"

Opening his eyes, he re-adjusted and finally slid a beer under Howie's sax, but it didn't stop the blues.

"You keep milkin' that chicken, you're gonna go blind."

Stevie waited for a reaction, but only got notes.

"I swear, that thing must give you a boner. Look at you. Holdin' it down low. Blowin' in one end like that."

Stevie started to imitate him, caressing an imaginary sax as if it had magically sprung from between his knees. Howie gave up. Stevie had won.

"Would you stop? I ain't in the mood for your jokes tonight."

"All right. Choke that chicken. See if I care. I bring you this nice beer here, and what do I get?" Stevie did a squeaky voiced mock impression of Howie's shallow attempt at toughness. "I ain't in the mood for your jokes tonight."

Both boys broke into laughter, and Howie reluctantly accepted the beer. They moved up to a precarious perch on the railing, the Sound swirling menacingly below and behind. It wasn't Howie's first taste of beer. It wouldn't be his last. He was raised in a Bronx Irish Catholic household and had been small-sipping at the table since before he could hold his own glass. After a second quick drink, Howie pushed his glass away and paused to look out at the sea.

"I'm playin for those guys on the ships out there, the soldiers and sailors."

"You don't even know those guys."

"Only a sailor named Fred, and we ain't met, yet. Figure there's gotta be a 'Fred' on one of those ships."

"Yeah, probably some guy with big muscles and lots of tattoos."

"Eats a lot of spinach, too. Three times a day." Howie took a pensive sip. "How many people you know, Stevie?"

"You got it all wrong. It's all about how many people know *me*."

"I used to remember how many I knew. But now I'm losin' count. I'm startin' to subtract. I gotta take Charlie O'Reilly and the other guys off the list."

"And now you got Magic Maggie."

"Yeah. Nice pup. Really broke."

"You had to tell his mom, and now you got his glove. That stinks."

Howie took a deep breath, sucking up a sudden wave of guilt. Stevie turned his face toward the starry night, parallelling Howie's gaze.

"You know what I think, Stevie? I think he knew he wasn't never comin' back. Nobody gives up their glove if they're comin' back. Nobody. Especially not Charlie."

"Yeah. Especially not Charlie. Not when he was goin' to the majors...I wonder if they got baseball in heaven."

"He'd play short stop," said Howie. "He was always the best at short stop."

"Or he'd be a catcher like me. You gotta admit, Howie, he was a great catcher."

"If they build him a monument, I'm gonna donate my glove... his glove."

"He *should* get some kinda monument, or ceremony, or somethin'. Anybody who plays ball that good can't just be forgot. It ain't fair. We oughta do somethin'. Old man Lubisch could make it happen. Ya know, Howie, he was a Rough Rider."

"Yeah, and he's got flypaper in every room. He must be rich."

They looked at their almost full beers, little men stuck in a little world sitting on the edge of endless darkness. A long quiet, only broken by Stevie's small beer sips, passed between them before Howie spoke again.

"Hate spinach."

"Yeah, hate spinach."

"Stevie, I don't think I can do this messenger thing no more."

"Hey, Squat-For-Brains! Your family's always been the messenger. You can't quit."

"When I get those telegrams, it's just me and Columbia out there all alone. And when I tell 'em that their sons are dead, it's like I killed those boys. In their mothers' heads, I killed 'em. Without me, they'd all still be alive to their moms, to everybody on the Island. Nobody'd know. When I have that yellow paper, I just wanna ride and ride and ride and ride and ride. And never stop. Never. The longer I ride, and the longer I hold on to that telegram, the longer they ain't dead."

"Who else is gonna do it? Mr. Nakamura? Can you imagine what'd happen if one Jap came to tell ya that your son got killed by another Jap? They'd hang him from The Big Tree. Think about it, Howie. You got no choice. You gotta keep ridin'."

"I know. I'm tryin' not to let Uncle Sam down. He wants me."

Stevie took a courage-building bigger drink, followed by a gargle and then a foamy spit over the rail.

"Okay. Tell you what. I'm gonna ride along with you. I'm backin' you up. I'm your back-up man. That's me: Back-Up Stevie!"

"Forget it. Sounds like you're constipated. Beside, that'll just stick a number two problem in your number one head. And I don't think you got too much room left in there."

"Then look at the good side: I hear you deliver two more telegrams and you get to keep the hat."

Howie, caught in the middle of a sip, looked at him for a second, then laughed a mouthful of Knickerbocker foam.

"Keep it? I hate it!"

"I know," laughed Stevie. "But it'd be fun to watch. Me, holdin' ya down on the ground, jammin' that hat on your head. You, kickin' and screamin', tryin' to kick me off. What's not fun about that? I could sell tickets."

The bubbly, coughing backwash started to knock Howie off the railing, but Stevie grabbed his shoulder reeling him back in. They laughed their way down to safer seating, just in case.

"Thanks, Stevie. You go over that rail at high tide, and you ain't never comin' back."

"Oh I'd come back from the dead, just to see you as an old man, takin' them old man baby steps, using two canes and still wearin' that Western Union cap. Besides, it ain't like anybody'd miss me."

"Yeah. Who'd miss you?" echoed Howie.

Stevie waited for Howie to answer his own rhetorical question. Howie held firm, as long as he could. Finally...

"All right. You know who'd miss you?"

"Who?"

"Pete the Dog, that's who. Pete the Dog would miss you."

"Yeah, I'd miss him, too."

"I...ah...I threw a rock at him today. Hit him good. He made this little dog sound like, 'What'd ya do that for?' Never told him I was sorry."

"Tell him next time he comes in for beer."

They clinked their glasses to a bond of friendship and pondered the ships, the dog and the high tide.

"Stevie, you think a German submarine could come up right over there and blow us all to smithereens? I heard they already sunk 150 ships in just six months."

"Where's 'Smithereens'?"

"It's not a place. It's a thing."

"What kinda thing?"

"I don't know. It's a thing. It's a small thing. It's just this...this small smithereen thing."

"How small?"

"Small!"

"*How* small?"

"Forget it. Okay?"

"Where do you get 'em? Sounds like Jersey."

"Stop."

"And it's not a *submarine,* Howie. It's a *U-boat.*"

"Shut up, Stevie!"

Stevie shut up. Howie had exiled himself to another indefinite silence. He needed the concrete, solid sound of a voice or a sax, if only to keep his mind off his dreams. But this time he was determined not to give in.

Stevie, unaware of Howie's little mental challenges, easily broke the silence.

"Sure, a U-boat could pop up and blow us all to some place...or some thing. Why not?"

"Maybe I should go up to big Fordham Road, hock this sax and get me a gun."

"Howie, that is the first smart thing you said all week."

"I gotta go. Ivory's gonna start."

"Ya' know somethin' Howie? I've been thinkin'. I bet ya that nobody could play that good like Ivory and be blind. I think he can really see...see somethin' at least. How else could he be the ump?"

"He's got powers."

"If he was really blind, he would'a told somebody about how it happened, somebody like you."

"Stevie, don't be a nincompoop."

"Yeah. Must be the beer talkin'. Wait a minute! It's gonna say somethin' else. Here it comes! Oh! It's for you. Telegram for Howie Logan!"

Stevie ripped off his best fart. Both boys laughed as Stevie leaned back and confidently cracked his knuckles.

"Back-Up Stevie!", he proudly beamed. "Now *that's* what I'm talkin' about! See? I got powers, too."

Howie took a drink, sent a laughing burp his way, then dunked his fingers in the beer and flicked it in Stevie's face. Stevie retaliated and laughed harder. They took last sips mixed with plenty of air and practiced their best beer burps.

"So, Howie, who's gonna talk to old man Lubisch about Charlie's monument? You know him pretty good from the store."

"Yeah, but he hired you to nail those boards up on its front door."

They stared at each other, waiting for a volunteer. With a sudden smile of enlightenment, they both spoke at the same time.

"Kim!"

"Yeah, Howie. All she's gotta do is listen to some old poetry, and she got him!"

"And you know she's a sucker for a ceremony!"

They clinked their glasses, took a final sip and poured their remaining half full drinks into the Sound.

Beer foam mixed with the water's swirl. And then it was gone.

# CHAPTER 27
# THE CRAWLIN' MAN
# JULY 6, 1942

Gene had carved himself a piece of floor. Dollars sprouted from between his fingers as his other hand let the dice fly into the center of this high-stakes crap game.

"Get hot! Mama needs a new wedding ring."

He lost, and Bad Bill's gnarled hands raked in the pot. Gene was anything but dejected. Instead his body rose to the challenge like hairs on a chained dog's back. Vinny tried to pull him away.

"Forget it, Gene. Come on. You've lost enough."

"No. I'm due. Watch this."

He threw most of his cash into the pot, and the surrounding crowd grew in proportion to his bet. A shower of dollars floated down to cover the wager. But now Bill held the dice, and he was not eager to roll. The antagonism between the two sides of the Logan family transcended any beer-soaked gambling game. It had grown from seeds planted 40 years earlier, nurtured by a love-hate relationship between brothers driven in opposite directions. Bill savored the moment, then rolled a nine.

The rest of Gene's cash hit the pot as he bet against his uncle.

Bill smiled and laid down his green, then added, "And ten more."

But Gene didn't have ten more.

"Vinny, give me ten."

Vinny came in close. "I...ah...I don't have ten."

"Vinny, I know you got bucks, and I know I can walk away with enough to get Teddy a new ring easy."

"I don't have it. Niagra Falls ain't cheap, you know."

Gene motioned for Bill to roll. "Go ahead. I'm good for it."

Bill smiled an inside-his-mind smile and rolled, making his point. Gene exploded.

"No! I was due! I'm still due."

"You wanna get back in this game, nephew, you pay up the ten spot first."

Gene looked around, saw Howie entering from the terrace. He pulled himself to his best standing position.

"Hey, shorty. You got any cash on ya? Nickels? Dimes? Anything?"

Howie shrugged, "No". He could see that the drinks were taking their toll on his oldest brother. Gene angrily crutched his way out the front door and headed for the Logan house.

A few minutes later, his green eyes edged from behind the back door. As he expected, Lillian's bridal shower was significantly more sedate than the party he had just left. The future Mrs. Vincent Logan sat in a lone chair in the center of the living room, surrounded by an array of presents. A dozen women ooohed and aaahed as each new article was unveiled.

Kim helped Mom in the kitchen while Teddy demurely poured whiskey into teacups for several of the senior ladies, distant relatives referred to only as "The Kissing Aunts". Once they saw a victim, they were known to surround and shower him with lipstick kisses up and down his cheeks. They would be tough to avoid.

Gene timed his entrance well, slipping in from the back yard, but not quite well enough. The *creak* of the screen door caught Teddy's attention as he headed for the staircase. The Kissing Aunts turned in unison and swarmed until Mom's grasp and Teddy's voice pulled Gene to safety.

"Eugene Francis Logan. I never thought I'd be seeing the likes of you sneaking into a bridal shower."

"Actually, Mom, I just need...ah...a lighter."

Teddy's look lingered as Gene crutched up the stairs. It was obvious that she was apprehensive about his sudden appearance, not to mention his drinking, but she turned to the aunts and covered it with a laugh that snapped a dozen eyes from furtive glances at the missing leg.

"Here I am with a melon on the vine and that man still can't stay away. But that's why I love him."

The Kissing Aunts' agreement flowed in on a warm tide of approval.

Once inside the bedroom, Gene reached the dresser and carefully moved his lighters to the side. First the gold, then the silver forming them into an equally military line. Next he removed all of Teddy's $110 that had rested underneath them, placing two ten dollar bills in a separate pocket. He paused long enough to admire Teddy in their wedding photo next to the lighters' new formation. Catching sight of his lipstick-christened face in the mirror, he wiped it clean and retreated for the door.

Gene reclaimed his piece of the Legion Hall floor and threw down all the cash in his fist. He threw it down hard and several players backed off with comments of "Too rich for me," and "I'm out." With a disapproving head shake and an exasperrated exhale, Vinny picked up the bills and started to pull Gene away, only to have the money slapped back to the floor.

"Come on, Gene. Let's go."

"I'm hot!"

"You're drunk."

"Maybe so. Or maybe I only want you to think I am. Did you ever think of that?"

"You lost your limit for tonight."

"Get off me, Vinny!"

Vinny backed off. "Okay. Okay. Go ahead. Beat yourself up."

Gene turned to the game. "Now who's gonna cover that? And who just wants a piece?"

"Try this on," said Bill as he laid out several presidents' pictures, carefully matching Gene's bet, then added, "And ten more. One shot. Winner takes all. And this time, no markers."

"I knew it!" agonized Vinny, his excited feet launching him off the ground.

"Vinny, please. You're sweating on me. And I'm trying to conduct a little business with Bad Bill, here."

Gene reached deep into his pocket and pulled out a ten, tossing it on the pile. Then he produced the second ten and threw it in Bill's face.

"And the ten I owe ya."

He laughed. Bill didn't. Gene shook the dice, blew on them and let his "come out" roll fly. He hit a six to set up a point with good odds. Vinny hushed the fringe crowd as quiet edged in from far corners of the room, but his eyes went wide as he saw the despicable seven dots of the second roll come up. Words blew out of Gene's mouth, propelling his prone body right into the crap game. He bounced, tried to get up and bounced down again, punching the floor.

"Damn it! You're killin' me here."

The gawkers started to disperse as Bill picked up his winnings. Gene felt panic rising all the way from the toes on his remaining leg. Vinny started to walk away in disgust, but Gene grabbed his ankle, slowing him down.

"That's...That's the money for the baby. I can't lose that money, Vinny. I can't...Bill, I need that money."

"So do I, Gene. Maybe you shoulda thunk of that before."

"No. You don't understand. It's Teddy's money for her baby. I can't lose it."

"News flash, kid. You just did,"

"Bill. Wait. Bill...At least lend it back to me."

Bill slipped his winnings into a money clip as quiet settled over the room. All eyes came to rest on his. Slowly in one fluid movement, the bodies parted, and Ivory cane-tapped his way through the gap. He stood looking around for a moment as if he were actually taking in the landscape, then spoke with authority.

"Give it to the boy, Bill. He's drunk…and it's only money."

"Give the boy my money?! Ya know, some people around here think that Bill Logan is lower than clam shit. I know what you say. I can tell. And you want me to give this drunken so-called war hero back *my* money? Me. The one you all call 'Bad Bill'...Yeah. Okay. You want this money, war hero? You can have it. It don't mean a goddamn thing to me. I don't need your godamn money. Here! Take it. Take it!"

Gene started to climb up one crutch. Bill's voice stopped him.

"But you gotta crawl for it like the sniveling excuse for a soldier that you are. A soldier who never fought nowhere and comes home with medals on his chest."

Bill laid down 10 dollars just out of Gene's reach, then kicked his crutch away.

Gene fell to the floor, raised his eyes and gave him a hard look. Clawing and sliding within reach of the cash, Gene picked it up. Bill dropped a small pile of dollars six feet away. By now the room was silent, except for the sound of Gene's military buttons scraping against the wooden floor. The only other movement was the smoke rising above the locked-in-place spectators.

"Come on, war boy. Crawl for it."

Gene felt his mouth go dry as he pulled himself over to the cash, just in time for Bill to drop another stack 10 feet farther. The distances were getting greater. As Gene struggled forward, Bill's voice overpowered the room.

"Who's the clam shit now?!"

He leaned down close to Gene, but still spoke loud enough for the room to hear.

"You and your fine, up-brung family. Dunny always thinkin' that him and his boys were better than me and my son. Well who's crawlin' now? Huh? Who's the crawlin' clam shit now?"

Bill spit on the next little mound of money and laughed.

Vinny interceded, but his words danced around inside Gene's head in vain. "Gene, don't."

"Get away from me, Vinny. Don't make this any tougher than it is."

Bill moved ahead and laid a path of singles across the floor. A few patrons turned away, but one or two laughed in Bill's support.

"Look at your war hero, people. Look at him...I said look at him!"

Bill grabbed several men and roughly turned them around to stare at the slow moving spectacle. Some looked. Some simply moved to the bar. Howie navigated the crowd and knelt down by Gene's ear, following the one legged crawler, his own face close to the floor.

"Gene, don't do this to yourself."

"I gotta."

"What would Pop say?"

"Pop's not here."

"He wouldn't take that money. Not this way. No matter what. No matter why."

"It's not Pop's choice. It's for my kid."

"What about your...your dignity?" Howie didn't know what dictionary he pulled that three dollar word out of.

"Dignity? Three months on a bedpan shot that to hell. So don't talk to me about dignity."

"Is this the way you want your kid to meet you for the first time? Broken? No pride? Even though you only got one leg, you're still this island's hero. Right Ivory? He's still our hero?"

It might have been fatigue. It might have been the drink. It might have been Gene's seeing himself through the eyes of his unborn child that brought him to a temporary halt, but it gave Howie enough time to kick the next pile of cash, spreading it into the crowd, beyond Gene's reach. Bad Bill's stare earned his name for him.

Ivory's broom handle slammed down on the cash already in Gene's hand, pinning the bills to the floor. The mystical move caught every eye in the room.

Gene lifted his head to see Ivory looking down, as if the blind man were actually staring back at him. He watched his own pitiful reflection in the dark glasses as Ivory's words fell on his head.

"Even a blind man can see the boy is right, Gene. It's time for you to go. But no matter what you be doin' here tonight, no matter how bad you be down on your luck, when you wakes up tomorrow, you holds your head high. Rest of the island gotsta make up its own mind, but you still gonna be a once-in-a-lifetime hero to me. End of story. Take your brother home, Howie. Now."

Ivory's makeshift cane lead him back toward the piano.

Howie glared at Bad Bill, then kicked the remaining dollars in his direction.

Bill started after Howie, but Gene edged his way up and balanced on one leg, blocking the big man's path. For a moment the scene froze, reminiscent of an old West bar just before the shoot out. No one spoke. No one moved, until Gene's fingers started to relax and the remaining money fluttered down to Bad Bill's feet. A dangerous smile worked its way across Gene's face until it formed its words.

"Keep your damn money. C'mon Howie. The ladies are brewing tea."

Howie helped him with his crutches and they headed for the door. Bill's cold eyes followed the pair. Men started to talk and drink again, and Bill gathered up his money. He laughed his way to the bar.

Howie held onto Gene. It wasn't like Gene to accept help from anybody.

"I just had to stand up for you, Gene. Not that you can't take care of yourself or nothin'. You don't mind. Do ya?"

"You're a real 'buttinski'. You're the only one I'd let get away with it, though. You know, some day you're gonna get your ass kicked. But if you're not doing anything tomorrow, maybe you can back me up when I tell Teddy."

"Tell her what?"

"That I lost all of her hospital money. Every damn dollar."

Howie could hear Ivory's piano start to sing behind them as they stepped out into the cool evening air. The buildings would have a lot to talk about tonight.

# CHAPTER 28

# HEARTBREAK ISLAND

## JULY 6, 1942

After he had guided Gene home, and after he had survived the onslaught of the Kissing Aunts, Howie carried blankets and lemonade to the Nakamura porch. This time, he even carried some for Stevie. Kim wasn't so sure about inviting him, but Howie had insisted. She filled the bowl up with extra popcorn, even if they had no butter. At least they still had salt. Howie didn't want to see Stevie leave City Island forever, which he probably would do anyway. More importantly he wanted to make things right between Stevie and Kim. Plus there were a few more reasons that he couldn't crystallize in his mind. Things always seemed to make more sense in the morning.

The more he thought, the more he realized none of these reasons was compelling.

In the final analysis, he really didn't know why they should invite Stevie. But maybe sometimes just for fun, it was good to do something for no reason at all. That had to be Vinny talking from a perch on one shoulder, because if Gene were on the other, he'd say never tolerate an illogical or haphazard action such as this.

One thing Howie was sure of. He'd have a better chance of avoiding that Nana nightmare if he moved his sleeping location farther from where she fell to her death, a few feet away from his sax practicing spot.

Stevie was flattered to join them, but he tried to hide it. He had no one waiting for him at home and wouldn't be missed. He knew it, and so did they.

They set up their rockers, ate the popcorn and prepared to wait patiently, but within a few minutes Howie started looking over his shoulder, back through the store front window. Although Kim was getting annoyed at his sporadic twists and turns, she knew what he was looking at and kept quiet. Stevie however, felt no such need.

"You're twitchin' worse'n Mable Trent. We ain't never gonna hear them buildings talk if you let 'em know we're here. What's the matter with you, anyway?"

Kim answered the riddle.

"It's the hat. Ain't it, Howie?"

"Yeah. It's starin' at me. Right at the back of my head. It knows I'm out here."

"Remember in The Big Tree? Didn't we figure out that it really can't stare."

"I don't care. It's starin', and I can feel it."

"Well, do you wanna leave? 'Cause you could leave if you wanna. Stevie and I can finish this popcorn all by ourselves. Or do you wanna face it down?"

Howie thought for a moment and then came up with a statement that would put fear in the hearts of City Island's boldest sons and daughters.

"I gotta take it to little Fordham Place."

Stevie slipped off his chair and hit the porch hard.

"You what?! You *have* gone nuts! I don't know what I'm doin' here. I shoulda gone home."

Howie distinguished among the three streets named "Fordham". City Island's Fordham Street held their local public school, but the much larger mainland thoroughfare, big Fordham Road, crossed the Grand Concourse on the other side of the shaky bridge in the real Bronx. This big Fordham Road was a shopping mecca with easy access to the Loew's Theater where Ivory had taken Howie to see the big bands, and where Vinny had taken Lillian to see this year's best movies: *Casablanca* and *The Road To Morocco.* From Fordham Road any ordinary person could catch the Jerome Avenue IRT elevated train, simply called "the el", from the bowels of the Bronx directly to the heart of Manhattan. Fordham Road was truly a highway of magic and wonderment, the type of place that would someday lure Stevie away from the Island, never to return.

The smallest Fordham, little Fordham Place running on the east side of City Island, lay adjacent to the cargo ferry pier for Hart Island. That almost uninhabited, almost treeless piece of land, a mile long and a quarter mile wide, home to only the Mortuary Man, was New York's City's Potter's Field, but the children called it by a more appropriate name: Heartbreak Island.

The island held the remains of an abandoned women's psychiatric hospital, and on nights when the wind blew just right, the children argued whether the whines they heard were the ghosts of the boxed up and buried, or the distraught spirits of the Crazy House Ladies. Either one was sufficient to keep even the most daring teenagers off the island.

Once a week in the summer, the Mortuary Man would offer high school boys 50 cents a day to work along side prisoners as they dug trenches long enough to hold 1,000 simple, children-size, pine coffins. The adult section limited its trench size to only 48 body boxes making it easier for theoretical later retrieval and identification. But in reality, nobody wanted these bodies back. The third section, the most feared of all, held assorted body parts. This was

City Island's worst form of employment and only the impoverished need apply.

Vinny and Gene had never even thought of digging the trench. They were always able to earn a solid two dollars a day as lifeguards at Orchard Beach, across the bridge and through the woods, and they each had drilled Howie to someday take their place.

As far as first-gamers knew, no older second-gamers had ever taken the Mortuary Man up on his offer. And if, in fact, any unremembered teenagers had actually gone across the half-mile strait of swift salt water, there was no known record of their return. All they knew was that Heartbreak Island was a spooky place filled with body parts and suffering spirits, a place to be avoided for all except the most desperate.

Howie was desperate.

"Are you sure? You know what's over there."

"Yeah, Kim. I know, but I'm the only one who wears that hat, so I gotta be the one to end all this. And I gotta do it now before it can suck another telegram through those wires up there. I gotta bury it, and I gotta do it where it belongs: off this island with the other dead things, so it knows it's dead. You don't gotta come."

"I'm goin'. No way could you do this alone."

Stevie got up from the floor and headed for the blacktop.

"Now? In the dark? Go ahead. Drown and kill yourself! See if I care."

"Be a flat leaver, Stevie. Or, scared or not, you can come with Howie and me across the water in the dark and if we drown, we all drown together, 'cause that's what buddies like us do. Besides, we ain't gonna drown. Right Howie?"

"I ain't scared," Stevied answered. "But I ain't stupid. Remember what happened to Old Pete the Clammer and Old Pete the Fisherman? They rowed out there one night and never came back. The Mortuary Man's probably made 'em slaves, if they ain't dead already. And even if you make it, Kim, there's bad stuff there."

"Oh, we'll make it to Heartbreak. And we'll make it back, too. Tell him, Howie"

"None of yous gotta come if you don't wanna," added Howie, ending the discussion. "But I gotta do this or drown tryin'."

Half an hour later, Howie and Kim reached the boat basin at the corner of Fordham Street and little Fordham Place. Kim carried the beaten up hat, and Howie held a shovel on his shoulder. Stevie waited next to an untied, two oared row boat. He tossed an old tin can in the stern as they met him at the bottom of the boat ramp, barely able to see in the light and shadows given off by the nearby homes. Their target across the white caps was the single distant light from the Mortuary Man's cottage, the only dim beacon on Heartbreak Island, a half mile away.

Stevie pulled out a handful of crushed popcorn from his pocket and loaded up his mouth. His words spilled out, dragging the puffed kernels with them.

"About time you guys got here. Gonna miss the tide. What took you so long?"

"Howie couldn't find his rabbit's foot."

Howie held up the old rabbit's foot and rubbed it between his fingers.

"Don't worry. I got it. See? Good mojo."

"This is gonna be a lucky trip. Right?" said Kim.

"Right," came the response from both her shipmates. They punched one another in the shoulders, splashed into the boat and shoved off. Howie and Stevie sat side by side, each manning an oar. Kim faced them from the rear seat. The wooden 12 footer bobbed in the small waves, but the ebbing tide was still with them, and they floated away from their island with relative ease. They'd need to pull a lot harder to get back.

Stevie had instinctively chosen the downwind starboard side seat. Being bigger and stronger, he would have to put more muscle into his stroke just to fight the wind driven drift and correct their course to the left. All Howie had to provide was forward motion. Howie threw a confident smile and a go-ahead nod in Stevie's direction, telling him that he had faith in Stevie's ability to get them across the running water and was thankful that he had a loyal crew for this important mission.

"You know it's all on you, Stevie, or else we're buryin' this hat over on Long Island," said Howie.

"This could end up a burial at sea, and I ain't talkin' about the hat. This is one dumb idea. One big dumb-ass, dumb idea. You had a lot of dumb ideas, Howie, but this one is the dumbest of the dumb. If we never come back, I'm gonna start callin' you 'Dumb Howie'. You just keep on pretendin' to row. I got this."

He fought the breeze and the little band headed into the choppy sea. Kim periodically extended her arm, pointing the hat toward the the left of the bow, aiming at the Mortuary Man's lone light, allowing the rowers to adjust their direction.

"Did you boys ever see the Mortuary Man?"

"No," said Stevie, "But I hear he wears a top hat so you can't miss him. He wants everybody to know who he is."

Howie had more information but was hesitant to share it for fear of intimidating his brave crew. But after another minute of rowing, he had to let it out.

"I never saw him come into the store, but I heard he had three kids when he moved over there five years ago. No wife and three kids. And nobody ever saw the kids again. I think he buried them. That's why nobody'll go dig the ditches. They don't wanna get buried."

"Maybe he ate the kids," added Kim. "Maybe he ate 'em and just buried their bones. Nobody'd ever know. Probably weren't even his kids. Maybe he's like Hansel and Gretel's witch, and he's gonna try and eat us, too. I bet he never comes in the store 'cause he just chews away on the body parts they ship over there every week. He's gotta be a real fat guy by now...and a slow runner. He'd never catch us."

"Don't worry. He ain't even gonna know we're there. I got the foot, remember?"

Stevie wasn't convinced.

"Yeah, what are you gonna do? Tickle him to death?"

In 20 minutes, they touched dry land. The high pitched sound of the late night wind whistled through the abandoned lunatic asylum, adjusting its tone with each little gust. Stevie anxiously searched the dark landscape as he beached the boat.

"Hear that? That's the dead Crazy House Ladies. I don't like this. I'm gettin'...nervous."

Kim didn't care. "We're all nervous. So what?"

"Yeah, but when I get nervous, I kinda...ya know...crap in my pants."

"You crap in your pants, I'm gonna whack it back up there with that shovel! Right, Howie?"

Howie was too busy concentrating on a single light in the small cottage.

"Shhhh. He might be in there. Let's go."

They pulled the boat up, hunkered down and sneaked on shore. After climbing a small eroded embankment, they reached a flat plain populated only by sporadic wild grasses, some over their knees.

"Boys, I think I see somebody walkin' back and forth inside."

"Inside's better than outside," Howie said optimistically.

Stevie urged him on. "Let's get this over with."

Howie walked inland, measuring twenty paces to get to deeper dry soil, barely seeing were to place his feet in the limited light falling from the stars. He found a grass-less spot and started digging, but his scoops were too small and his hole too shallow for Stevie.

"Where'd you learn to dig? In a sand box? Here, gimme that!"

Stevie grabbed the shovel, drove the point in with the weight of his foot and dug furiously. The sand and dirt mixture flew in the air showering Kim and Howie. They stepped back.

"Make it deep. I don't want this hat scratchin' its way out."

"Shut up, Howie. I know what I'm doin'. You dig too deep, you're gonna hit water and then we gotta move closer to the center of the island…near that house."

The shovel hit something solid with a *THUNK.*

"Whoa, shit!" screamed Stevie as he dropped the shovel. Kim and Howie spontaneously screamed behind his scream, but even louder.

They suddenly froze, looked at the cottage, then dropped to the ground. The silence only served to compound the sighs of the Crazy House Ladies, floating in the wind. The trio's close-together, hidden-in-the-grass faces finally whispered to each other.

"I must'a hit a bone, or a box, or somethin'. Think it's alive?"

"Did it grab the shovel?"

"No, Howie. It did *not* grab the shovel. If it grabbed the shovel, I'd be in the boat by now."

"Then it's probably a root."

"It ain't a root, Howie," countered Stevie. "Look around. There's hardly no trees on this island. Bet it's Old Pete the Clammer's head. Maybe I broke his brain."

Kim settled the argument.

"Probably an old dead root. Everything here is dead…except 'him'."

She nodded toward the cottage. After a tense moment, she grabbed Howie's shoulder. "I think I saw the door open, and there's nothin' movin' inside now."

"Are you sure?"

"No."

"Stay down anyway."

Howie peeked over the grass, slowly stood up and surveyed the terrain. He motioned for the others to rise and rubbed his rabbit's foot, directing it toward the cottage.

"Whatever you hit, that's deep enough. Give me the hat, Kim."

She did, and Howie started to toss it in, but Kim stopped him.

"Wait. We need a ceremony."

"No, we…"

"You're only gonna do this one time, so do it right."

Stevie was shifting into panic mode. "Make it quick. I'll be in the boat."

But Kim would have none of that. "Stevie, stay!"

He stayed. She brushed herself off and straightened up to her full height, facing the hole.

"We're here tonight to bury the Western Union messenger's hat. It lived in the store its whole life, as long as any of us can remember. It used to be a good hat. Gene wore it. Vinny wore it. Tatsu wore it. Then the war came along, and it turned into a bad hat. We gave it a chance. And then we gave it another chance. But it's still a bad hat, and we can't fix it. Howie tried to drown it...OK. I helped...Then he beat it up with a bat and broke it, which he's sorry for 'cause he was just mad and knows it wasn't the right thing to do. Right, Howie?"

"I don't know that!"

"So we're puttin' you to rest on Heartbreak Island here, where all the other dead stuff is. Hat, I hereby declare you dead. Stay dead. Stay with the dead stuff. Don't ever come back. Sorry we got no music, but…well, we don't. Amen. Goodbye. Throw the hat in."

Howie dropped the hat into the hole. Stevie started to fill it back in.

"Wait!"

Stevie stopped. "What now, Howie?"

"My rabbit's foot. I think I threw it in with the hat."

"Leave it."

"No!"

But Howie hesitated. Touching the hat was acceptable, but he didn't want to stick his hand down there to touch something that made a shovel go "thunk".

"Do it or forget about it, cause I'm shovelin' it in."

Howie lay on the ground, closed his eyes, stuck his arm into the dark hole, felt around and came up with the rabbit's foot. He stood up in time to see a swinging light coming from the cottage, working its way in their direction. His jaw locked and eyebrows rose as Stevie obliviously shoveled dirt on top of the hat. Kim saw Howie's motionless expression and followed his stare toward the cottage. Her eyes picked up the light growing closer and brighter. She whispered to Stevie as she backed toward the boat.

"Let's go, Stevie."

"Almost finished."

"Let's go *now.*"

Stevie pounded the top dirt in place, completing a job well done. He looked for approval from his comrades but found them already slowly retreating in the boat's direction. The swinging lantern grew close enough for Stevie to have his handiwork reflected in its glow. Suddenly he turned around, saw the light in full view, and bolted in the opposite direction toward the water. He easily screamed passed the other two, jumped down the embankment, threw the shovel into the boat and pushed off from the beach.

Howie and Kim scrambled downhill on his heels, but by the time they reached the water, Stevie had the boat turned and was already rowing away. They splashed in pursuit, shouting over the sound of the wind, waves and Crazy House Ladies.

"Stevie! Stevie! Wait up!...Stevie! Come back!...STEVIE!""

Stevie could see the light approaching the beach behind them. He seriously thought about pulling for the open sea, but summoned his courage and pushed his oars in reverse, backing the boat up. Howie and Kim climbed in over the stern.

"Don't worry. I wasn't gonna leave ya."

"Yeah, you were," replied Howie as he slid onto the middle seat manning the oar on the starboard, upwind side for the return trip.

The swinging light reached the beach. It raised up higher and made a large arc, as if signaling them in a slow, welcoming motion. They were momentarily intrigued, wanting to distance themselves from the looming menace a few yards away, yet fascinated by its unknown, even friendly beckoning. Howie reached for his rabbit foot. Suddenly an eerie voice rose above the Crazy House Ladies' sighs and drifted out from the lantern holder's direction, calling them back to land.

"Stevieeee...Stevieeee...Come back."

"He knows my name! He knows my name!"

Stevie's panic gears screached into overdrive. Both boys pulled as fast as they could, but Stevie's wild strokes made the boat circle. Howie released his oar, rocking the boat as he gallantly jumped to his feet. He held the rabbit's foot extended like a sword aimed at the moving light, and rubbed the remnants of the soft fur harder than ever before. His body twisted as Stevie drove the boat in its curving route, and he started to lose his balance. Kim grabbed Howie, pulled him back down to his seat, then shook Stevie's knee, pointing toward City Island.

"Boys, we're turnin' around!"

"Stevieee," echoed from the shoreline.

They adjusted, stroked, fought the current, and slowly Heartbreak Island with its scary words and swinging lantern faded behind them. White caps splashed over the bow and water ran down to the stern, but Kim used the tin can to bail out the puddle accumulating at her feet.

"He knows my name, Howie! The Mortuary Man knows my name! You two had to go callin' my name, and now he knows it. Next thing he'll know where I live. And lots of nights I'm there by myself! Why'd ya have to go callin' my name for?!"

"You were leavin' us!" shouted Howie over the open water's wind.

"I wasn't gonna leave ya. I was just givin' us a head start."

"You were scared, and you were leavin' us."

Kim joined in. "Yeah, you were scared and I'm tellin' everybody that you were gonna leave us for the Mortuary Man so he could eat us alive. Everybody...or nobody."

"Nobody," said Stevie. "Let's not tell nobody that we were even there or what happened. It's a secret. Our secret...Buddies. Right?"

Howie and Kim looked at each other, then gave Stevie a double "Okay".

The increasing wind swept even more water into their little bobbing vessel, and Kim had to bail faster, using two hands as the boys put their backs into the stroke.

"Besides, none of that means nothin' now," said Stevie. "What matters is the Mortuary Man knows my name. I swear I could see his top hat behind the light. He looked like the Mayor of Uglyville! And he was sniffin' the air like he was gettin' our scent. He's gonna track us down like a bloodhound! I'm gonna remember that voice forever...How old you gotta be to change your name? I'm gettin' nervous."

Never slowing down, Kim delivered her daily dose of hollow reassurance.

"Don't go shootin' nothin' out, Stevie! 'Cause I can still reach that shovel, and I *will* whack it right back up your butt. Besides, maybe what we heard was only a Crazy Lady ghost. Maybe a *ghost* knows your name. That's not so bad. Right? It's just a plain old ghost."

"You tryin' to be funny? 'Cause that ain't funny."

Howie burst into laughter at her ridiculous suggestion.

"Yeah. It is."

His laugh was contagious, and Kim broke up, too. Stevie was a reluctant third as they all laughed and rowed and bailed their way back to the glowing warmth of City Island's lights and its faithful promise of unbuttered popcorn.

## CHAPTER 29

# THE RING BEARER

## JULY 7, 1942

As expected, none of the three exhausted midnight arrivals lasted long enough to hear the old Legion Hall speak of the family rift that had cracked still deeper and wider during the evening's crap game. And none heard the general store relay its apprehensions about the telegrams it may receive within the next few days, or even hours. The aged store said it was starting to sag a little, leaning into the sea under the weight of these new messages it had to bear. It was a task that had never been experienced by any other building either of them had known. In fact, if it had the power to do so, the old general store would have ripped out those wretched wires and terminated its association with this message delivery system that same night. But in reality it knew that it would have to wait until the next major storm. The East Coast hurricane season was a month away, and by then it would be too late. Boys would still die, and families would still have to be told.

The Legion offered its support as best one stationary object could for another, and pledged still more beams to shore up the smaller, ancient store if the need arose. At least they could take solace in the faith of this new generation of sleepers who always waited and never heard. As their creaking ended with the approach of the warmth of daylight, they smiled down at the motionless children and listened for the tide to change. But a lone figure corrupted the sanctity of their silence.

The tap-tap-tap of the broomstick-cane echoed in the predawn stillness as Ivory followed an unseen path to the small beach, his favorite place to greet the rising sun.

Those subtle sounds failed to rouse Howie from his well-earned slumber, but the morning's first rays did the job, hitting his eyes and jolting him awake. It took a few seconds to establish his surroundings, and he felt relieved that he was not in the midst of a Nana experience. That was a good thing. The events of last night's triumphant burial detail flashed back at him. That was a very good thing. The hat was gone. Everything would go back now, back to the way it was before the war. Everything would change.

Except the war.

Next, he felt the bulge in his crotch trying to stiffen its way through his pants. That could be a bad thing, a very bad thing if his sleep mates noticed. It was starting to become a morning habit that he couldn't control. He knew it would probably relax if he could just get around the corner to the bushes and pee. But that first rollover would stand a good chance of waking at least one, if not both, of his fellow crew members.

The sun wasn't waiting for him any longer. As it climbed above the horizon, his opportunities for an easy solution were fading away. He had to take his chance now.

Howie found himself facing Kim on his right. To his left Stevie was slung over two wooden high-backed rockers with peeling green paint, in an uncomfortable looking position. *How could he sleep like that?* Howie slipped off his blanket and edged off his rocker, onto his feet. Both resting bodies stirred. He looked around for something, anything, to cover his crotch and found the only shield available. He reached for the empty popcorn bowl. It was a little too big, but he was out of options. This was no time to be choosey. Making sure his fly was tightly sealed against any possible embarrassment, he strategically placed the bowl below his waist. His feet tiptoed off the porch as he ignored one last Kim stir.

Howie made it around the corner and stepped behind the scraggy foliage. The early morning breeze washed his face. He needed two free hands but was now stuck holding the bowl. He was getting urgent and felt the need to dance. In desperation he flipped the empty bowl upside down and set it on his head. It gave him that British soldier look, and for the first time in several days he felt jaunty again. And for the first time in several months, he was glad they had no butter.

Down came the zipper, and his little dance ended as he took quick aim, but nothing was working. Howie squeezed inside, then squeezed again. Finally a crooked dribble hit the bush and grew to success. He wondered if Vinny and Gene and Tatsu had gone behind the same bush years before as they waited for the buildings to talk. Probably not, because the poor bush most likely would have been killed long ago, or at least stunted like one of Mr. Nakamura's bonsai plants. And he wondered if they had to deal with this same early morning pants problem that was becoming such a frequent part of his daily routine.

The slightest motion, caught in the corner of his eye, made him turn away. He found himself peeing into the breeze, and had to dance a little more just to stay dry. He didn't know whether it was Stevie or Kim behind him. It really didn't matter. Both options would be embarrassing. He semi-closed his eyes. It was the next best thing to hiding, which also hadn't worked out well for him so far. But then again, being a squint-eyed, dancing, peeing, bowl-wearing boy seemed like a celebratory way to start off this new hatless day.

"It's me. I gotta go bad, and I can't wait! Move over."

He did as Kim slid in and squatted behind him back to back, separated by a frail, under appreciated bush. Howie knew better than to look over his shoulder because first, he'd have to go to confession and second, Kim would slug him, and this time not necessarily in the shoulder. He didn't mind the confession part, but Kim was getting stronger than she looked.

*This peeing-on-opposite-sides-of-the-same-bush has to be something that would bind us together forever, sort of like that blood-brother cutting thing, but painless.*

His little soldier with the German helmet stood at ease.

He shook.

Kim bounced.

"Howie."

"What?"

"Nice hat, dumb-ass."

He zipped up, turned around, and she removed the inverted popcorn bowl from his head. The moment was over.

*So maybe we won't be bound together forever, at least not by this bush. It was a stupid idea anyway.*

"You want breakfast, Howie? I'm gonna make some for Stevie or he won't eat."

"Nah. I told Gene I'd go up to big Fordham Road with him early."

Howie gathered his blankets and lemonade pitcher, looked through the store window, saw the empty hat shelf and smiled. "Some night, huh Kim?"

"Yeah, some night. Good thing you had that rabbit's foot."

A few hours later Howie and Gene got off the bus-that-ran-whenever-it-wanted and stepped onto the amazing big Fordham Road in the real Bronx. Howie had slept all the way. He wondered who this Fordham hot-shot was and how come he got so much named after him.

As Gene, in full uniform, crutched down the busy sidewalk, gentlemen respectfully removed their hats, and ladies looked away, reminded of their brother or lover or son. Seeing their reactions drove home how much Gene had sacrificed, and Howie was proud to be by his side. It was guys like his big brother who would make sure we won this war. But it just might take a little longer now that Gene was on the bench.

Howie carried a khaki knapsack over his shoulder. Gene had given it to him years ago for playing war, but since the real war started, "playing" didn't fit into Howie's daily routine anymore. Today, the bag took on a new life.

They passed near Loew's Theater and Howie detoured a few steps to look at *The Pride of the Yankees* posters under the marquee. He promised himself that he'd come back to see it after the wedding, twice. Gene was on a mission, and even on crutches, he never slowed down. Howie ran to catch up

Across the street loomed the Holy Grail of their quest, the three dull hanging balls of the 24-hours-a-day, we-never-sleep, it's-your-money-so-come-and-get-it Empire State Pawn Shop. Gene stopped in the middle of the street, held his stomach and turned around. Howie, only a step behind, nearly bumped into him and had to juggle the knapsack.

"What's the matter, Gene?"

Gene doubled over and heaved. He threw up the best parts of last night's liquid menu, forcing Howie to jump back.

"Take my advice kid. Don't drink. Write that down."

"I can remember it."

"Not for you. For me. I think we oughta do this another day?"

"I don't think we oughta do it at all. What's Teddy gonna say?"

"Let me worry about that. I don't feel so hot. Let's come back tomorrow."

"Hey, if you're gonna do it, do it! I didn't come all the way up here just to watch you puke. The light changed, Gene. What's it gonna be?"

No cars were coming in any direction. Gas limitations had convinced most of the motorists that only essential driving should be undertaken. Besides, even if there had been a car, no one would honk at a one-legged soldier in uniform.

Gene crossed the street. They entered the pawn shop to the noisy clatter of several over-resuscitated junk-heap fans. They didn't help. It was still hot inside. The real Bronx was always a few degrees warmer than City Island. A bald, thin-lipped pawnbroker looked up from his newspaper. It was easy to see that the thirties had not been good to him. Too much inventory. Not enough redeemers. He pushed falling eyeglasses back up his landslide nose.

Howie stared around the room at multiple hanging flypapers sporting hundreds of expired residents, then whispered to Gene, "This guy's gonna be tough."

"What can I do you for, sergeant?"

Gene took a deep breath. The whole idea sounded so good when he first explained it to Howie, but now the execution of the plan proved a little more difficult. Gene glanced at Howie for support and got a thumbs-up in return. Gene looked back at the pawnbroker, changed his attitude and with one deep breath, Sergeant Logan was back.

"What'll you give me for these?" Gene challenged.

Howie pulled out the sack's first offerings and handed them to his brother. Gene slammed down two medals, the Purple Heart and the Silver Star. His jaw was set for competition but the pawnbroker was unimpressed.

"Ten bucks, and I'm not even sure if that's legal."

"Twenty."

"Watch my mouth...leee-gal."

"Hey," Howie chimed in, "You're talkin' to a war hero here!"

The pawnbroker peered over the counter, his eyes fixed on the missing leg.

"Roll up that pants leg, soldier."

"What?"

"You heard me. Roll 'em up. You're not the first Joe to come hobblin' in here with some chest salad claimin' to be a war hero."

"I ain't no hero."

"For all I know, you got your old lady's garter belt holding your bent leg up."

"Show him, Gene," encouraged Howie.

Gene threw a mind-your-own-business look at Howie, then reluctantly rolled up his pants leg to reveal his stump. The broker looked satisfied.

"Gotta check, ya know. You want 20? You got 12. Don't give me no more agita."

Gene signaled Howie who reached into the sack's deepest pocket and pulled out all six lighters, which had kept their half-year vigil on top of the bedroom dresser awaiting their owner's return. Gene lined them up on the counter, from smallest to largest, first gold, then silver. A little army of lighters ready and willing to set his world on fire.

"How much? And don't low-ball me."

More than a question and not far from a curse, it verbally grabbed its receiver by his lapels.

The pawnbroker tried each one, and each one lit on his first attempt. As he tested the last lighter, Gene caught the broker's hand and brought it down like an arm wrestler. He leaned in, speaking through his teeth.

"How much?"

"Two bucks."

Gene slid his arm across the counter and started to scoop them back, but the pawnbroker's final word changed all that.

"Apiece. Two bucks apiece."

Gene fondled the largest of the gold lighters, then fired up a cigarette, inhaled and smiled.

"Done!" belted out in a puff of smoke.

Gene moved them to the side, setting his eyes for the next intense confrontation. He motioned for his sidekick to empty the knapsack on the counter. Howie dumped it upside down, and out tumbled Gene's recently acquired, and as of yet unused, artificial leg.

"One below-the-knee prosthetic device. What's it worth to you?" Gene said, slapping his hand down hard.

The pawnbroker didn't answer. He was lost in a stare, eyes locked in amazement on the object laid out before him.

"I...I...don't know, exactly."

"It's brand new, mister," Howie added. "It's gotta be worth 100 bucks."

"Not much call for 'limbs'."

"There will be," muttered Gene.

The shopkeeper picked up the leg and ran his slender fingers up and down it as if he were examining the workmanship, making a good show. His glasses slowly slid down his nose.

"Ten dollars. That's it."

"Make it 80." Gene was haggling for anything he could get.

"Ten, and I'm doing you a favor."

"Twenty."

"How am I gonna sell this thing? Who wants a...a leg? Ten bucks or nothing."

Gene shook his head in despair and gave in.

"Ten bucks it is."

Gene pulled a handkerchief from his pocket, carefully opened it and produced the engagement and wedding rings that were too small to fit on Teddy's finger any longer. The pawnbroker shoved his glasses up to his forehead and used a jeweler's eyepiece to examine the stone, nodding his approval. It would be small but flawless. Gene's life had always been small but flawless, until Pearl Harbor.

Howie put his hand on Gene's muscular arm.

"You sure you wanna do this?"

Gene dismissed his brother through a jaw locked grin. "Don't give me no agita."

Howie turned away, digging a canyon between himself and the transaction. His eyes fixed across the room on a shiny, almost new, dent-free tenor sax that hung in the window, picking up the morning light, a sparkling angel sent to guide this young knight on his musical mission. Drawn like a moth, he approached the instrument, gently rubbing his fingers up and down the fine brass work. But background haggling drifted into his ideal world.

"I'll give you 50 dollars. They're not hot, are they?"

"What? I'm looking for at least a hundred and ten."

"Sixty. And that's only because you're a steady customer and my new best friend."

"I'll take a hundred, and that's only because you've got a kind face."

"Yeah, Sergeant. I get that a lot...I'll go 70."

"Make it 90, and I'll throw in my kid brother."

The pawnbroker laughed. Howie didn't. Gene pushed the rings across the counter.

"It's a good price, 90."

The broker pushed them back. Gene leaned in close.

"Let's drop the dance. We both know they're worth at least 80. Eighty will do it, right Howie?

Howie snapped out of his saxophone daydream, did the mental math and reluctantly nodded his approval.

The broker nodded to Gene in return. "I'll go 80...if you keep the kid."

Gene pumped the broker's bird-like hand, but then pulled him in tight, never loosening his grip. Gene's words oozed through a grin that was anything but friendly.

"I'll be back for those rings the day the war ends. If they're not here, I'm coming back for you. Pearl Harbor will look like tea-with-the-queen by the time I get done with this place. And Gene Logan is a man of his word."

The shopkeeper pulled back a handful of sweaty fingers. He made out the tickets and counted up the cash, but kept a wary eye on this strange duo.

"And don't even think of putting them in your display case."

The first smile of surrender appeared on the broker's lips. "Okay sergeant. The rings'll be in the safe until the war is over." He slid the glasses up to the bridge of his nose one last time, throwing a two fingered salute as he finished.

"Corporal, American Expeditionary Force, Rainbow Division, 69th Infantry, Meuse-Argonne back in '18."

Gene nodded back. "When the war is over."

Without turning from the shiny sax, Howie called across the room.

"Give him the diamond one. Keep the wedding ring."

The transaction thundered to a halt and all smiles disappeared.

"Don't listen to the kid, mister."

"Gene! It's her *wedding ring*!"

"That would knock 30 bucks off the deal, Sergeant."

Howie crossed the room, leaving the prized saxophone slowly swinging in the sun's rays, heightening their reflective powers. He pocketed the wedding ring.

"I got your 30 bucks, Gene," said Howie, ending the debate.

Gene was caught off guard. "You got 30 bucks."

"Yeah. I've been savin' up."

"You heard the man," Gene acquiesced as he neatly folded the now reduced bills and slid them into his pocket.

Howie returned to stop the slight motion of the sax, but the price tag underneath continued to swing. His hand stopped that one, too.

It read "$52.99".

The duo headed out the door, back to the Island. They still had important business to tend to this morning. Once outside, Gene raced for the curb, held the cigarette out of the way and then threw up in the gutter. It wasn't much, but it reinforced his earlier words.

"Hey, Buttinski. Remember what I said about not drinking?"

"Yeah."

"You write it down yet?"

"Nooo."

"Write it in big red letters. Next time I take a drink, kick out my crutch, hold me on the ground and shove those words down my throat. Get Vinny if you need help, or Kim. She's pretty tough... This all started 'cause I just wanted to get Teddy a ring that fit. Guess I failed at that...Where'd you get 30 bucks from, anyway?"

"Been savin' buffalos."

Howie felt a little loss as he saw his hero brother who had crawled across the floor last night, now further reduced to vomiting in the street...twice. It hurt, and he changed the subject as they re-crossed Fordham Road.

"Gene! We should have tried for some flypaper! That guy had a lot. Probably give us a half-used one."

"Probably charge us for each dead fly, too."

"Did ya know that stuff'll stick in your hair if you just walk by it?"

Howie's glance caught the pawnbroker's talon of a hand shifting the silver sax to make room for the new artificial leg among a collection of braces, crutches and canes.

# CHAPTER 30

# JUST A GAME

# JULY 7, 1942

City Island's weather had turned hot. Yesterday's sea breeze was only a memory, and this morning's balls flew high and true. Howie had snagged several line drives as they flew past the hypothetical pitcher's mound, blasts that normally would have sailed to second base. Magic Maggie had spawned a powerful fielder drawing comments from admiring second-gamers. Even Gene was impressed. He lifted his catcher's mask, struggled up and crutched his way to the un-mound.

Howie moved in close to Gene and spoke in an uncharacteristically secretive tone.

"How'd Teddy take it about the engagement ring?"

"So far, everything's good."

"You didn't tell her, yet. Did you?"

"Well, not in so many words. But I did get the wedding ring and the dollars back onto the dresser. Thanks again, but you could'a told me your 30 was all in change. I'm praying she doesn't count it before I convert those coins to bills."

"Did you tell her or not?"

"Sort of. After we got back from the hock shop, I lit my cigarette *with a match.* She saw it. Oh yeah, she pretended that she didn't, but she saw it. She knows."

"Gene, that's not tellin' her."

"But it's a start. I figured I'd open with the lighters and work up to the ring."

"The longer you wait, the worse it's gonna get. She's not gonna take it too good either."

"I know that, too. But that's when I tell her that you made me do it."

"Oh, yeah. That'll work for sure."

"At least you, she won't hit. Me, she's going to kill."

"So for now, Gene, what are we gonna do with Stevie?"

"Time for a little catcher intimidation. Watch me destroy him with my silver tongue. Nice mitt work today."

"This glove's like a ball magnet. I never played so good."

Howie looked down at the mitt as if he were holding a religious relic. "It was Charlie's."

"Yeah, I know Maggie. Charlie and I took turns oiling her when he was breaking her in. Kept her tied up tight with a ball in the pocket for three weeks. He used to sleep on her like a pillow. Had linseed oil hair for a month. Said he couldn't wash that smell out, but I think he liked it."

Gene leaned forward and sunk his face into Howie's mitt. He inhaled a deep whiff and savored the aroma, letting time stop around him. He closed his eyes, momentarily transported back to a less complicated world, when life was only a mile long and half a mile wide.

"Mmmmm. Smell that? That's Charlie. Insisted on 100% linseed. The good stuff. We put it in so deep that she'll never dry out. This mitt will last forever. He loved her, so you treat her right. Can't believe Charlie's gone. I'll tell ya, he had an arm."

He produced a baseball from his pocket, tossed it into Magic Maggie and crutched his way back to home plate. Ivory had cleaned off the old cardboard that served as a base, as well as any seeing ump could have done. It had been pegged down last week but was now ripping at the corners. Gene pulled the catcher's mask over his face, dropped his crutches and squatted on one knee into a painful but necessary position, ready to receive the ball. Ivory rested his hands on Gene's arms and said his traditional words with the power of a much younger man.

"Play ball!"

A last minute dirt-rub coated Stevie's palms as he picked up the larger of the only two bats that the combined squads possessed. Sue Ellen, the Lombardi twins and half a dozen other teammates began an active chatter of support as he surveyed the opposition in the field. The target was readily visible: Kim guarding second with Mungo behind her in center field.

Kim sized up the batter and took a few just-in-case steps back.

Gene smirked at the glow of confidence spreading across Stevie's face. He'd soon erase that.

"So Stevie, how's your mother?"

Stevie wasn't about to play Gene's games. He ignored the catcher's comment and worked his fingers around the bat perched high above his shoulder, eyes fixed on Howie at the mound-less mound. Then he double-checked the Louisville Slugger label, making sure it was face up.

"They tell me you never knew your father."

The slightest of distractions worked, and the ball sailed into Gene's mitt as the swingless Stevie blinked. Ivory's resounding voice pierced the still air.

"Steeeee-rike!"

Gene tossed the ball back to Howie for the next attack. The pressure was mounting. If he could strike out Stevie, the game would be over. If Stevie scored, they'd at least tie, if not defeat Howie's team. There was no time for extra innings. The older players, delighted to see Gene home again, were anxious for the next contest. He had been a second-game player when they were still firsts.

Gene rolled out phase two.

"As a matter of fact, Stevie, I heard that your dad was just some guy who worked a fishing trawler for a season and then moved on."

Again the ball sailed back into Gene's mitt, and again the batter failed to swing.

"Steeeee-rike two!"

Gene's confidence grew as he sent the ball back to Howie for possibly the last time. Stevie kicked the dirt and spit. His sideline rooters and several second-gamers called for a long ball. Howie never paid any attention to them as he went into his windup. And Gene went into his.

"You know, they got a name for a boy like you."

Stevie swung and connected, sending the sphere deep into center field, and he raced down the base line. Gene yelled after him.

"Hey! Come back here. I wasn't finished yet."

The word was the same, but the tone was one of disappointment.

"Bastard."

Stevie didn't hear it. He was over halfway to first.

Kim never had a chance as the ball flew over her head, and she yelled for Mungo to scoop it. Scooping, however, was not Mungo's forté, and he chased it down as it went through his legs on a bounce, then threw it in Kim's general direction. Stevie had already rounded first. She leaped, trapped it in her glove and landed bracing herself, blocking Stevie's path. For an instant, she pictured a giant target painted across her chest, but some deep determination made Kim plant her feet exactly how her brother Tatsu had taught her, ready to take the runner's best hit.

Stevie plowed through her and slid into second as she tagged him in a smooth, sweet motion. Her light frame lifted completely off the ground, went horizontal and then came down. A cloud rose, fermented by the dry heat of that July sun, covering both of them in a blanket of haze. Just as quickly as she disappeared in the dust, Kim snapped back up again, holding the ball high, still firmly in her mitt, as firmly as when it had made contact with her runner. Big Stevie was out. She knew it. He knew it. And so did every player in the first and second games.

Kim smiled down at the her victim.

"Boop-boop a doop."

From his vantage point at home plate, Gene calmly agreed, "He's out."

Ivory's echo was deafening, an indisputable sound for all to hear.

"You're out!" came loaded with a full umpire air-punching, side-step dance.

But then he threw an addendum onto his statement for Gene's ears only.

"Ain't nothin' but a game, Gene. Sometimes the winnin' and the losin' get more high monkey-monk than the playin'. But in the end, it ain't nothin' but a game. Don't ruin it for 'em."

Gene thought for a moment, analyzing his competitive zeal. The words "only" and "a game" didn't seem to go together. But Ivory had a wisdom behind his eyes that earned him the respect of several Island generations. Gene acquiesced. He righted himself with his crutches and shook Ivory's hand.

"Yeah, what the hell. It *is* only a game."

Howie saw Stevie nod to Kim as he dusted himself off, acknowledging the gutsy way she stood her ground. A few days ago he would have decked her. A few days ago he *did* deck her.

Howie lifted his foot and looked at the sole of his shoe. The V, I and E were worn away from Stevie's name. Mom was right. But that was no surprise. Mom was always right, unlike Gene who always thought he was right, and Vinny who just didn't care.

Second-gamers crowded around Gene, showering him with questions about the war and Pearl Harbor. But Gene's war had been fought from the business side of a bedpan, and Howie could feel him drowning in a sea of youthful enthusiasm. Oddly enough, it looked like he was going down a happy victim. Howie waded into the small crowd, launching his brother in the direction of home and the general store. It was too late. He had already been infected by their euphoria.

Howie lifted his bike out of the grass and walked with his brother. Gene pointed at Stevie.

"Hey, kid. Nice swing."

Stevie smiled at Gene's approval, but then glanced over at Howie, remembering his own home plate verbal bashing a few days before. Their eyes said what their mouths didn't need to. Stevie stood a little taller, receiving acknowledgment from a certified Island hero. Gene never noticed.

"Poor bastards. Those second-gamers all can't wait to enlist. They don't know how bad the war is going to chew them up. Once it spits them out, it's coming back for me, and it'll be my chance again."

"You?"

"Yeah. That's how war works. When the young ones are used up, it comes back and takes the old and the 'amps' and the women. I'll be called back up. You'll see. Six months from now, a year tops. Sure, maybe I'll be pushing paper somewhere at first, a regular 'Remington Raider', but you'll see. Leg or no leg, I'm going back, and before it's over, I'll get in that fightin' war, too."

Kim fell in by their side.

Behind them, an elevated Stevie sat down to watch the next contest. The youthful Mungo sat next to him, debating whether to pick dandelions or his nose. Just by observing Howie, Stevie and Kim, he knew life would inevitably get more complicated the day his birthday cake held 12 candles. He had made a conscious decision to enjoy nine or ten, or maybe eleven, and right now observing a bumblebee choose its flower took precedence over the rest of the many exciting offerings in his wonderful world. He watched Howie pushing Columbia, then closed his eyes, made a wish and blew a dandelion fuzzball into the sky. He was lucky to find one this late in their season.

*I wish that someday I get to be the messenger. I'll get me a bike, and I'll ride all over this island like Howie. But when I hold onto the bus, I'll coast from the Legion Hall way up to the shaky bridge, from one end of the island all the way to the other. And everybody'll wave at me 'cause I got the Western Union cap on. And the best part is I won't be allowed to talk to any of 'em 'cause it's Western Union business...Then I'll let all the mamas find out that all their kids are dead.*

The ultimate conclusion sent his eyes popping open. Maybe that wasn't such a great wish after all. His gaze fell on Stevie, completely content to watch the second game.

*Or maybe I'll just throw firecrackers like Big Stevie.*

Mungo had plenty of time before he had to pick his heroes.

He searched for another fuzz-topped weed to unwish his wish, but there were none. The blood drained as he went extra pale at the thought of being stuck with that Western Union committment. Mungo silently ambled away in search of a late-blooming dandelion patch that had the power to release him from his self-imposed bondage. *Gotta be one more fuzzball on this island somewhere. Help me! Anybody!*

Several minutes later Howie, Kim and Gene approached Mrs. Trent's house.

Lubisch, Antonsic plus half a dozen other Legionnaires gathered on the front porch and draped a flag over the railing. Mable Trent stood solemnly in the center, her spotted companion, Pete the Dog, by her side. Her gnarled hand patted the dog, then steadied itself against a rocker limiting the tremors, and it worked as poorly today as it had for the last few years. The rocker vibrated quietly as the men made their comments. Pete the Dog's head cocked to the side with each spoken phrase, as if he were following the Legionnaires' conversation.

Kim was the first to see the unfolding drama.

"What are they doing?"

"Mable Trent's getting the gold star," Gene explained.

"Yeah. I saw it at Danny Giardello's house," added Howie.

Kim looked to Gene for a better explanation.

"What's the gold star?"

"Her son died for his country. Everyone will know of his sacrifice when they see the star in her window."

"But everybody already does know." It didn't make much sense to Kim.

"It's a symbol," added Gene, "so we'll remember him everyday. Every time we go by his house, we'll remember. It doesn't bring him back. It just brings his memory back. Eddy was a good guy. I'm going over there."

"Not me," admitted Howie. "It's too sad."

Brought up in a household of men, "sad" was not a word that Howie used freely.

Gene turned toward the ceremony, his mitt strapped to the crossbar of one crutch as Howie and Kim continued along the small dune line. Gene crossed the roadway, mounted the porch and pulled himself up to his latest version of military attention. Lubisch stepped aside, and Gene stood shoulder to shoulder with the old Spanish-American War vet, each proud to be in the other's company.

"You're right, Howie. It *is* too sad."

One look at Kim's belief in him, and Howie decided he had to make up for his lack of nerve.

"I guess they'll do Charlie O'Reilly next. I'll be there for that one. Charlie did give me this glove and all. But I don't know if I can face his mom."

He looked back at Gene, so at ease with the group of old soldiers, so anxious to face the challenge of kill or be killed. Howie found himself on the brink of emotions that he didn't understand and couldn't hide.

"I mean, there's so much death around here now, and I bring it all. All of it. I'm the death-bringer, you know. That's what I am."

"No, you're not."

"Yeah, I'm like an infection. People close their doors when I come ridin' down their block. They pull their little kids inside. They don't think I see it, but I see it."

"It's not your fault."

"They're afraid of me."

"Howie, it's not you. It's the war. Everybody's afraid of the war."

With the bike still moving, Kim hooked her mitt next to Magic Maggie hanging from the handlebar, and slipped her arm around Howie's shoulder.

He felt close to her, emotionally close. They had grown together for years, but this week had made them two matching pieces in a 642 piece puzzle, with no other possible mates in the entire box. He wanted to say something nice, something to make her forget about her mother in a California detention camp, or her brother she never spoke about, far away somewhere in the service. He wanted to say she was pretty, or smelled nice, or how that little bounce in her walk made him happy when it was hard to be happy. He wanted to tell her he loved the way she smiled when she punched his arm. It came out:

"You played good today."

"Better than you?"

"Better than...Mungo."

"Mungo?! That is the dumb-ass-est thing you ever said!"

She punched him in the shoulder, staggering him back half a step, dragging his bike with him. He looked for her smile, but she was already running in the direction of the out-of-sight general store. After a few boyish strides, she glanced over her shoulder to see if he was in pursuit. Despite her best effort, that Kim smile was creeping out.

Howie hopped onto Columbia and chased her down. She climbed on the cross bar and they imitated the cries of the overhead gulls as he slowly pedaled her home.

The commanding noise of a motorcycle roared down City Island Avenue forcing everyone in ear shot to involuntarily stop for a moment, then resume his or her ongoing activities, including Columbia. It rocketed passed Howie and Kim without the slightest slow down, finally coming to rest when it ran out of road at the general store. The rider lifted his circular, leather goggles and balanced them across his forehead, showing the worn face of a man too old for his job, who had performed his task so long and so well that he had permanent indentions orbiting his eyes. He set the kick stand, removed a package from his saddle bag and stepped onto the porch, stopping to take in the strangely boarded-over front door. Nakamura, alerted by the loud noise, stood in anticipation as the rider entered, holding a yellow paper.

He stopped short. With a disdaining look, he took in the spector of Nakamura in a white apron, pencil behind his ear.

"Where's Operator 1432?"

"I am Operator 1432," responded Nakamura.

"You ain't the operator. You're a chink."

"True, I am Japanese by birth. But I am also Operator 1432 by profession."

The rider casually spit on the floor. Nakamura stared at the small wet spot, then shifted his eyes back to the rider.

"And you are...?"

"Senior Messenger 64. American...just like Western Union. War Department know about you?

"Grocery clerks are of little interest to generals."

The rider's eyes glanced around the store looking for something out of place, then reluctantly handed Nakamura the yellow paper.

"Fill this in, sign here, initial here and here, check the correct box and hand over the damaged uniform. You do write American?"

"I write 'American'."

Nakamura initialed, signed and reached for the old broken cap but found an empty shelf instead.

"It's...ah...gone."

"It's not 'gone'. I don't have a box for 'gone'. I have 'damaged'. I have 'discolored'. I even have 'burned'. But I don't have 'gone'."

Nakamura wrote one word on the paper.

"Now you have 'gone'."

He exchanged the paper for the package. An unhappy Senior Messenger 64 returned to his ride. His weight hit the pedal with a loud blast. He spit on the blacktop and sped around the circle, heading north for the shaky bridge. A sand storm flew in his airborn wake.

Nakamura removed a new Western Union cap from its wrapping. He breathed on the visor, polished it with his sleeve and reverently placed the hat on its shelf. The strong, late-morning light hit the visor with a reflective, look-away gleam.

Howie had to steer Columbia into the grass as Senior Messenger 64 roared by, leaving a noxious blue vapor trail behind.

# CHAPTER 31

# PETE THE DOG

# JULY 7, 1942

Howie and Kim entered the store, hoping that Nakamura had not yet noticed the missing hat, but the new replacement stared down at them from its place of honor. Howie's eyes fixed on this intruding representative of Western Union and the war and everything that was wrong with his world. He braced himself against the counter, rubbed the back of his neck and let his eyes shift to the floor. Defeated, his shoulders slumped and he walked out the door, gluing himself to a compassionate, waiting rocker. Kim tried to read her father's expression.

"Dad..."

But Nakamura cut her off.

"It's 'gone'. Let us give this new hat a chance before we judge it."

He stuck his head out the doorway and extended a white apron in Howie's direction, delivering a prescription of his keep-busy medicine.

"Come Howie. I've told these peas and carrots all about you. It's time you met them in person."

An invisable jack hammer wrenched Howie out of the chair.

Barely two hours had passed before the ringing sound locked Howie and Mr. Nakamura in a catatonic stare. Both looked up as if they could actually see the bell through the rafters, and both simultaneously turned toward the chattering telegraph as they realized they could not.

"It's never gonna end," Howie whispered to himself.

Neither made an instant move to fulfill his duty and acknowledge the message. Nakamura stared off into the distance, momentarily imagining no wall between him and the sea. But just as quickly he snapped back, regaining his height and his composure, marching himself across the canned goods, through the produce and behind the counter. Two customers parted to allow him access. A third simply placed her few groceries back on the shelf and left.

Howie forced his hand to reach for the new symbol of his office. He tested the fit and adjusted the rear strap. It was stiff and inflexible, not at all like the pliable comfort of the old cap. This hat had a different smell, the smell of new wrapping paper and old warehouse shelves. It told a story of a dozen cigarette smoking workers carelessly shifting it from place to place until it was needed for its thankless mission. It felt awkward on his head, and he guiltily hoped that it might fly off in the breeze. Something inside him missed the old hat, and something else hated it and all it had done.

Within minutes, he was riding away from the storefront, gleaming cap square on his head, tears working down both cheeks. The feet that had effortlessly carried both Kim and him home, now labored under a heavier burden. His legs felt so weak that he could not find the strength to drive the pedals down without standing up, putting his weight into the circular motion.

There was no bus to hold onto yet. It was even later than usual. And this was a good thing, for although his ride was exhausting, the bus would have only increased the speed of his delivery.

As they saw his anguished face approaching, old women turned their downcast eyes away, and apprehensive mothers once again pulled small children into their homes. Neighbors peered through closed curtains behind opened windows, protecting themselves with a shield of drapes from the harbinger of death. He had braved this spectacle before, but this time Howie was too driven to notice. With his insides churning, he knew he had to develop an emergency plan to protect the telegram in case he threw up. His body was getting the best of his mind. His legs, his stomach, his watery eyes all rebelled, and he fought each one as he rode forward into an invisible storm of silent screams only he could hear.

*That is one deed that no man should have to do for his fellow man more than once in his life.*

Ivory's words wedged themselves into the corners of his memory, hoping to be forgotten. But Howie didn't have that luxury. He had done this before, and each time it had killed a little piece of his heart. After this delivery, he knew he could never do it again.

Mrs. Trent's house came into view. The porch was empty now but the railing was still draped in the red, white and blue flag. In her window the gold star, her sentinel of sorrow, stood its lonely vigil. Pete the Dog's ears stood up at the distant but familiar sound of Howie's bike, and he rose to greet the rider. His barking drew Mrs. Trent to her window, and she watched through the screen as the dog bounced out into the road.

This time Howie wasn't stopping.

Today the-bus-that-was-late-when-it-wanted-to-be-late had become very late. Joe tried to make up time as he drove across the shaky bridge just a little too fast. The war-time national speed limit had been set at 35 mph, and he pushed over the edge. He was nearing the end of his run as the bike approached from the opposite direction.

Howie's physical and emotional distress was temporarily diverted as Stevie and Mungo stepped from behind The Big Tree, throwing strings of lit firecrackers at his tires. He swerved to successfully avoid the explosions, but found himself headed for the oncoming bus. Instinctively he swung Columbia back again, out of harm's way.

Pete the Dog bounded into the air at the bullet-like sounds, then bolted across the street, directly into the bus's path. Joe hit the brakes hard. Pete the Dog looked up in time to bark at the offending tire, but his challenge was silenced as this rolling agent of the big city snuffed out his life, like an old shoe crushing the last spark from an old cigarette.

Howie careened to a sand-in-the-road stop, sprawling to the ground, stretching out his protective hands and losing his hat, all in one motion. The telegram spilled to the black top. He hustled to retrieve his charge, hiding in its now slightly stained yellow envelope, then stood transfixed, not even realizing that his hands bore tell-tale sand and gravel scrape marks. But the small red streaks that transferred themselves to the envelope, betrayed the roughness of the day's ride. He froze on the sudden horror behind him, confused and torn in which direction to go.

Joe exited from his bus to find Pete the Dog motionless.

Mungo slowly slid down to a crouch behind the tree with his thumb in his mouth and eyes closed. Stevie's first intinct was to run, but his feet nailed themselves in place. The faithful muscles strung on this strong adolescent frame refused to answer his call. In what seemed like slow motion, Stevie turned his head in Pete the Dog's direction. As his feet regained mobility, they led him back into the street, to Pete's side. He stepped in front of the bus driver, picked up the limp body and carried it to meet usually stoic Mrs. Trent as she ran from her porch. Howie had never seen her move so quickly or cry so loud. No one had.

"Pete! Pete! Oh my God!"

She sat right in the middle of the road and cradled the lifeless form in her arms, reminding Howie of a picture of Mary holding the body of Christ from a forgotten book somewhere in another time. She screamed to the heavens, then hid her face between her trembling hands, rocking all the while.

Howie stared at the woman who had been more concerned with getting him his tip than expressing her emotions when he had delivered her son's death telegram. Now she exploded with grief at the death of a dog. Howie tried to understand whom she was actually crying for, but it would take more time than he could afford.

Stevie sat down by her side and slowly petted the lifeless form, brushing a trickle of blood from Pete's mouth, showing more empathy than ever before. He looked up and his eyes locked on Howie's, 50 feet down the road. Neither one had any words that could make this right again.

Howie looked away. Pete the Dog was dead. If the animal had not heard the bike, if Howie had not come that way, he would still be alive. But he *had* ridden by, and the dog *had* died, caught in Howie's wake of death.

There was only one explanation. Death was the ultimate result of war, and there was no escaping it, not for City Island boys, not for City Island dogs.

The last thing Howie saw was Mungo emerge from hiding behind The Big Tree and sit in the street on the other side of Mrs. Trent, his thumb never leaving its assigned oral position. Howie picked up the hat, no longer polished or new, and slapped it against his leg to shake the road dirt off, possibly a little harder than he had to. He smoothed the telegram into the cap, threw it on his head, gulped air and peddled as fast as he could, bungalows, trees and porches blurring past. He had to get away, and he didn't know where. He didn't care, as long as it was "away".

When his one deep breath finally gave out, he looked up to find the shaky bridge looking back. He fishtailed Columbia to a sliding stop, daring himself to cross into the labyrinth of the real Bronx. *A boy could get lost there, lost forever.*

Maybe he didn't have to go that far.

*The bridge. The bridge could end this all right now. All I have to do is stand in the middle and drop this envelope over the side. Let it sail free. It'll get swept away, along with all the sad stuff wrapped up inside. No one will ever know that another Island son is gone. And if no one knows, and no one cares, no one's gonna scream in the middle of the night...until the war is over...and this son doesn't come back home.*

That ultimate conclusion made Howie slowly turn his bike in the other direction. Finally, he coasted into the cemetery that bore Irma Lubisch, his Nana and Ivory's wife. His speedy-delivery pledge be damned. He needed time to breathe again.

Columbia rested against the white shakes of the chapel wall, standing guard while its owner sought the gift of a private peace from a greater power.

Howie sat alone in the back pew of the empty little church long enough to lose track of minutes and hours; in one hand his cap with the telegram wedged up into the lining, in the other, the rabbit's foot. His hand contracted as if trying to squeeze the life out of that little piece of fur and bones, but it still innocently looked back at him through a five-fingered cage.

He stuck the rabbit's foot back in his pocket and ran his fingers across the name on the telegram.

This time he would make death wait for him. And if he delivered the telegram late, then a boy would live in the heart of the opener that much longer.

*Light a candle and burn this awful yellow paper. Light it now. For two cents, he can live another day.*

But how could Howie face Pop when he came home, knowing that he had failed in his duty and dishonored his family? It was this shared faith in the values of duty and honor that bound his father so closely to Mr. Nakamura. They held a common belief in the Code of Bushido, the way of the warrior, the rules by which all worthy men should conduct honorable lives. Nakamura by birth. Pop by design.

Destroying the telegram was not the answer. It would bring no honor to his father, nor to the boys who had sacrificed their lives. It would only deprive their families of the gold stars for which they had already paid the price.

He remembered how hard it was to wait for a telegram about Gene after Pearl Harbor, not knowing if he had survived. When he brought Teddy the message that he was only injured, it was the greatest day a Western Union messenger could ever have.

Good telegrams didn't come anymore. Too many Islanders had died, and he had lost count of the number of living people he still knew. He would never again add them up. Them or their dogs. He had lost count and he was glad.

Even though he didn't have his two cents, Howie lit a candle for Pete and the boys. Exiting the chapel, he stuck the cap on his head, dipped his palms into the small holy water font and rubbed them together washing the blood stains from his road scraped hands.

Howie mounted Columbia. He had no more inside tears left to drown him now and didn't care who saw the outside ones. It was time to stand up to the lie. The lie that had been living inside him for months. The lie that could kill a friendship forever.

Death had waited long enough.

# CHAPTER 32

# THE MAGIC OF THE BLUES

# JULY 7, 1942

Howie stood before Ivory in the doorway of his small bungalow. For the first time, he was glad that the blind man could not see his face.

"What is it, boy? Am I late for somethin'?"

"A telegram...for you."

"Now who'd go payin' for a telegram for me? No, no. It cain't be for me. Nobody I know would squeeze a eagle for Ivory Keys."

"It is for you."

"It is, huh? Well then I guess you gonna have to read it to me."

"I...I can't."

"You got the eyes to read the paper, so just read it. These dead lights of mine ain't gonna shine no more."

Ivory cleaned off his sunglasses as if it really mattered.

"Ivory, don't make me do this."

"Just do your job, and read the damn paper."

Howie's lip quivered, but he composed himself long enough to carefully open the envelope. With a final silent, pleading look in Ivory's direction, he began.

"Mr. Ivory Keys, City Island, The Bronx, New York ...Mr. Keys: The Secretary of The Navy regrets to inform you that Corey Keys, Navy Cook serial number 32960975, was killed in action...Stop."

"Corey? My son, Corey? No. I don't believe it. He's a cook in San Diego, California!"

"I'm sorry, Ivory. I'm so sorry."

"But he ain't in the shootin' war. He ain't. He's in San Diego. You read it yourself...in his letters, remember? He is cookin', ain't he?...Ain't he?"

Howie couldn't answer. Ivory's hands reached out through his emptiness and found Howie's shoulders. He tilted his head as if he could actually see the target of his next words, but this time they limped out softly, little broken whisper-soldiers sent on a thankless mission.

"Ain't he?"

"He didn't want you to worry. He wrote not to tell you, at the top of one of his pages, so I didn't. They got orders for Hawaii. He was cookin'...on the Yorktown."

"You lied to me? Every time you read me a letter, you was fabricatin' another falsehood?"

Howie carefully placed the telegram back in the envelope, ran his finger around its perimeter and sucked in a deep breath. It was face-up time.

"I...lied."

He tried not to break down. Slowly, he put the telegram into Ivory's gentle hand. The old man used it to brush away one sliding tear, then kissed the yellow envelope, folded it neatly, and slipped it into his shirt over his heart.

Ivory slid downward against the wall until he landed in a sitting position. New tears flowed in pursuit of their missing leader.

"Yeah. I guess I been lyin' to myself, too. Believin' what I wanted to believe. But I know my Corey, and I know he ain't gonna sit someplace safe when there's a fightin' war callin' his name. Truth is, deep inside, I knowed he ain't in California. Not Corey... I been fabricatin' that lie, too, and prayin' every day that you wouldn't come in here and read me a letter where he says different."

He pulled himself to his feet and began to walk inside, but there was no aim, no direction, and he stumbled. Howie followed him in.

"Corey is my life."

"What are you gonna do?"

"A piece of me just died, a big, thumpin' chunk. Don't know if there's enough left to go on livin'. And what for? I got nothin' now."

"You got me, Ivory...if you still want me around."

Ivory reached into a cabinet and fumbled for a pint of whiskey, but dropped it, and the half-empty bottle shattered on the floor. Disoriented, he started for the door without his broom-handle cane. Howie lifted some broken glass and grabbed a dish towel to sop up the alcohol, but Ivory's voice stopped him.

"Leave it be. It don't make no nevermind. Don't even know if I'm rightly fixin' to ever come back at all."

"But Ivory, I lied to you. Let me do something. I cheated you out of knowin' about your son. Don't you want to hit me, or yell at me, or...throw somethin'?"

"You did what you thought was right, little man. And that's all part of growin' up. This island is doing a heap of growin' up this week. Well, I ain't ready for it. But I cain't make it stop any more than I can hold back the rain or rub out the clouds."

Ivory stepped out into a strong July sun that would have made any seeing man shade his eyes.

In desperation, Howie called to him, blurting out the day's hardest words.

"But I got his foot, Ivory!...It's my fault he's dead."

The words locked Ivory in his tracks. He turned to send a silent, blind stare in Howie's direction that lasted too long and spoke too little to justify its duration. He slowly moved back to the boy whose hand now held out the rabbit's foot.

"Take it back, Ivory. I don't deserve it."

Howie braced, ready to be either absolved or condemned, but no judgement was pronounced. The wait for this verdict grew painful, until broken by Ivory's simple words.

"Need my cane."

Howie reached behind the door, picked up the broom handle and placed it in Ivory's hand. Howie pocketed the rabbit's foot and wheeled his bike around behind the man who had given him so much. He had just returned those years of kindness by taking away his son.

Before Ivory had led him half a block, Howie knew their ultimate destination: the Legion Hall. Ivory's three day drunken rampage after his wife had died had become an Island legend. He got his hands on at least a dozen bottles that first day, and those he didn't drink, he smashed. He wondered if Ivory would repeat the assault. It would be cathartic for both of them. And he wondered if the blind man got "blind drunk", would Lubisch pick up the tab again. And he still wondered how Ivory got blind in the first place. It seemed like a long walk today. It gave him too much time to think.

Ivory finally spoke over his shoulder.

"Go home, boy."

The unthinkable had suddenly crashed down on Howie. Ivory was rejecting him for what he had done. For his lie. And he deserved it.

But then Ivory added, "Go home and get your axe."

The request of the second part wiped out the rejection of the first. Howie rode home to wake up his musical instrument.

By the time Howie showed up at the Legion with his tenor sax, Ivory was alone, seated at the piano, an open quart of rye carefully placed on top, two filled shot glasses by its side. He played *The*

*Saint James Infirmary Blues* the way he had learned it as a boy before the century turned. He played it and tried to hold back his tears. Howie joined the sorrowful tune, watching his musical idol lose himself in the past.

As the song ended, Ivory let his forehead sink, clinking the keys, and he wept. When he finally rose, he took one shot glass and held out the other for Howie.

"How old are you again, boy?"

"Twelve."

"For a 12-year-old, you plowin' that row and steppin' in that shit like you was a man. If 12 is old enough to do a man's workin', I 'spect it's old enough to do a man's drinkin'. Drink up. To my Corey...Go on messenger boy. You earned it."

Ivory drank. Howie tried to sip, made a face and put the shot glass back on the piano.

"I can't drink this stuff, Ivory. I know drinkin' makes you a man, but it only makes me sick."

"You got it ass-backwards, boy. It's the sayin' 'no' to the drink that make you a man. A strong man. Stronger than me. Sayin' 'yes' to the drink just make you human."

Ivory groped for the bottle, then handed it to Howie.

"Best put this away...Hold on. I'll do it myself."

The piano man pulled the bottle back, poured himself another sloppy pour and downed that one. Ivory hurled the bottle across the room. It shattered against the Uncle Sam poster, running long liquor rivers down the length of the paper. He erupted like the sound of the smashing glass.

"Jesus, why'd you take my Corey!"

Sobs and moans mixed with his tears as he slammed his fingers into the keyboard, purging what was left of his heart, singing the blues as strong and clear as he could manage. He was alone in his void, darkness in a dark world, and there was no room for anyone else.

Howie sank down to the floor, resting his back against the piano, leaving his Western Union cap on top. But the earthquake vibrations of the angry notes sent shockwaves down his spine, and he had to shift his weight forward, pulling his knees up to his chest. His eyes closed, and he wiped the back of his hand across his mouth, half-revolted, half-savoring the bitter reaction his taste buds sent his brain.

Lost in his own collapsing world, he tried to hide from the disaster of the day, a day that had started out to be such a good thing and somehow turned into another day of death. His mind wandered though a list of telegrams that he had delivered, the ones that used to elicit such joyous responses, and the more recent ones to Mrs. Giardello and Mrs. O'Reilly, to Mrs. Trent and Ivory. Pete the Dog was killed again before his eyes, his closed eyes. He heard Pete the Dog scream, then Mrs. Trent scream. Then he heard Nana scream, and he looked up, envisioning an empty window.

Her scream echoed again, and then she fell from above. Bill's face and hands peered out behind her. Howie's eyes popped open with a small scream of his own.

"She screamed before she fell! She screamed *before* she fell! He pushed her out!"

He looked around, re-establishing his locale. Ivory's music blew through his ears once again. He wiped the sweat off his face and pulled at his strangulating collar. With labored breathing, he tried to stand, but sank back to the plank floor and gave up, staring vacantly through the glass doors, beyond the terrace and out to the Sound, muttering to no one.

"He pushed her. Bill pushed Nana out the window."

His eyes refocused inside the room and settled on Kim standing a few feet away. Her silent entrance, masked by the piano's slamming music, had gone unnoticed, but from Howie's point of view her small frame dominated the almost empty hall. She didn't greet him. She didn't comment on Ivory's blues. She never questioned

Howie's disheveled look or his loss of breath. She simply stared down at him.

"I need you."

Howie got to his feet and walked right by Kim without acknowledging her presence. He exited the Legion and crossed the street to the general store. She followed carrying the sax. Howie bore another, more important object in his hand, the unforgiving symbol of his terrible office.

The store was temporarily empty of customers, and he found Nakamura behind the counter. Howie stood in front of him, holding his Western Union cap.

"I can't do this no more."

"Then it will be as you wish."

"I mean, I tried. I tried real hard...hard as I could."

"I understand."

"I know all about the bananas. And I know what you did for me and about the debt to you...but I just can't."

"You owe no debt."

The edges of Howie's mouth started to turn down.

"Every time I deliver a telegram, every time I look into their faces, it's like...it's just that...I don't want to kill nobody."

Nakamura extended his hand.

"Give me the cap, Howie. It's okay."

"It's not okay...but it's the best I can do. I'm sorry I let everybody down. I guess I'm just not man enough for it yet. The job, I mean."

He surrendered the cap, glad it wasn't the one which had been handed down from Gene to Vinny to him. It was a terrible thing to do on a day filled with terrible things. He turned to leave, but Kim blocked his path.

"I said, 'I need you'."

She handed him the sax and walked out, Howie just a step behind.

Pete the Dog's lifeless body, covered in wild flowers, rested on the ground in Mrs. Trent's tiny front yard. Stevie climbed out of the grave he had just shoveled and bowed his head, taking his place next to Mrs. Trent, Mungo, Kim and Howie. The flag-draped porch railing painted a colorful background for the somber scene as Kim stepped forward and stood over Pete the Dog.

"We're here today to bury Pete the Dog. He was a good dog. He...ah...He never chased cats. Well, not too much anyway. Maybe a bicycle sometimes. He never peed in my father's store or ate any of the groceries. The whole island thanks him for that. And he never bit nobody."

Stevie looked up, obviously questioning Kim's last statement. She rephrased.

"Nobody that didn't deserve it. And he was always a good friend to Mrs. Trent, here, who loved him very much, until a dunce head...No. He's too dumb to even *be* a dunce head. Until some idiot, knuckle draggin', pod brain, mushy head, jerky dodo...and his friend..."

She gave a kinder look to Mungo.

"...his quiet friend, scared him with a firecracker."

Stevie's words spontaneously slipped out, "I love you, Pete the Dog."

"So now, God, we're sending him up to you. Please watch over him and be good to him. He likes his evening beer, but maybe he ain't gonna do that now. And Buddha, I know you're up there, too. Send him back as somethin' better than a dog this time. I mean, bein' a dog is good, I guess, but he deserves a promotion. He earned it."

She looked around for nodding affirmation and got it.

"And Saint Donovan, maybe you could watch over him too, a little. Amen."

A general "Amen" echoed in response. Mungo just nodded.

"Saint Donovan?" questioned Howie.

"Yeah. Dad says that Saint Donovan is taking care of him and me. So I figured, why not?"

"You know who Saint Donovan is?"

"What do I look like? A bible? Just play the music."

Howie leaned over Pete and spoke softly.

"I'm sorry about hittin' you with that rock. If you get sent back as somethin' better than a dog, let me know, and I'll make it up to you...Promise."

He raised his sax to his lips and played the soulful sounds of *The Saint James Infirmary Blues,* and his music mirrored the tune emanating from Ivory's piano several short blocks away. The old blind man's melody magically matched the timing of the distant notes from Howie's instrument, as two of the island's most beloved were mourned by those who loved them the most.

Stevie gently lowered Pete the Dog's body into the sandy soil, while Mrs. Trent dropped in his leash, bowl and bone. Then he shoveled dirt on top of it all. Mrs. Trent began to cry, but the sounds of the sax masked her sobs.

Mungo took her hand. As far back as could be remembered, he had never taken anyone's hand before. He always sniffled, but this time he looked up at her tears and sniffed back those of his own. His lips prepared to form a sound, but no one noticed. He could have gotten away with retreating into his own world. He could have turned back and no one would have been the wiser. Instead he tugged on Mrs. Trent's trembling fingers until she finally looked down. He wanted to speak, to say anything to make it right once again. He moved his lips, but no sound came out.

Slowly, his fingers slipped away from hers. He picked up two handfuls of flowers that had covered Pete's body, held them high and sprinkled them onto the grave.

Mungo felt an overwhelming urge to slide his thumb between his lips. He ambled back to The Big Tree. Sitting out of sight, he closed his eyes and lifted that old friend of a thumb to his mouth, but just as he started to suck, his eyes popped open and focused on a weedy spot between his shoes. There, almost trampled, was a soft dandelion fuzzball sitting on a delicate stem.

*Wow! Must be the last wishin' fuzzball for the whole summer!*

This had to be his final chance until next year to correct that wish he had made in such haste: to someday be the messenger. His thumb left his lips and reached for the wish-maker. He held the plant up to his mouth, but the notes from Howie's sax forced him to peek around The Big Tree once more, taking in the sadness from which he had attempted to distance himself. It didn't work. Maybe this was the only way he could fix what he had done and make sense of a senseless day.

He prepared his last precious wish, blew hard and watched the fuzzball fly, drifting apart in a hundred different directions.

*I wish Pete the Dog would come back as somethin' better'n a dog.*

# CHAPTER 33
# THE MISSING LETTERS
# JULY 7, 1942

Howie, Kim and Stevie shared one common thought. Ivory should not be left alone. His prior rampage was not a happy chapter in his life, and he didn't need to regret another. After Pete the Dog's funeral, they returned to the Legion Hall just as the sun set over the mainland, casting a long salmon-colored glow back across the Sound. The most beautiful pastels were always found in the opposite direction from the sunset. Most off-Islanders never looked in that direction. It wasn't the money view.

Ivory's silhouette outlined his bent and beaten posture as he played on in the growing darkness. His music was softer, slower and filled with blue melodies, hung on a flatted fifth note, that Howie could not identify. A new bottle of rye sat on the piano, replacing the one Ivory had smashed against the wall, but it was yet to be opened.

Stevie turned on one dim light.

"I guess we don't gotta give them U-boats any more targets than they already got."

"They don't want us," Howie said turning on another.

Kim finished the trio's statements.

"Sometimes I wish they did. Go ahead, Stevie. Turn 'em all on."

Howie moved close to Ivory and let his sax slowly wander into the never-ending blue melodies that seeped out of the old upright piano. Ivory was so lost in his pain that it was impossible to tell whether or not he was even aware of Howie's presence.

Stevie went behind the bar looking for the main light switches, but found Bartender Johnny's cigarette pack instead. He quickly forgot about his mission and made one of life's momentous little decisions. He filtched one cigarette and a pack of matches. The tobacco manufacturers were supplying cigarettes free to the boys overseas, so liberating one on the home front wouldn't be a big deal. He stuck the cigarette behind hid ear.

The taps had been turned off, but he held a saucer underneath a Knickerbocker spicket, pulled the handle and watched the last beer dribble down, then carefully balanced the plate all the way to the end of the bar. Kim watched as Stevie approached her. He waited for her to move.

"You're standin' in Pete the Dog's spot."

"Pete's dead, Stevie. You don't gotta do this."

"Yeah...I do."

Kim stepped aside, and he placed the beer saucer on the floor.

Stevie turned away concealing the redness in his eyes. He silently walked outside to the terrace, propped himself up against the railing, close to the swirling tidal rush below, and lit the cigarette like an amateur, taking a timid puff. Then another. Enamored by the cigarette's glow, Stevie held onto the match too long and burned his finger tips. He frantically threw it over the railing, and it immediately disappeared. Kim, following behind him, laughed at the grimace on his face, fingers now stuck in his mouth. She glanced over the edge at the swift dark water.

"First smoke, huh?"

"Maybe."

Stevie motioned knowingly with his cigarette.

"They do want us, ya know, those U-boats. I heard they already sunk 200 ships. They could just blow us all the way to Smithereens." He casually flicked the ash. "That's some small place over in Jersey."

"You're supposed to inhale, Stevie. You're not inhalin'. I can see your cheeks puffed up."

"I can inhale."

"You can't inhale."

"Can, too. It's not good for you to do it all the time, just some of the time."

"Go ahead, Stevie. Do it."

"*You* do it."

He held out the cigarette in her direction.

"I'm not stickin' that thing in my mouth. It's disgusting."

"You're just afraid of my boy cooties."

"No, I'm not."

"Yeah, you are."

Stevie shoved the matches into his pocket. When his hand emerged, it brought a long string of firecrackers with it.

"If it wasn't for these, Pete the Dog would still be barkin'...Eat-pay the og-day."

Stevie held the first fuse close to the cigarette's ember, but changed his mind. He balanced the cigarette on the railing, and unwound all the fuses, freeing the firecrackers one by one. He tossed each little unlit explosive into the swirling water, watching them get swept under by the tide's tremendous strength. When he finally finished, he turned to Kim, unashamed of his saddened expression. The powerful Big Stevie, the professor of Pig Latin, the batter of long balls and bicycles alike, slowly shook his head back and forth, now on the verge of tears.

Little droplets tried to peek out of both eyes, silent harbingers in place of dashed hopes and foiled plans, but before they ever appeared, willpower blinked them away. Pete the Dog and Big Stevie would have no more confrontations, nor would they ever have the chance to someday simply play like a boy and a dog.

Kim moved closer. She knew Stevie was brought up to be a fighter, not a hugger, but she hugged him anyway. And he couldn't fight it. He wasn't sure what to do, but his emotions overcame his awkwardness and he wrapped his arms around her. She had cried and Howie had cried, but she had never seen Stevie so upset before.

Stevie took a deep breath. He had to either talk or make tears. He chose talk.

"Pete the Dog was the closest thing I ever had to havin' my own dog. I know I'll never really get one. Oh yeah, I fool myself sometimes and pretend that someday I'll get a dog, but I know my mom. I know her. She's always workin'. Just tryin' to keep the two of us alive, she says. She don't got no money for no dog. And she says I'm not the best kid to take care of a dog, anyway. I said I would, but... Know what?..She's probably right. And I'm probably wrong. Most of the time I'm probably wrong."

They held onto each other in the sunset's dimming light as the music drifted out from the Hall. Slowly, they relaxed, sliding apart but still holding one another.

"When I grow up, Kim, if I ever have a kid, I'm gonna name him Pete...Pete the Kid."

"When Pete the Dog comes back, Stevie, maybe he'll come back as Pete the Kid."

"I'd treat him right, my kid."

"Suppose Pete the Dog wasn't your fault. Suppose it's the way the future was meant to be. Did you ever think that the future is just...just already out there? And maybe we sorta walk into it, and by the time we get there, it's not even the future anymore. It's right now. Maybe we got no control over it. The future's comin' around every day, with or without us. Whether we like it or not.

Submarines and firecrackers and dogs are all out there, waitin' for us, and we can't change nothin'. Maybe you didn't have no choice, Stevie. It's all meant to happen, so it happens."

"Ya think so?"

"Maybe we're sorta like actors in some kinda play they write in heaven. Who knows? The future's like religion. It's real confusin'. Did you know that the Buddhists let you be a Catholic, too? But the Catholics don't let you be a Buddhist? Who makes up these rules, anyway?...I wonder what religion dogs are. Think they say dog prayers?...If Pete comes back as a dog, we could call him 'Repeat'!"

"Yeah, but how we gonna know it's him?"

"Easy, Stevie. The beer. Betcha he's the only beer drinkin' dog in the world."

They held onto each other, afraid to let go, their bodies slowly moving to the rhythm of the blues. Kim watched a long-hidden tear finally fight its way to freedom, escaping from some secret recess inside Stevie that only today's events could have forced him to explore. He blinked it away.

"I ain't never gonna see him again. Am I, Kim?"

They swayed in the dance of compassion, yet in reality it was no dance at all, only two spent children slowly drifting together on a sea of loss. When the blues ended, so did their youthful, loose embrace.

Kim gave Stevie a quick kiss on the lips.

"I ain't afraid of your boy cooties."

She headed inside but Stevie's words stopped her at the door.

"Kim."

"What?"

"Don't forget me. Okay?...'Cause I ain't never gonna forget you."

His voice was soft, but the words rang clear. He would leave the island someday, probably sooner than the others realized, but like Howie and Kim, his memories of this week would never fade.

Howie had seen the kiss. He had attained his goal. Kim and Stevie accepted each other, perhaps more than he had anticipated, and he felt good about it and a little left out all at the same time. He looked at the sole of his shoe. All the letters of Stevie's name were missing, completely erased, taking Stevie's meaness with them just as Mom had predicted. He smiled the first smile he had been able to rally in many hours. Kim broke his mood.

"Step in somethin'?"

"No, I didn't step in somethin'. Just checkin' my shoe. Okay?"

"Well it must be a happy shoe, the way you're smilin'."

Outside, Stevie prepared himself to take his first full drag on a cigarette. He made sure no one was watching through the door, then sucked in all the smoke his lungs could hold. But his attention was quickly diverted as a car with military markings made the circle around the flagpole. He looked up just in time to see a familiar face in the rear passenger's seat. His puffed cheeks doubled him over as they exploded in a gagging sea of smoke. But it didn't stop Stevie from stumbling to the doorway and shouting to Howie inside. Kim sent a bouncing laugh back across the room.

"Howie! Howie!" he yelled coughing smoke. "It's your Pop. I just saw him in a car. He's outta jail!"

For a second, Howie stood rooted. The electricity set in. He let go of his sax, but Kim caught it as it slid from his fingers. At first he moved slowly toward the door, but by the time he reached the street he was running faster than he ever remembered running before.

Stevie coughed again, spit out the foul tobacco taste, made a face and flicked the rest of the cigarette into its watery grave.

"Uck. Disgusting."

He'd have to work on making better momentous decisions.

# CHAPTER 34

# THE HOMECOMING

## JULY 7, 1942

The Military Police vehicle stopped in front of the Logan house. Ryan, the tall, uniformed, All-American farm boy, exited from the driver's door, a pistol strapped to his hip. He surveyed the surroundings like a stalked animal approaching a waterhole. Satisfied, he nodded to the other members of his herd, two occupants in the back seat.

MP Sergeant Polcheck, short, stocky and tougher looking, stepped out and adjusted his sidearm. His steely-eyed, confidant expression said he was a man who enjoyed adjusting his sidearm.

The last door opened, and a full head of fox-gray hair emerged, attached to a tall, rugged-faced Dunny Logan. He stretched and looked over his familiar neighborhood, smelling the salt air that he had missed for half a year. He didn't paint the portrait of a captain of industry, nor a mere sailor in the captain's crew, but more likely a mutineer on the ship of life, anxious to be about his business.

"Smell that, Sarge? That's the salt life calling."

Rushing footsteps caught their attention, and Polcheck stepped in front of Dunny, hand on his weapon.

"Reel it in, cowboy," said Dunny. "That's my son."

Polcheck stepped aside as Howie bypassed him, no longer caring about the hugging and no-hugging rules. He threw both arms around his father.

"Pop! Pop! You're home!"

Pop returned the hug with patting hands that betrayed a longshoreman's story, but a wrist with handcuffs clinked against Howie's back. As they separated, Howie's eyes caught a glimpse of the cuffs. A partially forgotten image flashed through his mind.

He remembered hiding behind the kitchen door as an MP snapped handcuffs on Pop's wrists the day he was arrested. He remembered holding mom's hand on the porch steps, then breaking away to grab Kim's arm as she tried to throw a rock at the military car taking Pop away.

But this time dangling from the cuffs was a small briefcase. Apparently Pop was up to something important.

"Take this thing off me. We'll deal with this tomorrow."

Pop held out his arm and Polcheck reluctantly unlocked the cuffs, then snapped them on Ryan's wrist, much to the younger man's disappointment. Pop whispered some last minute instructions.

"What's in this case could mean life or death for a vast number of...vermin."

Polcheck shot back, "Just get this visit over with."

Pop signaled for the car's trunk to be opened. Ryan did so, and Pop handed Howie several packages of food and presents, taking the heaviest ones himself.

"For the wedding tomorrow. Greek olives. Russian beluga. Spanish sherry. Swiss cheese. Everything Mom could want. God, Howie! We've turned into the hoi polloi. What happened to good old American cheese, huh son? American ham and American cheese, some Jewish rye and a cold Knickerbocker, or maybe a Pabst. Now there's a New York meal! Grab that last wee bit like a good fella, Sarge."

With an exasperated head shake, Polcheck reluctantly hefted a large box of exotic edibles onto his shoulder.

Pop juggled his mound of packages to touch the "Home Sweet Home" sign, then savored every footstep as he climbed the stairs.

Polcheck moved ahead, motioning for Ryan to stay with the car.

His MP voice drummed out, "This ain't gonna take long."

"We're staying overnight," countered Pop.

Polcheck countered Pop's counter with, "An hour, tops."

Pop answered Howie's quizzical expression with a furrowed brow and a negative head shake that advertised the sergeant's poor grasp of the older man's master plan.

"Go on in, Sarge. It won't be locked."

Polcheck carefully opened the door, his eyes searching the living room before his body set foot inside, but Pop's entrance brought squeals of delight and screams of joy. Except for the season and the lack of a red suit, Santa was out of the chimney.

Pop put down his packages and held out his arms. Smiling, Mom never said a word as she marched across the room, grabbed him by the back of his hair and swallowed his lips with hers. She pressed against him long enough to make Lillian look away. Gene gave a little throat clearing cough, but Vinny laughed and applauded until Mom stepped back and took a Broadway curtsy.

Taking Pop's hands in hers, she gazed back into his gaze and spoke softly.

"Welcome home, Dunny."

Time became unimportant as the family reunited, a living, hugging portrait with everyone congregating in the kitchen. It seemed that no matter what the occasion, festive or otherwise, it always ended up around that big circular table.

Pop looked at Gene's missing leg, then embraced him.

"Did you give them hell?"

"I gave 'em my leg. I'll give 'em hell next time. You already knew about this?"

"I know more than they know I know."

Vinny couldn't let that go. "...than they know I know? Pithy. Very pithy."

Pop tapped his fist against Vinny's jaw. "Yeah. You're full of 'pith'. Ain't ya, college boy?"

Although Pop never made it past eighth grade, he was a student of life who appreciated the value and vocabulary of a university education.

Sons Howie, Gene, and Vinny, plus present and future daughters-in-law Teddy and Lillian, were all eager to learn where Pop had been and why. It took an event with the magnitude of Pop's return to keep Lillian out the night before her wedding.

Polcheck stood disapprovingly aloof, periodically checking his watch, while Mom beamed that every chick in her brood was finally back in the nest. She glowed as she prepared a meal for the new arrivals.

Pop put down his beer long enough to notice Lillian's painted-on stockings, accurate right down to the imitation seam.

"Lillian, what the hell have you painted on your legs?" he questioned.

"It's all part of the war effort. Really. Everybody's painting their stockings on."

"Everybody who's got the legs for it," added Vinny.

"The head silk importer for Mitsui for 20 years, biggest in the East, and here I am, replaced by a paintbrush. War *is* hell. How about another beer there, Anna my love?"

Pop was the only one that ever called Mom "Anna". Mom got him the coolest one.

"If you had only let me know you were coming home, I would have put them on ice. Next time, be more considerate."

She winked at the family, and Pop gave her another long kiss, this time drawing a raised bottle cheer from the viewers. With a slight clearing of the throat, he congratulated himself on sustaining his virility and made silent plans for the two of them later that night. Then he turned to the family and lifted his bottle. The others followed suit.

"A special toast for the bride and groom. May the road rise up to meet you. And may the wind be ever at your back. May the sun smile upon your face, and the rain fall gently on your fields. And may the Good Lord hold you in the palm of His hand, an hour before the 'divil' knows your dead."

"Pop, that's the same special toast you gave us!" shouted Teddy.

"You're all special to me, dear. Besides, that and L'Chaim are the only Irish toasts I know."

The room filled with laughter as everyone joined the drinking except Polcheck.

"Come on, Sarge. We're with family now. Relax. Have a drink," exhorted Pop.

"We've been here over an hour."

"For the last time, I'm not leaving 'til I see these two kids get married tomorrow."

"That was not the deal we made. We agreed that we'd drop off these 'supplies' of yours on our way from Boston to D.C., and that was that."

"Next time, don't trade horses with a mick."

"If you don't get in that car..." Polcheck threatened.

"What are you gonna to do? Shoot me? Explain *that* one to the colonel."

"Godamn it, Dunny!"

Mom gave the sergeant the dreaded Mom-stare.

"We'll have none of that profanity in this house, young man."

"Sorry, ma'am."

Pop looked out the window as much checking the street as he was observing the other MP by the car.

"Get used to the idea, Sarge. We're staying. Now call in Ryan, or he'll stand out there 'til Tojo grows hair."

The mention of Japan's bald prime minister drew a snicker from Gene as he muttered, "Cue ball."

Polcheck protested, "Dunny, you're gonna get my ass court martialed."

"I'll gladly take the rap for this one."

"No loose lips," Polcheck warned, reluctantly heading for the door. "Now I'm gonna have to notify the colonel we'll be a day late. Godamn it, Dunny!...Sorry, m'am."

Vinny was the first to take advantage of the sergeant's absence.

"So Pop, where have you been since December?"

"Yeah, Pop. Are you a prisoner?" added Howie. "Those guy's got guns."

Gene blurted out, "Colt 45, M1911. Seven round mag, single action, semi-automatic. Recoil operates with a five inch barrel and weighs 2.44 pounds empty."

That crashed the conversation sending quiet stares back in Gene's direction. He self-consciously looked around the table and tried to get the momentum going again.

"I hear they're working on an eight clip." Silence. "What?"

The tempo was still lost. After an awkward pause, Pop picked it back up.

"They're not to shoot me with. They think they're protecting me. Sometimes they forget and *treat* me like a prisoner. But no, I'm not a prisoner."

"So where've you been then?" asked Howie.

"Funny but sometimes I don't even know. They ship me around so much, from the basement of one building to the basement of another. Mostly in Washington, though."

"Sounds dangerous."

Howie realized he had said the wrong word. It made Mom turn away to move some nondescript nothing around in the sink.

"Nah," lied Pop. "They just play like it is 'cause it keeps them out of the real war. Who'd wanna bump me off? Besides, I'm riding with St. Christopher."

Pop flashed a medal from around his neck. But an image of the patron saint of travelers didn't satisfy Howie. "Then why can't you call us, or send a letter, or somethin'?"

Pop leaned in slightly, drawing his listeners closer.

"They got this crazy idea that it's better that you don't know. They're afraid that the Japanese could get to you and use you to prevent me from giving the War Department...'information'. It's just a precaution, that's all. But I do keep up to date on all of you. I got my spies. I'm taking names, so watch your step!"

Mom finally turned from the sink. "Well it still sounds dangerous to me."

"Easy as killing dock rats with a billy-club, Anna. I'm just helping them kill a different kind of rat this time."

His ragged explanation failed to pacify Mom.

"What kind of information, Pop?"

He pushed in to the center of the kitchen table, and his listeners gathered even closer as he answered Howie's question in hushed tones.

"Like what blocks in Tokyo really have the government offices. Like drawing maps of the smaller cities from memory. Like pinpointing production targets for...someday. The War Department's so desperate it's asking the public for post cards and family photos from anybody who visited Japan. They don't even have a Tokyo street map, and they'll never trust any info they get from the Nisei. That's why they got me, and I'm the right color. Mostly though, I'm matching names of Japanese businessmen to their pictures and weeding out the legits from the illegits. You don't hear about it, but a lot of them were picked up as spies the same day they took me. And the War Department's not even really sure who they got. So they just hold onto them. Them and their families. I know, or know of, almost every one of them on the East Coast. They're crazy for golf but the country clubs always barred them from membership. That's why I belong to a dozen courses and why I had so many friends. I hate golf but love the 19th hole. Played it with most of these guys. Eaten in their homes on both sides of the Pacific. Anna, remember Hidi Otashi?"

"Nice man. He sat at our table at the Lido golf dinner last summer."

"I loved interrogating him. It completely made up for that seven stroke drubbing he gave me. I pretended that I thought he was somebody else for an hour or more."

"Dunny! That's just mean."

"Oh you had to see it, Anna! I made him stand up and take practice swing after practice swing with an imaginary driver until he sweated up a puddle. Even had him tell me the par for each hole on the front nine. All of a sudden I 'remembered' his distinctive style. So I took him out to dinner. Me and him, and watchdog-Polcheck of course...Talk about a great job. I love my work! The War Department actually calls me 'unique'."

Mom looked on disapprovingly and asked, "Is Mr. Otashi a spy?"

"Otashi? I cleared him, so I hope not. I want him around for a rematch. But some of them *are* spies. More than you'd think. They've been sending home pictures and bits of information for years. They're actually proud of it. Anyway, none of this is for public broadcast. It stays inside the family. Got it?"

Group nods assured Pop that his family would abide by his wishes. Even though Howie's nod was enthusiastic, he had a broader sense of "family" than Pop.

"They look at photographs of these guys, and they can't even tell who's Japanese, Chinese or Korean. Last week, they brought in a Filipino! Some of my bosses grew up in a turnip patch. They're not too happy when I tell 'em so, either. Guess it's all who you know. But that'll change soon. Next, I have to work on convincing them to recruit those loyal young second-generation Nisei. Some of them have that warrior mentality. That would be a good unit for, Tatsu."

Howie ended that plan.

"You're too late, Pop. Everybody knows he already joined the army. Kim's pretty proud of him for that."

"No problem, I'll get him transferred."

Gene crutched over to the window and watched the two MPs.

"Never did like MPs."

"Don't worry about them, Gene. They think they're job is to make sure I stay alive. My job is to make their job difficult. Otherwise, we'd all get bored."

Howie had slowly realized that in spite of Pop's casual bravado, he was in a dangerous situation. They were both fighting the war without benefit of uniforms or guns, both soldiers on a home front that showed no feeling for the sacrifices they made.

*I should put a big sign on the porch that screams, "My father is not a traitor or a prisoner! He's a hero!"*

Pop was ready to go back and keep fighting the good fight. He was willing to do whatever it would take to end this war. He was capable of doing what Howie could not.

Howie knew that, sooner or later, he would have to tell Pop that he no longer possessed the courage to wear the messenger's hat. But for now, he was only able to get out, "When are you coming home for good?"

And Pop answered simply, "When Uncle Sam doesn't need me anymore."

Slight cramps in Teddy's abdomen had kept her a quiet listener throughout the audience with Pop, but now she had to excuse herself and work her way into the living room just to sit alone for a while. She anxiously awaited the birth of her child, but she wanted to be at the wedding too. She hoped she wouldn't have to find out if MPs were well trained in delivering babies.

# CHAPTER 35

# THE BANANA BANDITS

# JULY 7, 1942

"Because of you, I gotta tell the old man that we got this here imaginary engine trouble," Polcheck called over his shoulder to Pop. "I'm tellin' ya, Dunny. I don't like this. I don't like this one bit. If we get caught in a lie...You sure this telegraph office'll be open?"

"If not, we'll open it," answered Pop.

Stars punched holes in the sky as Howie and Pop followed in Polcheck's sandy footprints toward the general store. Ryan, still handcuffed to his briefcase, walked silently behind.

"Relax. Sarge. Enjoy the air. I should bottle this. When was the last time we had a day off?"

"We ain't never had a godamn day off, Dunny! And you know it! Seven days a week since I arrested you. We ain't getting' no leave, either. So you can smell that night salt air all you want, but come the dawn, we're burnin' outta here."

"Right after the wedding, Sarge. It's dead around here, Howie. Where is everybody?"

"We try to keep most of the lights out now, Pop, 'cause of the submarines. They say they're sinkin' ships. Maybe they'll try and sink us, too."

"There used to be such life here in the summer. Dances every weekend. Beach fires. We need a party!"

"Pop, what do you know about the bananas?"

Caught off guard, Pop laughed aloud as if recalling a long lost happy memory. "The bananas!"

"Yeah, the bananas. Gene told me that I needed 'em bad when I was a little kid and that you and Mr. Nakamura used to get 'em right off the ships."

"The bananas. That was a long time ago. Yeah. It was the Depression and sometimes they were so scarce that we actually had to steal them."

"You stole 'em?!"

"They didn't always want to give them up. So, yeah. We stole bananas."

"No...At gun point?" Howie's eyes were getting wider.

"Nooo...Well, mostly 'no'...Okay. Once in a while 'yes'. We were the 'Banana Bandits', so what do ya want? If you're gonna be a bandit, you gotta have a gun. And I only used to shoot in the air, just to get their attention...most of the time anyway. I think we were starting to get famous. I mean, who steals bananas? The cops probably thought we had a pet gorilla or something. One day my work at Mitsui sent me to Japan. So Nakamura got the bananas any way he could. Nobody asked how, but he got them."

"But, Pop! Stealing?"

Pop stood still, halting the little column. His voice turned stern, and he looked forcefully into Howie's face, leaning so close that MPs could not possibly hear.

"The Japanese man of honor lives by the Code of Bushido, the way of the warrior. Without honor and duty, life would not be worth living. That code will make the Japanese soldier fight even when all is lost. He's not gonna surrender. Nakamura and I both hold ourselves to that standard. You do what you have to do. A man takes care of his family, just as a man of Bushido does not let his friends and family suffer. Nakamura had the power and he used it. You're alive and there's a debt to be paid...You think those stevedores didn't know it was me? They sure as hell did, but wharf rats don't squeal. And yeah, I would have shot somebody for the bananas if I had to. But so would Nakamura."

"He said I owed no debt."

"He didn't do it for you. He did it for me."

They started to walk again but only got as far as the bench in front of the Legion.

Howie hesitated, and Pop sensed it as the boy dropped back a step. Pop stopped walking.

"Pop."

"What, son?"

"I've...I've been havin' this dream, this nightmare, and I tried to talk to Mom and Gene about it, but it ain't workin'. I'm still gettin' it, even in the daytime, now."

"Nightmares *and* daymares? Okay. Try me."

"This is gonna sound real bad, but I half-dreamed, maybe half-remembered that...that Uncle Bill pushed Nana out the window. And I know he's a great man, and I know all about him building the Panama Canal. But I keep on seein' him at the window, smilin'. I was there when she fell."

Pop sat down on the bench, took a deep breath, looked out at the water, then closed his eyes. Lights from Queens dangerously betrayed the shimmering outline of a ship unshielded by the night, a vulnerable target to any German U-boat that might somehow slip into the Sound. He patted the bench, and Howie sat next to him.

"It's time I told you the facts of life."

"Not that birds and bees stuff."

"No. The real facts. The Dunny Logan facts. Your Uncle Bill is a no-good bum. He'll tell you that his son got drafted before the war started, but if you ask me, he volunteered for the army just so he could get away from his old man. When Bill gets drunk, I think he beats his wife. Way back, when we worked on the docks, he started to beat on Nana. One night when Bill was in his cups, I heard him bragging he was gonna go home and have it out with her. But as he left the bar, I snuck up in back of him and... Bam! I bashed him on the head with a bottle and dumped him on the next ship out that night. Didn't know where it was going. Didn't care. Turned out it was carrying laborers bound for Panama. Never thought we'd see him again. Figured he'd get yellow fever or malaria or snake bit. Probably would have killed the snake first."

"But he came back."

"Yeah, six years later. Surprise, surprise, huh? And he was just as ornery as ever. He figured he got shanghaied and started calling himself 'Panama Bill', but I nicknamed him 'Bad Bill' 'cause he came back like a bad penny. I think he actually liked it. But somehow in his twisted mind he blamed his little boat trip on Nana, guessing that maybe she put somebody up to it. Maybe he figured me. Maybe not. When I found out Nana was dead, I knew that somehow that drunken son of a bitch was involved."

"He couldn't be. I mean, to just go and kill your own mother? No. Nobody could do that. In a nightmare maybe, but not for real."

"It wouldn't be the first time. He was there when my dad fell down the stairs and broke his neck. I'm ashamed to have the same blood as him running through me."

"What are you gonna do, Pop?"

"It's not your worry anymore. I'll take your nightmares over."

"You can do that?"

"It's done."

A sad silence wrapped around father and son as they stood and walked again. The general store had one light on, and Polcheck could make out Nakamura inside.

"Hey Dunny. There's a godamn Jap in there!"

"Don't worry, Sarge. He'll send your message. But I want to talk to him first...alone."

"I'll go with you, Pop," added Howie. "I think maybe you, me and Mr. Nakamura should talk about the telegrams." Howie took a deep breath. "I quit deliverin' them...Are you mad?"

That took all Howie's nerve, but Pop's words offered him a stay of execution. "I never said you had to be the messenger. Get on home. We have a big wedding day tomorrow, and I want to hear you play your best saxophone at the chapel. Mom says you got pretty good. And there's no way Ivory will be there, so you'll have to play that wedding march by yourself."

He tousled Howie's hair and got a chuckle for payback. Howie hadn't had his hair mussed like that since Pop left. He gave a boyish swing once around the flagpole and landed on the run in the direction of home, looking forward to a good night's sleep.

# CHAPTER 36

# TATSU'S LAST LETTER

# JULY 7, 1942

Pop entered the store like he owned it. Nakamura kept his head down as he worked on the monthly ledger, perhaps expecting a late shopper before he closed. Pop's voice had all the raw energy of a rising curtain at opening night Kabuki.

*"Homu wa funanoridearu. Umi kara no ie."*

Nakamura's head snapped up, and his startled expression transfixed him for an instant, then quickly slid into a broad welcoming smile. He responded by translating Pop's Japanese.

"Home is the sailor, home from the sea...*Oka kara hanta no ie.*"

"And the hunter home from the hill," answered Pop. "Yoshi, my good friend!"

"Donovan!"

"You still remember our Robert Louis Stevenson."

"And I am humbled by your skill of a language that is not your own."

"You taught me well. I use my Japanese every day."

The men met, clasping hands as if magnetized by a force stronger than blood.

"When you went missing, at first I feared you were dead. Then in prison. But no prison could hold you."

"It feels like prison. How are you?"

"How am I, Dunny? Sometimes I am scared. Always I am lonely. But I have truly believed that it could only be you who is responsible for securing my position here."

"From the looks of that broken door, you might be better off in internment."

"That is the work of your brother, Bill. But he was drunk at the time."

"I know, but that excuse wore thin a lifetime ago. As long as you're safe."

"Safe, yes. But no matter what, I would not abandon my station, just as you would not abandon your friends."

"I'll get your wife released yet. Army's like a business, all angles and percentages."

"It would be be difficult for a Japanese woman to travel alone across this country in these times."

Pop slipped back into his authoritarian voice, as he recited his credo for existence.

"Do *not* give up, Yoshi. *Never, never* give up. I'll make it happen."

Pop glanced out the window at the MPs. "I got my guys. She won't be alone. *Keizuko wa nari chikara.*"

"Yes. Perseverance is power".

"Have you heard from Tatsu?"

Nakamura took the box down from the shelf and removed its third letter, but there was no comfort in his face as he untied the red ribbon.

"I received his last letter before the war began."

He lovingly opened it and began to read:

*November 1, 1941*

*Father,*

*I have been accepted into the Imperial Army to serve my emperor. It was with no little difficulty that I overcame the handicap of my American birth. I curse the day that you and your parents left our homeland. Why did you have to come to the aid of Mr. Logan in that Yokohama shipyard, or accompany him to New York? It would have been better for us all, had you let those thugs kill him and steal his precious silk. You're quick, foolish decision set in motion the two decade chain of events that are now the cause of my loss of face. Because you choose to remain there, I have been advised that I may never rise in rank or responsibility. Upon completion of my training, I must accept a translation post as a radio operator, which will remove me from the empire's heart. I only trust that my new-found spirit will allow me to compensate for my ancestry. It is my fervent wish that, as long as you choose to remain in decadent America, you do not attempt to contact me again.*

*Tatsu.*

The empty sound of nothing stalked both men as they waited for the other to speak. Their sons would be directly or indirectly attempting to destroy each other. Perhaps it had already happened. No family bonds, no talking buildings, no Code of Bushido could unroll the wheel of time. This was one reality that Pop could not make right. He stood there, always a powerful man, now powerless. He had set these forces in motion, and their destination was mutual destruction.

Pop awkwardly looked away.

"I'm...I'm sorry. I never should have suggested that he attend school in Japan, or set up the interview with Mitsui's head office in Tokyo."

"It was I who sent him there, Dunny. Not you."

"Well, you'll be at the wedding tomorrow, right?"

"I think perhaps it would be better if I attended from here."

"Then Yoshi my friend, I will miss you."

"And you, Donovan. I will carry you inside me."

"Be careful."

"Be brave."

They shook hands at first, but moved into a backslapping embrace. As Pop stood in the desecrated doorway, he wondered what the two buildings had said about Bad Bill's handiwork, and wished he had the time to hear them. An anxious Polcheck intercepted him.

"Come on in, you two. You can send your telegram now, Sarge, but add that I need that internment camp meeting with the colonel moved up. Make sure you include that part. Got it?"

"Yeah, yeah. I got it."

Pop turned to Ryan.

"Bring over that briefcase. Give me the key."

Polcheck surrendered the key, but stared at Nakamura and held Pop's arm back, before he could unlock the briefcase.

"You sure you wanna do that right here, in front of...him? This stuff means life or death, you said."

Pop laughed, turned the key, and the briefcase clicked open. He lifted out a small, unmarked cardboard box and handed it to Nakamura.

"You don't have to wear those cuffs anymore, Ryan."

The young MP was glad to unlock the bulky case from his wrist, but Polcheck still stared at the box in Nakamura's hand. The storekeeper started to unwrap it, and Polcheck slipped his hand to his side arm.

"I'm not gonna have to shoot him. Am I, Dunny?"

Nakamura's eyes brightened as he opened the package to find six small cylinders of precious flypaper. "Ah, Donovan. Once again you ease my burden."

Pop's laughter merged with Nakamura's as Ryan fixed on the box's amber colored contents.

"I've been carrying *that* around all this time?! Flypaper!...Go ahead, Sarge. Shoot 'em. Shoot 'em both."

Polcheck's volcanic voice erupted.

"Dunny! You're gonna get us busted! You know that? Life or death for a vast number of vermin?!"

"Vermin means bugs, Polcheck. Bugs," laughed Pop. "Good work, Ryan. I owe you a commendation. Make that a beer."

"Get this wise-ass outta here, Ryan!" ordered Polcheck.

The MPs dragged Pop outside for an animated scolding in the middle of the street. Still laughing, Nakamura turned to see Kim standing in the rear doorway.

"Donovan? Saint Donovan, watching over us?"

"Donovan is a good man, Kim. He repays honor with honor, even if it places him in danger."

Ryan marched Pop in the direction of the Logan house. Polcheck re-entered the store, suspiciously eyeing its Japanese proprietor and his daughter. Hand still on his gun, he pulled himself up to his full height. His no-nonsense expression made five-foot-six look like a solid six feet.

"I gotta send a telegram."

# CHAPTER 37

# THREE MOONS OVER THE LAND BEFORE

## JULY 8, 1942

Howie never knew whether it was the dawn or Gene's distant, good-morning scream that shot him out of bed. Gene's wife rolled on her side and buried her head in the pillow. Teddy was getting used to this wake-up call by now. Everyone else slept through. Everyone, but the groom.

Vinny rounded up his brothers without waking the household. Dressed only in bathing trunks, he and Gene convinced Howie to slip into the livingroom where Polcheck and Ryan slept on the couch and some pulled-together chairs. Stifling their laughter, they peeked back in through the porch window, encouraging Howie to approach the end table and steal the military vehicle's keys. They grinned with pride when their young brother appeared victorious through the need-a-paint-job front door. Within seconds, they had quietly pushed the MP's car down the block, cranked the engine and pulled out with Vinny behind the wheel, laughing and howling at the success of their minor special forces operation.

They didn't travel far, only to the north edge of the Island, only to the shaky bridge. The car pulled over, and the barefoot brothers bounded out, Gene crutching a little slower than the others.

Vinny showed no mercy. "Come on, Stumpy! You still got one good leg!"

Gene crutched faster, rising to the challenge, pushing the limits of common sense up another rung. They stopped at the sand's edge and dove into the cool salt water just as they had for years. Before the war. Before Gene went to Hawaii. Before everything. Howie laughed and splashed. Vinny dunked and dove. Gene learned how to tread water all over again. As lifeguards, both older brothers were proven powerful swimmers. By his own count, Gene had saved seven lives at Orchard Beach. Vinny never counted. He just swam the big swim, pulled them out, then posed for pictures.

"This is the way things are supposed to be," said Howie after he had finished sending a fountain of water over his brothers' heads. "No war. No dyin'. No telegrams. No internment camps. Just us."

"Don't get philosophical on me," said Vinny. "Not on my wedding day. It's just three guys in the water. Have some fun for a change."

But it wasn't just three guys in the water, and they knew it. The world had come to an inexplicable stand still. It may actually have started to spin in reverse. It wasn't 1942, or even 1941. It was the way it was "before", and Howie closed his eyes, holding on to every moment. He'd never let it go. No matter what happened to him or his brothers, this would be the memory, the image that he would pin on a page of that mental scrapbook that would get him through the war.

"Come on. We don't want to miss the bus," urged Vinny. "You, too, Howie."

"But I never climbed before."

Gene pushed him toward dry land.

"Today, you are a man!"

Howie looked up at the bridge. "We don't even know for sure when it's comin'."

Vinny's words brought them out of the water and onto the shore.

"Move it, Howie. It'll be here. The first one's usually on time. And if we miss it, we'll never get another chance."

The pebbles under their feet made them nimbly dance until they reached the base of the bridge and climbed the ironwork. It was still early, and the metal had yet to absorb the heat of the day. The old structure wore a bonnet of criss-crossed girders rising 15 feet above the roadway. For the older brothers, climbing it barefoot had always been a test of their agility, but now Howie, the novice who had never ventured up into the steel, helped crutchless Gene adding a new comical dimension to the adventure. Vinny and Howie precariously passed him along, then edged higher to repeat the process, until finally they looked down at the swiftly runnning water 20 feet below.

Howie was nervous."It didn't look that high from down there."

"It never does," Vinny answered. "A lot of things look different when you're on top. Maybe better. The widow's walk on our house back there, and the Legion Hall. Even Heartbreak Island looks sort of happy. It's all...I don't know...peaceful. Wish we could just stay here. This is my favorite spot on the whole island. I used to climb up here with Danny Giardello at night. We'd moon the cars, just catching the top of their head lights. Always said we'd sleep up here. Never figured out how...We gotta do that when I get back from wherever they send me. The three of us."

They sat down on the aging metal girders and patiently waited for the bus-that-comes-when-it-wants-and-doesn't-when-it-doesn't, all well aware that these fun times might prove to be their last days together.

Gene had spoken little, and that was hard for Howie to take.

"You think we're gonna get in trouble for stealin' the MPs' car, Gene?"

"Nah, Vinny can commandeer anything he wants. He's a new-minted lieutenant."

"Hey, being a non-com is good, too," countered Vinny. "Besides, you worked your way up before they were giving rank out to just about anyone who looked good in khaki. I walked in. They took one look at this face." He poped his lips. "Bang! They offered me a commission right on the spot. Can you blame 'em? I tell ya, Uncle Sam knows what he's doing. I bet I get picked for one of those recruiting posters."

"It has nothing to do with 'working your way up," answered Gene. "It's ...It's...Forget it."

But Howie couldn't. "What's wrong with being a lieutenant?"

Gene didn't respond. Finally Vinny supplied the answer.

"Gene thinks they get picked off first. If you're aiming to pot-shot somebody, you aim at the officers, and the lieutenants are always out there with their men. But I don't intend to be a second lewey for long. I'm moving up fast. Probably even before I get over there. So don't you worry. And Gene, remember I can pull rank. So suffer."

"It was Pop who wanted the officer in the family," Gene added. "I told you not to do it. Why didn't you listen? Why didn't you just listen to me for once? If I knew you weren't going to listen, I would have...I would have..."

"You would have what, Gene? Gone to OCS yourself?"

"At least Pop would have got the officer he wanted."

"And that was supposed to do what? Take the pressure off of me?"

"Yeah...I don't know...You just shoulda listened better, Vinny."

The older brothers had run out of words. Howie had to fill them in.

"Don't die, Vinny. Promise?"

"I have no intention of dying, but I can't promise anything for sure, kid. I could tell you I promise, but then if that promise gets broken, you'd only be that much madder at me. But I'll do my best. Okay? I'll keep my head down. Hey, I'll be a captain soon and before you know it my guys will be calling me..." He popped his lips again. "...the old man."

Howie didn't like that answer. "You ain't even old."

"But you gotta promise me something back, Howie."

"What?"

"In case things go wrong, and in case my best's not good enough...You know, just in case I...I don't make it back, then you gotta be there for me."

"How?"

Howie waited while Vinny composed himself. They had just talked about the most serious subject brothers could talk about. He wondered what could possibly make him hesitate after that. Vinny's words came slower now.

"You got to tell Lillian. You're the one. I don't want somebody outside the family handing her a yellow piece of paper and taking off. I need you to be there, to do this. Will you do this, Howie?... For me?"

"I...I...told Mr. Nakamura that I can't do it no more. I can't."

"Do it Howie, for me."

Gene's words brought them to their feet as he pointed toward the mainland side of the road. "Here she comes!"

The bus bore down on the shaky bridge.

Motion in the metal caught Joe the Bus Driver's eye as he approached. He always slowed down when crossing the aged span, almost always. This time he was taken by surprise. He looked up to be greeted at eye level by three bare butts. In an instant he was passed them and tried to check his rear view mirror to validate what might have been an early morning illusion. The bus wobbled, and he turned back to his task at hand: running the length of City Island, turning around at the Legion flagpole and getting back to the mainland without hitting a Pete the Dog wannabe. In his mirror, he caught the vibrating reflection of three butt blurs on the shaky bridge swaying to and fro' behind him.

The girder dwellers laughed with excitement. The discussion of a minute ago was lost, and triumphant joy over a meaningless act reigned supreme. They threw their trunks out into the inlet, cheering in their nakedness, masters of their world. Joining hands, the trio hung 25 toes over the girder's edge.

"The Flying Bare Ass Logan Brothers!" cheered Vinny.

With a laugh and a look, they launched themselves into the abyss, sucking in all the oxygen they could consume, then disappeared into the blue water below.

They plunged deep into their liquid world, staying under as long as possible. Howie's saxophone lungs easily held the most air. He relished the idea of outlasting his lifeguard brothers, and he outlasted them by a lot. They were alive in the land of "before". Here, nothing mattered. Nothing would ever change.

The current had grown unusually strong overnight, and when they rose to the surface they found themselves already carried under the bridge. Even these three seasoned swimmers had to fight to find calmer water on the structure's other side.

*The high tide would be especially dangerous today.*

Howie dove down and watched through underwater eyes, three guys just having fun.

This was a good thing. This was a good day.

# CHAPTER 38
# THE SACRED CHARGE
# JULY 8, 1942

The lead team designated to set up the tables and chairs for today's wedding consisted of Lubisch and Antonsic. Lubisch had delayed his trip to D.C. as long as feasible just to see two Island children wed. He had watched them grow through the changing seasons, and now it was time for the harvest.

The exhausted sounds of Ivory's bloody fingers crawling across the keyboard caressed their ears as the two men opened the Legion's front door. Stevie was asleep on the floor in a contorted position. At first, they thought old Ivory was drunk as he swayed before the piano, but as they approached, it became obvious that he had replaced the external drink of rye with the internal taste of devastation. Lubisch interrupted the melody.

"Ivory, it's time to go home."

The piano player lifted his head like a man who had lost all track of time and was looking for the sun to establish the approximate hour of the day or the length of the night.

"Is the sun up?"

"Yeah, for a couple of hours now."

"The kids still here?"

"Just Stevie. He's sleeping."

"Let him be. I gotsta get home and clean up. I be playing the big weddin' today, ya know."

"I'm sure they'd understand if you don't want..."

Ivory cut Lubisch off. "Them Logans is the only-est thing I gots close to family now. There ain't nobody left, but I s'pose you heard that."

"I'm sorry about Corey. Do you need anything?"

"Yeah, maybe when this whole thing be over, you and me, we can sit down at the bar, have us a drink and talk a bit. That'd be nice. Just two old fools who lost their families, with nobody left for them to bury, and with nobody left to bury them."

"I think I'd like that, Ivory. Yeah, I'd like that a lot. Come on. I'll walk with you."

Lubisch helped Ivory to his feet and pointed him toward the door, but Ivory hesitated.

"Ya know, I gots this telegram what Howie brought me. It's a precious piece of my life now. I wants you to do somethin'. Sit with me a spell."

Ivory lifted his substitute cane out of its old gun holster on the side of the piano. Lubisch guided him across the room, finding two stools at the bar.

"You can't go around with this broom handle forever. Let me buy you a new cane."

"No. This'll do just fine for now. 'Cause someday the 'cane-taker' gonna be the 'cane-giver'. If'n the cane come from some-body else, well then the circle be broken. It ain't about the cane. It's about the circle."

"Ivory, you know your words are always honey to my ears, but when they come out in riddles like this, they give me a headache. How long you been up?"

"Makes no nevermind...Now I'm not a will-makin' man. Never was. Never thought I would be. You got a will, Lubisch?"

"Yeah. I got a will. I got lawyers makin' wills for me that I don't even know I have. My will's probably even got a will. I know my lawyer's got a lawyer."

"Don't think I ever met a lawyer. Leastways, not one that would fess up to it in a church meetin'. But tonight I had a heap of time to think, maybe too much time. Thinkin' 'bout Corey brought me to some speculatin' 'bout my own mortal remains. I want you to write 'em down for me, right on the back of this here telegram. Write 'em, and I'll make my mark at the bottom."

Ivory carefully entrusted the paper to Lubisch. Howie's small blood stains from when he had tumbled off his bike marbleized the envelope, but a rub of Lubisch's thumb testified the spots were dry.

When Ivory had completed his dictation, and Lubisch had written it all down, Ivory made a small X on the paper. Lubisch framed it with "His" above the X and "Mark" below. To the left of the X, he wrote "Ivory" and to the right "Keys". He witnessed and dated the document. Ivory spit in his hand and waited until Lubisch realized he had to do the same. After they shook hands, Ivory kissed the paper, refolded it into the envelope and put it in his breast pocket.

From behind the counter, Antonsic looked down to find Mungo silently staring up at him. Antonsic motioned with his head toward the flagpoles by the double glass doors. Mungo fetched the American flag and held it at attention behind Lubisch, awaiting further orders. Antonsic respectfully removed the old bugle from the wall, dusted it off with a bar rag and stood it in front of Lubisch, letting him know it was time to go.

Half an hour later, Lubisch led a single-file, Pied Piper's parade toward the sandlot. He carried a large canvas sack hanging from his shoulder and a shovel under his arm. In back of him, Mungo marched holding the American flag on a staff a little too heavy for him to handle, followed by Kim juggling a baseball mitt, a small book and the bugle. Next came Howie and Stevie, strung out with a ladder stretched between them. Finally, Antonsic hefted a three-foot-long wooden sign and a few tools.

The odd looking marchers halted at home plate. Stevie moved the cardboard and dug a two-foot-deep hole, making sure he stopped before hitting water.

Howie and Kim held the ladder and passed up material to Antonsic. When his mounting job at the top of the back-stop was complete, they stepped away to admire his work: a gold-lettered sign, facing the street, proclaiming "Charlie O'Reilly Ball Field".

Gathering to surround the hole, they stood quietly, waiting for someone to speak. Kim stepped forward.

"If Ivory was here, he'd say some words that would make us wanna sing and cry all at the same time. And whatever he'd say would be better than what we could do, and then he'd play some sad music. But he ain't here, so all we got is Howie."

As Mungo dipped the flag slightly, Kim handed the bugle to Howie. He had played this instrument before, but not well. Ivory had delegated that duty to him five weeks ago, on May 30th, for the traditional Decoration Day ceremony at the flagpole. Ivory's cigarettes had taken their toll, and he no longer had the wind power required for the task. Howie had to spit in the bugle to coax a sound. Reeds were so much easier for him than no-valve brass. He held it to his lips and blew the few C, E, G notes of "Taps". It wasn't his best work, and when he finished, he looked around to see if it had been acceptable.

"I coulda done better on the sax."

"You did just fine," lied Lubisch.

Mungo elevated the flag back to its full height. Kim stepped forward again, holding the mitt like a food tray.

"We're here today, to bury Magic Maggie. She's a good mitt. She never let Charlie down, took him all the way to the pros. He got her new and broke her in just right. So get ready, Charlie, 'cause here she comes."

Howie traded her the bugle for the mitt. He spoke to the hole.

"This is your mitt, Charlie. She's 'the kind'. You gave her to me, but she ain't really mine. I've just been holdin' her for you. I never played so good 'til I put her on. But no matter how good she makes me look, I can't get her to work her magic like she worked it for you. Even Magic Maggie ain't takin' me to the pro's so I'm givin' her back. You're gonna need her for your games up there, more than we do down here...And we know you're up there 'cause you gave more than you took. And that's all any man can ask for."

He glanced over at Kim and added, "*That's* what Ivory woulda' said."

She smiled agreement, then motioned toward the hole.

"Go ahead, Howie. Put her in."

Howie stepped to the hole, knelt down and gently laid Magic Maggie to rest. Then he pointed his rabbit foot toward the hole and gave it a few good luck rubs. Stevie shoveled the dirt on top and smoothed over the surface, stamping it down for good measure. Lubisch opened his book.

"I'm going to do what I do best, read. Here's the words to what Howie played.

Day is done. Gone the sun.

From the lakes, from the hills, from the sky.

All is well. Safely Rest. God is nigh.

Sleep in peace, comrades dear.

God is near."

Lubisch dumped the contents of his sack. Out spilled four used, but professional looking bases. He distributed them, and the three older members of the squad ran to their respective positions, placing the bases at first, second and third. By the time they returned, Lubisch and Antonsic had successfully pushed home plate's stake into the ground, above Maggie's resting place. While Howie and Kim were impressed, and Mungo just grinned, Stevie belched out his amazement about this new addition to the field.

"They look like the real McCoy! Where'd you get 'em from, with the war on and everything?"

"They're old practice ones from the Stadium," answered Lubisch.

"Wow! You mean the Yankees stepped on this? The real Yankees?"

Lubisch began to laugh. "Yes, Stevie. Even Joe DiMaggio. Maybe someday he'll come and sign. Who knows?"

"Boop-boop-a-doop! I'm sitting here all day! Right on home plate. Sleepin' here tonight, too. How 'bout you, Howie?"

"Can't. Got a wedding. Remember? And you're playin' drums, too...if Ivory shows up."

A few hours later, above the general store, Kim knelt before her Buddha shrine. She wore the only good dress she owned. Her mother had specifically bought the yellow polka dot frock with small padded shoulders and cut just below the knee, for today's wedding before leaving for her "short trip" to California. But that was one of several Kim-things that had not worked out for her. Incense rose in a stream around her pinned up hair.

*So what if I don't got Columbia. I don't need wheels. I'm the fastest runner on this island. I could do it...Yeah, the next time we get a telegram, I'm the messenger.*

She lifted the new Western Union hat from the floor, wafted the incense around it and placed it on her head, the only logical alternative to putting her father in harm's way.

After Howie had left her at the baseball diamond, he also went home to change into his good clothes. Next, he headed to Ivory's bungalow for one purpose: to find out if Ivory was coming to church, preferably on time, preferably sober, but right now that last one was optional.

The sleepless musician was already following his broom handle toward the chapel. Seemed like his good cane used to travel faster. His head was down and his feet dragged a little but he still had direction. Howie's voice slid in beside him.

"You okay?"

"Do I look okay?"

"You look like...You look bad."

"I look like I feel. Like I was s'posed to die a piece ago, but was too ill to meet the obligation."

"Yeah. That's about it."

"I cain't find 'the face', boy. With my Corey joinin' all his boys, goin' south like that, I just cain't find that 'gig face' no more."

"You don't hafta come."

"If I don't go, I gonna crawl in a one-way hole and pull a rock in behind me. Maybe I wake up, and this all be one big dead-ass dream. Or maybe I don't wake up at all. But then, this ain't no turtle-stuck-in-the-mud dream. Is it?"

"No. It's just what we got."

"Life's a bitch, Howie. And she throwin' all kinds of shit in our rows. You and me, we either gotsta plow through, or get plowed under. So hitch your mule up another notch, boy. This ain't gonna be no hay ride. Giddyup. We mourn tomorrow."

"But Corey was your son and you don't hafta..."

"We mourn tomorrow. Corey'd be sayin' that hisself if he was here. Maybe he is. We mourn tomorrow."

"Is there anything I can do for you?"

Ivory's slow-walking feet stopped.

"Yeah...I've been thinkin' a lot about the tomorrows. And I come up with the goods and the bads of it all. When I pass, there be one good thing happenin'. Nobody gotsta notify nobody, 'cause now I'm the last of the last. No death messenger lookin' at nobody. And no shock-face lookin' back. That's a big worry-weight off my mind. But then since I got no someones left behind, I got no buryin' person to look after these earthly remains. So, I conjured up two things. First, you wanna play ball instead of playin' the sax, then you go ahead and follow that dream, wasteful as it be, or else you gonna turn into some old dried-up, lookin'-back raisin-man, all mean spirited and sour souled. And second, I want you to take this here telegram sayin' what to do with me after the passin', right there on the back. And you be the one what gotsta do it. Only you and your own self."

Ivory pulled out the telegram with Lubisch's writing, still pressed against his heart. By now, the red stained envelope was starting to crease. He felt the folds and stopped to smooth them out before relinquishing it to his companion.

"You put this sacred charge in a special, safe place 'til my passin' come."

"But why me, Ivory? I'm a kid."

"You more man than most I know, and some I done forgot. You been to a place where few real men go, and fewer come back whole. You just ain't figured it out yet, but I be lookin' in your soul, and I know that you got the pluck."

Howie felt nervous about removing the last connection between father and son.

"I don't think I can take this envelope, Ivory. It's addressed to you. It's kinda like takin' *back* a telegram instead of *deliverin'* a telegram. I don't think Western Union lets us take 'em back. Anyways...I quit the job."

"You don't quit that job, boy, and that job don't quit you! 'Cause you *is* the job. After that first one...that Danny one...that be inside you forever. All them telegrams and all them mamas' looks and even old Ivory. We be stuck in there, in your heart and in your soul, and you gotsta live with that for the rest of your life. You cain't get away from it no matter how far you run or how fast you ride... or how big that hidin' tree grow. And you is the only-est one on this island who gots the pluck to do it. So, yeah, you *say* you quit. But the sayin' and the doin' is a wishin' world apart. Now take the damn telegram."

"But there's Western Union rules."

"This ain't the *rules* time! It's the *doin'* time! This here only be a little piece of paper with some scrawny scratchin' on it. Here. See how light it be? It ain't nothin'. So don't be a'scared. It only gonna weigh what you want it to weigh...Besides, you owe me."

"For what?"

"For lyin'."

That did it. Howie reluctantly tucked the telegram away. They headed for the chapel.

"You trust me with this?" Howie asked.

"I do."

Howie summoned up his nerve. He ran through the litany of the last seven days. He had been beaten up three times, shoved a firecracker into a kid's mouth, kissed a girl, run one brother's underwear up a flagpole, then hocked the other brother's wooden leg, played music for money, peed into the wind with a bowl on his head, swallowed hard liquor at the Legion Hall, buried a dog, stolen a car from an armed MP, mooned a bus driver, jumped naked off a bridge, stepped foot on the sandlot during the second game, escaped being eaten by a hungry Mortuary Man and delivered death notices to the innocent of the Island. A week ago he would have cringed at any one of these thoughts, but this was an extraordinary week. It made the next task look so simple. He spit it out.

"Then how come you don't trust me enough to tell me about your eyes?"

On any other day Ivory would have laughed at his courage, and kept his mouth shut. But not today. By the time they reached the chapel, Howie would know more than he wanted to know, and be sorry he had ever asked.

# CHAPTER 39

# THE POKEY BOYS

# JULY 8, 1942

*Now this be one long bunch of words that I never 'spected to hear my lips set free. It ain't a sharin' story. And Howie didn't need nobody else's number two problems stuck inside that number one head of his.*

*Still I figure I owes him somethin'.*

*So I baptizes him into this brung-down story fit for a brung-down week. And Lord knows, this was the worst of weeks that ever there was on this watery little dirt freckle we all called home.*

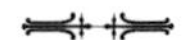

As Howie came in sight of the chapel, he felt Ivory take his arm. This in itself was unusual since Ivory took pride in his independence, and Howie sensed the uniqueness of the moment.

The old man had never spoken about his eyes. Over the years, both adults and children had put forth endless speculations as to how Ivory lost his sight, and if, in fact, he really was blind. He had wanted his story to die with him, but now he would be bonded with this boy-man messenger for the rest of his life. Maybe longer.

When Ivory's cane tapped the stone bench facing Irma's graveyard statute, he sat down. Howie sat beside him. Ivory cleared his throat, then unfolded his tale like a parable, even calling Howie by his name, and not just "boy" or "son".

"One mad-hot night when I was still a seein' boy just your age, Howie, I found myself by a window at a big elegant house sittin' in the middle of a green valley. There before these very eyes was a young naked white woman playin' the most beautiful thing I ever could imagine...a piano. A beautiful, candle-lit piano. I tried to count the keys, but got lost in the magic of the music. The only piano I'd ever seed 'afore was one my Pa drawed in the dust of our Road To Nowhere. I was in love, hypnotized and fixed to that spot. The greatest hope I had in my so-far life was to see, touch, even embrace a real piano. It was what I lived for, and here it be, just a spec more'n a gotcha-length away. If ever my fingers truly danced on them keys, nothin' else in this world would'a been left for me to want.

"I sat and I squatted, and I watched till I seed small beads of sweat slippin' off of that young missus' face, fallin' down onto them keys. I wished that I could be just one of them wet drops, brushin' the ivory for the first time, even though I would fail to make the slightest of sounds. Time folded into time as I breathed the music in. Pretty soon, I heard my own little voice startin' to make it's own little throat throbs to match them piano keys, just like my Pa taught me. I couldn't control it and I believe that was my undoin'.

"I never heard the steps behind me. I never heard them cusses as a crashin' blow struck across the back of my skull. I never felt myself being drug away by my feet. And I never knowed them drunken wretches what cussed at me, as they buck-tied my limp boy-body to the big grindin' stone in the plantation mill.

"When I waked up, they had my britches down and a long-knife blade to my privates. Hamstrung or not, I shook with all my fearsome might to break free. My wiggles meant nothin' to those two men fixin' to amuse themselves at my expense.

"'God almighty! If it ain't still alive!' I heard the red-headed one laugh.

"His pig-faced friend with the thick hands sucked down a long drink from a corn jug, then spat a line into my face. My eyes burned, and I screamed, 'Pa!'

"Red hit me across the face with a stick or a pole or maybe a length of rope, and I tasted a trickle of blood in my mouth.

"Fat laughed and shared a second stream of corn liquor with my eyes. He was yellin', 'Some-bitch nigger don't know 'nuff to keep his mouth shut.'

"Red scratched the blade across my thighs 'til a thin blood-leak hit the mill stone. He start laughin', 'You like goobers, boy? 'Cause you 'bout to swallow two of 'em.'

"I shuddered at the slice of the cold steel across my hot skin and screamed again. Red hit me hard, and I begin to dazin'. Every ounce of energy inside my beaten body tried to stay awake, tried to break free. Fat leaned in close, his stanky breath smothering mine.

"'You scared boy? You look like you scared. Rightly so, I 'spect. You never be lookin' at no nekid white woman again.'

"Red scratched his scraggy beard. 'Hold on there. Maybe we workin' the wrong end, 'cause his eyes still gonna be seein' what they seein'.'

"The truth in Red's statement must'a dawned on Fat.

"'You right. Give me that pokey stick, there.'

"Fat took his time sharpening the wood to a fine point, enjoying the useless whittlin' craft that it musta took him decades to perfect. Finally, he smiled at Red. 'Hold the boy still.'

"I screamed one hellacious scream, 'No! Please mister! Let me be! Let me go home!'

"Red near tore my ears off as he pinned my head back against that mill stone.

"I felt the pierce of pains that no man nor boy should be made to endure. Fat drove that stick down into my eye as easy as if he was pokin' some bug to his little bug end. He pushed into my other eye as simple as pushin' some nameless dust off a nameless shelf. I screamed the scream that lived somewhere else, but not inside me. I screamed for my Pa, tryin' to imagine him comin' down from The Road To Nowhere. Comin' to save me.

"I screamed for my Pa, and I swear I felt his strong hand take hold of my small one in some mystical, mysterious way, reachin' out to save me. But it weren't so.

"My father wasn't there when I was 12.

"Two house boys heard my fussin', and early the next mornin' they come lookin' for the source of that discomfortin' sound. They cut me down and carry me inside. A woman in the kitchen tell me, 'Don't go frettin' child, 'cause I gonna be your savin' woman.' And she was. She commenced to do her work, pullin' that pain outta me and somehow gatherin' it into her own self.

"Fat and Red must'a thought better of what they done 'cause they was long gone from the farm even 'afore I was discovered and brung in to that servin' kitchen. And they took two of mister's best riding horses with 'em.

"When missus found out, she had me washed and sent for my Mama. And like I told you before, bein' a messenger, bringin' such bad news, is a weightful bag of bones. This messenger, he went up that hill a boy, but he come down near a man.

"While she was waitin' on my Mama, the missus looked me over and sighed, 'Boy, you brought a heap of hurt on this house, but that ain't nothing compared to the lifetime of sorrowful grief ahead of you. Why'd they do this fearsome thing?'

"'Cause I spied on you,' I says.

"'You spied on me?'

"'Yes, 'um. I was crouched down like a jumpy frog outside your window. And I spied on you.'

"'Like a jumpy frog.'

"'Yes, 'um.'

"'And what was I doing?'

"'You was playin' the piano, naked as a new bore'd babe. I just wanted to see the piano, is all. I meant no harm nor disrespect.'

"Well, I guess they didn't see it that way.'

"I could hear my savin' woman gasp at the words that slid over my blood-caked lips. The missus, she left to send for the mister, and for the sheriff. The savin' woman what took me in, whispered in my ear.

"'Don't never tell that naked talk to nobody again, son, or you be losin' more'n just the light of day. Now we could all be in trouble, now that the sheriff be comin'. Anytime the sheriff be comin', there be hell to pay.' Then she say, 'What be your name, boy?' I just wanna say 'Boy' 'cause that's all the name I got. But 'Boy' stay hushed up inside, and 'Ivory Keys' come out instead.

"And she say, 'What kinda name be that? One of them African names?' I says, 'No, M'am. It just be me." But she don't believe, and she announce that she gonna call me 'Blind Boy', instead, 'cause she don't want no African names 'round her inside servin' kitchen, nor even her outside cook house neither.

"The mister come in after a bit, and I could hear the hush of him starin' down at me. Finally, his shoes shuffled back toward the door, but he stopped and mumbled to himself, 'Damn...Damn. Damn. Damn. Those be two fine horses.'

"The next persons to arrive, sometime in the afternoon, was the sheriff and the doctor-man who poked rough 'round my face for a bit, then put a new bandage 'cross my eye places and mix me up some medications and elixers. The sheriff, he asked me questions 'bout what I be doin' round the big house, down from the hill at night all by my lonesome. But I remembered what my savin' woman said, so I keeped my mouth shut and my ears open. The sheriff go mumblin' to himself and walk away none too satisfied.

"'Should've just tied this boy up to a whuppin' tree and laid his back open. Would'a saved us all a shitload of trouble. Now I gotsta go lookin' for them two pony boys. And I hope for all our sakes that they be long rode out of Lumpkin County, Georgia.'

"They was.

"When my Mama got to the servin' kitchen, she held me, and she cried. I could feel her tears on my cheeks mixin' with my own, ebbin' into that new rag bandage.

"'I'm sorry Mama. I'm sorry.'

"'Hush, now, sweetness. We goin' home.'

"And we did, Mama leadin' my blind body through the smell of that sweet grass, up into the pines, stoppin' every sometimes just to hold each other. By the time I sensed we was gettin' close to The Road To Nowhere, I knew that I was but useless to my Mama from that day on. 'Ceptin' she ain't seed it that way.

"I tells her, 'I cain't do nothin' to help us now, Mama. I cain't even work the mule. What are we gonna do 'til Pa git home?'

"Well, Mama didn't want to talk that talk. Ignorin' my recent state, she shook me 'round like she was churnin' butter, and there be nothin' wrong with my body. I was scared.

"'You stop feelin' sorry for yourself, Boy! It's a poor broom what gots but one straw. You'll find other ways of livin' that you never knew was there. Some blind people even gets this special power. They gets so they can see without seein'. Yes, yes. Right into another man's soul, and that's a heapful of responsibility. Now, you gonna fall down a lot. I ain't about to lie. But don't ever let me see you get up empty handed. You understand me?'

"I nodded my head 'yes' but had no idea what she was ravin' 'bout.

"Finally, my feet found the dry ruts of The Road To Nowhere. I pressed that Georgia clay against my cheek, and its warmth kissed me home. The porches, the old folks and the children all come to life, watchin' me, right in my mind.

"One day soon after, the missus her-own-self appeared on The Road. She didn't have no matching grays pullin' no high wagon, and she didn't come for to pick no magnolias. She come for to pick me.

"All the folks gathered on their sorry-ass porches to see such a fine-dressed lady walk the ruts. From their sighs and gasps, it must have been a vision to behold, her petticoats hiked up to her knees, my savin' woman shooin' the goats and children out of her way. By consensus of most seein' souls in attendance, it created one of the all-time great pictures in the history of history.

"She stopped at our door, and I felt the savin woman's healin' hands brush across my eyelids. I heard Mama invite the missus in. I wished so much that I could have seed her with her clothes on, gussied in her finery, standin' on *my* Mama's porch! I was smilin' proud for Mama. I knew that the folks would all be waitin' and watchin', and they be rememberin' the day that the missus climb the hill to pay respects to *my* Mama. I was damn proud.

"Mama and the missus repaired inside and commenced negotiations. I could hear some of their talk.

"'He'll be of little use to you in the house or in the field. But from what I've been told, he has quite a proclivity for music.'

"'That he does.'

"'Then I'll take him off your hands.'

"'The valley is a place of temptation and nowhere for a boy who cain't see.'

"'I'll be his eyes, and I'll teach his hands.'

"Mama thought for a long spell.

"'Only 'til his Pa git home. Then we'll see.'

"'And I'll send up a basket of food twice or thrice a week to make up the loss of his works.'

"'Agreed,' said Mama and she spit in her palm. I cain't be sure but I think I heard the missus spit too, and I was sold on a handshake, as simple as that. Sold for a basket of food, twice or thrice a week. I don't know who felt more guilty: the missus for what had happened to me, or Mama for what she was about to do. I was took to the big house in the green valley, and thereby strange and wondrous things transpired.

"I passed the summer with my fingers on those ivory keys, the last thing that I had seed 'afore my ordeal. The missus taught me every day to touch the smooth surfaces that sung back to me like magic. And even though my savin' woman still call me 'Blind Boy', I become known to all the other farm folk, black or white, as 'Ivory Keys'.

"Finally, when the days grew shorter, my father come to fetch me. He had a long parlay with the mister. Then he grasp me tight to his chest, kissed my forehead and he walk right off by his own-self. I couldn't believe that he wasn't takin' me with him, and my heart fairly sank down within my belly. I thought maybe he don't want me no more 'cause I got the blindness. Then 'bout a fortnight later, he come ridin' up on one of mister's fine horses with the second hitched behind. How he got 'em, he wouldn't say, but just like when he'd backtrack home with a squirrel or a fox, the smell of death was on him. I bumped up close to my savin' woman, and I whispered did she smell that, too. But she say, 'You don't smell nothin, Blind Boy, and you keeps your mouth shut.' And I did.

"While the mister thanked Pa for the return of them two animals, the missus leaned into my ear.

"'Play your best piece.'

"When I heard their footsteps approachin', I played my ultimest *Beautiful Dreamer.* I played it good, and when I finished, nobody said nothin'. I waited and listened, and it was plain quiet. I think somebody was cryin', and I was afeared that it might be my Pa. I'm mighty sure it was. I didn't know what to do, then my fingers started movin' and I was playin' *Camptown Races* and *Get Out the Way Ole Dan Tucker!*, and my mouth was hootin' and clickin' and singin' the words! When I finish, he scoop me up and kiss me! And we cried a real good cry.

"I knew right then, and I knew right well that I was forever a man of music. I was a piano playin' man.

"When it come 'round to leavin', everybody ask my Pa to let me stay, but he say it time for me to learn the circuit. Pretty soon, all the folks be wavin' at us, and my savin' woman, she be makin' a prayer and brushin' her hand over me like a wand in the air. She hug me and and say so loud that everybody listen up.

"'Farewell, Ivory Keys!'

"Now Pa, I felt him puff himself up proud, 'cause he know that I found a name fit to grow with me for a hundred years.

"My savin woman, she take a leather cord from 'round her neck, and she drape it 'round mine. I let my hand run down that thin line to find a rabbit's foot hangin' at the bottom. She hold my face and whisper her breath into my soul.

"'You had a run of bad ju-bob, Ivory Keys. Take this here good luck foot, and don't let nobody steal it or they be grave cursed like a walkin' dead man. You gonna need all the luck you can git. This here foot be a new one, so maybe it don't got all its juice up yet, but you just wait 'cause it grow stronger as it age. May you do the same.'

"Then she rest her hands over my eye places, whisperin' some words that I don't ken, but maybe they be African words after all. She kiss me and send me on my way.

"Pa led me home, but even the smell of the high sweet grass could not replace the scent of death around him. Maybe it was the blindness workin', but I smelled that smell for sure. Finally, by the time we reached The Road To Nowhere, I could contain myself no longer. I knew better than to ask questions, but I failed to heed my own advice. Stoppin' right in the middle of the rut, I turned as if I could look at him and said, 'Did you kill those two men, Pa?'

"He put his big hand on my shoulder, and his deep molasses voice roll out slow.

"'I told 'em I was fixin' to bring two animals back with me... them or the horses. They chose the horses.'

"His hand slid down to my hand, and we held on tight as we walked the last walk home. Him in his rut. Me in mine. Him in his world. Me in mine. And we spoke of it no more.

"That winter, my father took me away to ride the circuit and learn the life. And since that summer, Howie, I ain't never played dust piano again...And that's how I got the blindness."

Howie couldn't respond. He wrapped his arms around Ivory and hugged him. No one had hugged the old man since Corey left for the war. Now, Howie had a number two problem imbedded in his head, and it could never be solved. He was glad that Ivory had seen fit to pass on his history and allow him to share his pain, and he hated it all at the same time. Howie silently walked away, toward the water. He could always count on going to Ivory when he felt this way, but today that wouldn't work.

He got as far as the grass at the cemetery's edge, laid down and spread his arms to study his old friends, the clouds, but this morning the sky was clear and blue. Even the purest of white, puffy shapes had been chased away by the death of innocence in Ivory's story.

Reaching into his suit pants pocket, he pulled out the old rabbit's foot and examined it with a new reverence. He could even envision the long lost leather strap that had supported it around the young Ivory's neck. He closed his eyes and rubbed the worn fur against his cheek, until the vibrant sound of Ivory's hands pressing down the chapel's organ keys brought him to his feet.

He brushed himself off and headed inside the church. His brothers were already there.

## CHAPTER 40

# THE WEDDING

## JULY 8, 1942

Father Aiello had arrived at the chapel early that morning to prepare for today's ceremony, anxious to get these two troublesome nuptial candidates off his hands. Chances of it going smoothly were slim.

A head popped up from the rear pew. Bad Bill wore a stubbly beard and tired eyes as he hefted his pillow and headed out the door.

Hardly turning around, Father Aiello called an unfazed, "Good morning, Bill," but was answered with a chorus of coughs, grunts and an unintelligible word or two. Bill shaded his eyes from the glare as he hit the sunlight, belching and scratching his way toward the black top circle.

An hour later, still carrying his pillow, Bill stepped off the-bus-that-knew-no-schedule at big Fordham Road in the Bronx. He dragged himself into the 24-hour Empire State Pawn Shop and let the door slam behind him. But, just as quickly, it opened again. Bill stepped out to stare at the shop's front window display of canes, crutches and an artificial leg. His breath fogged the window as he stuck his nose against the glass.

As the sun got higher, it found Howie standing at his post inside the chapel entrance, looking in the direction of the general store. His only suit fit better before the war, and he pulled his jacket sleeves down, trying to stretch them out.

Ivory had poured out a full bowl on their morning walk, and Howie had a lot to digest. He had asked, and he had been answered. He realized that sometimes you *can* know more than you want to. But he also knew that he would have climbed that hill as the messenger, carrying the bad news to Ivory's mother, no questions asked. And he knew that, just as he did with all his telegrams, he would keep Ivory's story sealed.

But he felt the seal start to loosen as he caught a glimpse of Kim hurrying through the graveyard.

The Legion Hall and the general store would have a lot to discuss tonight. Earlier that day, a steady stream of bridal party friends had flowed in and out of the Legion, setting decorations, furniture and food at all the prearranged times and locations. It was a precision operation exactly the way Mom wanted it. Even Polcheck and the briefcase-less Ryan had been drafted for lifting and carrying, keeping their minds occupied as the hours ticked by.

Pop enjoyed Sergeant Polcheck's periodic rantings about the stolen car and the time delay. Their colonel would have to wait a little longer, but Pop's cover story would be well-rehearsed before they arrived in Washington late tonight or early tomorrow morning. Dunny Logan had adroitly sucked the MPs into the role of co-conspirators.

Howie heard Ivory's hands kiss the keys of the organ at the little church. They wanted to play the blues. They wanted to play *Sometimes I Feel Like a Motherless Child.* They wanted to hit all the minor chords and mourn. But they knew they had to pull themselves together, gig-face or no gig-face, and play a pre-bridal procession. Ivory found his fingers, and they responded, finding more keys in return.

Wildflowers decorated the altar, and white ribbons hung from the pews. Gene, in dress uniform with a bow on each crutch, waited patiently at the foot of the small altar as the best man should. Only, the groom was not by his side.

Howie felt a happy breeze flow through his head as he escorted Kim down the short aisle. He could not remember the last time he had seen her in a dress with her hair pinned up. A white scarf fulfilled the hair covering requirement. She looked so grown up overnight. Kim sat on the right, the Joseph-the-worker-statue side, where guests of the groom would go. The bride's family had appropriately positioned themselves to the left, on the Mary-statue side.

"Where's your father?" Howie asked.

"He ain't comin'."

The confessional curtain pulled back, and Vinny stepped out with an embarrassed grin. Father Aiello exited from behind his curtain, shaking his head in disbelief. By the time they reached the altar, Howie had already moved to Ivory's side at the rear of the chapel.

As he picked up his sax and wet his lips, he caught a glimpse of Uncle Bill and his wife rushing in, off to the side. He looked tired and needed a shave, but he was here. Howie promised himself that he would write Bill's name on the bottom of his shoe when he got home. That simple act had changed Stevie and would hopefully do the same for Bill. It could probably wait until tonight.

All eyes were glued on Vinny and Gene, simply because there was no bride to yet admire. Gene whispered to his brother as Mom, Pop and finally Lillian's mother came down the aisle.

"What *is* the matter with you, Vinny?"

"I can't help myself. I think it's hormonal. You remember what it was like between you and Teddy."

"It was *never* like that. Dogs in heat are never like that."

"I just hope I can get through the ceremony."

"Cold feet?"

"Hot rocket."

"Vinny, you got a serious problem. You need help."

"Yeah? Well you...you limp."

"I should be so lucky."

Vinny looked to the doorway, anxiously anticipating Lillian's arrival. He wiped his sweaty hands against his jacket pockets, felt something out of place and pulled out the white rabbit's foot.

"You put that in here?"

Gene gave him a who-do-you-think-I-am look. "Gotta be Howie."

Ivory interrupted the conversation as he began the wedding march with a flurry, and all rose turning toward the rear to see Teddy's nine-month pregnancy filling the entire doorway.

Gene whispered to Vinny," I might have to go help her."

"Oh, great. Then who's gonna help you?"

But Teddy portrayed the perfect wife, with perfect balance and a perfect smile. Behind her, Lillian and her father moved slowly forward. She: the radiant beam of light in Vinny's fun-filled world of conjugal fog. He: a necessary ornament by her side, expected to be ignored. And Vinny easily fulfilled his duty to mentally dispose of her father. His mind was only on Lillian, with the possible exception of a quick mini-stop back in the confessional.

Once her father had released Lillian with a kiss, the music stopped and her white gown floated up next to the groom. Father Aiello was ready to begin. But a glance at Vinny, sweating, red hands discreetly folded across a growing Mt. Vesuvius of a crotch, and he knew that action was required or he'd never finish. He moved close to Vinny and made the sign of the cross.

"Ego te absolvo in nomine patri..."

"Thanks, Padre. I owe you one. It's like we got this amazing mental thing going on between us, me and you." Vinny gave a wink, designed to get a chuckle out of the reverend. It didn't do its job. Lillian didn't give it a chance.

"Ah, Father, I can't go through with this. Not unless you give me one, too. You see, when I came down that aisle and just saw you there, Vinny, all I wanted to do was climb all over...Sorry, Father... But that would be sacrilegious, so..."

"Enough of this meshugenah nonsense!" erupted the priest. He took both their hands and administered an instant version of absolution. The assembled audience, somewhat familiar with the traditional Roman Catholic Latin wedding ceremony, looked at each other, perplexed. When he was finished, he put his arms around the bride and groom, pulling them in closer, and he whispered.

"There. I just absolved you *and* married you. It wasn't pretty, but it did the trick. Now you can think whatever you want, pure, impure or otherwise. I don't care, and I don't want to hear it. Understand? If you'll excuse me, I have to put on a show for these good people here, so sit down and shut up, or I'll put a curse on you."

Both bride and groom broke out in muffled laughter, much to the consternation of the assembly out of earshot. Vinny and Lillian sat down, but contrary to popular practice, the bride had to help the rotund matron of honor, and the groom had to help the unbalanced best man, eliciting a round of laughter from their well wishers.

Father Aiello drew himself up in front of his audience and pinned his temporary happy face back on. It was only a short-lived façade.

"Dearly Beloved, we are gathered here today to join this man and this woman in Holy Matrimony. These are truly unusual times in which we live, and just as unusual is the request that the bride and groom have asked me to make. They wish to dedicate this ceremony, not to each other, or to their parents, but to their life-long friends who cannot be here to celebrate with them today...Danny Giardello, U.S. Navy, killed in action..."

As he announced the name, Howie heard a gasp, and someone started to cry. He couldn't see who it was from his place at the back of the chapel, but he imagined Danny's mom wiping her eyes. She was here, as were many linked to those names on the death-grams that he had delivered. Their presence was expected, based on the long traditions of City Islanders mourning death and simultaneously rejoicing in life. There was a respectful pause before Father Aiello continued.

"Charlie O'Reilly, U.S. Marine Corps, killed in action..."

More tears. Howie had none left to give.

"Eddy Trent, U.S. Marine Corps, killed in action..."

Mrs. Trent's trembling hand automatically reached for her anchor, but Pete the Dog was no longer at her side.

"Corey Keys, U.S. Navy, killed in action."

Howie saw Ivory take a deep breath, then produce his small flask. He took a swig as Father Aiello concluded, "May the Lord have mercy on their souls."

This was met with a chorus of "Amens". As the priest started his next sentence, he was cut off by Ivory's raspy voice overrunning the pews and surrounding the altar. His organ music coincided with his vocals, and Howie spontaneously followed him on his sax.

"Amazing Grace
How sweet the sound
That saved a wretch like me.
I once was lost
But now am found,
Was blind,
But now I see."

# CHAPTER 41

# THE KISS

# JULY 8, 1942

Nakamura ceremoniously thumb-tacked a strand of his beautiful, virgin flypaper to the ceiling, but this time he only pulled out part of the sticky substance from the cylinder so it hung well above Howie's height. Satisfied with the day's culminating activity, he stepped onto the porch and settled comfortably into one of the well-worn high-backed green rockers. He still hadn't received his window glass order to heal the old general store's wounds inflicted by Bad Bill. Always on the low end, City Island's supply list had finally fallen off the desk of some nameless ration clerk ensconced in some nameless office, where he anonymously eliminated items, probably crossing them off with a bright red pencil.

Empty cars nestled along the road's edge. Music from Ivory's thrown-together band rolled out of the Legion Hall and crossed to Nakamura's ears. He had heard the old man's notes for the past 24 hours, with the exception of when Ivory left to play the organ at Vinny and Lillian's wedding. But Ivory's sleep deprived body was back now, and he brought his musical henchmen with him. His rag-tag band of musicians, including Howie and Stevie, somehow complimented each other's pluses and minuses, bringing forth a good sound.

Nakamura rocked and listened, missing the company of his old friend, Dunny, his worthy companion from a simpler time. He missed sailing the Sound at sunset, perfecting his English laced with Pop's contaminated second generation New York Irish accent. He missed pilfering Connecticut fishermen's lobster pods at two o'clock on a moonless morning without a light to betray them, and hoping they still had their fingers when they lifted the motley brown creature from his trap. But especially he missed the fun, silly and exciting days of the Banana Bandits, when life was raw, fed with the force of sheer nerve and electricity driving through their veins. And he missed imitating the swagger in Dunny's walk as they departed on the last escapades of their younger selves.

Nakamura knew that although they had done for each other in the past, and would do so again in the near future, the actions of their governments and their sons alike, would never allow them to so deeply intertwine their lives again. It left an emptiness in his chest. He grieved that he was growing old and his wife wasn't there to share it.

Inside the Legion, guests danced and drank until the music slowed to a stop. Stevie knew his drum rhythm had improved over his previous performance, and he rewarded himself by sideling to the bar, hoping to snag a beer. Ivory felt the sting in his overworked fingers, but his eyes could not see the small red streaks of his own blood that stained several keys before him.

A sheepish Bad Bill stood in the doorway. Next to him Cathleen crossed her arms, then elbowed Bill in the right direction. He straightened himself up and took a strong stride toward Ivory's piano, then leaned in close and produced his pawn shop purchase.

"Ivory, I bought you this here cane. It ain't exactly new, but it's better than that old broom handle you're usin'. And just so's you know, this ain't my idea. The only reason I'm doin' it is 'cause... well...Cathleen keeps kickin' me out, and man ain't meant to sleep in no church."

Bill removed the broom handle from the piano's holster and slid the "new" pawn-shop cane in its place. Ivory nodded to him, but the relative importance of a cane had been lost in the recently rewritten hierarchy of his life.

Bill stepped away with a "Sorry about your Corey."

He looked toward his wife who sent back her own look of approval.

Howie, with his suit jacket off and dress shirt sleeves rolled up, had already started outside to join Kim who appeared more like an isolated on-the-terrace guest, than an insulated in-the-kitchen worker. She sat on the edge of the railing, looking down at the dangerously swirling water. Although he and Stevie had perched there before, all that went through Howie's mind was: *That's not a good place for Kim to sit.* He'd never say that to her face. Instead he'd casually maneuver her to a little safer spot. Maybe a shoulder punch would do it. But when he executed the punch, it turned into a gentle touch instead, a touch that made her look around without being startled.

"Run out of excuses to stay in the kitchen?"

She greeted him back with, "I found Saint Donovan. It's your Pop."

"Even a dumb-ass like you should've figured that one out."

"Yeah."

"I said 'dumb-ass'."

Howie waited for a reaction.

"So?"

"Ain't you gonna punch me?"

"Grow up, Howie. That is so immature."

"*Im*-mature? You don't even know what *mature* means."

"Yeah? I'll tell you what mature means. Last year I was worried about havin' friends at school and what Sue Ellen said at lunch.

Now I'm thinkin' about life and death, and stuff like that. *That's* mature."

"So no punch, Kim? It would make me feel better."

"Alright, but no backs. No backs. No penny tax."

"Then forget it." He slid out of distance, hoping she would follow.

"You should get mature, Howie. I mean, you got everything goin' for you now. Think about it. Vinny's married. Gene's home. Pop's not in jail. And you're not deliverin' no more telegrams. Everything worked out just the way you wanted. So stop feelin' sorry for yourself. You got both parents, and your brother's a hero."

"It's not that."

"You got everything, Howie! Everything! What more do you want?!"

"I don't know...I see everybody doin' their jobs. Pop and Gene and Vinny, they're all fightin' this war. Even your dad, tryin' to keep food on the Island. I told him I'd do my duty like a brave soldier on the home front. Some brave soldier. You know why I walked out on the war?...'Cause it made me cry. I'm a jerk, right?"

"So it made you cry. So what? I seen you cry a million times, Howie. It don't make you a jerk. You're a jerk for a lot of *other* reasons, but cryin ain't one of 'em."

Kim turned her attention to the party-goers inside.

"Lots of happy faces laughin' now. Bet they're all gonna be cryin' before the war's over. Maybe you and me, too. Get used to it, 'cause that's our tomorrow. We can't stop it."

Howie could see his father talking to Sgt. Polcheck at the bar.

"I think I cried enough...There's somethin' I gotta tell you, Kim. And you can't tell nobody. Okay? My Pop's not arrested. He's workin' with those MPs, helpin' 'em find spies. He's a hero, like Gene and Danny and the guys who died, and like all the guys still fightin', like my brother Vinny and your brother Tatsu."

Kim turned away to hide her own tears that were crying to come out. She pretended to admire the calm evening scene of ships and the sea, but Howie knew this girl-woman before him well enough to cut right through her masquerade.

He put his hands on her shoulders and pulled her off the railing in time to see a solitary droplet wander aimlessly down from her dark eyes.

"Weddings get to you. Don't they?" he smiled, knowing it was more than that.

Kim came in and rested her head on his shoulder. For what she was about to say, she could not face even her best friend. Howie would have felt more comfortable with a punch, but accepted her closeness as second best.

"No, Howie. It's somethin' else, somethin' *I* gotta tell *you.* I've been tryin' to tell you for days and I still couldn't."

"You already told me I'm a dumb-ass, I'll never make the pros, and I'm goin' crazy. What's left?"

"It's Tatsu...The army that he joined..."

"Yeah?"

"It's...It's the Japanese army, Howie. The Japanese army! All along it's been Tatsu who's the traitor. Not your father. I didn't know 'til I read it in a letter he wrote to my dad. I figured people would leave us alone if they still thought he was in our army, fightin' for us. But he's not. He's trying to kill us! My own brother! All the time everybody thought your family had the traitor, and all the time it's been mine."

She got the words out through her emerging tears. Finally the thoughts of her brother's betrayal and her mother's internment, the anguish of shame and dishonor and suicide, all made sense to Howie. He had no words to make it better, so he just closed his eyes and held her tighter, listening to her quiet cry.

"But what about me, Howie? What about me? You saw how Bad Bill beat up my father. If anyone finds out about Tatsu, they'll kill my dad. I know it. I'll be left with no one, like Ivory and Mr. Lubisch and Mrs. Trent. No one! I don't want my dad to die."

She broke down and her words ran out. Howie felt her thin body heave against his, as if floodgates in her lungs were cracking open. He, too, had exhausted his words. He had wanted to tell her about Ivory's eyes. She had pushed him to find out the truth, but now that he knew it, he couldn't put that number two problem inside her already over-loaded, number one head. Maybe some day, but not today. Finally he whispered:

"It's gonna be okay. Come on, now. You got me, remember. I'd never let anybody kill your dad. I promise. You're not gonna be alone. We're always gonna be there for each other. Nobody else is gonna do it, so it's up to us to make each other laugh."

He rubbed his palms into her damp cheeks with a lame version of The Three Stooges: "Nyat, nyat".

She stared into his eyes and laughed through her tears.

"You're still my best friend, right Howie?"

Their lips were so close now that even the slightest motion, or maybe one more word would have made them meet.

"I may not be your true love, but I'll always be your best friend. Who cares if your brother is a stupid, dumb-ass traitor? He ain't you, and you ain't him."

An innocence inside them edged their lips together until they finally touched, weightlessly brushing across each other. In an instant the fleeting wisp was over. They had kissed a simple brief breath of a kiss that could not have been rehearsed on some movie sound stage nor written into a playwright's page. It was the kiss that gives adulthood and takes away youth in every one it touches. The moment their lips parted, they knew that they were children no more.

"I really am proud of you for what you did, Howie. Those telegrams and all. I know I told you before. But I am."

"Don't say that no more. You're gonna make me feel guilty for quittin'."

They held hands all the way back to the glass doors. Vinny and Lillian met them as they entered the noisy room. Vinny dangled the rabbit's foot in front of Howie's nose.

"I know you stuck this old thing in my uniform, Squirt, but I don't need any luck. 'Invincible Vinny', remember? Besides, I got Lilly now. She's my lucky charm."

The bride and groom laughed as Vinny shoved the rabbit's foot into Howie's shirt pocket.

## CHAPTER 42

# THE '40 PACKARD

## JULY 8, 1942

Earlier that morning, after the mourners had returned from the burial of Magic Maggie, and while the two unwilling MPs were helping to set up for the wedding reception, Pop had broken his word to them for the umpteenth time, slipping away to the small cemetery beside the chapel.

He found his mother's grave, just where Mom had indicated it would be. The flowers she had put on it a week ago were now brown and withered. Pop had picked a single fresh wildflower along the way. There was no headstone nor marker, and there would be none until Antonsic, the local jack of all arts, eventually finished another station of the cross and moved on to his next project. This one. Pop liked it that way. It was plain and it was private.

Lubisch rested on his ever-faithful stone bench by his wife's statue reading the morning's poetry. Pop slid down next to him, spinning the lone flower slowly between his fingers. Lubisch closed his book, admired the flower and couldn't resist offering an old quote.

"A rose by any other name would smell as sweet."

"It's not a rose. I think it's some kind of daisy," quipped Pop.

"It's the Bard, Dunny."

"No, it's not a bard, either. It's definitely a daisy."

"The Bard of Avon...Shakespeare!"

Pop broke into laughter as Lubisch reacted to his teasing.

"You're a rascal, Dunny Logan. Poking fun at an old man."

"Old man? Really? When I left, you could still take a joke. How old did you get, in six months? The war's ruined your sense of humor, Lubisch. War *is* hell."

"It seems like you've been gone a lifetime."

"Next time may be even longer. This war's only getting started. People don't know how bad it already is. Between you and me, in the last six months we lost almost 500 tankers and cargo ships to U-boats right along the coast. Germans even laid mines in Delaware Bay last month. Took out three freighters and a tanker. But the public doesn't know the numbers. Probably better that way...And I never said anything. Capisci, old man?"

"Capisco, Dunny."

"When you get to D.C., Lubisch, push for those sub-chasers. We have the yards to build them right here."

"It's on my list."

"Push hard. The German u-boats always attack at night and on the surface. These cities are so bright, they outline every ship perfectly, and the politicians are too afraid to impose a real blackout. I'm making waves but nobody's listening. When the officers replace the silk hats, you're gonna see a different war, a winning war...Thanks for keeping me informed about my family...and the lack of flypaper.

"My condolences for the loss of your mother. She was a strong woman."

Lubisch patted Pop on the knee and walked toward the Legion Hall.

After a few seconds Pop moved to Nana's grave. He spoke to no one. And no one listened. He laid the new flower across the dead ones and knelt down, his voice hovering just above a whisper, as if he were about to deal with a subject that he thought he had dismissed from memory forever.

"I know what Bill did, and I know what I have to do."

Pop looked around to make sure he was alone. The graveyard was still empty, at least on the surface.

"I used to shake when Bill would come home drunk, until the day I bid him *bon voyage.* I never looked back, never regretted it, until yesterday. Yesterday I knew I should have killed him instead of hitting him on the head and shipping him out...just like Cain and Abel. Cain always gets a bum rap, but he did what he thought he had to do. In the big book, that's gotta count for something."

Pop heard footsteps behind him. He looked up in time to see Polcheck and Ryan running along the dirt path, angry enough to give no quarter and take no prisoners. Obviously someone had squealed. Pop put his hands in the air, and surrendered.

But that had been early in the day and now the sounds of Ivory's band re-filled the Legion. Pop looked over at Mom, asking the question to which he already knew the answer.

"You sold me out this morning, didn't you? To the MPs."

"What if I did? You were too maudlin. Today is a day of joy. Mourn tomorrow."

Pop smiled at the old Island maxim, gave in and echoed "Mourn tomorrow."

Mom turned to Polcheck and used her Mom voice.

"Did you two gentlemen *have* to wear those guns in church today?"

Polcheck adjusted the pistol on his hip.

"They're for your husband's protection, ma'am. If I didn't carry it, I wouldn't be doing my job."

Mom saw a few of Vinny's friends start to toss wax paper wrapped sandwiches across tables much to her dismay.

"See! See that! That's what Hitler's done, turned this into a football wedding!"

Her sour sounding words actually came out with a smile on this day of joy. The shortage of supplies meant that any reception was a good reception. There were still a few things that hadn't been red-lined, and whatever eclectic stores could be rounded up, would be served with no apologies, flying sandwiches included.

Kim approached Pop, but the MPs were staying so close this time that she had to wiggle between them. She gave Pop a hug.

"Thanks for taking care of my dad. And for trying to get my mom home, too. You're like a saint."

"Every saint's a sinner, Kim. But don't worry. Your mother's coming back home."

"I believe you," Kim said as she moved back into the crowd of well over a hundred. She passed Bad Bill drinking at the other end of the bar. It struck a nervous chord and she detoured into her kitchen safety zone where she felt most comfortable. As she disappeared, he drew laughs with a comment about Kim, his door and a baseball bat.

Cathleen, dragged him off the bar stool and in Pop's direction. He wasn't staggering yet, but it appeared he would be before the evening was over. Bill put his hands out in greeting and Pop took them but did not pull him in close. Polcheck could sense Pop's change of mood and stayed warily by his side.

"Well if it isn't himself. It's good to see you back home, Dunny, brother of mine."

"Nothing could have kept me away."

"I just wanna say...great wedding. Yeah. It's a great wedding."

Cathleen came to Bill's support.

"You'll have to excuse Bill. He's been swimmin' in the sheep dip again."

"That's a load of dung, woman. And a mean spirited thing to say about your husband. I don't need you makin' excuses. I'm as sober as I've ever been at this time of day."

Pop changed the subject.

"How's Bill Jr.?"

"He don't write much." Bill looked away as he spoke, either ashamed of his son, or ashamed that his son may be ashamed of him. But Cathleen rescued his statement.

"...'Cause he's so busy defending the nation, don't ya know."

Pop put his hand on Bill's arm and took him aside, motioning for Polcheck to give them some private time. They stepped away from the bar, close to the American and Legion flags, hanging on pointed six-foot wooden staffs near the open glass doors. Polcheck was at a distance and an uneasy ooze seeped through his military bearing.

"Glad you could make it, Dunny. God knows those boys of yours need a man's strong hand."

"Glad I got here, too. I'm just sorry that I missed our mother's funeral."

"Aye. It was a sad passin', so sudden like."

"But today, Bill, today is a happy occasion. And even though I know how you humiliated my youngest son, Howie, with the back of your hand as he delivered his telegrams. And how you disgraced my oldest son, Gene, with your crap game money, making him crawl the length of this very floor. And even if you bring shame on our house and humiliate my middle son, Vinny, by disrupting his wedding with some drunken behavior, I will overlook it, because you are my only brother."

Bill wasn't sure what to make of this half statement of love, half underscored threat. He tried to laugh, but it stuck in his throat.

"Even as I overlooked it, Bill, when you said you tried to save our Da', as he broke his neck taking a drunk dive down those cellar steps.

But what I will never forgive, is what you did to our mother. You killed her sure as you're standing here looking at me today."

"What?! No, Dunny. You got it all wrong. Sure I was drinkin' but...I wouldn't hurt the old dame. Not me. I was tryin' to...to save her."

"Whether you remember it or not, I know you Bill, and I know what you can do. What you did back on the docks, it trained you well. I may never be able to prove it, but in my heart I know, and so do you. And may that last scream of hers burn through your ears as long as you live."

His final phrase carried an ominous tone as he patted Bill's cheek and forced a public smile.

"Enjoy the wedding." Pop walked away.

Bill started to follow but stopped after a step or two, sensing it was fruitless. He headed for his end of the bar and ordered up a double. Lubisch obliged. Pop didn't stop until he reached his wife. Her eyes questioned his.

"What was that all about?"

"Loving a brother can be...demanding."

The noise from the party-goers grew louder as the dancing and laughter increased in near geometric proportions. Vinny and Lillian sat lost in each other's eyes, simultaneously groping under the table. Without a word to anyone, and as casually as possible, they stood, meandered around to a few older couples and quietly slipped out the kitchen door. Gene, however, knew their destination.

Lubisch's five-passenger, black 1940 Packard touring sedan, stabled 160 screaming horses. On short loan to the newlyweds, it bore the freshly soaped words "Just Married" across the back window. This was not any old scrawl, but rather had the professional flare that Antonsic put into all his work. While the average car cost $1,100, this vehicle at $1,600 was a monument to successful small-town America.

Old tin cans and the occasional worn out shoe had been tied to the rear bumper. From his rocking chair on the storefront porch,

Nakamura laughed as he caught sight of Vinny and Lillian rushing for the auto. Vinny tripped over the cans while circumnavigating the car, sprawled to the road, rocketed back up and climbed into the back seat. Muffled chants of "Oh, Vinny!" and "Oh, Lilly!" crept through the tempered glass.

Inside the Hall, Gene and Teddy sat at a corner table, she massaging her bulging belly and he nervously trying to get his point across. This was the hour of fess-up, and he was sinking in the quagmire of honesty.

"See, Teddy. There was this crap game at Vinny's bachelor party. Right over there. Yeah, right there where Howie's playing."

"Gene, I don't feel so good."

"It's the beer."

He downed her half-filled glass.

"It's not the beer. It's..."

"Honey, this is hard enough to say without being interrupted. Let me finish, please...So I had a run of bad luck and lost all the money I had."

"Gene..."

"Please!...All the money, plus ten I didn't have.

"Gene..."

"So I went to our dresser looking for some more cash. Only 10 bucks is all I wanted."

"Gene!"

"But then I remembered that $110 that you had saved up for the hospital."

"Damn it, Gene! I'm having a baby here!"

"That's nice, hon'...So I remembered the 100 and...A baby? Did you say a baby? Here? Well, I'll make this quick then. I took the 110 with me to the crap game..."

"Gene, I have to go to the hospital right now."

"Oh! Oh! Yeah! The hospital. Come on, I'll tell you the rest on the way."

Gene crutched, and Teddy waddled out the front door. The Packard rocked like the shaky bridge in a September nor'easter. Vinny and Lillian were heavily into deep breathing exercises made mad by lovers' passions and promises of earthly delights. Their clothes started coming off, amidst moans, groans and wild gyrations.

Gene, never big on timing, knocked on the back window.

"Go away!" Vinny's yell was breathless.

"Vinny, it's Gene."

"Get the hell outta here, Gene! I'm trying to jump start this marriage, and I don't need your help."

"Ahh, Vinny?...I...ah...I need the car."

"You what?!!!"

"Yeah, I...ah...I really need the car."

"*This* car?!"

"Hey, it's not me. It's her."

Teddy, propped up on one of Gene's crutches, produced a moan quite unlike Lillian's. Vinny stuck his head out the steamed window and immediately felt her pain.

"Oooh! Oooh! Here. Take it. The car's yours."

Vinny jumped out of the back seat, buckling his belt, putting on his dress jacket, and fishing the keys out of his pocket. Lillian looked on in shock as she gathered her wedding dress around her. She assessed the emergency, then called to her new husband.

"How's he going to shift?"

"He'll use his crutch. He's a resourceful guy."

"Oh, right, and I'm frigid. Vinny you gotta drive them. Get in."

"Tonight?!"

"Yes, tonight...Now!"

Gene and Teddy got into the back seat as Lillian flowed out of the car, white lace and exposed body parts mixing like an albino tossed salad. She propped her dress up across her breasts and helped wedge Teddy in. Vinny jumped into the driver's seat. But

Nakamura managed to catch Gene's last words through the car's rolled-down window.

"Nice car. So, Teddy, there was this crap game and I took all the baby money..."

Teddy drowned him out.

"Gene, I'm pregnant, not blind! I know you took the ring and the money. Whatever you do, I'm there for you. Now be there for me, and *shut up!* And I'm not naming this kid Higby!"

Once the foursome was finally seated, Vinny cranked the engine, found first gear and pushed the pedal to the floor. All 160 hungry horses answered, bucking away in a trail of flying sand. Vinny answered them back.

"Yahooo!!"

"It's bad luck to kill the newlyweds, honey." Lillian hung onto his arm.

The cans and shoes rattled in anticipation, then lurched forward. The lone member of their audience nearly laughed himself off the rocker as the Packard finally shot by the general store on its mission to increase City Island's shrinking population by one.

The car disappeared from view, lost in the evening shadows. Nakamura smiled after them, but the smallest of sounds, the most corrupt of all noises that he could have heard that day, crashed his world around him. The tinkling of that simple bell, perched on the peak of that simple roof, tolled, "War has come back to City Island."

*How could such a beautiful sound carry so much sorrow?*

Nakamura closed his eyes and rocked, letting the bell ring... and ring...and ring.

# CHAPTER 43

# THE BIG SWIM

# JULY 8, 1942

The Legion Hall could have plunged into the sea that very evening knowing it had done its job and spent its life well. The band filled the floor with dancers. Ivory ran on automatic, but Stevie beat the drums with a newfound freedom that even Howie admired. He wasn't good, but he was loud. Outside against the railing, Mungo sat alone, shyly clapping to his version of the beat.

Behind the bar, Lubisch pulled two beers, while Antonsic listened to the laughter and conversations that colored in the background of this painting spread before him. It was reminiscent of a masterpiece he had copied half a dozen times while studying at the Kunsthistorisches Museum in Vienna. Pieter Bruegel the Elder's 16th, century multi-peopled celebration, "The Peasant Wedding" had come to life just for him. Although peasants at heart, these Islanders were rich in many ways. And although he had only lived among them for six years, since Lubisch brought him to sculpt the marble monument to their Irmagard, he was accepted as a local instead of a resident, for Antonsic was also a peasant at heart. He and Lubisch clinked their glasses, toasting each other and the success of their efforts on behalf of the newly married couple. This was finally a good, good day.

Mom noticed the absence of Vinny and Lillian, as well as Gene and Teddy. Her eyes searched in vain, finding only one son, Howie. She took comfort in knowing that at least the baby of the family was nearby, still playing in the band.

"Howie's only happy these days when he's making music," she commented to Pop. "I can't believe old Ivory dragged himself out like this, after what he's been through."

She caught sight of a familiar face coming through the front door and tugged on Pop's sleeve, making him turn away from the bar.

"Look. Yoshi Nakamura did come."

Pop's eyes lit up. His oldest friend had found the courage to brave the possible wrath of his fellow Islanders just to show his love for the bride and groom. But when Pop focused better, he found Nakamura silhouetted in the doorway, removing his Western Union cap and tucking it under his arm.

Nakamura's eyes canvassed the room, too, but they were stalking prey. The smoke that rose from random cigarettes threw an eerie haze across his face, hiding the movement of his pupils and challenging anyone who tried to follow their deadly hunt.

Howie was the first of the band members to see Nakamura, thereby the first to notice the subtle hint of menace behind his humble expression. The cap made it clear that this was, after all, a business call. In his hand, hidden down by his side, hung that dull, yellow telegram, feared by every Island family. Howie slowly lowered his saxophone, and one by one the other band members followed his eyes, coming to a similar conclusion: the sounds they were making were of no consequence when compared to the sobs and cries pent up in that thin little envelope.

As each instrument found its rest, so did the dancers, wondering what had caused such a break in the merriment. Only Ivory, unable to see, unaware of Nakamura's presence, played on. Not until Howie leaned down and whispered in Ivory's ear did he stop. He reached to his heart for his own telegram, felt a pint bottle instead and quickly realized he had already passed the paper on to Howie. It was the closest thing he had to a last will and testament, and he felt confident knowing that he had given it to the little man he trusted the most.

"A Jap with a telegram, Howie. This is bad. This is real bad," whispered Stevie. "I'm gettin'...nervous."

Kim cracked the kitchen door and stuck out her head as she heard the music trail off, stunned to see her father and the hat entering the reception. She stepped from the kitchen and walked forcefully to him, intent on fulfilling her role as the new messenger, but as she reached for the telegram, her father raised a hand motioning for her to stop.

Nakamura crossed the now silent room, every eye fixed on each fateful step. No mother nor father could stand his or her ground as the new Angel of Death came nigh. And each moved out of his way, before he could arrive within touching distance. He stopped in front of Pop. Nakamura's eyes spoke before his lips set that soft voice free.

"My apologies for intruding."

"You're welcome here, my friend."

Nakamura faced the Islanders, eyes still searching for one target, and one target alone. As he pushed closer, husbands' hands clutched wives', and wedding guests tried to melt into amorphous, nondescript beings. The entire assemblage slid back an invisible step like confused children in a game of "Mother May I" or "Red Light, Green Light". Those on the fringe fought the urge to flee to safety, bystanders at an accident, able to leave at any time, but lacking the nerve to pull themselves away from the scene until the victim had been positively identified.

Suddenly, Nakamura found his target, and the witnesses easily sensed it. They had watched those dark orbs from the moment he entered the Legion, and now, for the first time, they had stopped shifting. A still tension blanketed the soundless room as Nakamura locked on Bad Bill near the open terrace doors. Cathleen blessed herself and squeezed her hands together, but Nakamura could not be dissuaded. His footsteps parted emotional oceans as they closed the deadly distance. Cathleen's eyes sought any avenue of escape, but saw the color drain from her husband's face instead.

Realizing who the target was, Kim shoved motionless dancers out of her way and bolted through the crowd, determined to capture the deadly hat at all costs and reap her reward, a more deadly yellow paper. But Nakamura only made it halfway across the room before Howie stepped into his path.

"I'll do it."

"Step aside, Howie. It is no longer your responsibility."

"I'm the only messenger these Islanders know. I ain't gonna walk out on them now. I got no tears left. I can do this."

"Not this one."

"You don't choose your row. You get what you get. And you got me. I'm the messenger 'til this war is over."

Howie put his hand on the telegram, and Nakamura reluctantly released it. Howie looked down at the name, then back at Bill. The envelope's victim was already sweating, and now he took another half step back. The telegram felt heavy in Howie's hand, pulling his shoulder down, but he braced himself to face Nakamura again, holding out his hand. He received the Western Union cap and straightened it on his head. Nakamura automatically gave Howie a slow bow, symbolic of his respect for young man's dedication, but drawing a distainful look from several bystanders.

Now officially the City Island messenger once more, he moved directly down an empty canyon path, holding the telegram at the end of his outstretched arm.

As they finally confronted each other, Bill whispered slowly, threatening through a tight jaw, "Stay away from me, boy."

"I'm sorry Uncle Bill. I hafta do this. I hate it, but it's just the way it is"

"Turn around, and walk away."

Howie locked onto Bill's eyes and forced the telegram into his hardened hand. Cathleen's scream came out in a gasp of words.

"Oh my God! No!"

Bill opened the envelope. He read every word, then slowly crushed the paper, dropping it to the floor. Rage flew from his eyes, and blood welled up high in his neck. As Howie bent down to pick it up, Bill looked beyond his nephew and found Nakamura directly behind. He exploded a backhand that sent Howie crashing across the room and into Stevie's drums. The Western Union hat flipped to the floor, lost among anonymous feet.

The hall erupted as women screamed, and Ivory yelled to find out what was happening. Before anyone could stop him, Bill picked up Nakamura and threw him toward the terrace. He plummeted through the open doors. More screams of protest, this time from some of the men, too.

Polcheck grabbed Pop as he attempted to break through the scattering human mass.

"You're not going anywhere, Dunny. Nothing's gonna happen to you on my watch. Ryan, get the car."

"Get off me!" came the instant response, but the sergeant held him all the tighter.

A rush of hands moved to stop Bill, but he grabbed the first weapon he found and swung it wildly, beating them back before he even realized it was the staff of the American flag. The top of the pole caught Ivory with a glancing blow as he wandered blindly into Bill's line of fire. Ivory instinctively reached out, grabbing the flag as he tumbled down, ripping it from the staff.

Nakamura struggled to his knees, bruised and dazed, scrambling away to the far edge of the terrace. Mungo sat on the ground, frozen against the railing, and Nakamura pushed him off a few feet to safety.

Bill pummeled Nakamura with the flagpole, driving him down onto the stone floor. Only the railing kept him from sailing into the swirling tide. As others ran outside to stop Bill, he flailed the pole in a huge arc like a baseball bat, forcing them back.

More screams and denunciations surrounded Bill with Kim's echoing above the rest. Yet one or two yells of, "Stick him, Bill!" mixed in with the crowd's noisy chaos. He towered over the semiconscious Nakamura, aiming the point of the flagstaff at his chest, challenging anyone nearby.

"You want a taste of this?! Come on! All of yous!"

No one moved to test him. Bill turned his venom on Nakamura again.

"You deserve to die, you bastard! All you Japs deserve to die! You killed my son! You're gonna kill us all!"

A few random calls of, "Do it, Bill!" and, "Kill the Jap!" bounced back at him.

Howie leaped forward out of the crowd, trying to grab the staff away from Bill. He felt the length of the pole across his back instead. He fell down onto Nakamura, half protecting him with his body, half scrambling for his own life. Howie screamed upward as the spear-like shaft pointed at his own heart.

"Bill, stop!"

"He has to die! He killed my son. Now I'm gonna kill him!"

"He didn't kill nobody."

"Get off, or die with him!"

Inside the hall, Pop wheeled around and worked one hand free. He swung a strong elbow against Polcheck's chest, knocking him down. Pop broke loose and flipped open the top of Polcheck's military holster. He grabbed the pistol, expertly sliding it upward with one hand, but a clear shot was obscured by the horde of partygoers turned in Bill's direction.

Bill took a strong stance, raised the pole high, about to drive the point down through Howie and simultaneously pierce the life out of Nakamura. He sucked in a breath and tensed his muscles for the powerful thrust. Howie never moved.

Pop aimed the pistol right through the wall of moving bodies. As the first of them saw the gun, someone screamed, and they pulled each other to the floor. Pop took a deadly bead on his brother, but Bad Bill suddenly dropped out of view.

A thrusting pain drove it's way into Bill's brain as Mungo sunk his teeth deep into the attacker's right ankle. Bill staggered, looked down, took a hand off the pole and swatted Mungo in the head. Mungo held on and braced for a second hit as Bill straightened up to hit him again, giving Pop a clear shot.

Ivory blindly rose directly in front of Pop, never seeing the weapon. Pop reflexively lifted the pistol upward as it went off, firing into the ceiling. The building reeled with an echoing groan.

The blast and its resultant screams momentarily distracted Bill enough for Howie to make an adrenalin-fueled choice. This one little momentous decision meant life or death, and he was getting good at momentous decisions. He pulled his legs in, frog-like, summoned all his power and sprung upward, wrapping his ever-faithful headlock around the big man's face. The momentum was so staggering that Bill lurched backwards. His hips hit the railing with a driving impact that flipped them both over before Howie even had a chance to touch the ground.

Howie felt his body drop, and he knew he was heading for the swirling water of no return, but he refused to release his grip. The flagstaff flew from Bill's hands and disappeared somewhere out of sight. Mungo catapulted off the ground. Bill's ankle slipped from his toothy vice grip, launching the boy back onto the safety of dry land. The last thing he saw was Howie grab the deepest mouthful of air that he could. Two interlaced bodies crashed as one, instantly swallowed by the watery surface.

Mungo crawled back and looked through the railing. His eyes tried to x-ray the liquid, but Howie and Bad Bill were gone. Mungo found his ugly face again. His angry lips slowly started to move. A word formed. Then two. His quiet sounds reflected Pig Latin lessons well learned.

"Umb-day ass-yay."

Below it all, Howie thought he'd stroked free of Bill as they quickly sank out of sight. But Bill refused to let go, pulling him down, trying to climb up his body. Howie kicked him off and Bill's grasp slipped down to Howie's leg, his ankle. Then, in a bubbly swirl, Bill was gone. But the parsimonious Sound was unwilling to give back anything it had earned, and this time it had earned Howie. He fought his way upward toward the fading light, but no matter how hard he kicked, how far he stretched or how ruthlessly he clawed, the best he could do was maintain his position. This time "best" wasn't good enough. His air slowly seeped out. This was the big swim.

*It's all about the lungs.*

*It's all about the lungs.*

*It's all about the lungs.*

Howie refused to go down and reached up one last time.

A hand splashed downward, driving through the water, searching for everything, finding nothing. Howie kicked harder than he knew he could. His eyes worked to focus, but by now, the salt was burning them shut. He squinted through it, and the hand came into full view. One finger glistened, as if catching a ray from some hidden sun. He touched it, and the small hand wrapped around his. He felt the form of a ring and immediately recognized it: the Irish Claddagh ring, the old-sod wedding ring that Nana had worn until she died. Searching upward, he could just make out her face above the surface, clearly smiling down at him. It was a smile of peace and confidence.

*Does she wanna save me, or take me? If I stay here, I'm dead.*

He grasped tighter, and Nana's hand started to carry him upward. Just as he was about to break the surface, a strong grip from below pulled him loose, dragging him back under. He looked down to see Bad Bill clutching at his leg, climbing up his body and reaching for Nana's hand. Howie kicked with every ounce of energy he had left, barely breaking free and pushing upward off Bill. Bill grabbed onto Howie's shirt but only ripped the pocket off his chest. The waiting hand locked onto Howie's, but this time it was big, it was strong, and it easily lifted him up out of the water. Beneath him, the Sound stole Bill, sucking the lifeless shadow down.

Howie burst through the surface, gasping for air.

# CHAPTER 44
# THE GETAWAY
# JULY 8, 1942

Pop's tall body, already slung across the railing and half into the water, was dangerously overextended, but Big Stevie's bulldog grip held his legs secure. Pop handed the sputtering, coughing Howie up to Polcheck, who lifted him to safety. The cheering noise level erupted, yet Howie still heard only silence. Stevie threw a tablecloth around Howie's shoulders, and Mom wrapped his wet body in her arms as Pop climbed back over the railing to encircle them both.

Howie gulped for air, his heart racing uncontrollably. He had seen death and lived to walk away. The reality of war had truly come to his island, and he had met it face to face. Somehow, the luxury of crying or not crying was unimportant now.

Pop held Howie's face to assure himself that his son had survived, and Howie nodded in response as his faculties returned.

Polcheck slapped Pop on the shoulder, proudly looked around and broke out the first laugh that he had set free since he landed on City Island. Back huggers and hand shakers engulfed the little band, but Polcheck leaned in close to Pop, slipping out his words through a motionless, steely grin.

"Next time you go for my gun, I'm shootin' ya."

Confusion followed the momentary horror as the crowd rushed onto the terrace, some to check on Nakamura, others to look over the side in a vain search for Bad Bill. The battered Western Union hat was kicked along with the foot traffic, trampled and re-trampled again. Forcing her way through, Kim rescued the crumpled hat, found her father and cradled him in her arms, getting some of his blood on her dress. She helped him to his feet.

Cathleen arrived to stare over the edge into the empty, racing rip current. Tears welled up as she silently collapsed downward, sitting with her back to the rail. The wreck-of-a-woman had lost her husband and her son in one wretched day. People swirled around her, pushing to look into the black water, as if she were invisible. Even in the wake of his death, she was unseen in Bad Bill's overpowering shadow, but one small body slid down by her side. She turned her eyes in its direction and met Mungo's in silent, sympathetic return. He drifted the back of his hand across her cheek.

She couldn't comprehend what that meant, but it was strangely soothing to know at least someone on this island might also understand her emptiness. His gesture was accepted, and he slowly locked his hand into hers.

Polcheck tried to hustle Pop away.

"We gotta get out of here, Dunny. Now. Before the cops show up."

"Yeah. Don't worry about it," muttered Pop.

"Worryin' is how I earn my 78 bucks a month. I'm gonna do my job."

"There won't be any cops, Sarge. Not on this island. I need a minute."

"No more 'minutes'. This one lasted 24 hours. Let's go, and that's not a request."

Pop kissed Mom and hugged Howie goodbye. But Howie wasn't giving up.

"Pop...I killed him."

"Don't make book on it. I shipped him out to die in Panama. Only stayed dead for six years. He's not dead 'til I see the body. Mourn his son tomorrow, but not him. You're safe, and that's all that matters."

Pop kissed Howie on the forehead, and moved to Nakamura, who released Kim's hand to accept that of his closest friend.

"Yoshi, you're okay?"

"I will live. Your son has redeemed any debt that you think you owe me. Let us speak of it no more."

Their eyes said farewell. Pop turned to Kim.

"And you, young lady. Don't grow up 'til I get back." He winked, forcing her to smile. "And cut some fresh flowers. I know your mother, and she won't be happy if she comes home to a house with no flowers."

Pop laid a lip lock on Mom that would have made Vinny proud. As they slid apart, she leaned close to his ear, leaving just one word for only him to hear.

"Oom-pah."

A sensual "mmmm" sound crept up from Pop's throat as Polcheck pulled him away, but when his father turned, Howie caught a swirl of light around Pop's neck. He saw the usual St. Christopher medal riding on its chain, but hung next to it was the source of the momentary flash, Nana's Claddagh ring. Suddenly, Howie had to reach his father to tell what he had seen under that deadly water. But Polcheck was already navigating Pop toward the exit, beyond a sea of moving body parts. By the time the sergeant fought his way to the front door, Ryan had the MP car heading for the Legion. Howie lost his tablecloth cloak as he broke loose from Mom and rushed after them, calling over the noise of the crowded bar.

"Pop! Pop!"

People separated slowly, jostling Howie in celebration of his survival. Ivory's hands reached out, grabbed his shoulders and momentarily stopped him.

"Let him go, boy."

"They're takin' Pop away! I gotta see him first!"

"It's his time."

Howie shook free and ran for the door, but speedy Kim, stealer of bases, runner of dunes, was a faster step behind.

Outside, Ryan pulled the car around the flagpole, and Polcheck rushed Pop in. The door slammed shut. Pop let his head fall back, exhaled and rubbed two slightly shaking hands through his gray hair, no longer mandated to appear the steadfast pilot of a family ship in motion and already missing it.

Ryan squealed the vehicle away from the circle as Howie reached the Legion doorway, calling after them.

"Pop!...Pop!"

He raced behind the car as long as he could. Ryan saw him in the rearview mirror, but lead-footed it for the bridge. Howie kept running through the oncoming darkness until he reached home, ignoring the chasing sound of someone cutting the distance behind him. With pain in his side, he charged up the stairs, bypassing the second floor to reach the widow's walk. He had to catch that last snapshot of his father, and this was the highest place around.

Howie plunged out onto the narrow walkway, but emerged too fast, crashing his weight against the aged railing. It snapped like an autumn twig, and his feet slid out from underneath him. For a split second he couldn't believe he was going to fall three stories, just like Nana had in his dream. But Kim reached out, only a running pace behind, and made a one-handed grab before his momentum pushed him forward.

"I gotcha, and I ain't lettin' go."

Kim held tight. She pulled him back, and he panted more from fear than lack of breath. Hands entwined for safety, they edged farther around the widow's walk. Their eyes hunted the horizon, finding the red tail lights as they reached the distant, shaky bridge at the north end of the island. In an instant the car crossed, lost forever among the shadows of mainland trees.

As horrible as it seemed, Bill was probably dead. Pop had saved Howie's life, and now his father was gone. Howie knew he would have to go to confession tomorrow, or maybe just to see Ivory. His music had always made the bad stuff not so bad, but who could tell what shape the old man would be in when the sun exploded over the morning horizon.

Howie stared after the car. There wasn't anything left to see, yet Kim mirrored his gaze. He finally broke the silence, their eyes still searching the darkness.

"I couldn't catch him...When I was in the water, I saw Nana, smilin'. She looked happy. I wanted to let Pop know, but I couldn't catch him."

"Maybe he already knows."

"Yeah. Maybe he does."

"Howie, you saved my dad, just like you promised."

"Guess I did."

"And you killed Bad Bill. Didn't you? Killed him dead. Maybe we should have a ceremony."

"Maybe he ain't dead. We ain't seen his body."

"Oh, he's dead all right, Howie. Question is, will he stay dead?"

"I wasn't tryin' to kill him. I was just tryin' to swim up and breathe."

"Did you cry?"

"Nooo. Everybody knows you can't cry underwater."

"You look a mess. You're all wet, and your shirt is ripped."

Howie felt his torn shirt pocket.

"The rabbit's foot! It's gone!"

"It worked when you needed it, Howie."

"But, it's...special."

"Probably all used up by now anyway."

"Older it gets, the stronger it gets. It's got powers."

"Then you don't gotta worry. If it wants to come home, it'll figure out a way."

She tried to prop up the remnants of his ripped pocket flap, but it wouldn't stay.

"You know you got blood on your dress?"

"Oh no. My mom's gonna be mad."

"We can fix it."

Howie spit on her dress, pulled a wet handkerchief from his back pocket and rubbed the red stain out as best he could. He glanced down to find the crumpled Western Union hat in Kim's other hand, peeking from behind her back. It looked worse than its predecessor ever had. She handed it to him, and he laughed at the hat's deplorable condition, running the handkerchief across its visor.

"I saved it, Howie. I had to."

"I guess this ain't the hat's fault. But it ain't our fault either. It's just what we got. After all that, it ain't nothin' but a hat."

"Ya think? Even a dumb-ass like you shoulda known that, way back in The Big Tree. What took you so long?!...Howie Logan, 'King of the Dumb-Asses'. Don't even know why I hang around with you."

Kim laughed and punched his shoulder. He smiled back, hit the hat against his leg, banging it into some halfway decent shape, and placed it square on his head. She turned it slightly to the side, putting the "jaunty" back in the boy. But his smile faded as he slowly pulled her hand down.

"They shoulda read his name in church today."

"Who's name, Howie?"

"Pete...Pete the Dog."

"They only read people's names."

"He was people to me. I miss him. I never really told him I was sorry for hittin' him with that rock. Only when he was buried, and that probably don't count."

"Don't worry. You can tell Pete when he comes back."

"I guess, if he still knows me, and I still know him. Things change, ya know."

"Not you and me."

"Yeah, but if he's a person, he'll be a stranger."

"Maybe he won't be a person yet. Who knows? It don't matter what he comes back as, Howie, as long as he tries his best. But if somebody starts sniffin' you one day, better say, 'Sorry 'bout that rock', just in case."

She rested her head on his shoulder and held onto his arm. This spot had become her favorite anchor. It was close, it was comfortable, and it let them both know that they would always be there for each other.

"We're gonna be okay, right Howie?"

"Yeah...We're gonna be okay."

They stood quietly looking at nothing, and nothing looked back. In six hours, the sun would splash tomorrow across the horizon, and another bucket-load of future would paint their lives. But for now, for this little piece of time, on this little piece of dirt, at the edge of a vast and dangerous sea, all was right with the world.

His father was there when he was 12.

# CHAPTER 45

# THE FLOATER

## JULY 9, 1942

Dawn's fireball chased away the remnants of last night's hectic air.

This morning, a new floater joined the Sound's usual flotsam and jetsam. It rode the early, incoming tide that always accompanied the calmest of waters, before the beating sun could bring forth the midday wind and its white-capped offspring. This newcomer had no movement of its own and rolled gently with the soft breeze. It bobbed past a solitary creature planted at the farthest end of City Island's small beach.

Ivory stood in the sand, feet spread wide, arms stretched upward, embracing the heat of a new day. He smiled into the sunshine, and its warmth smiled into him in return, flooding his mind and washing his soul. Exciting rainbow vistas filled his horizon with more vivid colors than any seeing man could imagine. All his family had left him now, and he savored both the beautiful memories and the unfulfilled dreams. He took comfort in knowing that his greater City Island family would be nearby until he and his lost loved ones were ultimately reunited.

The slightest unfamiliar sounds, out-of-place wave breaks, penetrated his meditation, telling him that the water was bearing something foreign on its surface. But the sun was too strong, and his need for rejuvination too demanding to even ponder what might be passing by. His voice rose loud and clear, wiping out all other sound.

"Good mornin', Mr. Sun!"

The floater continued undisturbed, finally touching shore at Heartbreak Island. It rocked to a landing on the same sand that had welcomed the trio of hat-buriers a few nights before.

Through his cottage window, the Mortuary Man had been watching this odd object drifting ever closer to his domain and finally went out to greet it. He pulled his top hat down to his oversized ears, entombing that disproportionately large face stuck on a head too small to support its component parts. Like so many feral animals, his large nose and bulbous lips were obviously bred for the task of filling his internal senses. Exterior beauty was not a concern.

He slid down the small embankment to the water's edge, and his shoes carved little heel-trails in the sandy slope. Holding his top hat in place, he bent his long frame to examine this new arrival.

The blank stare of Bad Bill, floating face up, looked straight through him. The waterlogged body appeared lifeless, just the way the Mortuary Man liked his bodies. The living made him uncomfortable. Dealing with the living came with decisions and consequences. His existence on this reclusive island, a realm of insulated freedom, was a never-ending game of solitaire, best played beyond the range of over-the-shoulder spectators.

Relieved to find the visitor in his present condition, he grinned down at the expressionless face, running his fingers across it to close Bad Bill's eyes. This digger of the dead had soil permanently locked beneath his nails, but the transient dirt on his fingertips smudged against the dampness of Bill's weathered face leaving muddy warpaint-like impresssions. Bill's own meaty hands were closed in tight fists clenched against his chest. The Mortuary Man tried to pry them open, but they were locked as if guarding some secret treasure.

"Relax, my friend. Don't you worry about nothin'. You've come to the right place."

He pulled the body onto the sand, grabbed the ankles and dragged it up into the wild grass. He had to take a few panting pauses due to the weight of his burden, but once he reached the level elevation of this treeless plain, the body slid along quite nicely, bumping every time it hit an old stump or clod of high grass. The jerking motion made water spout from Bill's mouth, and that spout made a laugh spill from the mouth of the Mortuary Man as well. He was a laborer who truly enjoyed his work.

"It's okay, big fella. I got you now. You rest easy 'cause all your problems have worked themselves out."

By the time he reached the burial trench, Bill had been bounced and banged enough to kill him again, if he hadn't drowned already. The little canyon was six feet deep. Only a sloping 10-foot section was still open and unused, awaiting its weekly arrivals, but the rest of the trench was filled with pine box coffins and covered with dirt.

The Mortuary Man maneuvered the body between mounds of excavated soil, pausing at the yawning hole before him. A nondescript tune whistled across his lips as he rolled the body on its side and searched the pants pockets for Bill's wallet, but he only found a money clip holding several small-denomination bills and no identification. The Mortuary Man smiled as he examined the little wad, holding it close to his nose and smelling the scent of the dampened cash. Saliva rose under his tongue as if anticipating the taste of the wet paper. He slid the dollars along his lips, then wiped the hint of moisture off his mouth with the back of his hand and stuffed the cash in his pocket.

His fingers hunted for a watch, but both wrists were bare. The body wore no rings, so the Mortuary Man examined Bill's polished shoes, finding only worn out leather and cardboard-patched holes.

His dirty hands patted Bill on the head, smoothed his hair and straightened his wet collar. Pulling a long handled shovel from a nearby mound, he stepped back, admired the serenity of the body, then casually kicked his guest into the ditch. Six feet seemed like sixty as the body flipped in mid air and landed on its back with an echoing thud.

A final fountain of water shot from Bill's mouth, followed by a gurgling groan.

The Mortuary Man, with a shovel full of soil already poised to follow Bill into the hole, stopped and cocked his head at the unexpected sound. He peered over the edge, looking at the motionless form below.

The blue lips on Bill's empty face might have actually moved, or maybe it was the light playing with a few remaining droplets. He knelt down to take a closer look. Suddenly Bill's eyes shot wide open, in a lifeless stare with no focus and no direction.

The Mortuary Man fell back half a step, knocking the hat from his head and the shovel from his hand. He quickly retrieved them both, this time pulling the hat down tighter. Holding the shovel up like a weapon, he summoned his courage and edged forward to take another peek.

Bill's fixed eyes silently looked up at the shadowy human outline that blotted out the morning sun. After a thoughtful moment's hesitation, the Mortuary Man glanced around, resumed his whistling and dumped a shovelful of soil on Bill's face.

One of Bill's eyes blinked the dirt away. The other merely contorted itself into a fleshy knot.

His right fist slipped off his body, hit the dark ground by his side and opened slightly. The white rabbit's foot peered from behind Bill's fingers, as if fighting for liberation from its impending entombment.

Another load of dirt followed right behind the first, pushing a dusty rattle from Bill's throat to his lips. It brought forth a dull, shallow sound. A sound new to the ears of this cemetery veteran. The sound of a dead man coughing.

The Mortuary Man readied another shovelful of dirt, started to lift it, but could not complete the motion. What would normally be an easy exercise for one so accustomed to the task, was now an arduous effort, as he found his shovel psychologically fused to the ground. He dropped the long handle and turned back to Bill.

"Why couldn't you just shut up and lay there?"

The dead were so much easier to deal with than the almost dead.

He slid into the trench and put his disappointed face close to Bill's. A subtle unpleasant odor snaked into the Mortuary Man's sensitive nostrils.

"Whew. How long you been in that water? You smell like a wet dog."

He leaned still closer, whispering into Bill's ear.

"Guess you've been rejected by heaven *and* hell. By all rights, I should dispatch you back with a shovel to the head, 'cause you sure don't look like no Christ worthy of resurrection. Let's see if you can convince me you're worth keepin'."

The Mortuary Man wrapped his hands around Bad Bill's wrists, pulling the arms over the big man's head. He dragged the dead weight the short length of what was left of the open trench and up the half-excavated slope at the end.

"You like to dig, wet dog? Yeah, I bet you do. Could use a digger around here. You look like a man who knows somethin' about puttin' people in graves. It's tough work, 'cause sometimes they don't wanna go."

By the time they emerged onto the scattered grass, the Mortuary Man was close to exhaustion, and his patience was equally used up.

"You ain't dressed for fishin', dead man. So, where might you be floatin' from?"

Bill could hardly send enough air out to form a sound, let alone an answer. His words were no more than roughly-formed moans birthed on two raspy breaths, and their tone gave away the limits of any oxygen-deprived intellect that might remain inside this semi-lifeless shell.

"What's your name?"

"Name," echoed Bill.

The Mortuary Man saw the rabbit's foot in Bill's hand and knelt down to pry it loose.

"Now, is this a lucky one 'cause it *brought* you here? Or is it a cursed one?...'cause it brought you *here*."

He squeezed the foot dry, smelled it and taste-tested the fur with his tongue.

"It don't taste cursed."

He stuck out his tongue again, this time taste-testing Bill's cheek with a long slow lick that left a clear trail where the cemetery soil had been. He spit the dirt out.

"But you do."

The Mortuary Man placed the entire rabbit's foot inside his mouth and rolled his eyes back into his head as he pulled the soft object out through pursed lips, savoring the moment as he cleansed the white fur. He tucked the aged talisman into the wide black ribbon that encircled the base of his top hat, then quickly slapped Bill across the face, snapping his eyes open.

"I asked you somethin', dead man! Now think."

He formed his words slowly, as if speaking to some foreigner who did not understand the language, yet still expecting a response.

"What's...your...name?"

Bill's barely mobile pupils tried to look around, yet his head refused to move. The Mortuary Man slapped him again, but this was not a wake-up slap. It rang of domination. Bad Bill had probably never been attacked like this before, without ending the existense of his assailant. But now even re-birth as an amnesiac cripple, a semi-lifeless slave to a perverse planter of nameless souls, seemed beyond his reach.

"Whatever your name is, your ass is mine."

Bill fought to lift his arms, but only a single shaky hand responded, slowly rubbing the dirt away from his re-closed eyes. After several false starts, one side of his mouth staggered awake. His drooping lips fell into an aimless, rambling mumble, finally putting two words together.

"My name...my name..."

When his eyes reopened, they glinted with the slightest, dull ray of enlightenment, offset by a feeble, crooked smirk from a face now only half alive.

"My name is...Pete."

# CHAPTER 46

# THE ROAD TO NOWHERE

# JULY 1, 1961

*I was bore'd on The Road To Nowhere. It weren't no more'n two wagon wheel ruts wanderin' through a maze of shanties, 'afore sidlin' down to a lone path, and that path trickled to a lazy trail. To the sunset side, the wagon ruts run up to a stand of magnolias, each bud as light as air, as beautiful as life itself.*

*I knowed that someday I'd be seein' that stand of flower trees one mo' time, and that it be up to Howie to get me there. Well, he be a howl-at-the-moon success now. Got hisself joined up to Local 802, the musicians union. And he be jivin' in all them Broadway playin' pits for all them Broadway shows like "The Pajama Game" and "Flower Drum Song" and half a dozen others he told me, but I done forgot. When you reach a state of dilapidation like mine, you be findin' out for your own-self that mind and memory fade by the minute, if not sooner.*

*Now Howie, he growed up to be a good man. He drive me all the way down here to Lumpkin County, Georgia just 'cause I ask him to. And he don't give me no excuses or nothin'. He just do it.*

*When I looked into that boy's soul, deep in the miseries of '42, I knowed he be a boy with pluck, and he gonna grow to be a man what gots direction.*

*He not the strongest soul on that seaside pile of dirt, and he sure not the wisest, either. But he make us all better folk just by knowin' him. He got the courage that make him that little island's rudder.*

*Truth be told, he remind me of my Pa, who was about the same as Howie's now-a-time age when he come home and teach me the dust piano. My Pa was a music man with direction. And that be somethin' to be proud of, havin' direction. 'Cept now and then, Howie lose his drivin' direction, and he stop to talk up the locals, and they point him this way and that. They all seem like good and harmonious folk. Finally, I feel us hit that same Georgia clay what stuck to my Pa's shoes, when he had 'em. And then we gets to high grass, so I tell Howie to go slow, 'cause I thinks I can start to smell that sweet grass still growin'. And he says he can see that sweet grass right there, so he must be listenin'. But now, where the big house stood, where them two boys sharpened up their pokin' stick, there be parking grass. It all look the same, but it all be different.*

*Sure 'nough that trail still be visible, stickin' it's windin' neck out of the hillside. I praised the Lord that this magic land of mine had not forgotten me, nor been forgot.*

*Howie, he pulls that car over to the side, and after he opens the door, he takes out a carryin' bag. But he gotsta carry me out, too, making for one heavy load. He be a strong young man, and he starts climbin' up. I try to tell him which way to go 'cause the trail be mostly overgrowed in places, but the sign say "State Hiking Trail", and we follows it upward again. All the time he carryin' that satchel, and he carryin' me, like Pop's St. Christopher medal come to life.*

*Half a hour later, we gets to what was once a fine set of ruts, but now be no more than two boney-ass dirt cuts crawlin' up the backside of nowhere. Right then, I know I be home, the sweetest place ever a man could wish to see. Sure, them shanties, they all fall down. Just some old rocks tell the tale of where their rough foundations might'a been. Sure, there ain't no knotty old boards makin' up no knotty old porches, but once there was. And once a proud people walked in these ruts, every day, come wind or water, mad hot or froze cold, keepin' weeds and such from fillin' them in. These were the footsteps of the people I love.*

*When I close my eyes, I can see them movin' all slow like, wavin' at me and smilin', and me, wavin' back. And my Mama as proud as she could be of her little music man, sittin' up on his papa's shoulder as we come high-steppin' down the Road. High-steppin'!*

*Howie, he sets hisself down, weary from the long hike and the burden he's carryin'. I looks to the sunset side and there I see but one lone magnolia tree survivin' on sheer power of will...a beautiful sight for these tired eyes that never thought they'd see again.*

*"You rest good after that climbin' chore," I tells Howie, but he don't hear me. His mind be lost between watchin' hawk circles in the blue sky and thinkin' 'bout the life that brung him here to do it. People tend to reflect at a time like this, think about life, and livin'...and dyin'.*

*So that be the whole City Island mess. One bad soul couldn't pull down all them good ones that gone glimmerin'. Thank God that cryin' week be over and done. But it never be forgot. No sir. Never.*

*Howie gets hisself up from his restin' rock and moves out into the middle of the Road. From a pocket in his jeans he pulls out the little yellow paper I give him that week back in '42, the telegram for my Corey. It be bent, and it be beaten, but it still got all that writin' 'bout where to go and what to do. But it don't tell him what to say. The sayin' part he gots to think up all by his own-self. So he clears his throat, coughs his cough, and speaks his words:*

*"There's nobody else to hear this, just you and me, but that's the way you wanted it. What I have to say wouldn't change, no matter how many people heard it.*

*"You're the ump, Ivory. You're always right. How'd you ever get so smart? Any reasonable nation would have placed you in a temple where scholars could have come to study at your feet. You never learned to read. You never learned to write. But you were truly the wisest, wealthiest man I ever met. And I am so honored that you shared even the smallest portion of yourself with me.*

*"You had no eyes to see, but you saw everything we couldn't. You gave us your music. You gave us your soul. You taught us that not to change is to die. You taught us to hoe our rows straight and step in shit when we had to. That it's not how many people you can count, but how many you can count on. And we could always count on you.*

*"You taught us the hardest lesson of them all, to give more than you take 'cause gettin' the best out of life means nothing, unless life gets the best out of you. And for that I am ever grateful. Maybe someday I can live up to it.*

*"You were my father when he wasn't there, and even sometimes when he was. What I owe you, I could never repay. The best I can do is help you ride your blues to heaven."*

*Then Howie, he open his satchel bag, and he takes out his sweet ol' tenor sax that he had as a boy. He sets his mouthpiece reed, and the next thing I hear be that haunting melody of* The Saint James Infirmary Blues. *He play it righteous, better than I teached him, better than I deserve.*

*Now, them words just rip right through me, givin' me a sort of swelled up kinda worthwhile glow. I swear I feel Howie reach right out and take hold of my hand. The same feelin' I got when them pokey boys was doin' their business, and I felt my Pa's strong hand grasp mine and give me the courage to go on. And I bet it was that same feelin' what Howie must'a got when his Nana come out of nowhere and grasp his watery hand. But I do know that after he seed her smile, he never dreamed that Nana dream no more. Maybe her spirit finally gots some peace, or maybe it was just Howie's mind finally comin' to rest. Either way, he never dreamed that Nana dream no more.*

*Slow-like, I come to notice it be gettin' harder and harder to see Howie for some reason or other that I shan't try to explain nor understand. I think I see him rubbin' his eye, but then again, I cain't be sure.*

*Howie's melody finish its ear story, and he come back to hold me close. Slowly, I feel a great relief come over me. And when Howie lift me up and take me into the Road with him, I know my time be at hand. Finally, my joy be complete as he sprinkles me down into the leftover ruts, and I can feel them. Oh! Can I feel them! Growin' up and surroundin' me. The warmth of the Georgia earth, and the smell of that last magnolia on the hill give me the good news that I have come home to rest in the bosom of my Lord.*

*I left down that Road as a child and returned as a man. And I have become, as a man, what I loved as a child. I have become the Road. My dust and my ashes and my being will forever live in The Road To Nowhere.*

*But the story I told you ain't about me. And I hope I didn't talk about myself so much that you think of me as some arrogant and pretentious waster of your time. And if you do think it was about old Ivory, then I ain't told my story right. 'Cause it ain't about me at all. It just be a simple, little story about bein' 12.*

*Every word was true, 'cept for them parts that I had to fill in 'cause I wasn't there when they was hatched, or for them parts that was passed on to me by somebody I deemed an unreliable prevaricator. But every word was true as best I can remember.*

*And that part what ain't word-for-word true was mostly true.*

*I know 'cause I was there.*

CPSIA information can be obtained
at www.ICGtesting.com
Printed in the USA
LVOW07s1742170817
545388LV00012B/1028/P